THE SOUL
OF
BETTY FAIRCHILD

THE SOUL

OF

BETTY FAIRCHILD

ROBERT SPECHT

ST. MARTIN'S PRESS NEW YORK

Design by Dawn Niles

Library of Congress Cataloging-in-Publication Data

Specht, Robert
    The soul of Betty Fairchild / Robert Specht.
          p.   cm.
    "A Thomas Dunne book."
    ISBN 0-312-05965-5
    I. Title.
  PS3569.P425S68   1991
  813'.54—dc20   90-26944
                                    CIP

First Edition: June 1991
10 9 8 7 6 5 4 3 2 1

For Judy

ACKNOWLEDGMENTS

Many people helped in the shaping of this book, sharing their thoughts and their privacy. Some gave hours and hours of valued information and expertise, others equally valued encouragement and support.

Special mention must go to Janet Wilkens Manus. She has been more than an agent, not less than a friend.

The hospitality of fellow writers Bruce and Katina Strauch was as generous as it was welcome.

No less helpful were Barbara Wanbaugh, a patient and discerning critic, Everett Chambers, who offered incisive comments at the very beginning, and Richard S. Miller, Ph.D., whose professional advice was indispensable.

I am also beholden to Police Chief Harvey M. Becker, Cyndi Bennedum, Nancy Boynton, Kathy Brinson, Guy Gardner, Rev. Johnie Johnson, Robert R. and Brenda Lee, Robert R. Maline, Leon McKelvey, Sandy and Patricia Mock, William Rifkind, Keith Stewart, Michael H. Sukoff, M.D., Jacob Weinless, M.D., and George W. Whaley.

All of them, and others not listed here, enriched this story, and I most gratefully thank them.

THE SOUL

OF

BETTY FAIRCHILD

THEN . . .

Back in 1967, if you'd asked any man in Greenview, South Carolina—young or old—who was the best-looking girl in town, he'd have said Betty Fairchild. She was too. But that's like saying magnolia smells like perfume. It does, but no perfume can make you recall sweet and romantic memories—memories you never knew you had—like the scent of that flower, so to say that Betty was the best-looking girl in town wouldn't have described her.

Betty was, to put it rightly, a hauntingly lovely girl just barely turned seventeen. She was sexy too, and not a boy who knew her didn't at one time or another picture her crying out in moist pink whimpers as he made love to her. She lived in one of the finest houses in town with her parents and her uncle, Raymond Ordway, and she drove a spanking new red '68 Mustang convertible. From all appearances, she had everything a girl of her age could want.

Yet she carried darkness near her.

Betty was never happy for long. She should have been. She had the richest, warmest smile you could ever see. It was a woman's smile, wistful and understanding, and a little skeptical all at the same time. When she laughed it was deep-throated, bawdy, the laugh of a generous, big-hearted person. But if you looked carefully into those huge blue eyes of hers, you saw a long-standing hurt in them that had never healed. She had a poor

1

self-image, as they say ("Low on self-esteem," were the words one of her kinder teachers used back then), and she was moody. Once in a while—just like her uncle Raymond—she'd light into somebody in a real mean way just when the person least expected.

Yet there was something about Betty Fairchild that was also naturally good—you felt that—a special kindness that she'd pushed down so deep inside of her that sometimes she didn't know it was there. It came out in the way she always stuck up for an underdog. She'd never join in making fun of a kid who wasn't too smart, or didn't fit in. And she didn't see anything terrible about integration either. In fact, she was outspoken about the civil rights movement—went and joined it even though her father and her uncle felt that Negroes were asking for too much too fast.

That might have been because of Arletta Johnson, the family's housekeeper. Betty was very close to Mrs. Johnson, and once when she was about fourteen or fifteen, Betty confided to her that Negro men scared her sometimes.

Mrs. Johnson asked her why, and she said, "The way they stare at you when you go by—like they know something you don't."

"They do, honey," Mrs. Johnson told her. "They do."

Most girls who had as much as Betty seemed to think that it made them special, or at least they acted as if it did. Not her. She didn't care about possessions. You could borrow her car or anything else she had, just for the asking. Her best friend Juleen, or even an acquaintance, only had to admire something of hers—a cashmere sweater, a ring, anything—and Betty made them take it.

She was sixteen when she fell in love with Lee Caldecott. Lee was nineteen, and they were a perfect couple—she rich, stunning; he promising, handsome. Lee was the big love of Betty's life—or so it seemed. He came from a fine old family, and everybody believed that

2

Lee would do well, including Betty's uncle. Raymond Ordway gave Lee a good-paying part-time job that summer and said he wanted to take him into business with him when Lee finished with college. Lee could have been more aggressive, Ordway said a few times, but he had a good business head and a fine future ahead of him.

Betty and Lee didn't last, which was too bad because everybody felt that Lee was good for her. He was a solid young man, whereas Betty was the kind of girl, adults felt, who did too many things with boys that she shouldn't. Lee was Betty's chance to prove to those people that all those stories about her weren't true, that she could hold a young man who had a lot going for him. But she and Lee broke off after six months, and Betty, always moody anyway, seemed to get even more so.

In 1967 the civil rights movement was as much in full swing in Greenview as it was in Selma or Montgomery. Betty had been interested in it starting when she was fifteen, much to her family's displeasure, and now she became actively involved in it. She also became friendly with twenty-year-old Ed Johnson. Ed was Arletta Johnson's son, which you could tell just by looking at him: almost all of her children were good-looking, bright, and talented, and all the boys took after her. But Ed was a standout even in that exceptional family. A little over six feet, he had a brown-sugar smile and a quick intelligence combined with a phenomenal memory. He had a natural ability to make money and was marked for big things.

Like his mother, Ed liked Betty, but his little sister GG couldn't stand her. GG said she was a spoiled tramp, and Ed said that for a ten-year-old girl who was as smart and pretty as GG, she could repeat some awful dumb things. Betty Fairchild was decent, he said, and she had guts.

Which indeed Betty did have. She was right there in the forefront of Greenview's first civil rights demonstration, for instance, a march down Main Street. When the police moved in to disperse the marchers, a few officers got carried away and Ed took some lumps, but they made sure not to hurt Betty. Her mother was worried about her marching like that, and her father didn't like it at all: He'd sold a restaurant chain rather than not be able to choose his customers. But even he couldn't influence Betty when she had it in her mind to do something.

It seemed to people that Betty appeared to be happiest around that time. If it was true, her happiness wasn't fated to last: On a warm, late afternoon in November, her nearby darkness closed in on her.

She was alone, sitting in her Mustang convertible, the top down. She was parked in a lonely area in South Fork, unaware that someone was coming out of the woods toward her. Whoever it was had on mechanic's coveralls buttoned up tight to the neck and was carrying a gleaming, razor-sharp hatchet. Face shadowed by the brim of a leather hat, black gloves covering the hands, and glistening black rubbers on the feet, the figure was beside the car and throwing open the door before Betty knew what had happened.

She saw the upraised hatchet, knew she was going to die horribly, but couldn't move at first. Then she was writhing and shrieking in agony, trying to get out of the car as the heavy blade repeatedly bit into her flesh and her bone. It missed a few times, took chunks out of the white genuine-leather upholstery, chopped a deep gash in the dashboard. But it found her head and her body again and again, and soon what was left of Betty was hard to identify as having been human.

The figure stopped, breathing hard, face spattered with blood, coveralls wet with it. But things had to be done: The top had to be raised and the windows rolled up. After doing both, the figure got in beside the grisly remains and drove for a short distance to Willow Creek.

Some time after that, Lee Caldecott reported the

4

murder. Still sick from seeing what he had, Lee told the chief of police that Ed Johnson had done it. Lee said he'd gone to meet Betty at Willow Creek to lend her some money, and he was late. When he got there he saw Ed Johnson taking a small blue case from the trunk of the car. As soon as Ed saw him, Lee said, he ran off, and when Lee went over and saw what was in the car, he threw up his guts.

Betty's open purse was on the ground, empty of all money but change, and Ed's key ring was found right under the rear bumper. Lee's story checked out: He had a thousand dollars in cash on him that he'd withdrawn from the bank that very day.

The chief immediately deputized twenty good men and formed a posse. Every other red-blooded white man went home to get a gun. A few got kerosene and rope.

Bloodhounds were brought in, and about half a mile from the scene of the crime, close by the Ashley River, they found some blood-soaked ground. A trail led from the blood, made by a body that someone had dragged to the riverbank.

The blood later tested out to be the same type as Ed Johnson's.

People thought that what had happened to Ed was pretty clear, especially after a young man named Mark Turnage was brought in to the chief's office. He'd been seen hunting in the area near where Ed's blood was found, and he admitted under questioning that he'd fired his rifle "once or twice" but hadn't brought anything down. Six-foot-two, close-mouthed, he also admitted that he'd fought with Ed Johnson two days before. Ed had beaten him badly: Mark's left eye was still closed, his lip swollen, and a couple of teeth were loose.

He maintained that he hadn't seen Ed, and the chief didn't pursue the subject at any great length. Nor was Mark questioned in any manner that might be construed as unfriendly.

The word got around, and a lot of men were disappointed: They'd looked forward to participating in the time-honored manner of dispensing justice.

The story carried by the Greenview *Sentinel* the next day made for good reading. It and every other newspaper in the Deep South carried the whole lurid, blood-curdling tale along with pictures: the Beautiful White Girl Hacked to Death; the Crazed Negro Seen Running from the Scene; the Negro's Key Ring Found; His Fingerprints Found on the Car; the Grieving Family, etc.

Betty's father was interviewed and said that, like everybody else, he knew Ed Johnson had done it. Betty's uncle Raymond, also interviewed, said that Ed had no doubt already paid for his crime, but in case he hadn't— and Ordway hoped to God he was still alive so he could be electrocuted—he was offering a reward of $10,000 for the capture and prosecution of Betty's murderer, whether it was Ed Johnson or anybody else. Not only that, but he called the chief of police and the county solicitor right away and told them they were to make sure that all the latest scientific methods were to be used in collecting evidence, and that as long as the case remained open that evidence was to be carefully preserved. If the county couldn't do it, he said, he'd foot the bill himself to bring in an expert.

The chief took Ordway up on it. He wasn't privy to the latest methods in criminal detection and he knew it. He was a good policeman, though, and he was conscientious. He called in a criminalist from Columbia and told him not to spare any expense in garnering all the evidence he could. The criminalist was thorough: He went over the crime scene, took photos, vacuumed Betty's car—even vacuumed her room. Before he was done, he collected a whole bunch of stuff in plastic bags and labeled it all.

People who knew Mark Turnage said that he was probably kicking himself all over hell and gone. There he was, sitting on $10,000, and no way to collect it.

6

After nineteen years loyal service to the family, Arletta Johnson was let go as housekeeper. As much as she had loved Betty and been loved by her, she was understandably not invited to the funeral. Just as understandably, Betty's father gave her two weeks' severance pay, and Betty's uncle vowed he would never employ another Negro for as long as he lived.

At the funeral Betty's mother said that Betty was not gone. A deeply spiritual woman, Mrs. Fairchild said that the physical portion of Betty had departed, yes, but her soul and her beautiful spirit would forever remain here on this Earth where she had been loved by so many.

Unfortunately, there was little to keep her and Mr. Fairchild together after that, and a year later they separated and divorced.

Betty's murder was never really solved, and the case was never closed. Her car was impounded and stored somewhere, the evidence was boxed and sealed, and it too was stored away.

People talked about the tragedy for a while, then as the years passed it was forgotten.

". . . look for me by moonlight,
Watch for me by moonlight,
I'll come to thee by moonlight, though
hell should bar the way."

—Alfred Noyes
THE HIGHWAYMAN

NOW . . .

1

A little more than twenty-three years later, a young woman named Drew Summers lay in an uneasy sleep in the semidarkness of her Manhattan apartment.

Drew had never met Betty Fairchild. She had, in fact, been born a couple of months after Betty was murdered. Yet she looked so much like her, she could have been Betty herself—same honey-colored hair, same skin, same features.

The digital clock beside Drew's bed read 1:14.

It had taken her a long time to fall asleep. She had gotten into bed about eleven, and for a while she'd tried to think of ideas, first for Belle's Kitchen, a new account her agency was trying to win, then for her main account, but she hadn't been able to concentrate.

Now she was dreaming: She was in her car, gliding like a blimp through a busy street in a southern town, and she was frightened. Her car was bloated and misshapen, the steering wheel was barely responding, and she had no brakes. Behind her a man on foot was following with measured tread. She was terrified of him and she wished frantically she could go faster, but the street was filled with traffic and milling people.

Somehow she managed to maneuver between pedestrians and oncoming traffic without an accident. Finally, with relief, she came to a stop when she bumped gently into some bales of cotton.

Her relief did not last long. People gathered around to stare at her accusingly, and beyond them she saw the man on foot still coming. He was wearing a floppy hat, and he was going to do something horrible. She even knew who he was, but she was a stranger here and didn't want to cause a scene. He was brandishing an ax, pushing his way through the crowd, and she knew that when he reached her she was going to die an agonizing death.

Fortunately, Drew started to wake up. Realizing it was only a dream, she tried to go back to sleep. To help, she thought about her boyfriend Jim, pretending that she was beside him. Somehow she managed to drop off again. But for the next couple of hours she dozed fitfully.

At 3:37 she began to moan.

"Uncle Ray? Uncle Ray," she called, "please help me." Her voice had a soft southern accent, something that Drew Summers normally did not have, and she sounded like a little girl. "Uncle Ray, I think I'm out way too far. I can't get back."

The wall between her apartment and the next was thin. Her middle-aged neighbor on the other side had an ulcer, and ever since his girlfriend had told him that either they got married or they weren't going to see each other anymore, he woke up at the slightest sound.

He knocked and complained. "Hey, miss, it's almost four in the morning. How about it?"

Drew's eyes popped open and she sat up. "Uncle Ray, I can't breathe," she cried. "I can't breathe. Help me, Uncle Ray. Save me!"

She twisted around and her shoulder hit the headboard, banging it against the wall.

11

Her neighbor groaned and said he didn't believe it, but Drew was already throwing the covers off and scrambling out of bed. Stumbling into the living room, she headed straight for the door, fumbled with the chain and burst out into the hallway where she was faced with seven locked apartment doors. She clutched her ankle-length nightie around her and looked around wildly.

"Oh, God, I'm gonna drown," she screamed. "I'm all alone out here and I can't get back! Uncle Ray, where are you?" She was choking now. "It's getting darker and I'm gonna die. Oh God, help me please. Help me!"

She was clawing at the air and shrieking when a door banged against its chain. Unable to see what was going on from her peephole, the woman behind the partially opened door shouted, "Leave her alone, you bastard! I just called the police and they're on the way right now, so you just leave her alone!"

Drew's next-door neighbor didn't know what to do. He saw through the peephole that Drew was terrified and that she was alone. She was a good kid from what he knew of her, usually very quiet, and he wanted to help her, but he was afraid somebody might come out and think he was molesting her.

A couple of other doors opened, and that decided him. He opened his own door.

"What's going on?" somebody said.

"I don't know," Drew's neighbor answered. "Miss, what's the matter?" he asked her.

Her back against the wall, she looked at him, but he had the feeling she didn't see him or anything else. As if to prove it, she turned to the wall, clawing at it.

"Uncle Ray," she screamed, "I'm drowning. Help me, please. Save me. I'm here! I'm here!"

Drew's neighbor felt a chill, and he was glad that more doors were opening. Three young people who lived together came out, two guys and a girl. "What's the matter with 'er?" one of the guys said.

12

A bald-headed man shook his head in disapproval. "Gotta be dope," he said to his wife.

Drew was coughing and choking now. "Please, help me," she sobbed, her voice getting weaker. She sank down to the tiled floor as a short fat lady—the one who had yelled through her door—came out of her apartment with a blanket.

"Be careful," the bald-headed man said, "she could be on crack."

"Your ass is on crack," the woman answered.

Kneeling down, she tried to put the blanket around the girl. "Sweetie," she said, "you're gonna get all dirty out here like that. C'mon, now . . ." With a grunt, she pulled Drew toward her and got the blanket around her. "There you go," she said. "You're gonna be all right, don't worry. You got nothing to be afraid of."

She stroked Drew's hair, comforting her, while Drew continued to cry softly.

"What happened to her?" somebody asked.

Nobody had any idea. But what happened next took everyone by surprise.

Drew stopped crying. Just like that she took her hands from her face and looked up at everybody. Tears were still rolling down her cheeks, but other than that it was as though nothing had happened. The change came so fast and was so striking that all anyone could do was stare. Even the little woman beside Drew was startled.

Drew gaped at her. "What am I doing here?" she said. The southern accent was gone.

"You came out here, honey."

"I did?" Drew said.

"You sure did, miss," Drew's next-door neighbor said. "You ran out your door screaming up a storm."

Drew touched her face and stared at her wet fingers. She let the woman help her up. "I'm sorry," she said to everyone. She looked lost.

"Ah, it's nothing," someone said, disappointed.

13

The woman started to guide her to her apartment, but stopped when somebody suggested a look inside to make sure nobody was there. Three people went in and came back to say the apartment was empty.

Drew and the woman went in, leaving behind sighs of relief and headshaking. As Drew's door closed, sirens were heard. "Here they come," somebody said.

The cop who questioned her was thinking that he had a distraught female. She wasn't on any medication, didn't show signs of an intoxicant—slurred speech, flushed face, bloodshot eyes, enlarged pupils—and she had her full faculties. His partner had taken the little fat lady out to talk to her and others on the floor.

"That's all you can tell me," he said, "that you don't know what happened."

"That's all I *know*."

"Are you afraid of somebody maybe?"

"Who would I be afraid of?"

"Well, you're out there yelling in the hallway, you musta had a reason. Maybe there was somebody in here and you're afraid he'll come back."

"There was no one in here."

"And nobody tried to break in . . . You were alone."

"I was alone."

"You sure you didn't leave the door unlocked . . ."

She shook her head. "I wouldn't do that. Ever."

"You remember unlocking it to go out in the hall?"

"I told you I can't remember *anything*. I wish I could. I got into bed, I had trouble falling asleep—then I was out there with everybody staring at me. Could you tell me why you're asking me all these questions?"

"We get a report of an assault in progress, we ask questions."

"But nobody assaulted me. I know you're doing your job and I appreciate it, but I have to go to work and I'd really like to try and get some sleep."

14

There was a knock at the door and the second cop came in. He reported that from what the neighbors said, Drew was a quiet person and nothing like this had ever happened to her before. "Where you from, miss?" he asked.

"Los Angeles." She was actually from Sherman Oaks, but it was simpler to say Los Angeles.

"Y'ever live down South?" he said.

"No."

"That little fat lady . . ." He glanced at his notebook. "Mrs. Metzger. Said you were talking with a southern accent."

"Me?" She shook her head no.

"Your neighbor next door said the same thing."

"Impossible . . . y'all." She didn't think it was funny and neither did they.

"Well, that's what they said. You got relatives down South maybe?" Another glance at the notebook. "An 'Uncle Ray'?"

"No."

"Your neighbor next door says you were yelling about an Uncle Ray."

She shook her head, and he didn't know what else to ask. The first cop said, "Would you excuse us just a second, miss?"

He took his partner over to the door, and Drew waited while they talked in low tones. When they were done the first cop came back to her and asked her for a relative's name, "someone we can notify in case this happens again." He was very nice, and before he and his partner left, he suggested that if she had any more problems like this she might want to call a physician.

Left alone, she glanced at the time on the VCR. Five thirty-four. It was getting light outside. She picked up the phone, hesitated, then touched the buttons.

"This better be good," Jim said in a sleepy voice.

"It's me."

15

He became more alert. "Anything wrong, honey?"

"A really weird thing just happened."

"You okay?"

"Uh-huh."

He relaxed. "Not hurt or anything?"

"Uh-uh, just . . ."

"Honey, I'm dead. Call you back when I get up?"

". . . Sure."

He did, but she realized he'd be picking her up in another hour anyway, so she said she'd explain then.

She was waiting by the curb outside her apartment house, and Jim saw even before the cab stopped that she'd had a bad night.

He hoped it wouldn't spoil their day. It was one of those perfect April mornings that made you glad you lived in New York, spring in the air, sunlight warm on buildings still cool from the night. And today, Friday, was Pig-Out Day, when instead of taking the subway, Jim took a cab downtown to work, dropped Drew off on the way, then picked her up later for dinner. After that they were going to take in a play, then go to his place. She got in and sank back against the seat.

"Poor baby," he said.

She returned his exaggerated sympathy with an exaggerated, sad face. "Major fright," she said.

He put an arm around her as the cab moved out into the nine o'clock traffic. She nestled her head near his collar, smelled the faint aroma of soap.

"Mmmm, you smell clean," she said. Straight from the shower. She'd taken a shower also, but she felt grungy. Exhausted. She could have fallen asleep if she let herself.

His hand touched her cheek. "Tell me what happened."

When she did he was amazed.

"You can't recall *any*thing? Not even now?"

"All I remember is waking up in the hallway with everybody looking at me. It was really embarrassing."

"And they said you were talking in a southern accent?" He smiled skeptically. "Somebody was putting you on."

"Jim, practically every tenant on the whole floor was there. . . . It's not funny. Maybe I have a brain tumor."

"You don't have a brain tumor."

"How do you know?"

"If you're really afraid then go see a doctor."

"I don't want to see a doctor," she said. "I want to go to sleep. I'm tired. You don't know what that's like to wake up someplace and not know how you got there."

"You could have been sleepwalking."

"I never sleepwalked in my life."

"I think you need somebody to take care of you."

She groaned. "Glug. Here we go again."

"If we got an apartment together we could walk around in our sleep in matching pajamas."

"You know, it really bugs me that you're not taking this seriously."

She was right, he thought. "What can I do?"

"You could be a little more sympathetic. If this happened to you I'd sure be."

Without saying anything, he drew her closer, and it made her feel better immediately. It made her feel guilty too, but she needed his support—even more now than when she'd first started going out with him.

At that time she'd been a little in awe of him. He made five times her salary, was almost ten years older, and he knew about theater and art, good music, everything like that. He didn't feel he was any big deal—an associate in an investment banking firm—but for a few weeks she wasn't even sure what to say around him, what he wanted her to be. She was quiet around his friends too—especially one who was an actor who worked steady, and a married couple who were artists. She felt they thought she was a nerd. She was surprised when Jim told her they thought she was intelligent.

It took her a couple of months to be herself with him, talk about what *she* wanted out of life, confide her doubts, her fears. Gradually he became less of an idol and more of a partner who had his own doubts, his own worries, his own ambitions. She didn't realize how deeply he felt about her until he suggested they get an apartment together. Drew had told him she wanted to think about it. Since then he'd asked her twice more.

The cab turned onto Fifty-eighth Street. She'd be at work in a couple of minutes and thought how great it would be to be completely irresponsible and not go in. Go right back to bed instead. Her eyes felt as if they had sand in them, and maybe it was the tension of the last few hours, but suddenly she wanted him. She lifted her head and gave him a kiss under his ear. For a bonus she licked his neck.

"Jim?"

"Hm."

"Let's take the day off."

Her hand was resting on his knee. She stroked the softness of his inner thigh and felt him stir.

"I think it's going to snow," she said.

It had been their catch phrase for making love ever since the middle of January when they'd driven back from the Catskills after skiing for the weekend. The road had been iffy and it was snowing lightly when they started home, then it really began to fly, and a little while later they were part of the straggly line of cars waiting for the plow.

The engine was running, the heater going, and the windows fogged up fast. Outside there were people within fifteen feet. Inside, they were totally isolated. She couldn't remember who started it, but within minutes she and Jim had their pants down. She had fooled around in cars before, but never like that.

18

Just thinking about it now turned her on. She'd never taken the day off just for fun. Neither had Jim. The two of them worked so hard, and Jim worked such long hours, that it was tough for them to see each other during the week. Often he even had to work weekends. The more she thought of how nice and bad it would be, the more the idea appealed to her. Bad Drew Summers. Had a ring to it.

They could go back to her apartment and sleep in her bed because her neighbor on the other side of the wall would be at work. Usually when Jim stayed over they had to sleep in the living room.

Jim wanted to, but he couldn't, he said. "Got a meeting I can't miss." He was miserable, and he felt worse when she put her lips close to his ear and told him what she'd have done to him if they'd gone to her place.

By the time they reached Fifth Avenue and stopped in front of her building, he was groaning and she was giggling. As she went out the door he yelled that he'd changed his mind, but Drew said forget it, he was too late.

She made her way through the revolving door and into the lobby feeling high, and all the way up in the crowded elevator she kept breaking out in a silly grin. She was still grinning as she entered the art-gallery quiet of Arkwright & Campbell's reception lounge. She breezed past the receptionist with a hi, getting, as always, that slight feeling of being special as she passed through the tall antique doors and moved along the carpeted corridor.

She bumped into her boss near the water fountain, and she said, "Norman, I adore you."

As she expected, he scowled. "Don't dump things like that on me before nine-thirty," he said.

He bent to drink from the fountain, the network of veins in his cheek darkening. He was blushing, she realized.

She was glad she'd said it. For a long time she'd

wanted to tell him how much she appreciated what he had done for her, but the moment had never been right. He'd hired her as a secretary at BBD&O almost five years ago, and ever since then he'd pushed her along as fast as she could go.

Two years after he'd hired her he promoted her to junior copywriter, and a year after that, when he left BBD&O and came here, Drew was one of the people he eventually brought over. He'd started her as a junior copywriter at twenty thousand, then three months later upped her to twenty-three. She was making twenty-eight now. The past Monday he'd called her and Susan in and told them the Belle's Kitchen account was up for review and the agency was being asked to present spec creatives. He was going to give them a crack at it. It was the biggest chance she'd ever gotten.

Finished drinking now, Norman O'Neill raised his head. "You look like hell," he said. "Hope you had a good time getting that way."

"Wish I did."

"You're putting me on. I heard about you—sex all night and dope all day. You and Susan got anything you can roll with on Belle's?"

"We have some ideas."

"When can I see your roughs?"

There was no panic—the agency would not be presenting to the account for another seven weeks—but Drew felt a twinge of anxiety anyway.

"Monday?"

"Ten-thirty," he assented, walking off.

Already at her drawing board when Drew walked into her office, Susan raised an index finger, signaling she was in the middle of a thought. Drew went out to the kitchenette, poured herself some coffee, and when she came back Susan was sprawled in a chair, looking blah.

"That good, huh?" Drew said.

"Gotta meet Aaron at the motel at three."

20

Drew was going to make a joke about it, but decided not to. Susan and her husband had been trying for some time to have a baby without any luck. For the past two months they'd been having sex according to a schedule, and it wasn't fun.

The two of them settled down to work and were soon kicking around ideas, oblivious of everything else but updating Belle Starr and her kitchen from Old West to New Healthy and Hearty.

They worked well together, as they had from the beginning. Susan had had another partner when Drew came to work here, and twice Drew had given them good suggestions during brainstorming sessions. Once she had even brought them a copy of an illustration that was perfect for a presentation they were working on. Helping another team was not something people ordinarily did: Competition at Arkwright & Campbell, like competition in every New York ad agency, was keen.

The more Susan saw of Drew the more she liked her and her ideas, so that when her partner was fired she told Drew she'd like to have her as a partner if it was okay with Norman. Drew jumped at the chance. It was a generous offer—almost unheard of—because Drew was very young and comparatively inexperienced. But Susan didn't feel she was doing anything special. She didn't have the pressures the other creatives did: Her husband had a terrific job, and she wanted to have a baby.

By lunchtime they had some more ideas, but nothing they felt was breakthrough. They decided to go to Belle's again for more background. Both were going out to dinner that night, so they agreed they'd settle for the salad bar.

On line, Susan picked up a cold plate, turned around to tell Drew something, only to see her heading for the hot foods. "Hey, I thought we were *both* going to have salad," Susan called.

Drew didn't turn around. Susan shrugged, made up a

salad and found a table. A few minutes later she watched in awe as Drew came over, set down the tray she was carrying, then unloaded a small salad, a plate of sauteed shrimp with brown rice, a slice of German chocolate cake, and a carton of milk. "Where are you and Jim having dinner tonight—Weight Watchers?"

"I just may, if you are real nice," Drew said with a faint accent, "give you a taste of the cake."

"Oh, 'may' you," Susan said, mimicking her. "Well I declayuh, I just may take you up on it."

Drew smiled. "Tell you the honest-to-God truth, I am not goin' to have the chance to eat this for myself."

"And why not, Scahlett?"

Drew reached over and touched her hand, and Susan had the feeling this wasn't Drew. Something in her eyes was different. "Susan, I'd be appreciative of a favor. Please?"

Susan was disconcerted. This wasn't a joke anymore. "What is it?" she asked.

Drew said. "Tell Drew not to be afraid."

Susan had the sensation she'd missed something. "'Tell Drew not to be afraid,'" she repeated. "Of what?"

"Tell Drew I am not . . . I am not . . . tryin' to—"

She broke off, and Susan was fascinated. Drew was suddenly herself again, but lost. Her eyes went around the restaurant, down to the food in front of her, then to Susan. This time it was Susan who touched Drew's hand.

"What's the matter, Drew?"

"I don't know." Drew shook her head. "How long have we been sitting here?"

"A minute maybe," Susan said. "You okay?"

". . . Yeah. I just felt a little dizzy," she lied.

Susan made a joke about it. "Well I'm suah glad about that, Scahlett. Y'all were talkin kinda peculiah theah for a moment."

Close to the end of lunch Drew said, "What did I say when I had that dizzy spell? I can't remember."

22

Susan told her, southern accent and all.

"Yeah, I remember now," she said.

Drew had barely touched the shrimp. She ate the salad, though, and had a taste of the cake. Susan tried a taste too, then went crazy and finished off the entire thing. "Look," she said, "if I can't get pregnant, at least I can enjoy the perks."

"I told her I remembered, but I couldn't," Drew told Jim that night. "I couldn't remember anything." They were at his place, and she hadn't mentioned it until he'd turned on the stereo and poured them a glass of wine. Now she was looking out the window. She took a sip of her wine and put it down on the sill.

Jim was concerned.

"You don't remember buying the lunch or bringing it to the table?"

"No. But I must have. It was right there in front of me."

He came over and drew her to him. "You carried that around with you all night without saying a word? My God. You've got a lot of guts, Drew."

His words should have made her feel better, but they didn't. He kissed her on the cheek and she hugged him tightly. "I love you," she said.

They kissed, and she felt the growing pressure of his sex. She didn't want to talk about this anymore. Her arms went around him, and when she felt his fingers hitching up her dress, she asked him if he remembered what she told him in the taxi that morning—about what she was going to do to him over at her place.

They didn't reach his bedroom until after they made love. They were finishing the wine in bed when he told her that he was going to call his doctor and ask him to recommend a specialist for her. She had to have a checkup, he said, and she was going to, and that was that.

Before turning out the light, he told her that his

parents wanted them to come out to the house for dinner the following Friday if it was good for her, and she said sure. She'd met his parents a couple of months ago and she'd liked them.

"I think my mother wants you in the family," he said.

"Why do you think that?"

"You're the only one she's ever invited for dinner a second time. . . ."

She was out of it. It had been a long bad day and she didn't want to talk about living together again. Or anything else. She snuggled close to him, wanting him.

She was glad that it didn't take much urging for him to want her too.

At first Jim had wondered what was holding Drew up. Then he'd been annoyed. Now he was worried. She wasn't late very often, and if she was going to be she always called.

He called home. His mother answered and he got as far as "Hi, Mom" before she said, "Oh, Jim. Good. I was just going to call you."

"Wanted to let you know we're going to be late," Jim said. "I don't know where Drew is."

"Don't worry, your father's not home yet anyway. I just called his office and he left a few minutes ago. I wonder if you'd mind picking up a jar of macadamia nuts on your way. I need them for the dinner."

"Sure. Drew didn't call there by any chance?"

"No."

"She was supposed to pick me up a half hour ago, and I'm getting worried."

"I'm sure she's all right. She's a very capable young lady."

"I know, but it's not like her not to call, especially as late as this."

"She's spoiled you, that's the trouble. When you men are late, we women take it for granted something came up. When we're late, you're either impatient or worried. Call me as soon as you hear from her so we know when to expect you. Don't forget the nuts, all right?"

"I will. I mean I won't."

As soon as he hung up the phone rang.

He said, "Hi—where are you?"

"Jim?"

Her voice sounded small, like a little girl's.

"What's the matter, hon?"

"Jim, can you call your parents and tell them we won't be able to make it?"

"Where are you?"

"I'm . . . at Kennedy."

"Kennedy Airport? What are you doing out there?"

"I drove out here."

"You *what*?"

"Jim, please, I'm kind of upset and I can't really answer any questions now." Her voice broke. "Could you call them, and then come out and pick me up?"

"Can't you drive back?"

"I'd rather not."

"You didn't have an accident . . ."

"No. I just don't want to drive. I'll be waiting near the baggage inspection at Delta Airlines."

He took a cab out, his thoughts spinning all over. What was going on with her? She'd been examined by his doctor and he couldn't find anything wrong with her, so he'd suggested she see a neurologist. She hadn't done it so far even though she was getting rings under her eyes. She looked like hell lately too. Now this.

Suddenly the thought occurred to him that maybe she was knocked up. Involuntarily he smiled, musing on it. If she was, that would be terrific.

When he thought about it, he realized that she was the first woman he'd ever seriously considered having a child with. She'd be a fantastic mother, no doubt of it. As young as she was, she was mature. It was one of the things that had attracted him to her, her seriousness and her maturity. If she was pregnant he'd consider himself lucky.

He'd have to move, trade up his two-bedroom co-op for a three-bedroom, maybe a four. If he couldn't quite make the down payment, his folks would lend him the difference. That was one of the best moves he'd ever made, jumping into the real estate market when he had.

He thought about income. He had four deals he was juggling, and one of them, the sale of Cleveland-Pacific, he had generated on his own. The fee involved was one percent, and he had three potential buyers. It would sell for fifty million, which meant $500,000 for the firm. Not bad for an associate. He wouldn't get any of it personally, but it would put him in line for a hefty raise and a V.P. position. And Cleveland-Pacific had to sell because he'd found out they were going to be raided.

He was thinking about which buyer was the best target when he saw the winking lights and dark shape of a jet floating down and realized he'd be at the airport in a few minutes.

Jim was looking for Drew when she called to him. She was sitting beside a uniformed black woman near the security check, and she got up and almost ran to him. She looked like a waif.

She hugged him as though she was drowning, and he said, "You okay?" She murmured an uh-huh, and he said, "Boy, you had me worried. What happened?"

The uniformed woman came up to them then. She was replacing a walkie-talkie on her belt.

Drew said, "Sheila, this is Jim."

"Pleased to meet you," Sheila said. "Drew had a little trouble, got kinda mixed up, but I think she's okay now." She looked at Drew, and Drew nodded.

She was with Alert—airport security—Jim saw from the cap she wore. "I radioed that officer," she said to

26

Drew. "He'll be here in a minute. Why don't you two sit down and relax?"

"Sheila, thanks for all your help," Drew said. "I really appreciate it."

"Forget it. Take care of yourself." She walked off, heading for the security check station.

Jim led Drew to a line of chairs, put his arm around her when they sat down.

"Why an officer?"

"He has my parking stub."

"Tell."

She took a deep breath, tried to be light. "Okay. I'm driving up Lexington on my way to pick you up, right?"

"Right."

"Wrong. The next thing I know, I'm standing in that gift shop over there looking at a copy of *Mademoiselle*."

"That's it?"

"That's it."

"You don't remember driving out here?"

"No."

"Do you have any idea *why* you did?"

"I do now." She opened her handbag and handed him a ticket folder. Her hand was shaking.

He took out the ticket. "Charleston, South Carolina? You bought this?"

"That's right."

"You're kidding."

"I wish I was."

"Do you remember buying it?"

"No. I noticed it in the gift shop." She showed him her handbag. "It was sticking out of this little pocket on the side here."

Jim examined the ticket. "The plane left fifteen minutes ago. Thank God you didn't get on."

"I know. I got so shook up I went over to a cop and told him what happened. He asked me a lot of questions, then asked me for the parking stub for my car. He said that for my own good he couldn't let me drive out of here. That woman Sheila offered to keep an eye on me until you got here. Jim, I think I'm going crazy."

He put an arm around her again and assured her she wasn't. "I've got two suggestions. First, you gotta see a neurologist." He tapped the airline ticket. "This is pretty hairy—I mean not what you call your everyday common cold symptoms." It made her smile and he said, "You have a beautiful smile."

That got to her. She had to clear her throat. "What's the second suggestion?"

"Maybe you ought to see a shrink. It doesn't mean you're wacked out," he added quickly. "Those guys are heavy into things like chemical imbalances these days, hormonal deficiencies, whatever the hell you call them."

"I thought about it," she said. "I'll try the neurologist first."

They lapsed into silence, and Jim wondered what was going on. This was getting serious. He cared for Drew more than he'd ever cared for anyone. Forget cared—he was crazy about her and he wanted to marry her. If she was all right. Once they were married, he would be as deeply committed to her as his father was to his mother. He didn't take that commitment lightly. Before he made it, he wanted to be sure that this was the woman he wanted to have children with.

Drew asked him what he was thinking and he said, "How much I care for you."

He opened his hand and hers slid into it.

A cop came over just then and when he made sure who Jim was he gave him Drew's parking stub. "Sorry to inconvenience you," he said to them both, "but I thought that under the circumstances, the lady shouldn't be driving."

They both thanked him, and Jim asked Drew if she knew where the car was. She said no, so he gave the stub and the keys to a skycap, described the car and offered him twenty bucks to find it.

Ten minutes later the skycap was back and handed Jim the keys.

The car was waiting for them outside the main doors.

"No trouble finding that baby," the skycap said. "Couldn't miss it. Lady, that's gorgeous."

Drew thanked him and patiently answered a couple of his questions about the car as Jim got in behind the wheel. Then she said that she had to go.

Ordinarily she'd have answered all his questions because she knew how the car turned people on. She'd spent a lot of money to restore it to its original condition, and from the canvas top to the gleaming chrome and the spanking red paint job, it looked as if it was fresh off the assembly line.

She got in beside Jim, settled back against the white leather upholstery, and the '68 Mustang convertible moved away from the curb and the few onlookers it had attracted.

2

A few days later she went to see a neurologist.

After she had filled out a five-page informational sheet, Dr. Wachs questioned her as to how long the episodes had been going on, their duration and frequency. He was particularly interested in whether she had any warning before the episodes occurred, headache, nausea, loss of urine, loss of consciousness. Then he asked her what she did during them—or what others told her she did.

When he was satisfied he'd found out what he needed to know, he gave her a physical examination, a series of tests that took about ten minutes. By the time he finished he felt he had a pretty good idea of the problem.

The way Alan Wachs gave a patient bad news varied: He could pussyfoot, be brutal, or be frank. This lady was together, he felt, and mature, so he decided to be frank. He told her that her examination was normal, which was good, he said, but it also indicated that perhaps her problem was psychiatric in nature. Just as he anticipated, she was worried.

"Are you saying there's something mentally wrong with me?"

"No, at this point I'm saying that something has gone wrong—wrong enough to bring you here to my office—and the cause *could* be emotional. But let's find out for sure." He wanted to do an EEG and an MRI scan, he told her.

Two days after they were completed, he saw her again. He showed them to her, told her they were normal. "So again, that's good," he said, "but I'm still concerned. The spells aren't going to go away. I think it would be a good idea for you to meet with a psychiatrist or a psychologist and let him listen to what's been happening to you. I could be wrong," he concluded, "but I think we need this evaluation."

She asked him if he had anybody in mind and he suggested a psychologist. He didn't tell her, but he was almost positive he had a multiple personality here, and he felt that Corey Berringer would be perfect for her. If she needed the assistance of medication a psychiatrist could be brought in.

His nurse wrote down Berringer's name and number for her.

Drew didn't call him until the following Monday—after she made a scene in Norman's office.

She and Susan were presenting their roughs to Norman and a few account people. Originally set for the previous Monday, the meeting had been postponed first by Norman and then by someone else, and it went well. There was general agreement that the concept wasn't there yet, but Susan and Drew were following the marketing strategy outlined by the account people—a homey, healthy restaurant for the modern family—and so everybody was happy. Susan had retained the old checkered tablecloth pattern, and Norman particularly liked the new logo: neon in place of wood.

As the meeting was breaking up, Graham, the management supervisor, was telling Drew he thought it all looked good, when Drew turned from him.

"Mr. O'Neill," she said, flashing Norman a big smile, "can I ask you a favor?"

Norman thought she was kidding. "Wrong accent, kid. This is a western restaurant, not southern."

"I wanted you to know I will be going home soon,"

Drew continued. "I am afraid you are going to have to give Drew some time off."

Susan stopped dead in the middle of collecting her line drawings.

Norman still thought it was a joke, but he didn't get it. "Sure, but let's talk about it when we're done with this. So far—"

Drew interrupted him. "I do not know when I will have another chance to talk to you, Mr. O'Neill."

Before she could go on, Susan put an arm around her. "Norman, you mind if I talk with Drew for a sec?"

Drew removed Susan's arm. "Susan, please be kind enough to let me finish."

Her southern accent was unmistakable now, and Norman realized something was going on. The management supe had left, fortunately, but the account supe and the new business guy were staring. "Private joke," he said to them. "Would you gentlemen excuse us?"

As soon as the door closed behind them, Norman said, "This is a put-on, right?"

Susan said, "I don't think so, Norman. I've met you before, haven't I?" she said to Drew.

Drew nodded.

Norman began to understand. "Ah-ha. I see. Well . . . You feel like sitting down?" he asked Drew.

"Thank you," Drew said, "I would rather not. I am sorry for interrupting your work."

"My pleasure," Norman said.

"I just wanted to tell you that Drew will need a leave of absence, and I hope you will understand."

"What does she need a leave of absence for?"

"That's for me to know and for you to find out," Drew said saucily. "Just remember what I told you."

"Uh, what *did* you tell us?" Norman asked.

Drew didn't answer. She glanced from one to the other of them, frowning, then around the room. They knew immediately that she was herself.

32

Susan wanted to make sure. "Drew."

Drew looked at her questioningly. "Where did everybody go?"

Norman had never seen anything like it. "Do you know what just happened?" he asked her.

"Graham was saying something to me . . . then I must have blanked out. Did I do something weird?"

"Not for this business," Norman said. "How do you feel?"

"Okay."

He told her what she had done, then asked Susan what she'd meant by saying she'd met "her" before.

Susan was uncomfortable, but Drew told her to go ahead and tell him. After she related the incident in Belle's Kitchen, Norman was genuinely concerned.

"You want to take some time off?" he asked Drew.

"No. Do you want me to?"

"No. But I think that neurologist is right. You better see a shrink. Do you good. Look at me. I've been going all my life."

Drew liked Corey Berringer right away.

His office was on Eighty-fifth near Columbus. His sixth-floor window looked down on a line of newly renovated brownstones across the street. Dr. Wachs had called him, he told her, and clued him in on the results of all her tests.

She asked him if it was okay if they just chatted for this first session, "so I can see what kind of vibes I get."

"Hey, why not?" he said. He threw one lanky leg over the arm of his chair and sat back. "If we happen to touch on any of my problems, I'll only charge you half price for this session."

She liked that.

They talked back and forth for a few minutes, and Berringer asked her what she did for a living.

"High pressure, I'll bet," he said when she told him.

She felt comfortable with him—enough to ask him if he minded if she called him Corey. He said not at all, and a few minutes later when he asked her if she'd changed her mind and would like to talk about the problem that had brought her, she said yes she would.

"Back to the grind," he said. "I like to use a tape recorder for the first couple of sessions. Okay if I turn it on?"

She said sure, and he reached over and touched a button on the phone cradle.

Beginning with the scene in her hallway, Drew described everything people had told her. She finished up with the incident at work.

"Do you have any relatives in the South?" he asked her.

"No."

"Going back to the airport," Berringer said, "you don't remember driving out there or buying the ticket—any of it?" Berringer asked her.

"Nothing."

"Anything like these episodes ever happen to you before? I mean before the hallway scene?"

"No."

"What do you think might be causing them?"

"For a while I thought that maybe I had another personality. But I don't really believe that. It has to be something else."

"You have any idea what?"

"Yes, but I know it's going to sound . . ." She let her voice trail off and shook her head.

". . . Sound way out?" he asked her.

"Way *way* out."

"Try me."

"Something is going on that . . . Okay. When I'm alone, sometimes I get this weird feeling that someone is nearby me, someone I can't see."

Berringer's expression was neutral. "And does that

34

someone have anything to do with what's been happening to you?"

"You mean like do I think they're beaming deadly radio waves at me? No."

He grinned. "Any idea of who this someone could be?"

". . . No. Crazy, huh?"

"Interesting," Berringer said. He squinted at her. She realized it was a habit he had when he was thinking.

"On the questionnaire that you filled out for Dr. Wachs, you said you had a sister who committed suicide. In nineteen eighty-two. In California. Is that right?"

"Yes."

"How old was she?"

"Three years older than me."

"That must have hurt bad."

"It did." She smiled softly. "Gena was terrific. . . ."

"How did she commit suicide?"

"Pills. I found her when I came home from school . . ."

She stopped. Even after all this time it wasn't easy to talk about it. Gena's letter popped into her head. It was on the kitchen table, exactly where Drew always put her books down. She still knew the letter by heart. *Dear Drew, I'm sorry to do this to you, but Mom just can't handle something like this. You can. Don't worry, no mess. I'm in my room. I took a bottle of tranquilizers this morning . . .*

She didn't know how long she stood in front of Gena's closed door, tortured, saying to herself that this was not real. She knocked softly a few times and called her sister's name. Gena, please answer, she begged silently. Oh, please.

The door stayed closed. Drew didn't move, listening for the slightest sound. She listened for a long time, until she heard what she thought was a humming inside of her head. It stopped suddenly and she realized it was coming from the kitchen. The refrigerator.

She couldn't go in. She'd call her mother at work, she thought. Then she remembered what Gena said in the note.

She wished she was somebody else, some other girl who could handle this better than she could. She should call the police, she knew that, but she also should make sure that Gena was in there first. Maybe she should go next door, she thought, ask Mrs. Remsen if she would go in and look with her. No, she couldn't bring a stranger into this.

But she couldn't go in by herself either. She turned away from the door and went into the kitchen. It was empty and silent, and when she turned on the gas flame under the kettle it sounded like a blowtorch. She got a cup and a saucer and a spoon and a tea bag and waited. When the kettle shrieked she made the tea, but when she tried to lift the cup, her hands shook so badly half the tea sloshed out. It scalded her fingers and made her realize that she was making a terrible mistake—maybe Gena was alive and there was a chance to save her.

She didn't think. She ran out of the kitchen and down the hall, opened Gena's door and walked in.

Gena's room was neat, like always. She'd even made the bed, and at first Drew refused to accept the fact that the still person lying on top of it with her clothes on was Gena.

Up until then Drew thought that death was make-believe. You saw people die on TV or in the movies, but you knew they weren't dead. She knew Gena was. Even before she touched her wrist and felt its awful coldness, she knew that what was on the bed was not Gena. Her eyes were open, but they weren't her eyes anymore. They were dead eyes.

She kept trying to understand what she was seeing, trying to figure it out. She couldn't.

She started out of the room, but then realized that she had to cover Gena up. It was another thing she'd seen on TV and in the movies, and she never knew why they did it. Now she did. It was as if Gena was helpless and naked. Staring at her was like taking advantage of her. Drew covered her, and when she looked at the outline underneath the cover she felt she had just buried Gena.

She got on the phone and called the police. Later, one of them asked her how old she was. Fourteen, she said. It sounded childish and faraway to her. She had been fourteen when she went into Gena's room, she knew, but from then on she was an adult.

". . . Drew?"

"Sorry, what'd you ask me?"

"If you knew why your sister committed suicide."

"Yes." She knew. She knew so well that once she was able to get past the jolting pain of Gena's death, she was grateful that Gena hadn't suffered any physical pain. She'd suffered enough.

"My father molested her," she said, feeling the old anger surfacing. "He molested her from the time she was nine."

"Can you tell me what you mean by that?"

She was infuriated. "I mean he fucked her," she said before she could stop herself. "Is that clear?"

"Yes."

"Besides fucking her, he did things to her that he probably never had the guts to do with my mother. Is that clear too?"

"Yes," he said quietly.

She felt tears starting and pushed them back. She wasn't here to cry over the past. "Look, I'm sorry," she said, "I'm not usually that crude, but every time I think about it . . . Gena and I begged my mother to have my father arrested, and she wouldn't. She even hinted that it was my sister's fault. . . . Want to know something? Gena left a note. For me. You know what she said at the end of it? She said, 'Tell Mom I love her.' 'Tell Mom I love her,'" she repeated. "Oh Jesus Christ."

Berringer waited until she was under control.

"How was your own relationship with your father?"

"Not . . . exactly . . . the . . . best," Drew said, clipping the words to be light. "Let's see . . . I was 'too smart for my own good,' to quote him, I had a big mouth and I was 'glib.'"

"What do you think he meant by glib?"

"I never got tongue-tied with him, like my sister and my mother. He used to get them into arguments all the time, then he'd say every nasty thing he could think of to make them cry. He was such a bastard. I always knew what he was doing, so when he'd start on me I'd say exactly what I felt, and when he got nasty I'd back off. So I was 'glib.'"

Berringer grinned. "Do you think you were?"

Drew thought about it, then grinned too. "Come to think of it, I probably was," she said. "In fact I *am*. I always know what to say in a meeting with a client, for instance. I think my brain is always ahead of my mouth."

Berringer found himself liking her.

"Did your father ever bother you?"

"No. I was lucky."

"I think you said on the questionnaire that you've never seen a therapist before . . ."

"That's right."

"Did you ever want to?"

"I don't think I ever thought about it. In my family you didn't talk about feelings—you know, like confusion, or doubts, or worries. That was 'counterproductive.' You talked about ambition, goals, achievement. And you didn't talk about family problems either."

"Is your father still alive?"

"No, he died a couple of years ago. My mother called me—and you want to hear something? She couldn't understand why I wouldn't fly back for the funeral. Why'd you ask?"

Berringer explained that if her father was alive, the law required him to ask her certain questions, questions that would help him decide whether or not her father was currently in any situation where minors were at risk. If he was, Berringer said, it would have to be reported.

"Nah," Drew said, "my father believed in keeping it in the family."

The session was up by then, and he made an appointment to see her again in two days.

Drew called Jim a little later and told him about it. She said she liked Berringer.

The following night Jim went straight from work to Drew's place. They planned to go to his parents' for the previously missed dinner, and he was outside her door by seven.

She'd left her keys in the lock. He took them out and rang, then went in when she didn't answer. He called a couple of times, then headed for the bedroom.

She was packing a suitcase, and when he appeared in the doorway, she looked a little annoyed, until she saw the keys dangling from his fingers.

She breathed a sigh of relief. "Jim, I have been looking all over for them keys. You are a darlin'."

All he could do was stare.

"Whut is wrong?" she asked him.

"You're putting me on," he said.

"About whut?" she said.

He pointed a finger that indicated her hair, took in everything down to her feet, then went back up again.

"Don't you like the way I look?" she said.

"You are beautiful," he said truthfully, "you're gorgeous, but—" Everything about her was changed, her hair, her eyes, her lips. Even the dress. She looked like a sexy teenager. And he meant *sexy*. "But we have to get out of here," he said finally, "and I don't think you want to go dressed like that."

The idea crossed his mind that she had gone insane, and he immediately rejected it.

She moved to the open closet door and looked at herself in the mirror. "Whut, pray tell, is wrong with what I have on?"

"Absolutely nothing," he said quickly. "It's just that I'm not sure my parents are ready—"

"I don't give a whip-snap about your parents. I am not going to see them."

He hadn't been sure before, but he was now: She had a southern accent. Something was terribly wrong, and he didn't know how to deal with it.

"Look, we broke the date with them once. We have to go."

"Let's not and say we did."

"What do you want to do?" he asked her.

"I am going for a drive," she said. He'd put the keys down on the low cabinet beside the door. She came over and took them.

"Okay. That's fine," he said. It was perfect, in fact. She couldn't go to his parents' as she was. "Just let me call my folks."

"I'm going by myself. *You* may leave," she said coldly.

"I'm not going anywhere without you," he said.

She deliberately looked him up and down, then smiled. "Why are you acting so mean to me?" She came over to him. She was being obviously seductive and it was kind of charming. Her fingers touched his chest then moved down to his waist, and despite himself he felt desire.

She raised her face to his and her lips brushed his own. The soft curve of her belly nudged him. "Jim, I don't

40

really want to go anywhere. Maybe aftawhile, but not right now. I just feel like being alone. You understand?"

"Of course, but you're not going out alone."

"You mean that?"

"I do."

"You are being a pest," she said with a half smile. "If you don't leave me alone, I swear I will kick you in the balls."

That made him chuckle, and it was a mistake. She got a nasty look on her face, and fortunately he saw it coming, twisted and took the knee on his thigh. It hurt like hell. She took the opportunity to try to shove him out of the room, but he grabbed her.

"You sonofabitch," she hissed, "you let me *go*."

"Drew, settle down," he said reasonably.

She struggled even more, tried to punch him, so he wrestled her back onto the bed. He lay down on top of her and stayed on top of her, the sensation strong in him— and frightening—that he was with a girl he didn't know.

Finally she stopped struggling. "All right," she said. She was breathing heavily. "Get off."

"No more fighting?"

"Get off me," she said quietly.

He caught the aroma of her perfume. She'd never worn it before. He raised himself on his elbows. He was surprised to see she wasn't angry.

"You have ruined things . . ." she said. "This time. I won't let you do it again."

Now he was positive he was not with Drew, and he was fascinated. "Who *are* you?" he said.

She smiled at him. It was a nice smile. He felt her fingers brush the back of his neck, and she kissed him. He was so surprised, he had no time to think.

A moment later he felt her tense up. Her lips left his.

Drew stared up at him.

Jim knew it was her. And he saw by her stricken look that she knew she had done something wacko again. He raised her up and they sat on the edge of the bed. He told her from the beginning what had happened. She kept shaking her head in disbelief until he said, "Drew, take a look in the mirror."

She glanced down at her dress, then her shoes, and murmured, "Oh my God."

She got up, and Jim said, "You better brace yourself."

As she stared at her full-length image, Jim appeared beside her. His arm went around her.

She said, "Jim, do me a favor . . .? Don't worry, I'm not going to hurt myself. I just don't want the neighbors to come running. Okay?"

She walked into the closet, shut the door and began to scream. She screamed so long that Jim became concerned, but she stopped a moment before he decided to open the door.

She was crying uncontrollably, and he had all kinds of conflicting feelings—affection, pity, and repugnance. He didn't like the negative ones. But he had them, and if this kept on he knew he'd have to do something about them.

As he helped her up he thought to himself that he had to call his parents and tell them that he and Drew couldn't make dinner for the second time. For the moment he'd lie to them, as he had the first time. Later on, when he was alone, he'd call and tell them what was going on and see what they had to say.

3

Corey Berringer asked Drew what the last thing was that she remembered about the episode.

"Getting ready for my date with Jim," she said.

"How did you feel?"

"Fine. I had no idea anything was going to happen. One moment I'm standing there wondering if a blouse would go with a skirt I just bought, and the next I'm on the bed kissing someone. I was panicked, I was praying it was a dream—until it turned out to be Jim. Even then I was still really scared. And when I saw that packed suitcase—that was too much."

"How's Jim taking this?"

". . . I think he's kind of . . . I don't know . . . getting nervous."

"In what way?"

"I don't think he can handle it."

"Have you two talked about it?"

"A little. Jim likes things to be a certain way—you know, appearance-wise, financially, blahblahblah. He's got a career, and I don't think he needs a flake around him."

"Let me see, you've known each other about six months . . . Are you in love with him?"

"I like him a lot, more than I've ever liked anyone else."

"Has he changed noticeably since these episodes began?"

"I can feel him pulling away."

"How does that make you feel?"

"Corey, I don't want to talk about Jim. I want to talk about what's happening to me."

"Maybe it's partly tied in with him. You told me how pressured you felt when he talked about the two of you living together. That kind of pressure and others like it can be very disturbing."

"Like what others?"

"Like your job. How are you doing at work?"

"Well, my boss brought in another team to work on a project my partner and I are on. We're still on it, but now we have competition."

"That really worries you, I guess."

"It does. I've been working late a lot, Saturday too—but I don't want to get into that. Corey, do I have another personality?"

"The truth? I don't know."

"Suppose I told you I'm feeling more and more that there's somebody near me—somebody I can't see."

"Can you be more specific?"

"Not much." Again she was silent, and finally: "Okay, suppose I told you someone was trying to possess me."

"Suppose you did."

"What would you say?"

"I'd say tell me more."

"Would you say I'm nuts?"

"Nuts isn't the issue. People who are nuts can't function. You seem to be functioning. Do *you* think someone is trying to possess you?"

Drew slid down in her chair. She shook her head wearily. "I don't know . . ."

"What do you think of the idea of putting yourself in a hospital for a week or so of observation?"

"I'm not crazy about it. No pun intended."

"It might be a good idea. Suppose you wake up sometime and the man beside you is *not* Jim?"

44

"You think that could happen?"

"It's a possibility."

After she left he took a few notes, looked over what he had written and shook his head in perplexity. If ever a patient mystified him, it was this girl. He understood Drew's problems—high-pressure job, a boyfriend pushing for a closer relationship, an abusive family history—but she just didn't seem to be the kind of person to be coming apart the way she was. She seemed basically too healthy. Usually he could pick up on defenses, see fear reactions in the eyes, at the mouth. Even when a patient was totally compensating there were signs of trouble, sexual problems, relationships with friends. But Drew Summers either had to be exceptionally well-defended—at least in his office—or he was missing something.

He imagined himself talking to his colleagues at the hospital about her. After they'd thoroughly discussed her case in scholarly, professional tones, he finally told them what he felt was wrong: Drew Summers just wasn't weird enough

The following Sunday was the softball game in Central Park between Drew's agency and Y&R.

Drew was playing third base and she'd done fine, got two hits for three times at bat. The fourth time she was up everybody was rooting for her. It was two out and an account exec on second.

The first pitch was a ball. A few people in the small crowd of onlookers applauded, including Jim, and Drew took off her cap and made a low bow of acceptance.

On the second pitch she ducked out of the way.

"Jeezuz, that was a perfect strike, Drew," Norman complained.

For answer, Drew threw the bat down and walked off.

"Hey, what'sa matter?" Norman yelled. "Hey, Drew!"

A couple of people asked her what was wrong, but Jim took one look at the way she was sashaying off and

45

had the sinking feeling he knew. He took off after her, but even when he called she kept going. Someone else was filling in for her at bat when he caught up with her at Turtle Pond and grabbed the back of her shirt.

"Hey, take it easy. Where you going?"

She gave him a backward glance and didn't stop. "Crazy," she said, "want to come?"

The look on her face told him he was right: the other girl was back. "Why'd you walk away like that?"

"Better than standing there like a fool and getting hit by that silly ball."

"Makes sense," he said. He tugged on her shirt. "Will you hold up for a minute?"

"Sorry, sugar, little Betty has things to do."

He forced her to stop and grabbed her wrist. "Be nice. Will you?"

"Do you want me to scream?" she said.

"Frankly, no."

"Then let me go."

He saw out of the corner of his eye that a couple of guys had stopped to watch. If she screams, he thought, I'll let her go and just follow her. But she didn't.

"Oh, you are so strong, aren't you?" she said sarcastically. "Well maybe Drew adores your wonderful manliness, but I don't."

"Who are you?" he said.

"Betty Boop, and in the future you watch out for me. You get in my way again and I'll make you sorry."

He felt a little tremor run through her, and then Drew was there.

She took in the park, the game going on a short distance away, and he felt that she was pretty self-possessed for what she had to be feeling.

"What did I do?" she said.

"I think you lowered your batting average."

That made her want to kiss him. "Tell me," she insisted.

"For right now, why don't we go back to the game? It looked to everybody like you just didn't feel good there for a minute. That's what we'll tell them."

"I didn't do anything way out?" she said.

"No," he lied. "We'll talk about it later."

It was the best thing to do for the moment, he felt—act as if nothing serious had happened. Later on he'd tell her what she'd done and they'd deal with it. For now he didn't want people feeling there was something wrong with her.

Jim put an arm around her and they started back. But he didn't feel close to her. Just the opposite. There *was* something wrong with her, he knew that now, and he felt as turned off by it as if he'd just found out she had some kind of communicable disease.

After Drew told Berringer everything Jim had told her, he said that things were getting a little spooky and she should definitely be hospitalized.

"I'd like to be able to catch you in one of these episodes and get some information from it."

Drew was silent, then she said, "I know this is going to sound really strange, Corey, but I think somebody is making me do these things. I'm sure of it."

"Betty?"

"That's the name Jim said she used."

"How do you feel about her?"

"She scares me."

"Why?"

"Look what she's doing to me! And if you tell me I'm doing this to myself, honestly—" She broke off.

"You're sure about this girl . . ."

"It's either that or I'm a lunatic."

"Let's try something. I'll ask you questions and you answer with the first thing that comes into your mind." When she nodded he said, "Can you describe her for me?"

"Some kind of a presence. I don't know what she looks like."

"Is she here now?"

"I don't know."

"Any idea who she is?"

"Haven't the foggiest."

"What makes you think she's responsible for what's happening to you?"

"Nothing that makes sense. It's a feeling."

"Give me a little more."

"I can't. She's like an imaginary friend you have when you're a kid. But she's there."

"What does she want?"

"Now remember," she warned, "even if it's way out you want me to tell you the truth, right?"

Berringer nodded.

"She's trying to connect with me. Sometimes she can and sometimes she can't."

"Do you want to connect with her?"

"Shit, no!"

The way she said it made him laugh. She found herself smiling too, and it put them in a lighter mood.

"Why not?"

"Are you kidding? That's all I need is to start trying to communicate with a ghost. Then we'll *both* know I'm ready for the funny farm. I'm telling you what I feel."

"*Is* she a ghost?"

"Ghost, spirit—I don't know what she is."

"Why does she want to connect with you?"

"She wants me to do something for her. Don't ask me what because I don't know."

"What happens when she connects?"

"She takes me over. I become her. Sometimes she can't take me over, though, and I'm conscious of her. I can feel her trying to get to me."

Berringer was silent, but she knew his mind was

48

working because he was squinting again. Finally he said, "Drew, are you saying that you are being possessed?"

She looked drawn. "If I'm not, Corey, then I'm really in bad shape."

He said: "Sure I can't convince you to go into the hospital?"

"No, but you can do me a favor."

"What's that?"

"Convince *her* to go. Without me."

A week later he did not need to convince her.

She didn't show up for a two o'clock appointment. With most other patients, Berringer would not have been overly concerned, but with Drew, he thought it best to check. He called Jim, and learning that he had not spoken with her that day, Berringer suggested that Jim try her at the office.

He had a patient following the call, and at the end of the hour there was a message from Jim on his machine asking him to call. When he did, Jim told him that Drew hadn't shown up for work. "You think there's anything to worry about?"

"I hope not," Berringer said. But he was concerned.

"Maybe I ought to call the police," Jim said.

"It's a little early for that. Have you tried her at home?"

"Yeah. I get the machine."

"It might be a good idea to go over there as soon as you can. Make sure she's not there, then if you go to the police, they might be inclined to give it serious attention."

"Dr. Berringer, do you know what's wrong with her?"

"I have some idea."

"You think it's going to get worse?"

"I can't give you an answer to that, Jim."

When he checked his machine an hour later, he jotted down the name and the ten-digit number that an Officer

Stoll had left and dialed the number immediately. While he waited he castigated himself for failing to convince Drew to enter a hospital.

"North Charleston Police, Sergeant Galladeau."

"May I speak with Officer Stoll, please? This is Dr. Berringer in New York returning his call."

"You can talk with me, sir," Galladeau said. "Officer Stoll called you when he detained Ms. Drew Summers here."

"Is this a police station?"

"Nossir. This is an office at Charleston International Airport. Ms. Summers says she is under treatment in your care. Is that correct, sir?" He said *suh*.

As a rule, Berringer did not readily divulge such information, but he decided it was necessary. "That is correct. May I speak to her?"

"You bet . . . Carl, take the handcuffs off of her," Berringer heard him say. "The lady was raising a bit of a ruckus in the airport, sir."

Berringer groaned inwardly. "Handcuffs aren't necessary, Sergeant. Ms. Summers is not dangerous."

"I didn't think so. She seems like a nice enough lady. Officer Stoll was following policy."

"I understand. What did she do?"

"She accosted a passenger at one of the departure gates, yelling and stuff. Hold on, sir. Here she is."

"Corey?"

"Drew, how are you feeling?"

"I'm sorry to bother you," she said in a tiny voice.

"Don't worry about that. Are you being treated all right?"

"Yes, they've been very nice. I called Jim but he said—" Her voice broke and she waited a few moments before she tried again. "Jim said that I should call y— Oh, Corey—" Before she could say anything else, she broke down and began to sob uncontrollably.

50

Galladeau came back on and Berringer asked him if any charges were going to be filed.

"I don't believe so," he said. "Ms. Summers says she has no memory of what happened. Now that you and I have talked, I believe her."

Berringer asked him if he could have a man keep an eye on Drew until she could get a plane back to New York. Galladeau said he could, they'd let her walk around some, then he explained that Charleston International was not a large airport and there weren't many straight flights to New York: Drew would have to change in Atlanta.

Berringer asked him if it was possible for an officer to accompany her to Atlanta, and Galladeau said he would have to check with his captain. "This is just a little office here," he said, "not much more than a desk and a phone."

He called Berringer back fifteen minutes later to say that they could do it, and Berringer told him sincerely how much he appreciated everything he had done.

Then he spoke with Drew again. She was calm by then and was able to talk. She sounded exhausted and told him that she felt sleepy.

Six hours later, when Drew's jet set down at Kennedy, Jim was waiting for her at the arrival gate.

He drove her directly to the hospital in White Plains that Berringer had recommended.

The next day, when Berringer visited her, he found that Drew couldn't remember anything that had happened in the hours before she took the plane to Charleston, or during the flight itself. She said she remembered leaving her apartment for work, and then nothing until she found herself in the custody of a cop.

He deliberated giving her medication, but decided against it. She was in the hospital: if she had a recurrence of one of these episodes, she would be taken care of.

After a few days Berringer was more stumped than

he had ever been. Nurses' and techs' notes, his own daily observations—all indicated that there was nothing seriously wrong with her; no evidence of psychosis, no abnormal behavior. The staff liked her.

She did have trouble sleeping, the nurses reported, and she was very preoccupied. She interacted with the other patients well, liked taking long walks around the grounds, seldom could concentrate on reading or anything else for more than fifteen or twenty minutes.

Her tension was obvious, and Corey started having her lie down on the couch during sessions. When he asked her if she knew why she couldn't concentrate, she said she was afraid to.

"I'm afraid to go to sleep, I'm afraid to take a nap, I'm afraid to read. I think that if I get too involved with something and let my guard down, our lil' ol' Betty gon' jump me."

"At least you haven't lost your sense of humor."

"Wanna bet?"

"You're not doing yourself any good by wearing yourself down, Drew. If this other person is going to appear, there couldn't be a better place for it to happen than here."

"I'm *scared,* Corey."

"You sound as though she's becoming more real."

"She *is* real. She keeps trying to reach me, wanting me to do something."

"In Charleston?"

"I don't know where . . . She's younger than I am . . . It's peculiar, but in a way I feel sorry for her."

"Why?"

She had no idea, she said.

The next day when he had her on the couch, she mentioned that she hadn't heard from Jim.

"Maybe he's not sure what to do," Corey suggested. "He might feel he's intruding."

"How could he feel that?" She pushed off one of her

shoes with the toe of the other. "He wanted us to live together, practically asked me to marry him." She pushed off the other shoe.

"Maybe you ought to call him."

"Why should I?"

"Do you do so normally?"

"I used to."

"Then why not do it now?"

"Because I'd like to feel he cares about me."

"I can understand that. On the other hand, you won't know until you do talk to him."

She was silent. Then: "Dr. Berringer?"

He heard his last name and the southern tone and was immediately alert. "Yes . . ."

"I feel . . . just awful. So alone." There was a helpless appeal in her voice. It was the first time he had ever heard her use a tone like that, and it made him look at her. She had turned her head and their eyes met. His first reaction was emotional and sexual: She looked vulnerable and in need of him.

"I never felt this much alone," she said.

"Because of Jim?" he asked.

"Maybe. I just feel like . . . Dr. Berringer, could you come over here?"

He heard the southern accent clearly now, and got up. As he came around his desk Drew sat up. Her skirt moved up her legs.

He sat down beside her, wondering if this had happened because he'd pushed her too hard to call Jim, underestimated how threatening it was to her. And he wondered who this girl was. She looked as though she had the weight of the world on her shoulders.

"You are a very understandin' man, Dr. Berringer," she said.

She rested her hand on his forearm. As objective as he was, he was not unaffected.

"I'm glad you feel that way," he said. He smiled,

thinking to himself how appealing the girl was, and seductive. "You seem much more relaxed now."

"I feel so afraid. I'm glad you're close to me." Her hand dropped carelessly onto his thigh.

That was it. "Who are you?" he said pleasantly. Getting up, he went to his desk and turned on his tape recorder.

"You know very well who I am," Drew said, sitting up.

"I'd like you to tell me."

"Elizabeth Alexandra Fairchild . . . Betty to you. Scared of me?"

"No, you seem very nice. I just felt a little uncomfortable. Where are you from?"

She got up. She acted younger than Drew, yet at the same time more experienced. "I didn't come here to answer a lot of questions like a little bitty girl."

"What *did* you come here for?"

"To tell you I mean Drew no harm. I want you to tell her that. Tell her to stop fighting me."

"What do you want from her, Betty?"

"That's for me to know and for you to find out."

On impulse he picked up a pencil and a pad from the desk, offered them to her.

"Would you write your name for me?" he said.

"Whut for?"

"In case you're famous some day, I'll have your autograph."

She made a face that said how stupid, but she took the pencil from him, leaned over the pad and began to write. She wrote a couple of words, then stopped and looked up.

It was Drew, he saw immediately. She glanced at the signature, dropped the pencil on the desk and sat back down on the couch.

Berringer reached for the pad. "Can you remember anything at all?"

"No."

He glanced at what she had written: *Elizabeth Alexandra Fai* was as far as she'd gone.

"What was she like?" Drew asked him.

"Hard to tell," he said. "She wasn't around long enough. . . . What's the last thing you remember?" he said.

"You were telling me I ought to call Jim."

He ripped out the page with the signature, and handed the pad and pencil to her. "Can you write the name Elizabeth Alexandra Fairchild for me?" he said.

She did it, and he compared the two signatures.

They were different.

After dinner Drew was in group activity—Bingo this time—when the headline came to her. She went over to Liz, one of the assistant therapists, told her what she wanted to do and how important it was. As a rule, you were only permitted to do something on your own during free time, which started at nine, but Liz understood. She told Drew to go ahead.

Bursting with excitement, Drew ran to her room, where she jotted down the headline and everything else that popped into her head, then called Susan. "What do you think of this?" she asked. "'Come home to Belle's.'"

Drew held her breath, and finally Susan said, "It's good."

"You really think so?"

"It may even be kick-ass."

It was. It didn't take them long to decide on the look they wanted for the ads, and to devise a couple of TV spots. Inside of an hour they knew for sure they had a campaign.

Susan came up with a tag line, "Home was never like this," and Drew lost all track of time until her roommate came in at nine-thirty and asked her if she wanted to take a walk. Drew thanked her, said she couldn't right now, then she and Susan worked for another half hour.

When they hung up, she felt as if she'd come out of a dark tunnel.

She felt so good, in fact, that before she could change her mind she picked up the phone again and dialed Jim's number.

As soon as she heard the first ring she winced. Hang up, she told herself. Susan and Norman had called, and a couple of friends. If Jim wanted to talk to her, he'd have called too. But before she could hang up he was saying hello.

"What's happening, dude?" she said.

"Hey-y-y, Drew . . . How you feeling?"

She sensed it right away. Distance. She'd made a mistake. "Not bad." She wanted to mention the break-through, but something stopped her. "Resting. How about you?"

"Missing you. That's about it."

That gave her a lift. "I miss you too."

"Like to get out there next weekend if I can," he said.

"That would be great."

"Any chance of you coming home soon?"

"I don't know. Corey wants to give it another week."

"Well, you're not missing anything here in town. Same old grind, and gloomy weather."

He told her about an acquisition he was doing an analysis for, then they talked about friends, and finally he asked her if she and Berringer had found out anything new. She felt he was asking for a progress report and it bothered her, so she said no.

"How are your folks?" she asked.

"Fine."

"Say hello to them for me."

He said he would, then she asked him if he'd warmed up her car. "Sure did. Started right away."

They talked a while longer, and again he said that he'd like to come out next weekend if he could, but that he might have to go out of town. He didn't say why he hadn't called her, or why he couldn't have driven out even for an hour, and she didn't ask. If he wanted to come out he would.

Before they hung up, she told him that if he did make it out over the weekend there was a terrific restaurant in town they could try. He said it sounded good. She wanted to say I love you, but she didn't.

He didn't either.

As usual it took her a long time to fall asleep, and she thought of Jim's parents. They were nice people. His mother had sent her a card, but when Drew called her to thank her for it, she realized it had been sent more out of courtesy than anything else. His mother had been pleasant but distant. Drew understood why, but at the same time she couldn't help feeling hurt.

When she gave it more thought, she realized that it wasn't really Jim's mother she felt hurt about. It was her son.

"What you got, Corey?" Albertson asked.

Berringer usually could have done without these Saturday morning staffings. His colleagues used them less for discussion and brainstorming, which he would have enjoyed, than for covering their collective ass. As a consequence, the meetings boiled down to everybody's routine diagnoses of their in-house patients, which justified their continued hospitalization or release.

But this week he had arrived in the hospital's conference room a little early and deliberately took the first seat on Albertson's left. The chief always went around the table like a poker dealer, and Berringer wanted to be first this time: He needed input and he wanted fresh minds.

He started with his two minor cases. The first was the teenager he had on 4B. Suicidal a few weeks back, he looked pretty stable now. Everyone agreed: keep him another week to make sure he was clean, then have some after-care lined up for him.

The old guy with the dementia had everyone in agreement also: there was little chance he would get any better. The family would have to be spoken to about putting him in a home.

Then he opened Drew's folder, and after he gave a brief history—twenty-three-year-old female Caucasian . . . good health . . . seemingly oriented as to person place and time, abusive family—he said, "I can't figure this one out. She originally presented in my office with a kind of bizarre story about fugue-state episodes. I mean I thought it was bizarre because she didn't seem the type." He went on to tell about her subsequent episodes, including the one he had witnessed here at the hospital.

"They're increasing in frequency and length, and I'm not sure what to do with her," he concluded. "I have her tentatively diagnosed as a brief reactive psychosis, but I'm having trouble holding her there."

"Why tentatively?" Albertson asked.

"For a couple of reasons. The first is this other personality she adopts. As I told you, she talked in a southern accent and gave me a different handwriting sample."

"You got her on medication?" someone asked.

Berringer said no. "If she manifested psychosis continuously I could see the rationale for using some antipsychotics, but she doesn't. It comes and goes. Besides, she doesn't want medication, and I don't want to pressure her any more than she's pressuring herself right now."

Joe Hutchins said, "What about hypnosis?"

Berringer wasn't surprised. Hutchins leaned heavily on hypnosis. He shook his head. "I don't want to do anything to encourage these hallucinations."

"Whether you want to encourage them or not," Hutchins said, "you've got some kind of a split or differentiated ego state here. Sounds to me like a perfect case for hypnosis."

Berringer said he wouldn't rule it out. "But I'm not ready for it yet. Once you start with hypnosis you're committed, and until I'm sure it's right for her I don't want to start."

"I'd certainly try it," Hutchins insisted. "She sounds like a multiple to me."

"That's what I keep thinking, but I've never seen a real multiple," Berringer said. "Anybody here who has?"

The youngest of the group, Bill Sargent, said, "I saw one once in training, but I don't think I can help you. Why aren't you sure she's a brief reactive psychosis?"

"Good question. I don't have a good answer. I just get the feeling that I'm missing something. The woman is just too basically stable."

"You're talking psychosis or multiple here and you're talking stable too?" Hutchins's expression indicated he'd heard everything now.

"This girl is different from any case I've ever seen, Joe. She's bright, she's open, she doesn't appear to have any sexual hang-ups, never came on to me."

"Except yesterday."

"Except yesterday. But all the reports on her verify my own feelings—stable, outgoing personality."

"Maybe she's shamming," Hutchins said.

"I thought about it," Berringer said, "but it wouldn't make sense. There's no pressure on her for that type of behavior."

Greg Wallace, the hypnotherapist of the group, spoke up. "It might not be a bad idea to think of her as a multiple," he said. "I mean in the sense that she may be having an intrusion from a past life."

Hutchins groaned. "Jesus, not that again."

Wallace didn't take offense. "You don't have to listen if you don't want," he said, "but Corey's asking for help, and there's stuff here consistent with a past life."

"Oh bullshit," Hutchins answered.

"Why bullshit?" Wallace said. "We're talking about a

young woman redoing her hair in a sixtyish style, and dressing that way too. How would she know what the style was then?"

"The way I would—go see a Beatles movie. Go see any movie from the sixties. You ever watch TV?"

Wallace was stubborn. "Joe, all I can say is that I've seen people before who looked like multiples and then turned out otherwise. Multiples are rare, but past life experiences occur fairly routinely. In fact," he said to Berringer, "if you find you're still not getting anywhere in the next few weeks, and your patient is amenable, I'd like to interview her. It sounds as though it's very possible she's retrieving data from a past life. Frankly, I'd like to see her regressed to that life under controlled conditions. I've done it before with some results that would amaze you. You too, putz," he said to Hutchins.

"Corey, have you considered the possibility that she's not telling you the truth?" Sargent asked.

"About what?" Berringer said.

"About her father only molesting her sister."

"I have considered it, yes. It's very possible the father bothered Drew as well."

"How about guilt over her sister's suicide . . . ?"

"I've considered that too," Berringer said, glancing down at his notes. "Drew found the body, and she and her sister were very close. The suicide note the sister left was addressed to Drew rather than to the mother, so there's no doubt in my mind she feels there was something she could have done. But I still don't get the feeling I've got a multiple."

"What's bothering you?" Hutchins asked.

"Well, for one thing, I can't find a stresser. She broke into this other personality just like that. I questioned her to find out if she'd felt threatened, or felt that she needed help, or was frightened. She said no, and it was the same with all her other breaks. She couldn't remember having the slightest feeling of anxiety before any of—"

60

The phone rang and Albertson picked it up. "Yes."

He handed it to Berringer.

"Dr. Berringer . . ."

Whatever was said to him, he was visibly upset. "When did it happen?" he asked.

He thanked the caller and hung up.

"Looks like it doesn't matter what we come up with at this point," he said to everyone. "My patient has disappeared from the hospital."

4

Once the New Jersey Turnpike was behind her and the countryside became all lush woods and rolling hills, she drove with the top down. Below Washington, D.C. there were intermittent sprinkles, but it was so warm that, except for when she was caught in a sudden shower near Fredericksburg, she didn't put the top back up.

Toward dusk, she pulled into a small service station a little above Richmond. Stopping beside the nearest set of pumps, she set about touching up her makeup. Even after she was done she didn't make a move to get out of the car, and the few people there—including a mechanic and a teenage attendant in a blue cap—kept looking over at her. She and the Mustang were something.

After a couple of minutes the young attendant went over. He'd been fishing the day before and was red from the first sun in a week.

"Do you want service, ma'am?"

"Indeed I do," she answered, as friendly as he thought she'd be. "Fill it up, please."

"This is self-serve."

"Self-serve? Whut is that, pray tell?"

"You have to pump your own gas at these pumps."

"I wouldn't much like doin' that. Can't you pump it for me?"

He pointed to the other set of pumps. "Over there I can. Where it says 'Full Serve.'"

She looked a little perplexed, but she started the car and drove where he'd pointed.

As he took the hose from the pump, she got out and stretched. Hands clasped high, breasts straining against her blouse, she was delicious. He felt it from his knees to his stomach and he wished he was standing in front of her.

She caught him looking and smiled like she didn't mind at all. He blushed even redder and she asked him where the ladies' room was.

He thought of all kinds of nice things as he watched her walk way, and when she was out of sight the ugliness of the station crashed in on him.

A couple of girls who'd been by the Coke machine went by. "Jo-o-o-seph," one of them purred. He knew her, and ordinarily he'd have been embarrassed, but he paid her no attention.

The lady got back behind the wheel just as he finished washing the windshield. She found her credit card in her handbag and gave it to him. Just standing next to her gave him a charge.

When she'd signed the slip and handed it back to him, he was about to rip out her copy, but didn't.

"Ma'm?"

She started the car. "Hm?"

"You didn't sign the right name here."

"Does that matter?"

"Yes ma'm."

He handed her the board that held the charge slip. "Well, you are absolutely right," she said. "May I?"

She held out a hand for the pen, and he gave it to her, watched her cross out the name she wrote—Elizabeth A. Fairchild—and put in Drew Summers above it. "I trust I may leave now without fear of arrest for petty theft, arson, or murder in the first degree?"

She didn't say it nasty-like, and he knew he should have asked for her driver's license, but she was just too

63

gorgeous. He grinned, and she rewarded him with another smile. It was the kind that made him feel closer to being a man.

He almost forgot to give her her receipt. He stared after her as she drove off, and he knew that he would not forget her face or that smile for a good many years.

She stayed in a motel overnight, and about eight o'clock the following evening she stopped for gas again near Manning, sixty or so miles from Greenview. As she had ever since she had written the wrong name the previous day, she signed the credit card slip correctly, got her receipt, and eased the Mustang out of the station toward the highway.

Something occurred to her and she slowed. Reaching under the dash, she pressed a button, and a spring-operated panel snapped down. Attached to the panel was a duplicate of the .32 that Raymond Ordway had had installed in Betty's car twenty-four years ago, easy for a woman to handle, and deadly. After she pointed the gun once at an imaginary victim, she replaced it and expertly snapped the panel up out of sight again.

Less than two hours later the Mustang was moving along the beginning of Greenview's Main Street, past car dealers and fast food stores that hadn't been there twenty-three years before.

Past Highway 78 the old town began. Hurricane Hugo had roared and rampaged through other parts of town, but had spared the white-painted stores and shops, and the old trees of this section.

She knew exactly where she was going. She turned right onto Cedar, passed trendy shops that used to be a sleepy row of tight little cottages, and headed for the elegant facade of the Spengler House one block down. She slowed automatically when she crossed the intersection, and the tires stuttered over one of the few cobble-stone streets left in Greenview.

She pulled up before the graystone front of the hotel, the polished brass lamps beside its doors gleaming with pleasant yellow light. There was no sign that indicated valet parking: at the Spengler there was no other kind.

Leaving the engine running, she threw an arm over the seat and stared up at the filigreed veranda as if hypnotized. She seemed hardly aware of the uniformed doorman who came around to the driver's side and opened the door for her. To his pleasant "Evening, ma'm" she said something inaudible, and continued to stare. "It has not changed one little bit," she marveled, "not one little bit."

"You've been to our hotel before, ma'm?"

"*Been* here! My daddy and my mama and my uncle Ray and me? We used to come here every Friday night for dinner."

She grabbed her handbag suddenly, almost bouncing out of the car. "I have a suitcase in the trunk," she said, heading for the arched entry door.

The lobby was unusually crowded for this time of night. Many people were in formal attire, and she attracted stares as she sauntered to the front desk. Part of the reason had to do with how she had done her hair and the way she was dressed. But there was something else: a combination of self-conscious innocence and sexuality that had always made men stare at Betty Fairchild—some with amusement, others with distinct interest.

"My name is . . . Drew Summers," she told the desk clerk. "I have a reservation."

While he consulted a card file, she glanced around the lobby. At first she didn't notice the short, pudgy little man who had stopped and was staring at her.

Harold Bream was fascinated. He thought he was seeing things. It was just not possible for someone to look so much like somebody else. And dress like her.

65

He kept staring, hoping he'd catch her eye. He did, but she passed over him, then came right back. With recognition.

He nearly shit a brick: she was smiling and waving to him. He turned to see if there was someone behind him. No one. He'd have sworn she even called his name before she turned back to the hotel clerk. Bream headed for the ballroom.

The clerk had noticed her wave to someone. "You've been to Greenview before, I take it."

"I used to live here."

"How long ago was that?"

". . . A long time," she said. "Why's everybody so dressed up?"

"We're having our annual Casino Night—in the Robert E. Lee Ballroom. It's for charity. Invitation only, I'm afraid."

He told her he hoped she was going to enjoy her stay, and after she gave him her credit card, he took the pen from the green marble inkstand and handed it to her.

While she was filling out the registration card, she was unaware that Harold Bream had returned and had brought a woman with him. Together they were waiting for her to turn, but it was taking so long that the woman, Juleen Caldecott, was getting ready to tell Harold to forget it.

Just then the girl finished what she was doing. She turned around and Juleen was astounded. Harold had said there was a resemblance. Resemblance my foot, she thought. The girl was Betty to a t, even to the Jacqueline Kennedy hairdo. And the dress looked like it was made for Betty. Juleen felt she was in a time warp.

"*Now* you believe me," Harold gloated. "And I'm telling you, I think she knows me."

He was about to suggest that they go over and talk to her when she spotted them. Her face lit up.

"Juleen," she called. "Juleen Willis!"

No one had called Juleen by her maiden name in almost twenty years, and as the girl started toward her, Juleen sensed that she should get away right now, that something unpleasant was going to take place. Yet she couldn't move. She couldn't do anything but say to herself, *No, this girl is not going to do what I think she is going to. She is not going to act like she's Betty and that she knows me. That is impossible.*

She was wrong.

"Juleen!" The girl said her name with Betty's voice, with Betty's tone, and she came up and hugged Juleen with all the impulsiveness of a seventeen-year-old. "Oh, it's so wonderful to see you!" she said.

Juleen disengaged herself and stared.

"Now whut are you lookin' at me like that for?" the girl said lightly. "Something wrong with me?" She turned to Bream. "Harold, have I got some kind of a rash all over me?"

Harold Bream, who like half the boys in Greenview High had had fantasies about Betty Fairchild, just gaped.

Juleen finally found her voice. "I'm afraid we've never met," she said.

"Never met! Juleen, are you kidding me? How can you— Harold, did you hear that?"

Harold nodded, still gaping.

The girl smiled faintly. "You better close that mouth, Harold. You remember whut Miss Beltrage used to say."

Harold Bream knew exactly what Miss Beltrage used to say. She'd been his fourth-grade teacher, and she'd said that if he didn't keep his mouth closed, she was going to rent him out as a Venus fly trap. He was so shocked that when the girl impishly put a finger under his chin and closed his mouth he didn't do a thing.

Juleen Caldecott felt her skin beginning to crawl. "We'd better get back," she said to Harold. "You'll have to excuse us."

"Juleen!" The girl said it so sharply that Juleen

automatically stopped. "You haven't changed a bit," she said reprovingly. "Same as always. I never saw anyone get so uptight for no reason."

Juleen had the presence of mind to speak quietly and firmly. "I don't know how you know my name," she said to the girl, "but I would appreciate it if you would not call me Juleen. I don't mean to be rude . . ."

So saying, she took Harold's arm and headed for a heavily curtained doorway on the other side of the lobby. But she had no intention of letting this drop.

"Harold, we have to find Lee," she said as he parted the curtain for her and she went past him.

Inside the Robert E. Lee Ballroom, standing with his back to the entrance, Sergeant Warren Hawkins hardly noticed Mrs. Caldecott and the man go past him, any more than he'd noticed anyone else coming and going for the past half hour. She was a good-looking woman, tall and built, and for a while he'd had a great time watching her and all the other stuff going by, but he'd been on his feet for three hours now, and Greenview's rich and famous no longer turned him on. He was tired.

Hawkins shifted his weight to his other leg and glanced toward the roulette table as some guy raised his voice. ". . . I can pick up my bet anytime I want," the guy was saying. Hawkins moved a little closer, saw that one of the hotel security guys was on the scene, and lost interest.

He looked at his watch: ten-twenty. One hour and forty minutes to go. He'd be glad when it was over. He didn't dig the sorority atmosphere. Maybe it was all for charity, but nobody here gave one good crap about charity. This was a social affair, and everybody was here to be seen. He'd been told it was a fifty-year tradition in this town, but there was some heavy betting going down, and it was still gambling and it was still technically illegal. If they'd just canceled the whole affair and donated all the bread they spent on gowns and everything else, they could not only build a new wing, but a new hospital.

Juleen Caldecott finally found her husband at one of the dice tables.

"Lee, you have to come out to the lobby, quick," she said. "There's somebody out there you just have to see."

Lee's murmur was something less than interested, but Juleen insisted. "Lee, you have to."

"Jules, not now . . ."

"Yes, now. Right this minute."

"Who is it?"

"Never mind who it is." She tried to pull him, but he resisted.

"When this roll is over."

She spotted Harold and called to him. He didn't hear her, so she made her way over to him and grabbed him. "I found Lee," she said. "You hurry on out to the lobby and see if you can't hold that girl there."

"What can I say to her?"

"Darlin', just be your own eloquent self. I'll be right out there with Lee. Go *ahead*." She gave him a push and sent him on his way, then turned to go back to Lee.

She let out a yip of surprise and nearly jumped out of her skin. The girl was standing right in front of her. If she hadn't looked where she was going she'd have run into her.

"Juleen," the girl said, "are you going to talk to me or are you not? You're not being very friendly."

People were staring and Juleen was embarrassed.

"I . . . You took me so by surprise," Juleen said. She looked over the girl's shoulder, saw that Lee was still involved at the dice table.

The girl took her arm. "Well come on and let's sit down and talk. My goodness I—"

Juleen took her arm away. "Please don't do that," she said. She wondered if the girl was disturbed.

"Juleen, what has gotten into you!"

"Nothing has gotten into me," Juleen said, gritting her teeth, "and I asked you not to call me Juleen."

"Well pardon me, Miss *Willis*," the girl said loudly, "I didn't know I was being so offensive!"

People were staring at them openly now and Juleen was getting claustrophobic. "Lee!"

It came out louder than she'd intended, and she felt as if everyone in the room had to be staring at her. "Lee!" she called again, and finally, thank God, he saw her. She waved him over urgently. *Now!* she mouthed.

"Lee?" the girl said. She looked toward the dice table, and when Juleen saw the expression on her face she felt caught in that same time warp: The girl was waiting for him expectantly.

Lee Caldecott, wondering what the damned emergency was, slowed down as soon as he spotted the girl. He had seen her before, knew who she was, and he knew there was going to be trouble. He wished he was anyplace but here, and when he reached them, he avoided looking at the girl. "What's going on?"

"This young lady will not leave me alone," Juleen said. "Maybe you can find out why."

Caldecott concealed his apprehension. "Is there anything we can do for you, miss?"

"Lee," the girl said, "don't be boring."

Caldecott looked at his wife, but her expression said, Handle it.

"Do you know me?" he asked the girl.

"Why shouldn't she?" Juleen said quickly. "She knows everybody else."

He tried again. "Can I be of any help to you, Miss, uh . . ."

He left the sentence unfinished, trying to stare her down. She just stared back at him brazenly, making him so uncomfortable—making him almost cringe inside—that he knew he'd have to speak first. Before he could, the girl began to giggle.

70

"Lee Caldecott," she said, "you have not changed one little bit either. That's whut you used to say at the soda fountain—give the girls that flirty look and say, 'Can I be of any help to you, Jo Anne? Can I be of any help to you, Bunny?'"

With Lee here, Juleen felt more sure of herself. "Just who are you?" she demanded. "Did you hear me?" she said when the girl paid her no attention.

She was looking over Juleen's shoulder and her eyes had lit up. "Hold the phone," she murmured. "Will you just hold the phone . . ."

She brushed past Juleen as though she and Lee no longer existed.

"Uncle Ray!" She said it so loudly that even over the sounds of gambling and the noise of a hundred conversations, people turned to look at her.

Raymond Ordway was among them. Usually he was as unflappable and quick in social situations as he was in business or on the tennis court, but for one of the few times in his life he was caught unawares. His mouth fell open and he felt his lips form an O of astonishment as he saw coming toward him, all aglow with happiness, a girl that could have been his niece Betty.

Luckily the glass in his hand didn't have more than ice in it, because when the girl threw herself into his arms the contents spilled.

She hugged him with all the fervor of a long-lost child, holding him so close he could feel the entire youthful length of her body along his own, smell her perfume. His long-dead niece's perfume. She lifted her face to his and looked at him adoringly. "You glad to see me?" It was Betty's smile, Betty's voice, and he felt something inside of him coming alive.

By then he'd recovered his self-possession and his eyes narrowed.

"Let me go," he said to her.

When she didn't, he dropped the now-empty glass and grabbed her arms in a painful grip.

"What kind of a stupid joke do you think this is," he said, shoving her from him.

Surprise and hurt appeared in her eyes. "Uncle Ray," she said, massaging her arm, "whut's the matter? Why are you being so mean to me?"

It was Betty's tone and Betty's look of hurt, but common sense told him this could not be her.

"You know who this girl is?" he demanded of Lee, who had come up to them. Lee said he didn't, and Ordway looked around. "Anybody here know her? Somebody has to. How did she get in here?"

"Uncle Ray," the girl said to him, her voice starting to break, "why are you treating me like this? You know who I am. I'm Betty. I've come back."

Silence was spreading rapidly through the huge room. A tall man who had seen the disturbance was shouldering his way through the onlookers. He was a big man, and people made way for him quickly.

"What's going on?" he said when he reached Ordway.

"This girl is making a scene. I don't know who she is, and nobody else seems to either."

"You want to tell us?" the big man said to her.

"Mark Turnage, don't you start on me now," the girl said. "You are supposed to be my friend. Or are you going to say you don't know me too?"

Turnage exchanged a look with Ordway before he said, "I'm afraid I don't know you, miss."

People were beginning to murmur. The few who had known Betty Fairchild were amazed.

The girl had lost her self-assurance, but she stood her ground. "Uncle Ray, are you mad at me or something?" she said. "Did I do something wrong?"

"You better take her out of here," Ordway said to Turnage.

72

The big man touched her arm. "Would you be kind enough to come with me, miss?"

She jerked her arm from him. "No, I will not be kind enough to come with you, and you keep them greasy hands to yourself!" She was starting to cry now. "Uncle Ray," she said to Ordway, "why are you acting this way?"

She wasn't a small girl, but she looked small and pathetic alongside of Turnage, and people began to feel sorry for her.

Turnage's mouth tightened and he grabbed her arm. "Miss, I'm the chief of police here, and you're causing a disturbance. Now if you'll just come with me we can have a nice little talk outside."

"Get your hands off me, I told you," the girl said dangerously. She tried to pull away from him, but he held her and she lost her temper. Her lips twisted into a sneer and, screaming and cursing, she turned on him like a crazed animal, slapping, punching, and kicking.

Turnage did the best he could to ward her off, but as big as he was he couldn't keep her away from him. He had to do a dance to keep from being kicked, and for a moment it looked as though he might have to hurt her. Fortunately, Sergeant Hawkins came up behind her just then and grabbed her arms.

"Okay, miss," he said, pinning them to her side, "just settle down now and take it easy. Easy does it."

The girl was too surprised to do anything until Hawkins pivoted with her and started heading her toward the exit. Then she let out a howl of protest, went limp and dug in with her heels.

Hawkins was forced to stop, was barely able to grab one of her wrists as she twisted around and almost got away from him. "Uncle Ray," she screamed, "don't let 'em take me away! Please Uncle Ray, stop them. My God. Oh my God, Uncle Ray, don't you love me anymore? Please!"

She was sobbing hysterically now, and like everyone else, Ordway was touched, almost tempted to tell the officer to get his hands off her. Hawkins himself, still holding on to her wrist, was getting a little concerned.

She held out her free hand to Ordway. "Uncle Ray, please don't let them do this to me! It's me, Uncle Ray—I've come back. I've come back!"

Hawkins held her tight, telling her that nobody wanted to hurt her and to settle down. Finally she made one last effort to break free. "Uncle Ray!" she cried at the top of her lungs. "Please—Uncle Ray, help me-e-e-e!" She followed it with a sobbing wail that sent chills through everyone who heard it.

Hawkins felt her stiffen suddenly. At the same time a look of stunned surprise appeared on her face and she shrieked in pain. Then her eyes rolled up until only the whites showed and she went limp.

Turnage reached Hawkins as he was easing the girl to the floor. "Keep everybody back," Turnage said.

Kneeling down, he pressed his ear to the girl's chest, then apparently satisfied with what he heard, he set about reviving her. Someone offered a rolled-up jacket and Turnage put it under her head.

The girl's skirt had ridden up. Juleen Caldecott knelt down opposite Turnage and pulled it down.

She was shaken. She felt guilty. Perhaps if she had been a little nicer this would not have happened. After all, the girl hadn't done anything terrible to her or anyone else. When she was screaming and carrying on, it had flashed through Juleen's mind that that was exactly the way Betty would have acted under the same circumstances, gone completely crazy. The thought occurred to her that maybe this was Betty's long-lost daughter. Betty had never been exactly stable, and this girl didn't seem to be either . . . But that was impossible. Betty had never been pregnant. At least not long enough for it to show. This was too weird. And what was most weird was how the girl seemed to know everyone, even Mark.

"Can I do anything to help?" she asked him.

"No, looks like she's gonna be okay . . . You ever see the likes of this?" he asked her.

Juleen knew exactly what he meant. She shook her head.

Turnage said, "Any idea who she might be?"

She shook her head again. "I met her out in the lobby only a few minutes ago. It was very creepy."

People were crowding in on them, and a photographer was taking pictures. Turnage glared up at everyone and raised his voice. "You people, and I mean every one of you, take one step back and take it right now."

Hawkins saw to it that they obeyed.

Juleen was smoothing back the girl's hair when she opened her eyes.

She saw Turnage first, then Juleen, and the expression on her face struck Juleen immediately: surprise. And fear. No recognition. No hostility. She was a different person. She took in the gowns and the tuxedos surrounding her, the faces staring down.

"Where am I?" she asked Juleen.

She spoke like a northerner, Juleen thought.

Turnage answered before she could. "Same place you were a minute ago," he said sarcastically.

"You're in the ballroom of the Spengler Hotel," Juleen said, trying to make up for Turnage's unfriendliness.

"Where? Where is it?" Betty was gone.

"In Greenview," Juleen said. Something made her add, "South Carolina."

"What's your name?" Turnage said.

". . . Drew Summers."

"Can you get up?"

"Give me a minute."

"Take your time," he said, "because when you're ready, I got some questions for you. The first one's gonna be how the hell you know my name."

When they helped her to her feet she paid no attention to the people looking at her.

Including Raymond Ordway. He was almost directly in front of the girl but she didn't even glance his way, and he was disappointed. Obviously she was not the least bit interested in him anymore. She wasn't interested in anybody, for that matter, and Turnage and his officer led her away without any resistance.

It left Raymond Ordway feeling let down, empty. He told the reporter from the Greenview *Sentinel* that he had nothing to say, then he told Lee and Juleen he was leaving. When they were ready to leave, he said, he'd like them to stop by the house for a nightcap.

"Tell Turnage to give me a call as soon as he has a moment," he told Lee. Then he went home.

5

She had a bite to eat with Turnage and Hawkins in the hotel coffee shop. With Hawkins anyway; Turnage had coffee.

Hawkins liked the girl. From what he'd seen of her in the ballroom he'd figured her for a snotty little bitch, but she was decent. Once she calmed down she was cooperative: showed them her ID, told them where she was from, where she worked, everything.

She was scared, he was convinced of that—scared and lost. She didn't seem to know anything, where she was, when she got here, how she got here.

He felt sorry for her, especially after she said that she'd been in a mental hospital before she found herself here, and that the last thing she remembered was going to her room after breakfast. She even thought it was still the same day, until Turnage told her that if she'd left New York after breakfast, the only way she could get here the same day was if she came by plane. He had to show her a newspaper before she believed a whole day had gone by. That hit her hard.

Turnage didn't care though. Even after she gave him her doctor's name and telephone number he gave her a bad time, acted like he didn't believe a word she was saying, asked for proof.

"Proof of what?" the girl asked him.

"Proof of this story you're telling us," he said.

"But I just told you I can't remember anything after I—"

"I know what you told me, but if you left New York yesterday, you stopped places, you stayed somewhere. Let's see something."

Hawkins thought the girl was going to come apart, but she was tougher than she looked. She dug around in her bag, started pulling out pieces of paper and examining them.

While she was doing it, Chuck Pennington came over, camera in hand, and asked if he might join them. Turnage said no he might not. This was police business and Chuck could take a walk.

Chuck got smart, told Turnage that if this was police business, did he intend to arrest the girl? It was the wrong thing to say, because Turnage did not like reporters in general and the *Sentinel* in particular.

"Not yet I don't, because I am trying to keep this friendly," he said. "But if people are gonna come over here and interfere, I just may take her down to the station and question here there. Now"—he smiled evilly—"you want to be the cause of me doing that?"

Chuck backed off, snapping a couple of fast pictures of the girl while he did. Then he sat down in another booth and joined everybody else in the place pretending not to notice what was going on.

The girl was lucky. She had a receipt from the previous night from a motel in Virginia and some charge slips for gas. She was relieved, and Hawkins felt it was more because she'd found out where she'd been than that her story checked out.

Turnage wasn't satisfied. "How'd you get in the ballroom? No one got in there tonight without an invitation."

"I don't know," she said.

"How'd you know my name?" he asked her. "And Juleen Caldecott's, and Raymond Ordway's?"

"I don't know what you're talking about."

"You know damn well what I'm talking about." He kept his voice down, but he was mad. "You sashay in here dressed like Betty Fairchild, looking like Betty Fairchild and acting like Betty Fairchild, and you—"

"Betty Fairchild?" The girl sat up. "Who's Betty Fairchild?"

"Who *was* Betty Fairchild, you mean," Turnage growled. "She's been dead over twenty years."

"You mean there actually was such a person?"

Turnage said yes and Hawkins thought the girl's chin was going to hit the table. *She* started asking the questions then, kept after Turnage until he told her the whole story. Hawkins was interested. He'd heard something about the case, but he never knew the details.

"My God," the girl said. "Ohmigod."

She had such a strange look on her face that Hawkins didn't know if she was going to laugh or cry, and when Turnage asked her why she was interested she said, "Chief, you wouldn't believe me if I told you."

Turnage didn't like that answer, and he started on her again: What did she want here? How did she know his name and everybody else's?

But now, for some reason the girl wasn't afraid. From what Turnage had told her, she said, she didn't think she'd done anything terrible, but if he wanted to bring some kind of charge against her, fine. In the meantime why didn't he just try to act like a human being? At least until she finished eating.

That made Turnage back off some. He calmed down and asked her why she'd been in a mental hospital.

She said she had blackouts, did things that she couldn't remember. Like this. She'd had a suspicion of what was causing the blackouts, she said, but up until now she didn't know for sure. Now she did: They had something to do with Betty Fairchild. At that point Turnage found a spot on the table that he looked at disdainfully, and even Hawkins had to admit that it

79

wasn't the best answer he'd heard. Still, he got the feeling she was telling the truth.

Turnage stayed on her case. It wasn't like him to be this mean, and finally Hawkins thought he understood: Raymond Ordway. Ordway was going to want to know all about this girl, so Turnage had to find out all he could. But he didn't have to be as hard-nosed as he was. He was acting like the kid was some kind of a threat. Hawkins wondered which one of them was going to blow up first.

He figured it would be Turnage because he was doing that thing with his head that he did when he got mad—tipping it to the side like he was listening to an invisible midget giving him a lot of bullshit. He was biting on his lower lip at the same time, which if you knew him, meant he was ready to lower the boom.

"Okay, you had your sandwich," Turnage said, "and I assume it is not going to hurt your digestion if we get down to cases. What are you doing down here?"

Drew turned to Hawkins. "Am I totally out of it or did he ask me that same thing five times already?"

Hawkins smiled. "She got you there, Chief."

The girl said, "For the sixth time—"

Turnage cut her off. "I know—you don't know."

"I not only don't know," she said angrily, "but I don't think I even want to talk to you anymore."

"Well, you better, young lady, because if I don't think I want you to spend the night outside of jail, you won't!"

Other diners were looking over at them, and when a girl in the next booth suddenly turned around, Turnage said, "'D you finish your banana split, pumpkin?"

Blushing, she said no and turned back fast. The other kids in the booth giggled and laughed.

"Chief—" The girl started to say something, then changed her mind and gave Turnage a funny look. She kept staring at him, not saying a word until he asked her if she'd heard what he said. She said yes.

80

"What are you looking at me like that for?" he asked her. "Or don't you know that either?"

"Something just flashed on me."

"Let's hear it."

". . . It's about you."

"Fire away."

She hesitated, then: "You were about seventeen . . . You wanted to get a football scholarship—to Notre Dame. And you wanted to travel—to Brazil, I think. You wanted to go down the Amazon. You saved up for a long time, then your father got very sick . . . He died, and it was one of the worst times you went thr—"

"That's enough." Turnage had turned red. He looked mad enough to hit the girl, and Hawkins was worried. He didn't feature tangling with his own boss. "Where the hell did you get that from?" Turnage snapped.

"I don't know. I just thought of it. You said you wanted to hear it, and I told you."

"What are you after!"

The girl was played out. "I'll tell you what," she said, "can we just hold all this till tomorrow? I don't even know what I'm saying anymore. After I get some sleep I'll tell you anything you want to know."

"You've got a reservation here at the hotel—for a week," Turnage said. "Did you make it?"

"No. At least I don't remember making it."

Turnage glanced at Hawkins. "I checked at the desk," Hawkins said. "The reservation was made on your credit card. You even asked for a veranda room."

"So we can assume you made the reservation," Turnage said. "Which means you planned on being here. I'm asking you why."

"And I'm telling you I don't know!"

"And I'm telling you that your story smells as bad as Warner's sawmill. You come in here acting like the long-dead niece of one of the most prominent and wealthiest men in this part of the state, and as soon as you arrive you make sure you get right to him. Well, young lady, it doesn't take an expert to know you're here for something, and it isn't to admire the azaleas! Did you hear what I said?"

Drew was looking at someone across the room. "Yes. I'm sorry," she said. "Who is that woman?"

"Which one?" Turnage asked her.

"The black waitress."

"GG Johnson," Turnage answered.

"She's been staring at me like she doesn't like me."

"Considering who you look like, I'm sure she doesn't," Turnage said.

". . . Does she have a brother?" Drew said.

"Two," Turnage said.

Drew continued to stare, then suddenly she said, "Edward . . . Is one named Edward?"

". . . She *had* a brother named Ed," Turnage said.

Their own waitress put the check on the table.

Drew reached for her bag. "Gentlemen, I'm beat. I want to go to sleep. I'll be glad to answer any more questions tomorrow. May I go?" She put some bills down. "That should cover my part. Good night, Mr. Hawkins."

She left them sitting there.

Hawkins said, "Uh, Mark—about how she got into the ballroom. That coulda been my fault . . ."

Turnage didn't say anything, and Hawkins said, "All that stuff about the football scholarship, and the Amazon, and your father—that true?"

"Yeah."

"How would she know that?"

"Beats the shit outta me . . . She might've found it out before she came here," Turnage said. Getting up, he threw a couple of dollars on the table, told Hawkins he had to make a call. Then he stopped. "That part about the Amazon, though," he added grudgingly. "Not many people I ever told about that. Meet me by the phones."

At the front desk, along with her key the clerk gave

Drew a funny look when she said she wanted to make sure she was registered.

As she turned away she almost ran into someone holding a worn briefcase under his arm—the reporter from the coffee shop. On the plump side and sloppy, he gave her a gap-toothed grin.

"Hi, Ms. Summers. My name is Chuck Pennington. I'm from the Greenview *Sentinel*. Like to talk with you for a minute."

Something occurred to her. She turned back to the clerk. "Excuse me, can I see the card I filled out when I registered?"

While the clerk went to get it Pennington indicated the ballroom. "I was in there when that altercation occurred between you and Mr. Ordway. I thought you might like to comment on it."

"Mr. Pennington, I'm the last one in the world who can tell you anything about anything right now."

The clerk handed her the registration card she'd signed. She looked it over, frowning.

"Something wrong?" the clerk said.

"No . . . no," she said, handing the card back. "Thank you."

Pennington kept asking her questions all the way to the elevator, but she shook her head wearily and said nothing. The door was open and she stepped in.

When she hit a button and he held the door, she said, "Mr. Pennington, be a nice guy. Not now?"

He wasn't happy about it, but he let the door close. Then he headed back for the desk, curious to take a look at that registration card if he could.

In her room Drew sat back on the bed for a while, going over what had happened and trying to calm down. When she felt she was in control of herself, she called Susan. Not getting an answer, she found her address book and dialed Corey's number.

"This is Dr. Berringer," his recorded voice said. She dialed the number the recording said to call if it was an emergency, left a message, then went in to draw a bath.

The phone beside the bathtub rang almost immediately. She turned the water off.

"Corey?"

"Drew, am I glad to talk to you! Are you all right?"

"I'm fine, Corey. I'm in a town called Greenview, South Carolina."

"I know. I just got a call from the chief of police there—a fellow named Turnage."

"He called you?"

"Yes. He wanted to know if you were my patient. I couldn't tell him that, naturally, so we had to kind of talk around it. First, though, Drew, when do you think you'll be coming home?"

"I don't know. I'll probably leave here tomorrow. I'm not sure yet. Did the chief tell you what happened?"

"Yes, he said you, quote, caused a public disturbance."

"But did he tell you what he told me—that I called people by name that I've never seen before in my life, and that I knew them?"

"Yes. He didn't sound very—"

"Did he also tell you that I look exactly like a girl who lived in this town and is now dead?"

"Yes he did."

"Did he tell you her name was Betty Fairchild?"

"Yes."

"Is that something or is that something?"

"I'm still concerned."

"Concerned! Corey, don't you realize what this means? For the first time in weeks I'm beginning to feel that maybe I'm not a nut—I can't tell you how—"

"Don't misunderstand me, Drew. If what the chief told me is the truth—and now from what you say, it is—I'm worried about what could happen to you."

84

"There's nothing to be worried about. I'm even getting flashes about people, Corey, picking up on things about them that I couldn't possibly know."

"I understand. The chief of police told me about that too. He also said that Betty Fairchild's family is very influential in that town. You're all alone down there, and if they were to get upset and decide that they don't like something you do, you could be in for trouble. That worries me more than anything."

"Corey, that's sweet, but you can relax. Tomorrow I'm going to take a walk around, maybe find some people who knew this girl and talk with them. Then I'm coming home."

"Well, I hope you'll be careful. You don't want to antagonize those people, especially the police."

"I won't. Corey, you do believe I'm not making all this up, that it's really happening . . ."

"Of course I do, but I don't know *why* it's happening, and if you get hurt, it's not going to matter."

"I'll be careful. I promise."

"I'm still concerned. What I'd really like is that you come home and we try to piece this together. If you have to go down there again, maybe Jim or someone could go with you to look out for you."

". . . Have you heard anything from him?"

"No, but that doesn't mean anything, Drew. He could have tried to reach you at the hospital."

Before they said good-bye, Berringer made her promise to sit down first thing the next morning and write him a one-line note authorizing him to discuss her case with the authorities of Greenview.

He put down the phone, frustrated. Not wanting to alarm her, he hadn't gone into his conversation with the chief of police. If Drew caused him any more trouble, he'd said, he just might have to put her in jail. The chief had asked him if there was any chance Drew was playing a game. Hampered by the law, he could only answer that the girl the chief was calling about did not sound calculating or malicious.

"If I had a patient such as the girl you are describing," he'd said, "I'd ask you to bear in mind that it is not illegal to be disturbed, and I'd ask you to tell your officers to look out for her." Well, whatever she is, the chief had answered, she stays down here and does anything again like she did tonight, she'll wind up in trouble.

The more Berringer thought about it the more he wished he was Drew's friend and not her therapist. Then he could call her back and tell her in no uncertain terms, *Drew, do yourself a favor. Get out of that place fast.*

Sitting beside Sheila in the small switchboard room adjoining the front desk, Hawkins kept taking notes even after the girl and her shrink hung up. Sheila's chair squeaked as she rolled beside him.

Her breast nudged his arm. "You have such a neat handwriting," she said.

He gave her a faint murmur, caught the musky smell of her. Finished writing, he took out the earpiece she'd given him. Her mouth was pretty near his own and he felt a slight—very slight—temptation.

"I shouldn't have let you listen in like that. It's against the law, you know," she said coyly.

"It was real nice of you, Sheila." He made his voice husky to give her a charge. "I appreciate it."

"How much?" she asked, and he wished he could be attracted to her, but her thighs were too meaty and her skin too pale. He liked darker girls. Didn't matter if they were white or black, just darker.

"We'll talk about that over a drink one of these days," he said, getting up. She asked when and where, and he was rescued by an incoming call. He whispered thanks and left fast, notebook in hand.

When Mark Turnage showed up and began to report on the girl, Lee Caldecott groaned to himself, went to the huge Victorian sideboard and poured another drink. A big one. Juleen flashed him a withering look which he disregarded with satisfaction: He hadn't wanted to come here to Raymond's in the first place—she had dragged him here—and he was not interested in any further discussion about the "mystery girl" in the second place. Everyone had talked about her at the charity gamble, Juleen had talked about her in the car driving over here, then Juleen had talked about her to Raymond and his sister Harriet. He was bored—bored with Harriet Fairchild's wide-eyed wonder and totally fanciful memories of her daughter, bored with Raymond's repeated insistence that this was a scam, and now especially bored with Asshole Turnage's droning report on the girl, to which everyone was listening with rapt attention.

Except himself. He didn't have to listen. *He* knew damn well who the girl was.

Finally Turnage finished up: He'd spoken with her therapist, he said, "fella named Berringer. He was cagey, wouldn't say outright she's his patient, but I could tell she is. He asked me to keep an eye on her, and that was the way we more or less left it."

"So she's crazy," Raymond Ordway said.

"I don't know," Turnage said. "She didn't act crazy when I talked to her, but from what she said, she believes that Betty has something to do with her being here."

"Oh, I do wish I had been there," Harriet Fairchild said. "Mark, did she really look exactly like Betty?"

"Harriet, you've already been told that," Ordway said to his sister. "What do you think of the girl?" he asked Turnage.

"Could be some kind of a con job."

"That's what I'm thinking," Ordway said.

"*I* think that y'all don't know what you're talking about." Caldecott glared at everyone except Mrs. Fairchild. "None of you. The girl is genuine," he said.

No one was offended. He was drunk, they realized. Juleen was surprised. Not that he was drunk, but that he

87

was drunker than usual, and belligerent. The girl's appearance had really set him off. Why, she didn't understand. If anyone had taken the brunt of it, it had been Raymond.

"How do you know she's genuine?" Ordway said.

"I *know*."

"The hell you do," Ordway said.

Caldecott gave him a wave of dismissal and went to the sideboard again.

"We could invite her here to the house and find out," Mrs. Fairchild suggested.

"Harriet," Ordway said, "that's the one thing we don't need."

"What ever possible harm could there be in it?"

"You didn't see her. In five minutes she'd have you convinced she is Betty herself."

His sister touched her wrist to her forehead and pretended to swoon. "My heavens, I do believe I am being overcome by the vapors! Please bring this reincarnation of Betty to me. I want to change my will in her favor. I may not have your keen facility for business, Raymond, but I do have a few brains left." She turned to Caldecott. "Lee, when you say the girl is genuine, what do you mean?"

"I mean that Betty was in that room tonight."

Mrs. Fairchild shivered. "You just gave me a chill."

The phone rang and Caldecott picked it up. He listened for a moment, then wagged it at Turnage.

Turnage took the receiver from him, and they all watched as he asked an occasional terse question, then finally hung up.

"My officer. She made a call to her therapist. He tried to get her to come back to New York right away. She said she wants to take a walk around town tomorrow, maybe find people who knew Betty and talk with them."

"So she's going to stay here," Caldecott said.

Turnage shook his head. "Sounded like she'll probably leave tomorrow."

Harriet Fairchild was disappointed. "Oh, I would
have so loved to meet her. But Mark, she is not really as
beautiful as Betty, is she?"

"Comes close." Turnage looked at his watch. "Got to
go . . . Good seeing y'all."

"Thanks for coming out, Mark, I appreciate it," Ordway said. "I'd like you to leave me some particulars about
the girl, name, address, etcetera. In case I have to check
on her."

"We should go too," Juleen said to her husband.

"I want to talk to Raymond for a minute," Lee said.

Ordway took him to the den. "You look like shit," he
said after the heavy door closed behind them.

"I feel like shit," Lee said.

Ordway eyed the drink. "That's not going to make you
feel any better, is it?"

"We're going to have problems with this girl," Caldecott said.

"What makes you think so?"

"I've met her before. About a week and a half ago, at
the airport."

"Are you serious? This girl has been here for two
weeks and you didn't—"

"No, she lives in New York."

"Then how did you meet her?"

"I'll tell you—but don't you tell me I'm drunk . . . I
was in the gift shop. I thought I heard someone call my
name, but I was in a hurry and I didn't pay attention.
Finally I hear, 'Lee-ee'—exactly the way Betty used to say
it when she was annoyed with me. 'Lee-ee, are you ever
going to turn around, or do you need a formal invitation
before you will deign to look my way?' I turned around
and there she was, one hand on her hip. I couldn't believe
my eyes."

"You talked to her . . ."

"Not because I wanted to."

"Why didn't you want to?"

"Why didn't *you*?"

"Because I thought it was someone's idea of a bad joke," Ordway said.

"What was I supposed to say to her—'Hi, Betty, what's happening, baby?' I gave her a fast hello and got out of the shop, but she wouldn't let me go. She came after me. She said she'd come a long way to talk to me and why was I so cold to her. I told her I was sorry and that I had to go, but she grabbed my sleeve and hung on. I didn't know *what* the hell to do—people were staring and I was embarrassed. Thank God a cop came over. I told him I didn't know the girl and had a plane to catch, and he asked her to leave me alone. She got hysterical, and he ended up putting cuffs on her, took her away cursing and screaming. You should have heard her. 'Lee, you bastard, you lying sonofabitch, you're gonna be sorry. I'm coming back and I'm gonna get you, you fucking shithead,' and so on. Exactly like Betty. I tell you, by the time I sat down in the plane, the sweat was pouring out of me."

"That was the last time you saw her."

"Yes. When I got back the next day I called the North Charleston Police and got the report from them, then I had her investigated."

"And . . . ?"

"I'll send everything over to your office tomorrow. You can read for yourself."

"Why didn't you tell me about this?"

"I didn't tell you, I didn't tell Juleen, I didn't tell anyone. Raymond, something very weird is going on."

Ordway smiled. "You've had too much to—"

"I told you, don't tell me I'm drunk. I couldn't get drunk if I wanted to."

"You *are* drunk." Ordway took his arm to lead him out, but Caldecott shook him off violently.

90

"Don't you indulge me, damnit!"

"And don't you get shirty with me!" Ordway flared.

Caldecott spoke more calmly. "Raymond, for one time in your life, listen to me. This girl is as much a con artist as you are a field hand. She's bright and she's hard-working—if you wanted a daughter, she'd be it. About a month ago she started acting strange. She went into a mental hospital the day after she came after me. Personality disorder. Now she's back. I don't think she has any disorder at all—I think this girl is Betty all over again."

"Those things don't happen, Lee."

There was a knock at the door. Juleen's voice was barely audible through its thickness. "Unless you gentlemen are in a discussion that cannot wait I would be delighted to chauffeur my husband home."

"Right away, Jules," Caldecott said. He lowered his voice. "I know what you think, but wait until I send the reports over to your office tomorrow and you see for yourself."

"Do they indicate what she could be after?"

"That's the point. She doesn't seem to be after anything. I'm telling you—something weird is going on."

"You said that already." Ordway took the drink from him and gave him a gentle push toward the door. "Go home, Lee. Make love to your wife. Sounds to me like you're going to get a mercy hump. You need it. Say good night to her for me."

Ordway stared at the closed door after Caldecott was gone, then he sat down behind his desk and put his heels up on it.

Lost in thought, he had been sitting there long enough so that when his sister knocked his knees were stiff.

"Come in," he said, easing his feet to the floor.

Harriet opened the door. "I'm going to sleep," she

91

said. She put a piece of notepaper on his desk. "Mark left this for you."

He grunted a good night and massaged his legs.

"I would so love to meet this girl," she said.

"Maybe you will," he said.

"Was she really that much like Betty?" she asked for the fifth time.

"She *was* Betty," he said, which was not only what Harriet wanted to hear, but the only way he could describe her.

Alone again, he thought of what the girl had called him. Ray. Betty was the only one he had ever allowed to call him that. Everyone else, even Harriet, called him Raymond. Was it possible . . . ?

Unconsciously he shook his head. No. This girl was not Betty. Betty was dead, and the dead don't come back, no matter how much you might want them to. At the same time, the girl had affected him a hell of a lot more deeply than he would admit to Lee or to anybody else.

He wanted to meet her again. Very much. But first he wanted to know more about her. In the morning he would go over whatever information Lee had. He was pretty sure it would not be enough. Except when it came to business, Lee wasn't too bright.

He picked up the piece of notepaper and glanced at it: name, address, driver's license and social security number. More than he needed if he wanted his cousin Wendell to find out about her for him.

"What were you and Raymond talking about?" Juleen asked as she drove home.

"Business," Caldecott said. He didn't want to talk anymore. He slipped his hand between her legs.

Juleen removed it and placed it firmly on his knee. So much for the mercy hump.

"Her expression was what got me," she said.

"What do you mean?"

"Don't you remember that look Betty had? *You* know—as if she was all alone, cut off from everybody?"

"Now that you mention it, I do," Caldecott said.

"She had it worse after she cut her wrists. It used to make me want to shake her sometimes, tell her to stop feeling so hellishly sorry for herself and get *with* it. I wonder what this girl is after?" she asked.

"What makes you think she's after something?"

"Everybody is after something," Juleen answered.

6

Taking a sip of coffee, Drew leaned back against the cushion of the white garden chair and savored the lay-back ease of a time long past. Wisteria framed the French doors that led to the hotel dining room, and in the center of the more-than-century-old courtyard, a carved fountain bubbled and splashed.

She felt rested. As bad as the night before had been she'd had a good night's sleep, the first in weeks. When she finally woke up she'd started to think about the previous night. Then she thought about calling Susan and said no: She wasn't going to think, or plan, or worry. Just for a little while she was going to say the hell with it and pretend she was a tourist.

With that in mind, when she came down for breakfast, she'd decided on impulse to have it out here. She was glad she had. A vine-laden brick wall separated the sun-splashed courtyard from the street outside, making it as quiet as a church. Except for a few other people having breakfast also, it was easy to imagine that the Monday morning high-tech world on the other side of the wall did not exist.

She loved everything about the hotel, thick carpets, polished brass, fine crystal and heavy silver tableware. Too bad it was so expensive.

She'd bought a local newspaper but deliberately left it folded on the peach-colored tablecloth until she had a second cup of coffee and half a grapefruit.

94

She saw the story right away—two columns on page one: WOMAN CAUSES DISTURBANCE AT SPENGLER FETE, the headline read.

> A glamorous evening dedicated to raising funds
> for the new hospital wing was in full swing when a
> young woman interrupted the festivities . . .

Fascinated, Drew skimmed what was on the front page, then turned inside. There, along with the rest of the story, was an accompanying one, this one with a photo of her and Betty Fairchild, each in an oval outline. DOES YOUNG WOMAN ACTUALLY RECALL EVENTS BEFORE HER BIRTH? the headline read. The story detailed the circumstances surrounding the unsolved murder of Betty Fairchild twenty-three years before, then went on to quote witnesses who stated that Drew had said things she could not possibly have known.

Drew had almost finished reading when a small potbelly in rumpled slacks stopped beside her. The face looking down at her wore a self-satisfied smile and needed a shave. It was familiar, but Drew couldn't remember its name.

"Chuck Pennington. I think I did a damn good job. Can I sit down?" He plopped himself down opposite her.

"Sure."

"Just got that piece in under deadline," he said.

"I think you did a damn good job."

The humor went by him. "Not bad, huh?" A waitress came over and he ordered coffee. "How do you like our little town?" he asked Drew.

"I haven't seen it yet."

"You know how to treat yourself good." He made a little motion that took in the courtyard. "What brings you down here?"

She glanced down at the story, found what she was looking for. "'When questioned,'" Drew read, "'Officer

Warren Hawkins said, '"She claims she has no recollection of anything that occurred over the last twenty-four hours."' Did you read this after you wrote it?"

"You're putting me on," he said. "You really don't remember . . . ?"

"I'm in a good mood, Mr. Pennington—"

"Chuck. Look, maybe I put that wrong," he said. "If you'd let me, I'd like to ask you a few questions, but just remember I'm a reporter and don't take them personally."

"Go ahead."

"Do you plan to leave town soon?"

"In a few hours, maybe less."

"And you have no recollection of what happened last night."

"None."

"You told Chief Turnage and the other guy—Hawkins—that things like this happened to you before. Were other people involved?"

"What do you mean?"

"I mean people like Raymond Ordway."

"I don't understand."

"Okay. Since you don't remember, I'll tell you—" He stopped when Drew frowned and put a hand to her forehead. "You okay?"

She took the hand away. "I'm fine. Go ahead."

"Okay. You know you look exactly like Betty Fairchild, fine. Did you also know that the man you threw your arms around last night—Raymond Ordway—was Betty Fairchild's uncle, and that he's a very, *very* wealthy and influential man?"

"I do now."

"All right—remember, I'm being devil's advocate. From what I heard, Betty Fairchild was the apple of Ordway's eye, so a lot of people might ju-u-u-ust . . ."

". . . Might just feel that I'm after the family jewels," Drew finished.

96

"*Quien sabe*, as the Chinese say."

"Let me tell you something, Chuck—" She stopped in mid-sentence as the waitress came over and set down a plate of eggs and toast in front of her. "May I have the check, please?" she asked.

"Don't you want your eggs, ma'm?"

"Thanks, I decided I'm not that hungry."

"Did I say something wrong?" Pennington asked as the waitress left.

"No, I just realized I want to go somewhere."

"We can talk about something else if you like."

"Talk about what you were talking about."

"All right," Pennington said. "Raymond Ordway is rich. Harriet Fairchild, Betty's mother, is also rich . . ."

"This may shock you," Drew said, "but before I came here, I never heard of Mr. Ordway or Mrs. Fairchild. Or your town. And the longer I'm here, the quicker I want to leave." She tapped a finger on the table and glanced off in the direction the waitress had gone.

"You really are in a hurry, aren't you?"

"Yes."

"Where do you have to go?" Pennington asked.

"Why do you want to know?"

"My car's outside. I could drive you and we could talk."

"I have a car. Thank you."

"Are you in any way related to Betty Fairchild?"

"Not that I know of."

"What do you do in New York?"

The waitress came up with the check just then. Drew wrote a tip and signed it.

Chuck stayed at her elbow all the way to the front desk. "Can you help me?" she asked the clerk. "I checked in last night, but I can't remember where I might have parked my car . . ."

"The valet would have parked it," the clerk said, "then returned your keys to you."

"The doorman'll get it for you," Pennington said.

Drew gave the clerk a fast thank you and headed for the door. But outside, when the doorman asked for her car keys, she searched around in her handbag and then let out a groan.

"Oh no, they must be in the room. How long would it take to get a cab?"

Pennington touched her arm. "Come on, I'm right across the street and I know this town. Come on."

He led her across the cobblestones to a Toyota as scruffy as himself, asked her where she wanted to go.

"Straight ahead," she said after they got in.

"Can you tell me where we're going?" he asked a few blocks later.

She was frowning. "Hang a right at the next corner."

"Can't—it's one way."

"Then turn right here."

He obeyed. "Care to give me a hint?"

". . . It's twelve forty-two Halstead Road," she said.

"Why didn't you say so?"

"Because I didn't know until now."

He let that pass, thinking that for a stranger, she sure knew her way around. The address sounded familiar. It was in the best section of town, small mansions and pockets of single and double houses rivaling the most elegant in Charleston—walled gardens and genteel indifference.

They picked up Halstead at the 900 block, and as they drove down the wide, tree-lined street Drew leaned forward, peering up at the branches that made a leafy cathedral for the next three blocks. Occasional bright vacancies were the only reminders that Hugo had once roared through. Even the birds sang quietly here.

When they stopped in front of 1242, Pennington took one look at the name on the mailbox and wondered what was going on. He let Drew get out first, joined her as she was ringing the door bell.

The door was opened by a teenager. Daughter, Pennington figured. From the look she gave Drew, he had the feeling her parents had told her about last night and that she'd seen Drew's picture in the paper.

Drew introduced herself, then asked, "Is Mrs. Caldecott home?"

"No she isn't," the girl answered.

"Oh." Drew was disappointed. "May we come in for a minute?"

"Sure." The girl made way for them, and they entered a spacious entry hall.

"What's your name?" Drew asked as they followed her up a few steps into the living room.

"Patricia."

Pennington didn't care for the decor—pastels and grays. The white rug made him afraid of leaving footprints.

Drew said, "I'm really sorry to barge in on you like this, Patricia. A few minutes ago I was having breakfast, and I don't know why, I just got this sudden impulse to come over here."

"It's true," Pennington said. "I was with her." He didn't want the kid thinking she had *two* weirdos here. She was taking it in stride, though. Interested.

Drew was frowning in concentration and looking around. "Is the kitchen over that way?" she asked Patricia. The answer was yes, and Drew pointed in another direction. "The family room is over there, I think, down the hall on the right." The girl nodded. "The master bedroom is upstairs. There. And there's a safe behind that," she said, pointing to a painting.

"Is that right?" Pennington asked the girl. She nodded again and he found himself getting interested.

"Second bedroom," Drew was murmuring, "guest room and—" She broke off suddenly and her eyes widened. "Oh my God," she said. "Chuck, *she* lived here. This was Betty Fairchild's house once. Betty lived here!"

99

Pennington was about to ask Patricia if it was true, but Drew said, "Chuck, I think I know why I came here now. There's something I have to find."

"Like what?"

"I don't know. It's—"

"Excuse me a minute," Patricia said quietly, and left.

"We better get outta here," Pennington said. "I think that kid just went to get somebody."

She didn't pay any attention to him. ". . . It's a book," she said.

"What kind of a book?"

Drew was looking up at the ceiling. "I don't know . . . It's up there." She headed for the entry hall.

Pennington tried to stop her. "Look—sweetie," he said, "you can't just go running around somebody's home like . . ."

"Please, Chuck." She got past him, and he followed her down into the entry hall. She was about to start up the stairs when Patricia came back.

"My mother is on the phone. She said she'd like to talk to either one of you."

"You talk to her," Drew said to Pennington. "Can you come with me?" she asked Patricia.

"Sure," Patricia answered.

"Will you wait," Pennington said. "Drew! Christ," he muttered. He ran back to the phone in the living room.

"Mrs. Caldecott, this is Chuck Pennington."

"Mr. Pennington, my daughter just told me that Drew Summers is there. What is going on?"

"I'm not really sure, Mrs. Caldecott," Chuck said hurriedly. "We just got here and Drew says she's looking for something—a book."

"Tell her to try the public library. Do yourself a favor, Mr. Pennington. My daughter is there alone, the cook is out shopping, and it's the housekeeper's day off. I've called the chief of police, so I would advise you and the young lady to leave as quickly as you can."

100

"We will. I'm sorry this happened. I'll go up and get her right now."

"Up? She's upstairs? What is—"

"Right now. I'm getting her right now. Wait—quick question—did Betty Fairchild ever live here?"

"A long time ago. Now do—"

"'Bye." He slammed the phone down. In the entry hall he took the curving stairs up two at a time.

Drew and Patricia were at the far end of the corridor, and when he reached them, Patricia was poking a slender rod at the ceiling. It was hooked at the end and she was trying to engage a metal ring.

"Time to split," Pennington told Drew. "I just spoke with Mrs. Caldecott and she wants us to—"

Drew cut him off. "Give us a hand, Chuck. We have to get up in the attic. The book is up there. I know it." He tried to say something, but Drew insisted.

"I don't believe this," he said, taking the rod from Patricia. He engaged the ring easily, pulled, and a stairway came down. Grabbing the bottom step, he lowered it. As soon as it touched the floor, Drew's foot was on it. Patricia followed right after her—enjoying herself, Pennington thought. Thank God somebody was.

He liked the attic: plenty of room to move around in, giant oak outside the window, and lots of furniture. All it needed was a bathroom, a kitchen, and a dusting.

"What kind of a book is it?" Chuck asked.

"I don't know . . . It has a date on it, and I think it has a leather cover."

"Maybe it's a yearbook," he offered.

Drew kept moving around, looking behind things, poking here and there. Finally Pennington couldn't take anymore. "Drew—"

"Chuck, I know it's here," Drew insisted. ". . . It's a diary, and the date is stamped in gold on— Wait."

She went to the fireplace chimney. "Here," she said excitedly. "It's right here somewhere. I'm sure of it." She searched along the brick surface, then moved around to one side and glanced down at the base of the chimney. "There. It's there. It's right there under the floor!" she said.

She started to stoop down when a voice from the stairway made them all jump.

"Hold it, Miss Summers."

Officer Hawkins, his revolver out, was standing at the top of the stairs. He advanced on them.

"Warren, it's okay," Chuck said. "Take it easy. Nobody's hurting anybody."

Hawkins looked at Patricia. "You all right?"

She nodded, her eyes glued to the weapon, and he said, "Okay then, we'll all go downstairs like ladies and gentlemen. You first, Miss Summers."

"Mr. Hawkins," Drew said, starting to stoop down again, "can you wait just a second? There's something here that—"

"Do as you're told!" Hawkins barked.

"Please, Mr. Hawkins," Drew said. "It's a diary and I have to—"

"Damn it, kid, do what I tell you! The chief is on his way here right now, and if he gets here before you're out of this house you are history. Now either you move down those stairs or I shove you down, so move!"

"I was really mistaken about you," Drew said, giving him a dirty look. "I thought you were nice."

He tried not to smile. She was a mental, no doubt about it, but he liked her. "Just move, girl. You too," he said to Chuck.

He made way for the two of them.

"Wait—Wait a second, everybody," Patricia called. She was still by the chimney. "It could be here. There's a loose board."

The board was about a foot long, right beside the chimney. She pried it up, but it caught and she dropped it. Getting a good hold on it this time, she lifted it all the

102

way and reached into the opening. When she withdrew her hand, she didn't have to say a word.

She blew some dust from the book she held. "It's a diary," she said.

For the first time, Pennington looked at Drew with respect. He thought she'd be flipped out, but all she did was let out a sigh of relief.

Hawkins wasn't impressed. "Move!"

Drew started down the stairs.

Pennington took the diary from Patricia and, as Hawkins hurried them along the upstairs corridor, he called to Drew, "you happen to know the date on this?"

"Nineteen sixty-one," Drew said immediately.

She was right. "Warren, do you have any idea what this lady—"

"Keep going!" Hawkins said. He could not have cared less. He wanted to get out of here.

They didn't make it. Turnage came through the front door when they were almost to the bottom of the stairs and he was as grim as Hawkins figured he'd be. "Got ourselves a clairvoyant here, Chief," Hawkins said.

"That right," Turnage said to Drew. "Last time I saw you, you were throwing your arms around Mr. Ordway. Kind of got an affinity for our leading families, do you?"

Pennington spoke up, told Turnage everything that had happened after he sat down with Drew in the Spengler. "She even called the date on it," he said, showing him the diary. "It's Betty Fairchild's."

"That's no excuse for breaking into somebody's house. Give it here." He indicated the diary.

"She didn't break in," Pennington said, reluctantly handing it over. "Patricia let us both in."

Patricia looked worried. "Yes, I did, sir."

Turnage opened the diary, glanced at a couple of pages. He gave it to Hawkins. "Run that over to Mrs. Fairchild. You can go," he said to Drew, "but I don't want any more trouble from you."

Drew turned to Patricia and thanked her. "I hope I didn't get you into trouble too."

"It was fun," Patricia said.

The front door was open, and Drew and Pennington started for it when Turnage said, "You leaving town?"

"Chief, I'm going to make your day. Yes. Right now. Does that make you feel good?"

"If I can depend on it."

Drew studied him. "Do you do it on purpose?" she asked him.

"What's that?"

"Act like the cliché of every southern sheriff I've ever seen in the movies?"

"You're seeing the real thing, little sister."

She kept studying him. "You were in love with Betty Fairchild, weren't you?" she said.

"What's that?"

After she said it, she looked as surprised as Turnage, and Pennington thought, *No. No, sweetie, don't say another word. Just go. Right now.* But she wouldn't leave it alone.

"That's why you get so uptight with me, isn't it?"

"How the hell would you know how I felt about Betty Fairchild?"

"You *were* in love with her. I feel it."

Surprisingly, Turnage forced a smile. "Got to admit I was—me and every other young stud in town."

"But *you* got into a fight because of her."

Pennington felt the size of the entry hall shrink. He had the vague fear that Turnage might hit the girl.

"Where'd you get that information?" Turnage asked her.

She was scared now, and Pennington was glad. *Be scared,* he thought. *Just shut up.*

"I asked you who told you that!" Turnage was furious.

Drew looked suddenly small. "Nobody. I don't even know why I said it. Honestly."

104

Pennington cleared his throat. "If you don't mind my saying so, Chief, I think you're being a little hard on this lady. She came over here and found something that Mrs. Fairchild will probably bless her—"

"Chuck, I saw your car out there. Do the lady a favor. Take her over to the Spengler. Take her over there and let her get her things, and wait there while she gets 'em. When she's got 'em, you carry her suitcase to her car as fast as you can and then wave good-bye to her. You do that before I do it myself."

Pennington took Drew's arm and steered her to the door. She called good-bye to Hawkins over her shoulder.

Turnage and Hawkins came out just as they drove off. "You're really down on that girl, Chief."

Turnage headed for his car. "Get that diary over to Mrs. Fairchild," he said, "then go on over to the Spengler. I want to know if she leaves town."

It took Turnage some ten minutes to drive to the station house. There, alone in his office, the door locked, he poured himself some bourbon and sat sipping it. He knew he shouldn't, but he needed it. Old memories were crowding in on him, memories of the way things had been, the way he'd felt about Betty, and the way he'd felt toward Ed Johnson when Betty told him she was in love with him. Up to then he'd never thought that much about Ed except that he was a smart, handsome sonofabitch for a Negro.

They'd been in a few classes together in high school, shot the breeze once in a while about this and that, sports mostly, played some basketball. Anyone asked him, he'd have said he liked Ed. He wasn't about to join the civil rights movement like Betty did, but he wasn't against integration. Get the race bullshit over with was all he thought, and go on to important things.

But then Betty had to go and confide in him. Like she always did—told him her troubles, told him how she felt about things, what she wanted from life, everything. Or almost everything. The one thing that hurt her the deepest she never even hinted at.

It wasn't a complete surprise to him about her and Ed. A lot of kids suspected it. For her sake he acted "mature" about it, told her she better watch her step and Ed better watch his. But then she dropped the bomb: she and Ed were going to run away. In two, three weeks. She had to get some money, she said. She had it in the bank, but she couldn't touch it on her own till she was eighteen.

Would you lend me some if I need it, Mark?

How much you need?

Whatever you can lend me, two hundred, three hundred. I know you're saving to take that trip, but I'd give it back to you in a few months . . .

He said sure, he'd do it, and she said there was just the chance she wouldn't have to take it from him because she was going to ask Lee for all of it. If Lee said yes, she wouldn't need Turnage's money.

Turnage said whatever she wanted, gave her some more fatherly advice, and she hugged him. *Mark, I just wish I had a brother like you,* she said. *You're the best.*

All she did was make him ache, and to this day Turnage sometimes wondered if she'd known he was in love with her. Probably not.

He hadn't been that jealous when she got involved with Lee Caldecott. Caldecott was a wimp. There was too much woman in Betty for him, too much emotion, too much hurt. When she dumped him Turnage wasn't surprised.

But Ed Johnson was a different story. He had it—brains *and* balls. Went off up there to Howard University for three years in a row, and only came home and went to work so he could go back again. And while Ed had been at school he, Turnage, spent his days on his back in his father's garage, looking up the fat metal ass of cars that

106

people like Betty and Lee—and Ed too—were driving toward a better life.

But he wrote it off. Or he thought he did. Told himself he was glad Betty found somebody who was good for her. But he ached bad.

He didn't realize how bad until a Friday night a couple of weeks later. He was in Healy's bar—gone now to another shopping center—and he got mean with three or four different faces. The faces kept backing off, and finally he challenged everybody in the place—called them all chickenshit. Thinking about it now, he realized they were all being nice to him because his father had died a few days before. Even when Healy threw him out he did it friendly. He and the bunch he'd come in with headed over to Fourth, jostling each other and bragging and shoving. But his blood was still up and he wanted a fight. He had to have a fight.

They stopped in front of Betty's father's restaurant to regroup. He remembered that because Fairchild's black-and-red For Sale sign was still prominently displayed a week after Ed and some other black activists had staged a sit-in there. The sign said he refused to serve customers that the federal government ordered him to, so he'd sell the place cheap.

There weren't too many people on the street. Everybody was either at the Empress seeing *Night of the Grizzly* or out someplace else, and the guys finally decided they'd get some six-packs.

Turnage said the hell with that, he wanted to head out for the roadhouse. He'd find himself a fight there for sure.

"Mark, you start something out there, you gonna wind up dead," one of the guys said. "We all wind up dead."

He argued, but he couldn't get them to go along. Then all of a sudden he knew where he'd find the fight he wanted, and he looked at his watch to see if it was too late—few minutes after nine. Duchaud's Department Store closed at nine tonight. Shit.

He started off, heading for Main, and the guys yelled, "Hey, where the hell you going," and he called back, "You want to see yourselves a fight? You come on along and you sure as hell gonna see a beaut."

They came after him, smelling blood, saying, "Who is it, Mark? Who is it, huh? Mark, where you goin'?"

He wouldn't say, and when he got to Main he looked to see if there was light coming from the store all the way near the end of the next block. There was.

The guys had no idea what he had in mind, and they kept asking him and making jokes about it, but all he'd say was don't y'all worry, just wait. Sure enough, the next time he looked up the street the sidewalk in front of Duchaud's went dark and people came out. He waited, not even looking that way anymore so that the guys wouldn't be able to tell.

"Here now," he heard one of them say. "Here here *here* now, will y'all look at what's comin'!"

He felt joy rip through him, and he turned and saw what he expected, the one Negro working in Duchaud's men's department—high-type, clean-cut, well-educated. Ed Johnson. On his way to the bus. Thank you, Lord.

He was with his little sister GG and three other Negroes.

The guys started making jokes about niggers and coons, smart-aleck stuff, and Turnage heard Harold Bream say, "Let's get 'em." He didn't like Harold, thought he was a weasel. But the other guys were for it.

"Want to, Mark?" somebody said.

Turnage didn't say anything. He didn't give a shit what they did. This was *his* fight coming, with this black sonofabitch that was doing everything to Betty *he* dreamed of doing, everything he was starving to do, and he was so sick and mad and jealous, he was set to kill.

Then Ed's face was right smack there in front of him saying Hi, Mark, saying I heard about your father and I'm real sorry.

Turnage didn't say a word. He just waited, waited for the right second to throw a punch and get the fight going. Beat the Betty-fucking sonofabitch to death.

He couldn't tell how long Ed's face was in his— couldn't tell—when he heard one of the guys say something to the other Negroes. There were snickers, and Turnage sensed that the fight he wanted was close, very close. And he was ready. All he needed was one wrong word from Ed, one wrong look.

He wasn't getting it. People passing were stopping, watching. The other Negroes were hanging back while he and Ed talked. It came to him that they were getting scared now. Little GG was already scared—Ed was pushing her in back of him—but Turnage didn't care. He got ready for what he'd come for.

But suddenly Ed was smiling kind of peculiar, backing off, saying I'll see you, Mark, and there was no way Turnage could hit him. Then Ed wasn't backing off either because he bumped into three guys behind him.

One of them was Harold Bream, and he and the other two were calling out names and cursing. Fuck you, Harold was saying to one of the Negroes, and the Negro answered Fuck you too, and the curse was barely out of his mouth when Ed turned on him, snarling Shut your dumb mouth. Then Ed turned on Harold and the other white boy, shoving them out of his face, and that surprised them. Ed was no pushover. He put one hand on his little sister's shoulder and another on the cursing Negro and said Let's go now, c'mon.

But some other guys blocked them, and Ed turned back to Turnage saying What's going on, Mark. This isn't your style. This is bad stuff.

You scared of them? Turnage asked him.

And Ed said, I am, yeah. Cool these guys down, man. You don't know what's happening.

Turnage saw the look on little GG's face then and dimly realized what was going on. Dumb bastards. He straight-armed one of the guys and gave Harold a kick in the ass. They complained and they cursed and said what the *hell* was he doing, but they took it.

"Now you got nothing to be scared of," he said to Ed and the other Negroes. "Except me. Me. I'm gonna take y'all on."

"Can't do that Mark," Ed said. "Your friends here, they gonna get into it."

"They won't get into nothing." He turned on them. "Y'all stay out of this, hear? I don't need you. Ain't a black sonofabitch in this whole town can beat me in a fair fight. Not a black sonofabitch in the whole country. You got that?" He glared at them all, challenging anyone to dispute him.

No one said a word. Except Ed.

"I think *I* can," he said in a quiet little voice.

Turnage heard the tone more than he heard the words, and he had a feeling that something had just gone wrong. He turned to face Ed.

"Just you and me," Ed said. He talked in that same quiet little voice. "Everybody else takes off."

Turnage said, "Just what I had in mind." Then they got rid of everybody, Turnage's friends going one way and the Negroes the other.

They agreed on the rear of Harrington's Warehouse, and they walked the three blocks in silence. All the way over something kept gnawing at Turnage.

110

With each block his head got clearer and the blind anger got lesser. And with each block he knew he had to sober up fast because he was going to need everything he had to win.

And with each block—all the way over—Turnage kept hearing that quiet little voice Ed had used. And he knew Ed was going to whip him.

He'd been right, Turnage mused. It still embarrassed him to think about it. Ed whupped him so bad that for a week it was painful to chew. And one of his eyes was closed.

It was his left eye, he remembered as he put the bourbon bottle back in the bottom drawer, and it was still swollen when the hunting season began a few days later.

The reason he remembered it so clearly was that when he was out in the woods and raised his rifle, he hardly had to squint when he took aim, exactly the way it was when Ed Johnson appeared in his sights and he shot him.

7

"How'd you know that diary was there?" Pennington asked as he was driving Drew back to the hotel.

"I sneaked up last night and put it there."

"I don't blame you for being mad," he said. "I'll be honest, I thought you were a phony, or a kook, and I figured what the hell, I'll go along with it, but now I'm inter—" He interrupted himself, picking up the minirecorder on the seat beside him. "You mind if I turn it on?" She shook her head, and he set it on the dash. "All I'm asking is how you knew that diary was up there. Did you hear a voice, was it a hunch, how did you know?"

"I don't hear voices, and I don't know how I knew. I just knew."

"Anything like this ever happen to you before? I mean relative to Betty Fairchild."

"I've had some problems lately."

"What kind?"

"The kind I'm not in the mood to talk about right now."

"I can see why. . . ." He couldn't get over it. "You really leaving town?"

"Right now."

That killed him. "You know, I didn't realize what you were going through," he said sympathetically. "I think I'm beginning to understand."

What he was really thinking was how he could get to

her. There was a story here. A biggie. He could smell it. Forget story. There was a book: rich family, beautiful daughter brutally murdered—and her exact beautiful twin who shows up over twenty years later and knows things only the daughter would know. Wild. If he could get her confidence, find a way to keep her here . . .

"There aren't many straight streets in this town, are there?" she asked.

"Not in this old section. They're wide and winding. They follow the old cowpaths and the wagon roads." As winding as they were, though, he had the feeling she'd have found her way to the Caldecott house without help. "What I said about you wanting to get close to Betty Fairchild's people—forget that. I don't think you're that kind of person."

She stayed quiet.

"Look, you didn't finish breakfast, and you have to eat," he said. "C'mon, we'll do lunch before you go."

"Thanks, Chuck. That's nice of you."

He gave her what he felt was a reassuring grin and she said, "I do appreciate what you did. I really mean it."

"Heart of gold," he said.

Not until late morning was Raymond Ordway able to concentrate on the investigative report that Lee had sent over. His day had started with an irritating breakfast meeting at which his bank people had given him a hard time. The savings and loan crisis had been bad enough—left them nervous as hens—but this damned recession had them downright scared. He'd finally gotten what he wanted by agreeing to cross-collateralize all his loans, then he'd walked over here to his office. He'd arrived only minutes before his 9:30 appointment with the owners of L'Esprit, which had left him little time to think about how much he really wanted to pay for the place.

Ordinarily he'd have left the negotiations to his subordinate. There was maybe two million five involved, but the owners considered themselves epicures and wanted to feel he wasn't treating this as just another deal. Which he was. Their restaurant didn't interest him, and he intended to sell it soon after he took it over. He wanted the chef. The man was superb, and Ordway needed him for the Spengler. Unfortunately, his contract with L'Esprit had another year to run.

It was a good meeting. On a hunch he'd offered a million eight and gotten it for two. After the meeting was over he'd leafed through a few more pages on the girl while he made some time-consuming phone calls.

Now he gave the report his full attention. He didn't know what he'd expected, but on paper at least, the girl didn't appear to be that much out of the ordinary—until he came to an interview with a neighbor.

Halfway through it his pulse began to race, and when he finished he went back and reread part of it.

. . . hardly ever heard a sound from her before, and believe you me, that wall between us is paper thin. The one who lived there before her was another story. Her and her boyfriends used to drive me up the wall.

Q. *I can understand.*

EAKINS: *Anyway, at first I wasn't even sure it was her. I thought it was some southern girl maybe who was staying with her.*

Q. *Just to recap: What you heard Ms. Summers do was start talking in her sleep, then she began to scream and run out into the hall. Is that correct?*

EAKINS: *Yeah. And she's screaming the same thing over and over. "Help me, Uncle Ray," she's saying. You know, like she's drowning. "Save me, Uncle Ray." I felt for her. Reminded me of when my sister was very sick once . . .*

114

Ordway could not believe what he had read. He glanced back at the first page, scanned the statistics and found what he was looking for: *Born: 1/12/68.* Two months after Betty died. How could she have known something like that?

He read a police report next, and finally the information on the girl's arrival and behavior at the White Plains Rest and Rehabilitation Center in New York. Not much information about her there.

He went back over some of the material he had skimmed the first time . . . *Subject's sister Gena committed suicide 4/13/82; Subject graduated Sherman Oaks H.S. 6/19/84, 3.7 avg.* Graduated before she was seventeen. Smart too. He kept reading: went to New York shortly after graduation; held two jobs for about a year; landed a job with BBD&O; stayed there until she moved to the advertising firm she was working for now. Steady worker. Rare for her age.

Two-week trip to Europe 1989; current boyfriend James Hendricks, 493 E. 92 Street, etc., etc.

He pushed his chair back and swiveled around, staring down at Courthouse Square and the harbor beyond. He called Lee. "This report only goes up to the girl's fifth day in this White Plains place," he said.

"I didn't see any point in continuing with the investigation while she was there," Lee said.

"That was penny-wise and pound foolish, wasn't it? If you're going to have someone investigated, you go all the way."

"I didn't expect her to drive down here."

"She *drove* down?"

"In a red 'sixty-eight Mustang convertible," Lee said.

If Lee expected a reaction, Ordway disappointed him. He fingered the pages. "Do you know anything about the girl other than this?"

"Isn't that enough? What else would you want to know about her?"

Everything, he thought, *and I will.* "For starters," he said, "where every cent she's got came from, and whether she has some extra money that can't be accounted for."

"You know what I think, so I won't say any more. Interestingly enough, I heard that she knew some things about Turnage that he didn't like hearing."

Ordway let that pass. He wanted to get off the phone, and was about to say good-bye when Lee said, "That incident to do with her crying in the hallway—the 'Save me Uncle Ray' stuff, does that have any meaning?"

"Not to me," he lied.

After he hung up, he called in his secretary. "Fax this over to Wendell Barnes," he said, handing her the report; then he took a secure phone from a desk drawer and dialed Wendell's number.

Whenever he ever needed to know anything about anybody—*anything*—Wendell got it for him. What kind of people he used to get the information, Ordway could only speculate about, but for over ten years now, he had done it.

"Wendell."

"Cousin Raymond."

"I'm faxing you over a report on that girl who showed up at the hotel last night."

"I can only imagine how deeply shocked you were, Raymond. For myself, I was transfixed."

Wendell was from his father's side of the family—all bullshit. Being naked in a hurricane might transfix him, but nothing less.

"I want you to read the report carefully," Ordway went on, "then find out what you can on the girl in the next twenty-four hours."

"Can you be specific?"

"I am being specific. She's from California. I want to know everything about her from childhood to the present. I want to know if there is the slightest chance that she is part of a scam. Find out about her family. She began

116

acting strange maybe five weeks ago and was in a mental hospital. It's in the report. Get all the information you can about her from neighbors in New York and California and from people at work."

"And you want this in twenty-four hours."

"Or less."

"You got any idea how many people have to be—"

"Do it."

"Are you aware of the cost, dear man?"

"Do it. And something else. The girl seems to know things about our police chief, Turnage. Find out what that's all about."

"Ah, you wealthy folk, you giants who with a simple snap of the fingers can command—"

Ordway hung up. Wendell would not be offended, and Ordway didn't care if he was.

He swiveled around in his chair and again stared out of the window, thinking of the incident in the girl's hallway. What she had carried on about had occurred over thirty years ago. Betty was probably ten or eleven then. The whole family had gone to Sullivan's Island and Betty had waded out too far. He'd seen her and ran to get her. When he reached her, she had swallowed some water and was white with fright, clung to him, shivering. There was little chance she would have drowned, but that day he was her hero. For days after she told the story of how her uncle Ray had saved her life.

He'd forgotten all about it, it had happened so long ago. Yet this girl knew about it. How? Who could have told her? Lee? He'd been a kid himself then, and he wasn't even there. Betty's father was dead. Harriet? No. Who would even remember something like that? Yet this girl knew about it. *How?*

He had never been a believer in the supernatural, and he was not going to become one now, but as much as he wracked his brain for a rational answer, he could not find one.

* * *

As soon as Drew and Pennington walked into the lobby of the Spengler, GG Johnson took her purse from where it sat beside her and put it on her lap. The revolver inside made it very heavy.

GG had sneaked the gun out of her parents' closet last night, and when she got it home and unwrapped the plastic, she smelled the fine film of oil on it. It was a good revolver. She knew that. Her father had bought it twenty-three years ago, when everybody in town was being mean to them. He cared for what he bought, and he did not ever buy anything that was cheap.

She'd never fired a gun, but early this morning she'd practiced holding it in both hands and squeezing the trigger with the bullets out.

She was ready now. She would do what she planned. When the bitch finished at the desk and went to the elevator, she would follow her. Upstairs, she would push the gun in her back and force her way into her room. There she would tell her how much she hated her for all the misery she had caused. There she would spit on her just as she had been spit on because of her. Then she would beat her till she begged for mercy.

Her mind started racing with anticipation, and before she realized it, her thoughts were getting all mixed up, coming too fast.

You stay away from my son! It was her daddy yelling at Betty that night. GG was peeking from behind the door. He was so mad, spit was flying from his mouth. *Don't you know what they do to him? Don't you KNOW?* he yelled.

GG tried to keep her mind blank. She couldn't.

You listen now, GG, Daddy said. *You don't tell a soul that girl come here that night. 'Less they ask. They ask, you say she come looking for your mama, hear? She come looking for your mama.*

Yessir, she said, scared so bad she almost peed her

118

pants. That was right after they murdered Sonny. She was only ten, but she wanted her daddy to know she would say it right: *Betty Fairchild, she come to the house looking for my mama that night.*

But nobody ever asked. Nobody knew. Not even mama.

Betty got murdered too, but GG didn't care. She was glad. But *did* she get murdered? If she did, then who was that girl standing there at the desk? *Had* to be Betty. Had to be.

There was a man came in with her, and GG hoped he wouldn't go upstairs with her. She wasn't sure what she'd do if he did. She forced herself to calm down, keep her mind clear. Get ready.

At the front desk, after Drew told the clerk she was checking out, he handed her two messages. Pennington glanced at them at the same time she did. One was from a Dr. Berringer, the other from Mrs. Fairchild.

She told Pennington she'd only be a few minutes—she was already packed—and he said he'd wait for her.

He walked her over to the elevator. The lobby wasn't crowded, and he noticed a woman coming from another direction, a black woman with a blond streak in her hair. She reached the elevator at the same time they did. Drew wasn't aware of her, but Pennington saw her glaring and sensed there was something wrong with her.

"One second," he said when the elevator door opened and Drew started to get in. He stopped her so that the woman could go ahead. She didn't move.

Drew turned around. It was the woman who had been staring at her in the coffee shop the previous night, GG, and her eyes were boring into Drew's with such intense hatred that Drew was paralyzed.

Immediately she thought of a woman who had almost attacked her on the second day she'd been in New York. She'd been wandering around Rockefeller Center when someone stepped on her heel. She'd turned to stare into eyes that glittered with hate, the eyes of a pale woman with matted hair and smeared lipstick. She was holding a dirty shopping bag. Drew tried to get away from her, but the woman followed her, cursing and raging, until finally Drew ducked into a restaurant. The woman watched her through the window for a while before she disappeared.

This woman confronting her now took care of herself, but there was that same raging madness in her.

"You Betty Fairchild."

Drew felt weak. "Excuse me?" she said.

"Why you looking at me like you don't know me? You know me. You know my whole family."

The elevator door closed. Drew said, "I'm sorry, but I don't know you. I don't live h—"

"You her daughter?"

"I think you're mistaking me—"

"Why you here—to hurt us all over again? Ain't it enough you got Eddie killed?"

Pennington suddenly guessed who she was. "You're Edward Johnson's sister," he said.

"I'm not talking to you," GG snapped at him. It crossed her mind that she could do it now. She had her purse under her arm. She could just reach in and—

"Can I be of any help?" The voice broke into GG's thoughts, making her wary. She knew who it belonged to without turning around. Security.

Drew didn't know who the man was, but she was glad to see him.

"GG, you got business in here?" he said.

"Why you ask me?" GG flared. "Why don't you ask her if she got any business here? Or him?"

"I'm askin' you," the man said, "and if you want to hold on to your job you'll answer me."

Between the tone of his voice and the woman's fury, Drew felt the closeness of violence.

"It's okay," she said to the man. "She just thought I was someone else."

120

"Don't you talk for me," GG said. She pointed a finger at Drew. "You hurt my family once, but you won't get a chance to do it again. Not while I'm here. You won't ever hurt anybody else ever."

She gave Drew a final vengeful look and headed for the exit.

The security man made sure Drew was all right and ambled off. Shaken, she jabbed the elevator button three or four times.

"I'll go up with you," Pennington said. He followed her into the elevator, touched the button for the upper floor.

Drew leaned against the wall. "What kind of a place is this?" she said. "Is everybody crazy here?"

They rode up in silence, and when they reached her door, Pennington said, "I noticed you had a message there from Mrs. Fairchild. Are you going to call her?"

"I don't know what for," she said.

Her open suitcase was on the bed where she had left it.

She called Berringer, but either he was with a patient or he was not in: She got a recording. "Corey, I'm sorry—I forgot to call you this morning," she said. "It's about eleven-thirty and I'm okay. I'm leaving Greenview now. I'll be home tomorrow."

"Your shrink?" Pennington asked her.

She nodded, then called Susan.

"Norman bought the concept," Susan said. "He told me to tell you, 'Come home, all is forgiven.'"

That gave her a huge lift. Without going into detail, she told Susan where she was and tried to assure her that she wasn't crazy. She could tell Susan was worried about her, and feeling guilty, she said she was going to try and get back to work as soon as she could. "I'm leaving here today."

"Look, Drew, we're over the tough part, and Norman's a very understanding guy," Susan said. "Don't worry, I can take up the slack. We'll make it. You just take care of yourself. And, uh, by the way . . . I'm late."

It took a second for it to sink in. When it did, Drew felt a surge of warmth. "Oh Susan, that's . . ."

"It's only been five days," Susan said, "but I think I'm pregnant. I know it. I can feel it."

Drew hung up grinning, then headed for the bathroom to wash her face and put on some lipstick. When she came out, Pennington held the phone out to her. He had his hand over the mouthpiece.

"It's Mrs. Fairchild," he said. "I called her. Give her the chance to thank you. She's a sweet lady."

"Hello. Mrs. Fairchild?"

"Oh. Miss Summers." The voice on the other end sounded uncertain. "My goodness, how your voice is like Betty's. I've been quite anxious to talk to you, and now Mr. Pennington tells me you are going to leave Greenview."

"I'm afraid so."

"I do wish you didn't have to. I wanted so to meet you, if only to tell you how grateful I am to you. I have Betty's diary in my hand."

"Is it really hers?"

"It is. Even if she had not written in it, I would have recognized it. I bought it for her myself, for her eleventh birthday. To me it is a treasure."

"I'm really glad."

"Young lady, what you have done is impossible for me to describe. I have had such a wonderful cry, and I am so happy I feel like crying all over again. You must let me do something for you."

"You just did, Mrs. Fairchild. Thanks."

"Then you must do something else for me. Mr. Pennington told me of some of the awful things that have happened to you in the short time you have been here. Last night, then with our chief of police, and now with poor GG—the Johnson girl. I would so hate to have you leave here thinking ill of us."

"Oh, it hasn't been that bad."

"That bad or not, won't you please come out to the house before you go?"

"Gee, I—"

"Miss Summers, please. I'm being selfish. Of course I want to thank you for this marvelous gift, but I also want to meet you, talk with you in person even if it is only for a few minutes. Mr. Pennington told me that you were going to have a bite to eat before you left. Why can't the two of you come out here and have it? It's only twenty minutes from town, and by the time you are here the cook will have a cold lunch already prepared. You can have a taste of genuine southern hospitality and then be on your way. Please, won't you?"

Drew smiled. "You don't make saying no easy."

"Believe me, I don't often act this way. I am usually so unassertive . . . but I so want to meet you that I'm being horribly insistent. I'll send our car for you if you like."

"Thanks, I have a car, or I can drive out in Chuck's— Mr. Pennington's."

"You'll come—how wonderful! What would you like for lunch?"

"Anything. I'm starved."

There was a moment's silence on the other end, then Harriet Fairchild said, "I do hope I haven't made you feel you must. I would feel awful."

"Not at all," Drew said sincerely. "I want to come. I really do."

When she put the phone down Pennington said, "Mad at me?"

Drew shook her head. "No. She sounds nice."

Pennington was relieved. "We can talk on the way out."

They took his car, and as they pulled out of the hotel parking lot he asked her if she happened to know the way.

She said no, she didn't, and he reached into his briefcase for his tape recorder, put it on the dash.

"You remember how you started to direct me to the Caldecotts' this morning?"

"Yes."

"Were you ever there before?"

"No."

"Then how did you know the address?"

Tightness crept into her voice. "I have no idea . . ."

"Did you get some kind of an image of the house?" he asked.

"No. I just knew where it was, like you know where you live."

Pennington said, "I swear, If you'd told me that last night I'd have laughed. Did stuff like this happen to you in New York?"

"It was different there. I don't mean like last night, when I was zoned out. That was the same—I did things I couldn't remember later on. But in New York I just had a . . . I don't know . . . a *suspicion* that something was going on. Here it's like I can really *feel* someone near me. Let's get off this part of it. It's making me nervous."

"What was all that you said to Chief Turnage about his being in love with Betty Fairchild and having a fight over her?"

"I just had a feeling about it."

"Some feeling. The man was ready to murder you." Pennington glanced at the rearview mirror, wondering if it was his imagination or if the police cruiser a short distance behind had followed them from town.

They fell in back of a loaded logging truck, and Drew glanced out at what had once been a stretch of piney woods. All the trees were broken off at the stump and a faded sign said LANDSCAPING BY HUGO.

After Pennington passed the truck, the road behind them was clear for a couple of minutes, then the cruiser

124

appeared again. He slowed and so did the cruiser. He didn't say anything to Drew about it.

"When you get these feelings like you had about the chief, how do they come to you?"

"They just come, like memories, like—" Drew broke off suddenly and leaned back against the headrest.

Pennington slowed the car. "What's the matter?"

"Don't stop."

"You okay?"

"She's after me again."

"What does it feel like?"

"She's noodging me to go somewhere."

"Where?"

"I don't know, but if it's up to me, I'm not going." Taking deep breaths, she braced herself against the dash and gritted her teeth.

Chuck waited. "What's happening?"

She didn't say anything for a few seconds, then she shook her head in defeat. "All right, all *right,*" she said to herself. "Chuck, there's a three-way intersection ahead. When you get to it, take a diagonal left."

He knew the intersection. "You sure you're okay?"

"Yeah. I was afraid I was going to black out." She was braced against the dash, head down, so when they neared the intersection, he was pretty sure she didn't see the sign. He took a diagonal left onto a dirt road that ran in almost the opposite direction they had been headed. They were veering south, and he could smell the Ashley River nearby.

He was leaving clouds of dust behind, he saw in the rearview mirror. He also saw that the cruiser had taken the same turn they had. He'd been curious before. Now he was worried. "Do you know where we're going?" he asked.

"It's just a little farther," Drew said.

He couldn't see behind him because of the dust, but he knew the other car was there.

"I don't suppose we could do this another time," he said.

"We're almost there. There— There it is." She was pointing to a clearing up ahead on the left, and when they reached it he thought, Good, plenty of room to turn around and get out if I have to.

"Pull in near that big willow."

He slowed, turned into the clearing. She had the door open as soon as he stopped and she slid out of the car like a ghost.

He turned the car to face the road: At least they'd be able to get the hell out fast if they had to.

He took the tape recorder and left the engine running and the door open. He turned on the tape recorder.

They were in a natural clearing; tall pines and the shifting haze of the woods loomed silent, a wall of watching stillness.

"Drew," he said quietly, but she was moving around now and paid no attention. He wanted to say let's get the hell out of here, but he followed, the feeling growing in him that they were not alone.

"Something terrible happened here," Drew said. She waited, motionless, then shivered suddenly and let out a sigh of pity. "Betty Fairchild may have died here."

She stopped, uncertain for a moment, then she pointed. "There's a car over there," she said, "near that stump. It's exactly like my car."

Pennington looked where she was pointing, almost afraid of seeing something. She started toward the stump, then halted, peering at whatever existed there for her. Pennington was fascinated. At the same time, the thought popped into his head that maybe she was acting. It was possible. He'd read all the accounts of the Fairchild murder, seen the glossies taken here at the scene. Why couldn't she have read the same accounts, seen the same pictures? But then there was the diary, and what she'd known about Turnage.

126

She turned to face him. It took him a moment to realize she was looking past him.

"There's someone there," she said.

He nearly jumped out of his skin, but when he turned he didn't see anyone. "Where?" he said.

"There," she answered, "behind that big tree." He was getting set to run, until he told himself she was talking about the past.

"I think he's waiting . . ." Her voice trailed off, and Pennington wanted to ask her what the guy looked like, what he was waiting for, but he was afraid of breaking her concentration.

"He *is* waiting. He's watching for someone," she said. "There, he sees the person now and he's ducking back—" She broke off and her eyes went to Pennington's left. He followed her gaze.

"It's a young man. Black. He's coming along a trail by the edge of those woods," Drew said. "I think he's carrying something. Now he's leaving the trail and he's coming this way. . . ."

Ed Johnson, Pennington said to himself. The black guy had to be Ed Johnson. But there was no trail there. Again he wanted to ask questions, and again he thought better of it. He watched Drew carefully as her eyes followed someone's invisible progress. She turned around to face the stump. "He's heading for the car. He's leaning down and peeking in."

She became silent, and Pennington came around her so that he could see her face. She was troubled. "I lost him," she said. "I—No, wait. There's something strange going on. I think there's someone else on the other side of the car. He's standing up . . . Now it's getting confusing. I can't really see. Somebody is taking something out of the trunk. Some kind of a small case . . . The young black guy has it. He's going away. He's running."

She started moving toward where the car had to be. When she reached it she leaned down, staring.

"There's someone inside of it . . . in the front seat. I think it—it's a girl. She's all crumpled up . . . She's— Oh . . . Oh my God, there's nothing left of— Oh my God, no!" She buried her face in her hands and began to scream.

Pennington was so terrified, he was ready to scream himself. He grabbed her, babbling that she had to be quiet. "Hey, take it easy." But she kept screaming, and he yelled at her that there was nothing to be scared of. "Drew, there's nobody there—nobody! Look for yourself, there's *nothing* there—no car, nothing. Stop, for Christ's sake!" In desperation he grabbed her and clapped a hand over her mouth. "God*damnit*, Drew!"

That stopped her. Pennington took his hand from her mouth, held on to her as much to comfort himself as her. He was wrung out.

"You all right?" he asked quietly.

"Yes. I'm sorry . . . You can let me go."

She was trembling, but at least she was quiet. Drew eased herself out of his arms.

Then he heard it: the snap of a twig or somegoddamnthing. There was no mistaking it, and he could see from Drew's expression that she heard it too. He was so scared he could feel his hair rising. He blubbered something wordless, grabbed her arm and started for the car. Taken by surprise, Drew nearly fell, but she stayed with him.

He almost flung her at the car when they reached it, and she was beside him when he piled in and released the emergency brake.

He hit the gas, not caring that the doors were still open. The rear wheels spun and spat dirt and the car fishtailed forward in agonizing slow motion before he thought to ease up on the accelerator. Then they moved forward steadily, and somehow he managed to swing out onto the dirt of the road and build up enough speed to stifle the hysteria that left him close to sobbing.

128

The rearview mirror was useless: dust obscured everything. He kept driving as fast as he could until he reached the Stop sign at the three-way intersection and slowed, then moved out onto the blacktop. Making an easy left, he picked up speed, keeping an eye on the side mirror.

Sure enough he saw the police cruiser pull up to the Stop sign. Pennington stepped on the gas as the cruiser moved onto the highway. It stayed with them for about a mile, then turned off.

Only then was he really able to question Drew coherently, and the first question he asked her was whether or not she knew that the place they'd just come from was called Willow Creek.

8

Now that she had met Drew, Harriet Fairchild completely understood what her brother and the Caldecotts had been talking about. She was quite pretty. She did not have Betty's inner beauty and sensitivity, of course, yet there were moments when Mrs. Fairchild truly believed she was staring at Betty reborn. She forgave herself for not having paid the reporter more attention: the girl was leaving Greenview in a little while, and she would probably never see her again.

After they finished eating and the table was cleared, she suggested that they have some lemonade out on the balcony.

"Gee, Mrs. Fairchild," Drew said, sitting back, "if we do, you'll never get me to leave."

"What a perfectly wonderful idea," Mrs. Fairchild said. "I'd love to have you stay."

"Ah, thanks," Drew said. "It's getting late and I really have to go soon. I have a long drive."

Harriet Fairchild concealed her disappointment. She had arranged to have lunch served here in the ladies' sitting room because it was her favorite room. Even on a hot day such as this fresh air was everywhere on this side of the house. It came in through the ceiling-tall doors that opened onto the north balcony, and through the windows that were almost as tall as the doors.

Outside, the grounds were in bloom, the air redolent

130

with their perfume. Mrs. Fairchild had wanted Drew to see how perfectly beautiful they were from the balcony. She had been sincere in telling Drew she would love her to stay. She would have so enjoyed talking to her about Betty and introducing her to the graciousness and cultured ease of life here.

"Well, before you go," she said, "you must let me show you something. And you, Mr. Pennington," she added.

Going to the antique desk in front of the bookcase, she took out a photograph album, brought it to the love seat, and had Drew sit beside her.

"It is absolutely uncanny," she said as she showed Drew photographs of Betty taken a few weeks before her death. "My brother was right. Drew, you *are* Betty."

Standing beside them, Pennington pretended interest as Mrs. Fairchild leafed through the photos, but his mind was on the portrait he'd seen when he came in. If he could, he wanted to get a shot of it before he and Drew left.

He waited for a chance to cut into her monologue. She wasn't bad for an old lady, Pennington thought, only boring. Besides taking a year to say something, she couldn't stop talking about herself and her daughter and she never listened.

When his chance came he said, "Mrs. Fairchild, I wonder if you'd mind if I took a photograph of that portrait out in the hall?"

"Not at all," she said.

"Can I take another look at it?" Drew asked.

"My goodness, of course."

They went out into the hallway. If you could call it a hallway, Drew thought. Twelve feet high, it was a trek from one end to the other, all polished wood and ornate Victorian carving. It would have been gloomy except for light that poured down the staircase well at one end and the two-storied windowed entry hall at the other.

"You know, you could put my whole apartment in here and you wouldn't notice it," she said.

"That's what you get for being born twenty-three years too late," Pennington said too low for Mrs. Fairchild to hear.

Just before the entry hall the three turned and looked up. Spaced along the hallway ceiling's entire length were octagonal, lighted recesses. The portrait was in the second recess, an enlarged copy of a drawing made shortly before Betty had died.

The lifelike quality was startling. The girl's character and haunting loveliness hovered above them like a living spirit.

Looking at the drawing again, Drew felt what she had the first time: without ever having met Betty Fairchild— without ever having learned as much about her as she had—she knew her. Not because of Betty's resemblance to herself, but to her sister—the wariness in the eyes, the slightly skeptical expression, and the warmth. And the pain. It was pain that she, Drew, might have carried if it hadn't been for Gena.

Pennington took some shots—he tried a couple with Drew and the portrait together, but they didn't work— then the three went back into the sitting room.

There, as Drew got ready to leave, and she and Mrs. Fairchild chatted, Pennington thought back to what had happened at Willow Creek. He wondered if it had been Chief Turnage who'd scared the living shit out of him like that. More important, why was Turnage so antagonistic to the girl?

The hell with him, he thought. What was really on his mind was how to keep Drew in town. She was a find. If what she'd said at Willow Creek was true—that both guys were in their early twenties, and that the black guy had come on the scene *after* the Fairchild girl was dead— there was a potentially big story here. Assuming Drew was right, the white man could have committed the

132

murder and Edward Johnson was innocent. Which meant that Lee Caldecott, who had accused Johnson, might have been lying. He could even have committed the murder himself.

Pennington loved it. It was juicy. Prominent family, old murder case reopened, scandal, gossip, the ghost of a beautiful girl. There was money here, big money. Definitely a book. *Sybil*—with a supernatural slant. A title flashed into his mind: *The Possession of Drew Summers*. No. *The Reincarnation of Betty Fairchild*. Better. But how could he keep the girl in town?

He couldn't go to Turnage, that was for sure. Arnold Stiggs was the guy. As county solicitor, Stiggs was head honcho. But Stiggs would have to have something solid, something to give him a reason to pursue a reinvestigation of the case. So far Pennington didn't have it. The diary wasn't enough. What happened at the charity gamble wasn't enough. What Drew said at Willow Creek wasn't enough. He needed something spectacular, something that would prove Drew was not guessing.

Drew was thanking Mrs. Fairchild for the lunch and saying what a nice time she'd had when he had a thought.

"Drew, when we were at the Caldecott house and you knew where Betty's diary was, could you have said what was written in it?"

"I never thought about it."

"Could you do it now?" Pennington said.

Before she could answer, Mrs. Fairchild said, "Haven't you seen the diary?"

"No, she hasn't," Pennington said. "Our chief of police threatened to arrest her, then sent it right over to you."

Mrs. Fairchild went to the desk. "Drew, you must see it," she said.

"Mrs. Fairchild, could you wait just a second?" Pennington said. "*Could* you describe anything that's in it?" he asked Drew.

She signaled him to cool it. ". . . I'd rather not try," Drew said.

Pennington kept on. "Why not?"

"I don't want to make a game out of this."

Mrs. Fairchild hesitated, then went to Drew and gave her the slender leather-bound book she'd taken from the desk. She touched Drew's hand. "It would not be a game to me," she said.

Drew glanced down at the cover, at the date in gold, and suddenly the inscription inside the diary popped into her mind. It was affectionate and loving, and the woman before her had written it when she was young and hopeful. Now she was old and alone, and it was as though she had never been in love, never married, never had a daughter. Drew repressed a surge of pity.

"What's the matter?" Pennington asked her. "What's wrong?"

"The inscription inside," she said honestly. "It's very sad."

"You know there's an inscription?" Mrs. Fairchild asked her. She had sat down again.

"Yes."

"Will you tell me what it is?"

Drew's eyes didn't leave Mrs. Fairchild's.

"It says, 'To my darling Betty—May this be the f-first . . .'" She had to swallow before she went on. "'The first . . . of many . . . wonderful years . . . to come.'"

Drew's eyes filled, and thinking she was going to cry, Chuck Pennington took out a clean handkerchief, but Mrs. Fairchild began to weep softly, so he gave it to her. Drew found a tissue in her handbag and dabbed at her eyes. Pennington pretended to look out the window.

A gold mine, he thought, a fucking gold mine.

When Mrs. Fairchild recovered, Pennington asked Drew if she knew anything else that was in the diary.

"Yes."

134

Again Mrs. Fairchild had to urge her to tell them and Pennington was astounded. He knew Drew hadn't seen the diary, yet just holding it, without opening it, she told of one entry where Betty was upset that her parents were arguing, of another where she wrote how glad she was that their uncle had come to live with them. She told of Betty's mother taking her to the county fair and how scared she'd been when the geese began to hiss at her. Mrs. Fairchild almost started to cry all over again, and as hard-nosed as he thought of himself, Pennington was touched. More than ever he was convinced that he had a once-in-a-lifetime opportunity here if he played it right. He saw himself saying good-bye to the *Sentinel* and hello to the Atlanta *Constitution*. He knew he had a best-seller.

He and Drew had agreed they would not tell Mrs. Fairchild what had happened on the way over because it might upset her. Now he said the hell with it. He described Drew's compulsion to go to Willow Creek and what she had sensed there about Edward Johnson arriving on the scene after the white man.

Mrs. Fairchild took her usual year answering, but what she said surprised him. "I never believed that Edward would do such a thing. He was not that kind of young man. Everyone else did, my husband and my brother Raymond. I did not. None of Arletta's children could have done something like that."

"It's too bad you're leaving here," Pennington said to Drew.

"Must you?" Mrs. Fairchild said.

"I'm afraid so," Drew said.

"Do you have to return to work?" Mrs. Fairchild asked her.

"If I still have a job," Drew said with a wry smile.

She told them briefly what had happened over the past weeks, and Mrs. Fairchild said, "You must know now, Drew, that there is nothing wrong with you and that you have been made to come here for a reason."

Pennington jumped in. "You stay and my paper'll pick up the tab," he said. He was sure his boss would back him up. "Hotel, food, everything—within reason."

"You must, Drew," Mrs. Fairchild said, then her eyes left Drew and she looked past her. "Raymond," she said.

Raymond Ordway was standing in the doorway, and as soon as Drew saw him, her heart gave a heavy thump.

His sister said, "Oh, Raymond, you are in for such a wonderful, wonderful surprise."

"Am I?" He acknowledged the reporter with a grunt. He looked at Drew without saying anything.

"Have you any idea at all," his sister asked him, "what has happened today?"

"Get to the surprise."

"First, I want to introduce you to this young lady. I know—you have met her before, but not really. Drew Summers, my dear brother Raymond."

"How do you do," Drew murmured.

"Raymond, you have every right to be standoffish," his sister went on, "and Drew would be the first to grant that. However—" She took the diary from Drew. "Look. It was Betty's. Drew divined that it was in the attic of our old house."

"I heard about it," he said.

His sister's eyes filled again. "I gave it to Betty myself, Raymond. You of all people will want to read it."

"Harriet," Ordway said, "this is neither the time nor the place, is it?"

She took his arm and led him to a chair. "This *is* the time, my dear brother," she said firmly, "and this is most certainly the place."

Ordway protested, but she shushed him. Opening the diary, she leafed through it and found what she was looking for.

"Raymond, this is dated Sunday, September twenty-third, 1961. 'I fell and cut my hand pretty bad today,'" she read. "'Daddy was angry and said I fussed too much and told'—Betty left out the word me—'told to put a Band-Aid on it. Uncle Ray was so funny. He pretended to be Dr. Elspeth and made a sling for me and said I would have to stay in bed for six months. "No school for six months," he said, then he wrote out a prescription for lollipops and chocolate creams. He made everybody laugh and me most of all. I love him so.' Do you remember when that happened, Raymond?"

"Vaguely," he said.

"Oh, I do," his sister said. "You were so funny. You imitated Dr. Elspeth to a T and you had us all in stitches. Wait." She turned the pages, found another place and gave him the book.

What Ordway read made him frown. But it was a cover-up. He was obviously deeply affected.

Mrs. Fairchild took the diary from him. "May I read this to our guests, Raymond? They are responsible for this wonderful gift."

He said nothing, not trusting himself to talk.

"This was written," she said, "when Raymond had the flu so badly that—" She interrupted herself and said, "Drew, have you any idea what Betty wrote here?"

"Why are you asking her?" Ordway said.

"To show you something. Mark would not let Drew see the diary after she told where it was. He sent it to me immediately. Isn't that correct, Chuck?"

"That's right, Mr. Ordway," Pennington said.

"Drew," Mrs. Fairchild asked, "do you think you might possibly be able to tell us what is written here?"

"Gee, I—"

"Try," Mrs. Fairchild said. "Here is a hint. It was written when Raymond was quite ill." Ordway started to say something, but Mrs. Fairchild shushed him.

Drew hesitated. An image of the page began to take shape in her mind. "Does it begin 'Dear God'?"

Mrs. Fairchild nodded, and Drew said, "I think it says something like, 'Please don't let anything happen to

Uncle Ray . . . I won't be able to stand it . . . Uncle Ray, I do love you so—'" She stopped.

"Almost word for word," Mrs. Fairchild said. "'You are kind and warm and—'"

"'. . . And I think of you so very often. . . .'" Drew murmured.

Mrs. Fairchild closed the diary. "Raymond, can't you feel it? Betty is here. Her spirit is within this girl."

Drew glanced at him, saw he was still unfriendly. "I think we should go," she said to Pennington.

"Please not yet," Mrs. Fairchild said. "Raymond, urge our guests to stay."

Ordway got up. "How did you 'divine' that it was in the attic?"

Drew shrugged uncomfortably.

"What else do you divine?" His tone was sarcastic.

"Raymond," Mrs. Fairchild said.

"Wait—I am very interested in any other bits of information this young lady might have about Betty."

Drew said, "Mr. Ordway, I don't blame you for being angry. Whatever I did last night, I'm sorry. It wasn't intentional. We ought to go," she said to Pennington.

Ordway had picked up the diary. *"How did you know this was in the attic?"* he asked.

Drew pretended not to hear. "I had a really nice time, Mrs. Fairchild," she said. "Thanks for that great lunch and for invit—"

"I am accustomed to an answer when I ask a question, young lady," Ordway cut in. "What do you want here? What are you after?"

His sister was incredulous. "Raymond!"

He motioned her to stay out of it and confronted Drew. "You're involved in some kind of scam, and you can't tell me otherwise. I know a lot more about you than you think, and you're not down here to perform some magic tricks and imitate my dead niece for nothing, are you? My guess is that you plan to somehow work your way into this house, which you have already started to do!"

"Raymond, Drew is leaving Greenview right—"

"Stay *out* of this," he said harshly. "You've been down here before, haven't you?"

Drew had turned pale. "Down here?"

"Yes, down here. You showed up at Charleston Airport about two weeks ago. Why?"

"I don't know."

She tried to get past him but he wouldn't let her. "Don't you tell me you don't know! You caused a scene there with Mr. Caldecott. And last night, you just *happened* to turn up at the Spengler and cause another scene. I'd say that looks like some sort of a game, doesn't it—enough to tempt me to get Police Chief Turnage on the phone right now and have him march your smart little behind down to the station to find out what it is."

Again Drew tried to get past him. This time he grabbed her wrist. Pennington loved it.

Drew was so pale now that Harriet Fairchild was afraid she was going to faint. What she did next, however, was more shocking than anything Raymond had done.

She gave Raymond a look of utter contempt and in a measured, warning tone, said, "Get them effin' hands off me, Ray."

Mrs. Fairchild felt a terrible foreboding. "Raymond," she said, "please let her go."

Ordway wanted to, but suddenly he'd have sworn he was holding Betty, and he couldn't think. "Just calm down, young lady," he said.

"Bugshit. Don't you tell me what to do, you sonofabitch bastard," the girl said through clenched teeth. "Maybe everybody is scared of you, but I'm not. You want to call Mark, you go ahead and call him. Just get your hands off me. Let—me—go!" she yelled. Wrenching free, she went after him shrieking and kicking, and as fast and as powerful as he was, he had trouble finally grabbing her wrists.

Mrs. Fairchild did not know what her brother was feeling, but she knew she had seen this scene in the past. Betty had had a horrid temper at times, and occasionally, when Raymond had tried to discipline her, she had become quite violent. It was becoming too much for Mrs. Fairchild to bear, and she was on the verge of putting her fingers to her ears and shutting her eyes when suddenly the girl stopped struggling. As quickly as she had become violent she was calm, staring at Raymond in hurt surprise.

"Please let me go, Mr. Ordway," she said.

He did, and she looked at the welts on her wrists. She began to massage them. "Why did you do that?"

"Are you joking? What did you expect me to do?" Ordway said. "You cursed me and tried to kick me."

"I most certainly did not. I tried to leave and you wouldn't let me." She looked at Pennington, who wasn't sure what to say.

"You don't remember what you did?" Ordway asked.

"I don't care what I did," Drew said, forcing back tears. "You had no right to put your hands on me."

Ordway concealed his awe. "I'm sorry. I thought I was asking you a reasonable question."

"And I gave you the only answer I know." Drew was furious now. "I don't have the least idea what I was doing at your stupid airport." She kept massaging her wrists, her eyes shifting from one to the other of them.

"Don't you understand?" she said to Ordway. *"I can't remember!* I can't remember going to the airport that time and I can't remember driving down here. One moment I was in a hospital in New York and the next I'm in a strange place with a whole bunch of people gawking at me. How do you think that feels?" she cried. "How do you think it feels to wake up seven hundred miles away and have people you never saw before in your life treat

140

you like a criminal? First your dumb chief wants to arrest me, then some crazy woman attacks me, and now you accuse me of having some kind of a plan to weasel my way into your family. Well let me clue you in, Mr. Ordway, I don't even like you much less want to be part of your family!"

She looked so pathetic and frail that Mrs. Fairchild wanted to console her. But Drew wasn't finished. "You want to know what I'm doing down here, mister? Well so do I—and if you can find out, please tell me," she pleaded, her voice breaking now. "Because I don't have any control over my own life anymore. I don't know what's happening to me and I'm scared, scared to death. So you do whatever you please—I don't care. Just leave me alone. Leave me alone, for God's sake!"

She broke down into sobs, and Ordway automatically went to her. As soon as he touched her, her legs gave way and he held her up, her weakness and vulnerability penetrating him as only one other person's in all his life. He held her close, moved by the tears streaming down her cheeks, wanting to kiss them. It was like holding Betty in his arms again, and he was overwhelmed by the emotions that she called up in him.

He was almost resentful when Harriet came over and helped him lead Drew to the love seat. There the two of them consoled her, and there, with Ordway's reassuring arm around her, she surrendered herself as though she had known them all her life. At this point she didn't care who was offering sympathy. So much tension had built up within her that she couldn't hold up any longer, and for the first time since the events that brought her here had begun, she cried as she had not cried since her sister had committed suicide.

None of them noticed that Pennington had left the room. He had gone to look for a phone, found one in the reception room, and had been lucky enough to reach the man he was calling.

141

At first when he told Arnold Stiggs that he had to meet with this girl, the solicitor's tone had been impatient. Yes, he'd seen the girl at the charity gamble and he'd read Pennington's story, and yes he knew the girl supposedly had ESP. Right now, however, he was having a sandwich at his desk and was very busy with half a dozen pressing cases, so if Chuck didn't mind . . .

But when Pennington told him about the diary incident he became mildly interested. The interest deepened when Pennington mentioned the events at Willow Creek. The clincher was what had happened not five minutes ago; not only what, but where and with whom.

"You gotta meet this girl, Arnold. Ordway and his sister are crazy about her," he said, using their names again, "and listen to this—Mrs. Fairchild says she never believed Johnson murdered her daughter."

As soon as Stiggs heard that, Chuck felt, his ears pricked up.

"Are you saying that Mrs. Fairchild wants the case reopened?"

"That's what she indicated to me."

"All right, I'll give Chief Turnage a call and suggest he have a talk with the girl."

"I don't know if that's a good idea," Pennington said. "Turnage isn't too crazy about her."

"Chuck, I've known Turnage a good many years," Stiggs said. "He's not the kind of man who lets his personal feelings interfere with his job."

Pennington didn't argue. Turnage was the least of his worries. First he had to figure out how to keep Drew in town. He asked Stiggs if there was any legal way they could do it and Stiggs said no.

When he came back into the sitting room, Drew was saying good-bye to Ordway and Mrs. Fairchild. "Thanks for being so nice about it," she was saying. "I'm really embarrassed. I didn't realize I made such a scene."

142

"You certainly had every right to," Mrs. Fairchild said, giving her brother an arch look.

Raymond Ordway took Drew's hand in both of his. "You're a fine and brave young lady," he said. "I had no idea what you've been through."

"I wish we could change your mind about leaving so soon, Drew," Mrs. Fairchild said. "Can't you stay just one more day?"

Chuck Pennington broke in. "The county solicitor would like you to stay too," he said. "I just spoke with him. He'd like you to talk to the authorities about what you sensed at Willow Creek." He avoided mentioning Turnage.

"What's that?" Ordway asked.

"Oh, Raymond, it was incredible," his sister said. "I'll tell you later."

Drew shook her head. "I can't stay."

"Can't you talk her into it?" Pennington said to Mrs. Fairchild.

"I tried. I have offered Drew dinner at the finest restaurant in town, I have invited her to stay with us overnight, and I have even thrown in a grand tour of Greenview tomorrow."

"Please," Ordway said fondly. "Let me make up for how I acted."

"Do I hear correctly?" Mrs. Fairchild said. "Raymond Ordway admitting he's wrong?"

"Thanks," Drew said to him. "I have to go home and get my head together. If I can."

"I hope you don't intend to drive straight through," Mrs. Fairchild said.

Drew said no, she'd spend the night at a motel and get into New York tomorrow.

She complained of a splitting headache as she and Pennington left. Mrs. Fairchild offered her some aspirin, but Drew said no, she'd get some if it kept up.

When the reporter's car moved out of the driveway,

Ordway was left thinking of how sweet the girl had felt in his arms when she cried. He was glad he'd come home.

She was ready to leave now, the Mustang's engine running, the top up. Pennington had driven her back to the hotel and all the way over he'd tried to convince her to stay, but she wouldn't. And when the valet had driven up in her car, he went apeshit.

He asked her if she knew that Betty Fairchild had driven a car like this, and she said not until she saw what she had at Willow Creek.

He pleaded with her: one more day—one, that was all—but she said she was getting too scared.

"How's the headache?" he asked.

"Still there."

"Maybe I ought to follow you a little ways."

"Thanks, Chuck. I'll be okay."

"Think you'll be home by six tomorrow?"

"Probably."

"I'll call you then. I don't want to let go of this. Sure wish you'd stay . . ."

She released the emergency brake, put the car into Drive. "'Bye, Chuck. Thanks for everything," she said.

"Good luck," he said. He took his hands off the door as the car eased out of the space and made a U-turn. And no sooner did it do so than suddenly it shot forward, sped past a few cars and screeched to a stop.

As soon as Pennington recovered from his surprise, he trotted after it, got alongside and looked in. He couldn't tell whether Drew was more scared or confused.

"You scared the hell out of me," he said. "What's the matter?"

She shook her head. "I'm not sure, I—"

Before she could finish, her eyes widened in surprise and the car shot forward again. Chuck thought Holy shit and ran for his own car.

Waiting half a block down the street, Hawkins

glanced at his side mirror as the Mustang sped toward him, then passed him going fast, far too fast for cobblestones.

He pulled out behind her. Turnage had told him to stay with her to the city limits and keep enough distance so she didn't know she was being followed, but he didn't think that was a good idea now. The way she was driving, he wanted her to *know* he was behind her. Once she was out of town she could dance on the roof if she liked, but while she was his he didn't want anything happening—to her or anybody else.

She drove all right for a couple of blocks, then twice at the next three intersections she hesitated, stopping a couple of times. Finally she sped up, made it through an orange light, and he skinned through after her.

She was well over the limit as she approached Macon, which was one way to the highway, and again the light was changing. This time it was red by the time she burned rubber turning onto it, and Hawkins said to himself, *One more, lady, and I cite you.*

Drew passed a couple of cars before she reached the highway ramp still going over the limit. He took the ramp after her, and she was fine until the highway divided, two lanes on each side of the grass-covered median. The median widened over the next quarter mile, pine trees scattered in the center.

Hawkins was not far behind when her brake lights flashed on. Her car started fishtailing, tires smoking. She came out of it and everything looked good until she hit the brakes again. This time the Mustang skidded, and if there'd been anyone near her, it could have caused an accident. She had to be crazy and she was endangering herself: He couldn't let her go any longer.

He called in a 10–54 to the dispatcher, then cutting on the blue lights and the headlights, he gave the Mustang's plate number and his location.

She was weaving, probably not even aware of him.

He hit the siren. If she saw him, there was no indication of it. She kept on weaving, each left bringing her closer to the shoulder and the median, and Hawkins had the feeling that something bad was going to happen. The median was at its widest here, sloping down to a heavily wooded center thick with scrub. If she drove down there going as fast as she was . . .

As if she knew what he was thinking, she swung onto the shoulder and rode it.

Then what he'd been afraid of happened: the Mustang moved over onto the grass and headed diagonally down the embankment.

Jesus Christ, he thought, one wrong move and she goes over. And if she rolled in that convertible . . . He didn't want to think about it. He slowed and eased onto the shoulder, pacing her, hoping she wouldn't lose control. The embankment was steep and she was going too fast to turn back up to the shoulder. If she used her head and slowed down gradually, she could stop where the embankment leveled out, close to the trees. But either she didn't want to or couldn't. Instead she braked.

That did it. She went into a skid.

Inside the car as it sped down at an angle, Drew was trying to control her panic. She'd gone off the shoulder too fast, made the mistake of using the brake, and now she was trying to correct, praying she could get some traction. She was still going too fast and she was scared to death of overturning, but it was too late to do anything about it. She reached the bottom of the embankment praying she could turn the wheel gently enough on this level ground to avoid skidding into the trees.

She saw the raised concrete drain too late. It was half hidden by scrub, and instinctively she wanted to twist the wheel to avoid it, but she knew she'd skid and slam right into it if she did. She turned the wheel lightly to the right and prayed. She was lucky. The front wheel hit, jolting her and making an awful sound, then the entire length of

146

the car was being scraped. But when she came to a stop she knew she was all right, and that was all that mattered.

Hawkins edged his cruiser over the embankment, made it down easily and pulled up behind the Mustang.

When he got out and approached on the passenger side he kept his fingers on his gun butt.

He heard her talking before she came into view and wondered if he'd missed seeing another person in the car when she'd passed him on the street. But she was alone, hunched over the wheel talking to herself. He called her name, but she paid no attention. He was about to open the door when somebody came slipping and sliding down the embankment. Chuck Pennington.

Hawkins waved him away. "Stand clear," he said sharply. "Back off right now."

Pennington did as he was told.

"Ms. Summers?" Hawkins said quietly. "You okay? Ms. Summers?"

She didn't raise her head, and he had to stoop over to see her face. It was wet with perspiration and she was trembling.

"I'll go back," she whispered. She said it as if she was giving in to him, and he wasn't sure what to say.

"I'll go back" she croaked, but not until he heard her next words did he realize that she was talking to herself. "Just tell me what you want from me," she said desperately, her voice rising. "Tell me what you want and I'll do it. You hear me? I can't go on like this! *Tell . . . me . . . what . . . you . . . want . . . from . . . me!*"

9

Chuck found a cheap car rental for her, then she followed him to the Marriott, just outside of town.

Drew asked the desk clerk if she had a single on an upper floor.

"Upper floor . . . upper floor," she murmured, consulting a red-and-green-lighted board.

"You're sure you don't want to stay at the Spengler?" Chuck said.

"I do want to stay at the Spengler, but I can't afford to stay at the Spengler."

"I told you the paper'll—"

"I want to pay for myself. I wouldn't feel comfortable."

"You bet," the clerk said. She and Drew exchanged a smile. "Got a third floor, 309. Nice room. My sister stayed in it when she visited us last Mother's Day."

"See?" Drew said to Pennington. "What's meant to be is meant to be."

Pennington carried up her suitcase for her, put it on the bed. The room was quiet, cheerful and light. It looked out on a cow pasture across the highway and a shopping complex right next door.

"Now, what's wrong with this?" she asked him.

"It ain't the Spengler," he said. "How's the headache?"

She touched her forehead. "I didn't even realize it—it's gone. You'd think it'd be worse."

148

She went to the door that connected to an adjoining room, tried the knob. It wouldn't turn. She made sure the dead bolt was in place.

"You feel like talking about what happened?" Chuck asked her.

"I feel like screaming, is what I feel like. I want to go home and this girl won't let me—and now even if I could go home I can't because I don't have a car. She wants something, and either she can't tell me what it is or she is telling me and I don't understand."

"Or maybe she doesn't want you to know. You ever think of that?"

"No. And I wish you hadn't thought of it either. Chuck, thanks for helping me. We'll talk later. I've got to call work, then I want to lie down for a while." She rubbed her shoulder. "Hurts."

"Lucky you're alive. I'm heading for the shop. After you catch some z's, come on over."

"She said that all she could remember was losing control of the car in the Spengler parking lot," Hawkins told Turnage. "She said that if she tried to slow down her foot hit the gas, tried to speed up she hit the brake. The next thing she knew she was going off the highway onto the median."

"Was she drunk?"

Hawkins shook his head. "Clean."

"Well . . . ?"

Hawkins shifted uncomfortably. "She said somebody else took control of her." He expected a pained look, but Turnage leaned back in his chair and kept a straight face. "Her car had to be towed, so I figured she had enough trouble already and I only cited her for driving on the shoulder. Chuck took her in his car and said he'd be responsible for her."

"Then she's back."

"She's back."

"Call Ordway and his sister and alert them," Turnage said. "And maybe you better warn the Caldecotts too. What do your instincts tell you about this kid?"

"*Some*thing's sure goin' on with her. I mean I got the willies when I approached her car and there she was yelling at somebody who wasn't there. Maybe she's crazy, Mark, maybe she's got ESP, I don't know, but I don't think she's faking."

"Why?"

"Just a hunch. Chucky baby offered to put her up at the Spengler. Have the paper spring for it. She said no, asked if there was a less expensive hotel in town, and he took her out to the Marriott."

Turnage leaned back in his chair, thinking, then told his secretary over the intercom to hunt up everything they had in the files on the Johnson case and have it on his desk in a couple of hours. "Check with the county too," he added. "They might have some evidence stored."

Hawkins said, "Mark, you think those records are still gonna be around?"

"Why not? Case was never closed."

"Yeah, but it's been over twenty years."

"Call the girl," Turnage said. "Ask her if she can meet us at Willow Creek ten-thirty tomorrow morning."

"What for?"

"Arnold Stiggs requested it, that's what for."

Drew had left a four-thirty wake-up call, and when the phone rang she thanked the clerk sleepily. There were two messages: one from Mrs. Fairchild, and one from Sergeant Hawkins. She jotted down the numbers they'd left, then lay back, grateful there was no message from Norman.

When she'd called and told Susan where she was, Susan had suggested that maybe it would be better not to tell Norman anything—let him assume she was still in the rest home until he found out otherwise. Drew thought

150

it was a good idea. She'd told Susan about her resemblance to Betty Fairchild and some of the things that had happened, and she knew that Susan had to be wondering if she was crazy. She'd stuck with her though. She'd been great. Drew felt really good about her being pregnant.

She closed her eyes, and as soon as she did, the accident came back to her and she was behind the wheel again, the car crunching into the concrete drain.

Dragging herself out of bed, she rubbed her shoulder where it ached. This better be over soon, she thought. She couldn't take it.

She almost fell asleep on the toilet, then dashed some water on her face. She glanced in the mirror. "Ugh."

She ran her tongue around her mouth, uncertain whether to brush her teeth before or after she made her calls. Before, she decided: keep the phone user-friendly.

She found the business card the tow-truck driver had given her—Stroud's Garage & Repair—and was told it would take two days to fix the front end. She gave the man the go-ahead, then called Harriet Fairchild.

Deeply concerned, Mrs. Fairchild offered to send a car for her right then, but Drew assured her she was all right and made a date to meet her for lunch and a "grand tour" of Greenview the next day. She'd pick Drew up at the hotel at twelve-thirty, Mrs. Fairchild promised, and cautioned Drew to take care of herself.

Hawkins was next, wanting to know if she could meet him and Turnage at Willow Creek the next morning. She said okay, then started getting ready to meet Pennington at the *Sentinel*.

At Stroud's Garage & Repair, Bill Stroud was lying under the front end of a tilted-up Mazda when a car pulled up at the entrance. The driver left the engine running, came in and stopped close to Stroud's head.

"Billy boy."

Stroud rolled out to see the only man he'd ever met whose smile scared him.

"Oh. Hi, Mr. Barnes." He made a move to get up, but Wendell Barnes got down on his haunches and put a finger on his chest.

"Don't bother," he said pleasantly. "I know you are a busy man. You checked out that Mustang yet?"

"Yes sir," Stroud said.

"When do you believe it will be ready?" Barnes asked.

"Day, day and a half, maybe. The lady just wants it in running shape, but I got a man out and—"

"Any chance it might take longer?" Barnes smiled. "I'm not talking about overcharging the lady, you understand. You just find a good reason to keep it a few more days if I tell you."

Reaching into his jacket for a billfold, he removed some bills. Fifties. Separating them, he placed them on Stroud's chest, pinned them there with the same finger. "That's for four days. I'll let you know if more time is needed." He got up. "Appreciate it, Billy," he said.

After Barnes drove off, Stroud took the fifties from his chest. There were four. He didn't want them, but like the last time he'd taken money from Barnes, he'd been afraid to say no.

That was a few years ago when he'd worked for Barnes's dealership in Charleston. Easiest job he'd ever had. Barnes and his manager never worried much about sales or repairs, and after Stroud had been there awhile he came to believe the rumors he'd heard that Barnes was into money laundering and dope. Too many people who came in gave off bad vibes, and there was always big cash changing hands.

Stroud decided to quit when he was heading for the washroom one night and saw two men hustle a guy out of Barnes's office. He got a quick look and he felt weak. If the guy was still alive he was going to need a face. One of the men saw him, and Stroud got into the washroom fast

152

and locked the door. When he came out, Barnes was smiling, asked if he'd seen anything that bothered him.

He said no he hadn't, and Barnes handed him a fifty-dollar bill. "You take the little woman to a rock concert," he said.

The porter was just as scared as he was, said he'd cleaned up a mess in the boss's office that looked like someone had been murdered. Stroud quit two weeks later.

The words leapt out at Pennington from the microfilm screen, and he was so happy he made the sound of a kiss. "There's the reason," he said.

"There's what reason?" Drew asked, not too interested. It was close to six. She and Pennington had been talking and going over the *Sentinel*'s files for over an hour now and she was drowsy again.

"The reason, my beauty, why Turnage got so pissed off when you said that he had a fight with a guy over Betty Fairchild." He manipulated the dial to bring the paragraph up larger. "Read."

"'. . . questioned by Chief Pinckney,'" Drew read, "'Mark Turnage, twenty, admitted that he fought with Edward Johnson two days before Johnson's disappearance. "But I didn't kill him," Turnage said. "I wasn't hunting anywhere near where he was killed.'"

"He had a fight all right," Pennington said, "and the guy he fights with mysteriously disappears two days later—the same guy who's accused of Betty Fairchild's murder. But why did Turnage fight with him, that's the question. Any idea?"

Drew leaned back in the old-fashioned wooden mahogany chair. It was smooth and comfortable and she could have fallen asleep in it.

"I'm too out of it."

"That bad?"

She rubbed her eyes. "I feel like a rummage sale."
She was quiet, then she said, "Why me, Chuck?"

"Who knows? Maybe it's some crazy cosmic mistake.
Maybe you and Betty were supposed to be born twins and
weren't, and now you're connecting through time and
space."

"That's very corny."

"Why? I'm telling you, Drew, when you lit into Raymond Ordway you were somebody else. I never saw
anything like it. You had a mouth on you like—"

"Don't remind me, please."

"I'm telling you what I saw, and what Ordway and his
sister saw—Betty Fairchild. I think you don't want to
know it because you're scared and I don't blame you. This
girl has some unfinished business, and whatever it is she
wants you to finish it for her."

"You're right, I am scared. Very scared."

"I don't blame you, blacking out like th—"

"It's more than that. I'm afraid somebody's going to
murder me, Chuck."

"What makes you think that?"

"If Edward Johnson didn't kill Betty Fairchild, suppose the guy who did is still around? And don't tell me
you haven't thought of it."

"I've thought of it," he admitted.

"If he thinks I'm liable to identify him, what do you
suppose he'll try to do about it?"

"Or them," Pennington said.

"Thanks a lot."

"I'm trying to be honest. There's something else too."
"What?"

"It was what I was thinking up in your room when I
said that maybe Betty Fairchild doesn't want you to know
what she wants. Maybe she's after revenge."

It took her a moment to get it. "You mean she might
want me to kill somebody for her? Oh my God!"

154

A figure appeared in the doorway, and they both jumped. "Can I see you for a minute, Chuck?"

It was Steve Roberts, the *Sentinel*'s managing editor.

Pennington got up and followed him through the composing room into the newsroom. It was busy at this hour, almost all sixteen partitioned desks in the center occupied. His own was one of the exceptions.

He grabbed a cruller from the stained bakery box beside the coffee stand and wolfed down half of it before he was inside Roberts's glass-fronted office.

"You did a good job on the Fairchild stuff," Roberts said as Chuck closed the door, shutting out the newsroom sounds.

Pennington said thanks, but he was insulted. The fucking morning edition had not only sold out for the first time in God knows how long, but the story was more than good. It was terrific. "I told you there was a fantastic story here," he said.

"Yes you did. How is tomorrow's looking?"

"Even better."

"Good," Roberts said. Pennington expected him to mention that they were going to print five thousand extra copies of tomorrow's edition—which they were—but instead he said, "Raymond Ordway wants to talk with you."

"Fantastic! I've been dying to interview that guy."

"He's waiting for you at his office in Charleston."

"Now? Shit, I'm supposed to take Drew Summers to dinner."

"This comes first."

Pennington went back and told Drew that something had come up and that he'd pick her up at the hotel in about an hour and a half for dinner. If he was going to be longer, he said, he'd call. In awe of Ordway, he hoped he'd have to call.

He realized he'd overestimated the length of the interview as soon as he was in Raymond Ordway's office.

Ordway gave him the kind of look you give an overflowing toilet and didn't offer to shake hands.

"I don't have more than a few minutes," he said, indicating a chair.

Pennington wondered what he'd done wrong. As far as he was concerned, he'd always admired the man. You had to. The guy gave a new meaning to the term Reconstruction—reshaped billions of dollars of southern real estate into soaring hotels and glitzy art centers, and had investors offering him money the way fields of flowers offered themselves to the sun. He exuded assurance and certainty—and right now he seemed to be exuding acute displeasure.

Feeling like a grub, Pennington waited for Ordway to say something. Even in shirt-sleeves and tie the man was impeccable. On his wrist, Pennington knew, would be the most expensive and slimmest watch money could buy, and the rest of him, Pennington felt sure—hair, fingernails, body—was trimmed, manicured, massaged, and clothed by solicitous and expert hands.

"Give me your personal feelings about Drew Summers," Ordway said without preamble.

"She's terrific."

"What makes her so terrific?"

"She just is. Straight-arrow—everything she does, everything she says."

"Could she be a con artist?"

"I doubt it."

"What makes you an authority?"

The challenge shook Pennington up until he remembered that he *was* an authority. "I did a three-part piece on psychics once," he said. "They were phonies who dealt in generalized bullshit. They made guesses, dropped names, key words, key phrases. If their patsy reacted to a name or a word, they embroidered on it. If not, they went on to other words, other phrases. This kid doesn't

156

do that. She makes a statement and that's it, and she hasn't been wrong yet."

Ordway seemed to soften. "I'm sure you realize my sister and I are very torn up by this."

"I can imagine," Chuck said.

"No you can't. If this girl has my niece's spirit inside of her . . . Does that make you laugh?"

"Not at all."

"If she is genuine, my sister and I want her in our family. If she's a phony, I'm going to cut her heart out. I want you to keep me informed of everything you learn about this girl—what she does, what she says, when she says it and who she says it to."

"I can't, Mr. Ordway. That's privileged information." Pennington felt good saying it, and he sat back in his chair. "I'm sure you understand."

"Of course," Ordway said. "You have ethics."

He opened his desk drawer, took out some sheets of paper and turned a few pages. "This is a report on you. Four years ago you wrote a series of articles for the Cleveland *Times-Herald.* Your editor allowed you to resign when he found you'd made up half the information in them." He turned another page. "You're also $7,642 behind in child support, and your ex-wife would like to know your whereabouts. . . . Do we deal or don't we?"

Pennington had heard that Ordway had a mania for this kind of thing, learned things about people and then used what he learned. "We deal," he said.

Ordway told him to write down two telephone numbers. "When you call, only use a pay phone. Be aware that you're not the only one I am getting information from. If I find you're lying or withholding, I'll have you fired from your job. Then I'll have you run out of the state. Is that clear?"

Pennington said it was clear, then Ordway questioned him extensively about Drew. "Did you know she

157

drives almost exactly the same car my niece drove?" he asked at one point.

Pennington said yeah. "She bought it about eight months ago—sold a new Honda she'd just bought, and everybody thought she was crazy. Including her. She had it completely restored. Now she knows why."

Ordway was interested in what Drew had said to Turnage that made him so antagonistic toward her. Then he wanted to know how Drew herself was taking all this.

"In a nutshell?" Pennington said. "She's scared and wants to go home. You saw that for yourself. She's afraid that somebody's liable to murder her."

"Murder her? Who?"

"The same person who murdered your niece."

"The scum who murdered Betty is dead." Ordway tossed the pages to him. "For your memory book." Whatever he was feeling he kept to himself.

Pennington let the pages fall to the floor. "Is that all?" he said, getting up.

"For now."

"I'm going out to Willow Creek with Drew tomorrow."

"Anything else?"

"I'm having dinner with her in about a half hour."

"Call me if you learn anything interesting. From a pay phone. And before you go, you little prick, bend down and pick up those pages."

Lee Caldecott was home alone.

Tricia had gone to the movies and Juleen was at a club meeting. At least that's what she told him. If she wasn't at the club, he didn't want to know about it.

He was in the den. He had just hung up the phone after a long, taxing conversation with a client, and wanted another drink. He was behind the bar refilling his old-fashioned glass with ice when the phone rang. He ignored it: This was the first time he'd been alone in days, and he was looking forward to reading a new thriller he'd

158

gotten. The machine could pick it up. By the time he'd poured himself a couple of fingers of vodka and squeezed half a lemon into it, the ringing stopped.

Five minutes into the book the phone rang again. The opening pages were slow, so he went to the bar and picked up the phone as he reached for the vodka bottle.

"Hello."

He heard her faint breathing on the other end, and he knew immediately who it was.

"Lee." As soon as she spoke the hackles on his neck rose. "Look out the window, Lee."

He did. The poplars lining the driveway and the lawn itself were coated with silver moonlight.

"Remember, Lee—that line from my favorite poem? 'Look for me by moonlight.'"

He remembered it perfectly.

"'Watch for me by moonlight,'" she went on. "'I'll come to thee by moonlight, though hell should bar the way.' Remember how I used to recite that, Lee?"

"Yes."

"Well, I kept my promise. I am back from the other side of hell."

"Look, Miss Summers, I think th—"

"Lee-ee," she said warningly, "don't pretend I am someone else—and whatever you do don't hang up on me because if you do I will come over there right this—"

"Tell me what you want, whoever you are."

"Well, for one thing I want to ask Juleen what she ever did with that emerald necklace she stole from me. Is she there?"

"No."

"You ask her. I never said anything to her ab—"

"Get to the point or I *will* hang up."

"My pleasure," she said nastily. "I am calling to let you know that you are a shitty cowardly bastard, and you are going to pay for what you did to me and to Eddie—"

He hung up and stood leaning on the bar, afraid he was going to cry or be sick.

The phone rang again immediately, and this time he had the forethought to switch the machine on and turn the volume up. He listened to Juleen's recorded voice saying they weren't able to come to the phone. Then there was Betty's voice again, threatening and vengeful.

"You just wait and you see what's going to happen to you," she sobbed. "You know what? That girl Drew is going back to Willow Creek tomorrow, Lee. Hear? Because of me. *I* am sending her back there, and I will find a way to let her know what you did. You remember what happened there, don't you? You do remember how I looked after—"

She broke off suddenly, apparently aware of what Caldecott heard in the background—someone knocking at her door.

"I am going to get you, Lee," she hissed. "You just wait."

She hung up, and Caldecott stood motionless, listening to the pumping of blood in his eardrums. Then he poured more vodka into his glass and squeezed lemon juice into it. He drank it all.

Look for me by moonlight . . .

He told himself not to think about it, not to think about anything to do with her.

He picked up his book again, willing himself to concentrate, but Betty came right back into his thoughts.

With her came an image that seeped up from the depths of his soul like poisonous fumes. He could not stop it from taking shape, and it made him groan. When he first saw it, there in the front seat of Betty's car, it was so hideous he refused to believe it was real. It wore what had once been a lovely dress but had become a torn and bloody wrapping for the meat and the gore that oozed from it. . . .

He could not stay in the house. She might come over.

160

Even if she didn't, he was too afraid to be here alone. He had the presence of mind to remove the tape from the answering machine.

He turned on every light within reach as he headed for the front door.

His car was in the driveway. Walking toward it in the bright moonlight—*Look for me by moonlight, Lee*—he was afraid that at any moment he would see a blood-soaked horror jump from the shadows shrieking and raging. He didn't, of course. He was not insane.

But he glanced at the backseat of the car before he got in, and hit the lock button for the doors.

Then he drove off, heading for a bar.

"I'm telling you," Pennington said, "you were crying and carrying on—and you weren't yourself." He stood in the bathroom doorway while Drew stared at her reflection in the medicine chest. There were still tears on her cheeks.

"Chuck, I can't remember."

"I kept knocking and knocking until you finally slammed the phone down like a maniac. What's the last thing you do remember?"

Her eyes met his in the mirror. "I put on some lipstick," she said, "then I went out into the room to wait for you." She moved to the door and he made way for her to pass. As she did he glanced at the wastebasket. There was a tissue in it with her lip imprint.

"I thought I'd call Lee Caldecott and ask him if I could talk to him tomorrow," she said, going to the phone. She picked up a slip of paper beside it. "I got his number from information and wrote it . . . Oh no. No." She groaned and sat down on the bed. "I couldn't have called him . . . I couldn't."

"Take it easy. Maybe you didn't," Pennington said. He took the slip from her, got the phone book from a slot in

161

the table and leafed through it. He found a number under *Caldecott, L* and compared it to what Drew had written.

"You called him, all right."

"And you said I was screaming at him? Chuck, I was going to apologize to him."

"Call him now."

"I can't. I'm too embarrassed. Let's get out of here," she said, getting up. As she was checking her handbag to make sure she had her key, she stopped. "'Look for me by moonlight.' That mean anything to you?"

"Uh-uh. What's it from?"

"I don't know. It just popped into my head."

Chuck jotted it down under Caldecott's phone number and added *check w/Ordway.* "Good title for a romance," he said.

"Chuck, what am I going to do?" she asked him.

He knew she meant Caldecott. "You'll call him again and tell him you're sorry."

"No way."

"I'll call him for you if you want." He opened the door. "Let's go eat. I want to talk about book rights to your story with you."

"A book? Forget it. I can't think about anything like that. All I want—" She stopped. "I just had a thought."

"About what?"

"About Willow Creek," she said. "I don't know why, but I really want to go back there tomorrow."

"Hope you feel that way in the morning. Come on."

After being in the bar a few minutes and having people around him, Lee Caldecott felt better. He had to do something about this girl, he realized. He had to. He thought about hiring someone to scare her, or kill her, and immediately rejected it as being stupid.

Later on, however, after he'd had a few more drinks and was on his way home, it did not seem stupid at all.

162

But first he'd see what she was going to say at Willow Creek.

Juleen was in the den watching TV and sipping a drink when he came in. She'd bathed and was in her robe.

She lowered the volume with the remote and asked him what was the matter. He flopped into a chair and said he was just feeling down.

"Poor baby. I'm having an old-fashioned," she said, getting up. "What would you like?"

He said he'd had enough to drink—he'd have a Perrier with a squeeze of lemon.

When she brought it to him, she gently pulled his head against the softness of her belly. "Patricia's staying overnight at Cathy's," she said. Her speech was thick, and he felt a stir of anticipation.

Upstairs, when he came out of the shower their bedroom was dark except for the light from the street. It was cool enough to do without the air-conditioning, warm enough for the overhead fan lazily turning. Juleen was lying on her stomach, the sheet over her.

He got into bed keyed up, but when he saw the open handcuff beside her—one was already on her wrist—his excitement was instantaneous.

He took his time, touched her shoulders, her back, ran his fingers along the sides of her breasts before he snapped the other handcuff on her, then he kneaded her behind and her thighs. She moved a leg to raise her buttocks, and he ran his fingers down, teased her until she was breathing hard.

"Don't take advantage of me," she whispered as he helped her up. Eyes closed, breasts offered, she pretended to be helpless, said he mustn't do anything to her she didn't want. He didn't answer, but what he did made her squirm all over the bed gasping No, he mustn't do that, she couldn't bear it. Oh no.

When they could no longer wait, urgency locked them

together, unable to tell where one's flesh began and the other's left off. Then they fell exhausted.

After a while he took the key from where she had put it under his pillow and freed one of her wrists.

"I need to ask you something," he said while she was freeing the other. "You have to answer me honestly. It's important."

". . . All right."

"Did Betty ever have an emerald necklace?"

She was surprised, but glad that she didn't have to lie. "Yes. It wasn't really emerald, though. We just called it that."

"This is the important part. Did you take it?"

"Yes."

"How old were you?"

"Fourteen perhaps. Why—"

"Do you think she knew you took it?"

"She knew."

"Did anyone else?"

"I don't think so. You know how Betty was. She didn't care. She told her mother she lost it."

"What did you do with it?"

"I kept it, then I broke it up and buried it."

Awareness finally broke through her lassitude and she realized why he had felt so awful. "That girl again," she said. "Did she get in touch with you? What did she want?"

He said that she'd called and spoken to him about the necklace. That was all. Juleen felt he was lying, that he was withholding something, but she couldn't get him to tell her what it was.

10

They pulled into the clearing a little before ten-thirty, and Pennington felt Drew tense up as soon as she saw Turnage's car.

"Relax," he told her. "Just remember—he's here to listen to what you have to say."

"Not because he wants to."

Turnage was nosing around near the edge of the woods, and Hawkins was sitting on a fallen tree having a smoke and reading the *Sentinel*. He got up, ground the cigarette under his heel and dropped the newspaper on the hood of the car. Pennington saw the headline in his mind: WOMAN FINDS DIARY OF VICTIM IN 23-YEAR-OLD MURDER, it read. *In a bizarre series of events climaxing in . . .*

"Good story," Hawkins said to him.

"Thanks."

"How's your car?" he asked Drew.

"Not as pretty as it used to be," she said.

"You are though," he said. "The car can be fixed."

"I think I met my first southern gentleman."

"I'm from Detroit."

"Thanks anyway, and for being so nice yesterday."

Hawkins waved it off as Turnage came over. He touched the brim of his hat. "Chuck . . . Miss Summers."

He got a "Chief" from Pennington and a murmur from Drew.

"So we understand each other," he said to her, "Chuck tells me that the two of you were here yesterday and that you felt or saw some things that bear on the murder of Betty Fairchild . . ."

"Yes, I did."

"We're here to check it out. We'll tape what you have to say, if you don't mind."

"Sure."

Hawkins came over with a leather-encased tape recorder slung from his shoulder.

Drew said, "I'd like to kind of get the feel of the place first. But I can't promise that—"

"When you're ready," Turnage said.

While Hawkins talked into the recorder, giving the date, their names, and other particulars, Drew walked away. The surrounding woods were sunlit and glistening. What she had said yesterday seemed farfetched now.

Hawkins ambled after her. Turnage folded his arms across his chest, shook his head.

"Give her a chance, Chief," Pennington said, keeping his voice low. He turned on his own tape recorder.

Drew looked unsure of herself.

"As soon as we got here I felt awful. Horrible." She didn't have to raise her voice. It carried clearly. "I saw Betty Fairchild's car over there," she said, pointing toward the stump.

"Kind of car was it?" Turnage said.

"A 'sixty-eight red Mustang convertible."

"How'd you know it was Betty's?"

"She was inside of it," Drew said quietly.

"She started screaming at that point," Pennington said to Turnage under his breath. "Scared the shit out of me."

"Show us exactly where you saw it," he said to Drew.

Drew went to the spot. "Here. The car was facing that way."

Hawkins had a clipboard. He made a mark on it,

166

spoke into his tape recorder. "Miss Summers is standing on the square marked C4, Drawing B. She is indicating that the car was facing north."

Good, Pennington thought. The boys did some homework. They weren't going to just brush this off.

Turnage said, "Was the top up or down?"

"Up," Drew answered.

"How about the windows."

"Up—closed. There was a man hiding behind that tree. That big one there." Drew pointed beyond him and Pennington.

"Young man or old?" Turnage asked as Hawkins spoke into his tape recorder. "White or black?"

"Young. White. Then I saw a black man coming this way, heading for the car."

"How old was he?"

". . . Maybe early twenties. He came along a trail that ran along the edge of the woods there."

"Can you describe him?"

She shook her head. "No."

"You just said he was in his early twenties," Turnage said. "Why can't you describe him?"

"I couldn't see him clearly. I just felt he was young. The way he walked. I saw him go to the car."

"Did he touch it?" Turnage asked.

"He . . . Yes, he put a hand on the top, the other just below the window, and peeked in . . ." She paused. "That was when somebody behind the car stood up."

"A third man . . . ?" There was skepticism in Turnage's voice.

"I think so. I mean I think it was man. I couldn't tell. I felt he had sunglasses on, and some kind of wide-brimmed hat. And I think he was holding a gun."

"Handgun or rifle?" Hawkins asked.

"I'm not sure," Drew said.

"You sure about anything?" Turnage said.

Tempted to return his sarcasm, Drew checked herself. "I'm telling you what I saw," she said.

"Well, what you're describing sounds more like Grand Central Station then Willow Creek."

"If *you* know what happened here," Drew flared, "what do you need me for? I didn't ask to come here," she went on, "*you* asked me. You want me to go into a trance and describe a murderer to you? Okay, here it comes. I see him clearly now. He's about six-foot-two, nasty as hell, and everytime I'm around him, he does a number on me. You want a better description?"

In the embarrassed silence that followed, Drew said, "I'm sorry, I'm just not picking anything up."

Turnage became more civil. "Go ahead and tell us the rest of what you saw."

"There's not much more," Drew said. "All three men were there by the car, then someone opened the trunk and took something out. It looked like an overnight case. The young black man ran off with it. . . . That's it," she said.

"I made a tape of it," Pennington said to Turnage. "I'll send you a copy."

"Told me that before, we'd have saved time."

Turnage made his way toward the edge of the woods while he asked Drew more questions about the men, but she didn't add much to what she had said. He looked along the line of the trees. "You said there was a trail here."

"Yes."

"Sure about that?" he asked.

There was no trace of one, but Drew didn't back off. "Yes."

"Maybe there was at that time," Pennington said.

Turnage's expression was unreadable. "There was—a riding trail. Anybody knew this area could tell you that . . . Anything else you can think of?" he asked Drew.

168

"No."

"I appreciate you taking the time," he said. "Get that tape to me," he told Pennington, then motioned to Hawkins: Let's go.

Drew said, "Would you want a feeling I have?"

"Let's hear it."

"I don't think Betty Fairchild died here."

Chuck Pennington hid his excitement. The girl was unbelievable. "Drew, are you saying she was murdered somewhere else?"

"Yes."

"Why didn't you say that before?" Turnage said.

"I thought you just wanted me to pick up on things that only happened here. But I feel it pretty strong."

"Do you have any idea *where* Betty Fairchild was murdered?" Pennington said.

"No. Is there a river near here?" she asked.

"The Ashley," Pennington said.

She looked toward the woods. "I remember now that I had an image in my mind of the black guy running toward a river."

"You done?" Turnage asked her. When she nodded, he and Hawkins said their good-byes and walked off.

Pennington left Drew at his car and caught the two men before they could drive out.

"I'd like to interview you when you have a chance, Chief."

"About what?"

"Betty Fairchild—just general stuff."

"We'll see," Turnage said.

"You didn't seem too impressed with Drew."

"I'm impressed with hard evidence."

"C'mon, Chief, this girl *knows*. That had to be Lee Caldecott standing behind that tree."

"What makes you think that?"

"Because according to Caldecott's own statement he was on the scene here—after Johnson murdered Betty,

169

he said. Only *Drew* says he was here before Johnson even showed up."

"Her word against Caldecott's. Who do you think has more credibility?"

"Yeah, but how about that guy behind the car. Lee Caldecott never said anything about him, did he?"

"We're talking about a girl seeing things."

"Chief, you have to allow her *some* credibility. You asked her if the windows on the murder car were open or closed and if the top was up or down. She answered you—bang, just like that. Was she right?"

"That's a police matter."

"She said that Betty Fairchild wasn't killed here. What about that?"

"What's your point, Chuck?"

"That what Drew said here yesterday and today calls for a reinvestigation of Betty Fairchild's murder."

"The solicitor decides that."

"And he'll be influenced by your report."

Turnage's head swiveled. His eyes were close to Pennington's and cold. "Get outta my face," he said.

Pennington felt intimidated and expectant at the same time. "Are you saying you don't want to see this case reopened?" he asked.

He was hoping Turnage would be mad enough to threaten him or say something dumb. Instead Turnage murmured a word to Hawkins and they drove off leaving Pennington breathing car exhaust.

"I didn't do too well, did I?" Drew said to him when he got into the car.

"You done good, as the Portuguese say."

It wasn't what he felt. He'd been hoping for more excitement. He didn't blame Turnage for being unimpressed.

He dropped Drew off at the hotel in plenty of time for her lunch date with Mrs. Fairchild, told her to say hello for him. After that he legged it to the courthouse to check

170

on warrants taken out or suits filed. Which annoyed him. Here he was working on the story of the year and they still had him doing shit work. Cheap bastards.

At the courthouse he called Ordway, briefed him on what had taken place, then he called Lee Caldecott and managed to get an appointment to see him at five.

Harriet Fairchild's Bentley pulled up before Drew's hotel at exactly twelve-thirty.

Inside the lobby, after waiting for quite a few rings, Mrs. Fairchild put down the house phone and went to the desk.

"I had an appointment with Miss Drew Summers," she said to the clerk. "She is not in her room and I don't see her in the lobby."

"I believe she went out, m'am."

"Are you sure?"

"Yes, m'am. She gave me her key not ten minutes ago."

"Oh dear. We are supposed to meet for lunch. Perhaps she left a message for me . . ."

The clerk glanced at the pigeonhole for 309, then shook her head. "You might like to wait a few minutes. She might just be on her way back right now."

"I wonder where she could have gone," Mrs. Fairchild said. "She hardly knows anyone here in Greenview."

Arletta Johnson was doing what she loved to do most all her life, working in her garden. She was down on her knees near the porch and had just tapped the pansies out of their plastic pot when she heard the car stop in front of the house. It wasn't GG's. She knew the sound of GG's car. She'd have gotten up, but she was in the shade, which made her joints extra stiff. Lot of work to get up.

She placed the pansies into the hole she'd dug, packed some dirt around them, then pulled the hose over

171

and let the water trickle in. Her husband was on the porch rocking.

"Who is it, Luther?" she called.

Someone got out of the car, hesitated, then came in the gate. "Mr. Johnson?" Young white woman's voice.

Her husband cleared his throat. "Yes."

"My name is Drew Summers. I wonder if I could talk with you?"

Mrs. Johnson knew who it was now. She'd read about her in the paper and heard about her from GG and Harriet Fairchild. Bracing herself on the ground, she got to her feet. When she saw the young woman, she could not move. Nowadays she was used to seeing youngsters who reminded her of people she'd known once. The older she got, the more it happened. But she wasn't prepared for this. This girl didn't just look like Betty. This girl made her want to say, *Betts! Betts, what are you doing here?* She felt dizzy from getting up so fast. "Miss?"

The young woman smiled. "Mrs. Johnson?"

Mrs. Johnson had to steady herself, and just like Betty would have done, the young woman came right over and took her hand. Her touch felt familiar, warm.

The unsteadiness passed and Mrs. Johnson started to take her hand away, but the girl held onto it.

"Arlie . . . ?"

Mrs. Johnson stood still, not wanting to believe what she'd heard and what she was seeing. One second she'd been looking into the eyes of this young woman from New York, and now the very next she knew with all her heart and all her being that shining out of those same eyes was the soul of Betty Fairchild.

"It's me, Arlie . . ."

Oh, it was Betts for sure. Betts's voice and Betts's smile, and Mrs. Johnson felt the presence of something dear and sweet from the past.

"It's me, Arlie. Please don't say you don't know me. Don't you say that to me too. Not you. Please."

Mrs. Johnson told herself that she was not going to answer. Not yet. If she answered it would mean she believed this was God's work, and she wasn't sure of that. She would answer when she was sure.

Impulsively the young woman brought Mrs. Johnson's hand to her lips. She kissed the back of it, then held it to her cheek. "I love you, Arlie," she said.

A wave of pity overcame Mrs. Johnson, and again the past tugged at her. She had the strange feeling that Betty was here, and real, and that she herself was a ghost.

"Are you all right, Mrs. Johnson?" the young woman asked her.

She said yes, wondering if her mind had played a trick on her. Because Betty was gone—just like that— leaving Mrs. Johnson all pulled apart inside.

The young woman was worried. "Are you sure? Did I do anything to—"

"No. No," Mrs. Johnson said. "You didn't do a thing." Until she was sure what was going on, she did not see any point in upsetting the girl.

"My name is Drew Summers," the girl said. "If you want to stare, go ahead. I'm getting used to it." She struck a pose, and Mrs. Johnson was tempted to chuckle.

"Why did you come to see me, child?"

"I'll tell you the truth—I wasn't sure until I saw your husband. Ten minutes ago I was at the hotel getting ready to meet Mrs. Fairchild, and I got this urge to come over here. I had no idea why until I saw Mr. Johnson on the porch. I think I came to see him, but I don't even know what for. I know who you are, Mrs. Johnson, and I'm really sorry for intruding."

Her husband had gone in the house. Wasn't like him to be rude.

"Mrs. Fairchild told me how you found Betty's diary," Mrs. Johnson said. She wagged her head. "'Arlie,' she told me, 'I am completely confounded and amazed. You are absolutely not going to believe this, and don't you for one minute think I am getting senile, but I met the girl and she is the spittin' image . . .'"

Drew chuckled. The imitation was perfect.

Mrs. Johnson took her arm. "Come inside."

"Are you sure I'm not—"

"Just don't you mind the mess," Mrs. Johnson said. "I wasn't expecting company."

"You want mess?" Drew said. "You ought to see my apartment."

Mrs. Johnson went up the porch steps slowly. Drew followed her into the living room. As she'd figured from the warning, the house was immaculate.

Mrs. Johnson called, "Luther?"

There was no answer. She excused herself and went into the kitchen. Her husband was looking through the cupboard. "Where you hide my cigarettes?" he grumbled.

"What's got into you?"

"Nothin' got into me. Haven't had a cigarette since yesterday and I want one."

"I'll get one for you." She lowered her voice. "Our guest came to talk to you, Luther. Talk to her. I think she has a gift."

The girl was looking at all the photographs on the mantel when he walked in. He didn't feel friendly and he didn't hide it. She brought back bad thoughts.

"I'm sorry for barging in on you like this, Mr. Johnson," she said.

"Why you want to talk to me?" he said.

She looked around the room. ". . . Was Betty Fairchild ever here?"

"Too many times."

"No, I mean . . . " She hesitated. "I mean once when just you were here."

"Don't know what you're talking about."

His wife came in with a cigarette, gave it to him along with a wooden match.

". . . I just get the feeling," Drew said, "that Betty

174

Fairchild came here once looking for your son Ed, and you got mad at her."

He lit up, gave her a disbelieving look and exhaled smoke. "Where you get an idea like that from?"

"I'm pretty sure of it," the girl said, turning to his wife. "It was a couple of days before she died. You weren't here, Mrs. Johnson. You were away someplace . . . I don't know where." She turned back to him. "She came to the door. You let her in . . . She told you something that scared you, made you mad. You—"

"Wait," Mrs. Johnson said. "She's right, Luther. About me being away. That was the time I went to my sister's house in Orangeburg. When she had that car wreck. I stayed overnight there. That was two days before they killed my Sonny. . . . Did Betty come here to the house while I was gone?"

"Arlie, that was a long time ago . . ."

Mrs. Johnson waited. "Did she come here, Luther?"

"Why you doing this?" he asked Drew accusingly. "Why you want to open up all them old wounds?" He turned away from her and went to his easy chair, sank down in it. "That was twenty years ago, and we got nothing but pain to remember from that time. They killed my Sonny, almost killed my baby GG, took away my job, made it bad for all of us. Couldn't go near a window 'thout—"

"Luther, this girl doesn't know anything about—"

"Then why she bringing it up!" he shouted. His hand was trembling so bad the ash fell from his cigarette.

"Mr. Johnson, I'm sorry. I shouldn't have done this," Drew said quietly. "I want you to know th—"

Mrs. Johnson shook her head, made a motion for Drew to wait. She knew her husband. She knew what he'd gone through. Then and for years after. He'd suffered. Like they all had. But he'd come 'round. He'd carried it a long time, whatever it was, and he wanted to unburden himself. She knew that.

175

"You want to hear it?" he asked her finally. She waited, and he started to say something, but clamped his mouth shut instead. When he started again he spoke slowly. "Like you said, you were gone over to your sister's house—" He stopped, and Mrs. Johnson thought maybe he'd changed his mind and didn't want to say any more in front of the young woman, but he went on. "Betty come here near suppertime looking for Sonny—my son Ed," he said to Drew

. . . He felt disgust just looking at her. Whenever Arlie brought her home he acted nice to her, but he never liked her. She wasn't a nice girl. Too bold. Dresses too damn tight.

Sonny wasn't home. He was going to tell her that and get rid of her, but he'd been told something that morning at work: there was talk about her and Sonny being seen in that car of hers a couple weeks ago, and the talk didn't have to do with civil rights work neither. He wanted to find out if there was anything to worry about.

"Not expecting him for a while," he said. "You can come on in and wait for him if you want."

"No, that's all right," she said. She smiled at him in a way she never did before. Personal.

It made him uncomfortable, made him feel more disgust for her, but he forced himself to smile back and he said, "Sonny's mighty fond of you."

"Did he tell you that?"

"Oh yeah," he lied.

"Oh I'm so glad," she said. "When did he tell you?"

"This morning."

"You're not mad?"

"Not much I could do if I was . . . ."

The way her whole face lit up he knew that the talk was true. "Mr. Johnson," she gushed, "he's such a

176

fine person. I never knew anybody like him. He's got so much feeling and he's so complex. I'm kinda simple, but Ed, there's just so much to him . . ."

She didn't have the least idea how much fear she'd set to churning in him. No idea at all. Just like that she threw herself in his arms and hugged him, saying, "Oh, Mr. Johnson, you don't know how relieved I am! Ed was so worried about how you were going to feel about us."

He stood there stiff, shot full of panic. The smell of the girl was so strong it made him nauseous. She had to be stupid not to know what could happen to Sonny, to the whole family, if people found out. She could walk in a protest march like it was a high school parade. She was white, and white people could do anything. They didn't worry about crackers taking them out somewhere and torturing them and lynching them. They didn't walk around the world afraid, like he did. They owned it.

He lost his temper, yelled at her to stay away from Sonny or she was going to get him killed. He went too far, he could feel that, scared the girl bad.

After she was gone he didn't know how long he stood shaking and sweating, until little GG came in. She was scared. He'd forgot all about her playing in the back bedroom there. She said she was hungry.

That night he went crazy. He whipped Sonny like he never whipped any of the kids before. *Don't you know what they can do to you?* he kept yelling. *Don't you know? Don't you know?*

"I whipped 'im with my razor strap, whipped 'im till he took it away from me. It was the last thing he knew from me before he died," Johnson ended miserably.

"Luther, you should have told me." Mrs. Johnson went to him and touched his shoulder.

"At least you should have told the police," Drew said.

"Why would I do that?" Johnson asked her.

"To let them know that your son would have been the last person in the world to hurt Betty."

Johnson smiled in spite of himself. "Hear that, Arlie? I coulda said, 'Chief Pinckney, sir, I *know* my boy'd never have harmed that nice white girl. He was in love with her, you see, and she was in love with him. That's right, sir, she was in *love* with him.' They'd of killed us all . . . You know what they did to my little GG—a little ten-year-old girl who never hurt nobody?"

"Luther . . ." Mrs. Johnson murmured.

"They took her right out from in front of the house. Had our eyes off her less than a minute and they got her. Four of 'em. Took her off someplace. Did things to her you don't do to an animal, left her in a ditch. And we couldn't do nothing to 'em because GG couldn't remember what happened—didn't want to remember . . . Had three operations before she looked like herself. They couldn't fix what happened to her inside." Johnson shook his head wearily. "I did what I felt was best," he said. "Sonny was dead, Betty Fairchild was dead. I had my family to look out for." He put the cigarette out in the ashtray, sorry he'd smoked it. Tasted awful.

Mrs. Johnson looked at the clock on the mantel. "What time were you supposed to meet Mrs. Fairchild?" she asked Drew.

Drew's voice was throaty. "Can I use your phone?"

She called the hotel to find that Mrs. Fairchild had left a message saying she would meet her at the restaurant. The clerk told her how to get there.

After Drew drove off, Mrs. Johnson stood on the porch thinking of the bad times and the long bitterness that followed Sonny's murder.

Raymond Ordway had done everything he could to hurt them, made Luther lose his welding job, lost the kids their part-time jobs. She wondered how they'd lived through it—garbage dumped in the front yard, rocks thrown at the house. And then GG. Only after what they did to her did it stop, did the newspaper write something, did a few people help them. Only then, when they were beyond any more hurt, any more pain. Bad times. Luther and the children wanted to move, and everybody else in town, white *and* colored, wanted them to move. But she wouldn't. She'd believed it would be saying Sonny was guilty.

She shivered when she thought of what might have happened if it came out that those two children were in love. Like Luther said, they'd of all been murdered.

She was about to go back in the house when GG drove up. She'd forgotten GG was coming over with groceries, and as her daughter came up the path, a plastic sack in each hand, Mrs. Johnson sensed from her expression that she had seen Drew leave and waited until she drove off.

She knew for sure when she called out a cheery hello, tried to take one of the sacks, and GG brushed past her without a word and went on inside. Mrs. Johnson followed. In the living room she motioned to Luther to come into the kitchen.

"That was a nice hello," she said to her daughter.

"What that girl want here, Daddy?" GG said as she took out the groceries.

"Talk about something happened a long time ago," Luther said.

"I'm going to make some lunch, GG," Mrs. Johnson said. "How about some tuna fish? I'll make it just the way you like."

Her daughter looked at her finally and Mrs. Johnson felt terrible. Her eyes were full of hate. It meant what she'd been afraid of: GG wasn't taking her pills.

"What'd she want, Daddy?"

While Luther told her, Mrs. Johnson started preparing lunch. She wondered what to do. She knew from experience that when GG was like this there was no way to reach her. As long as she kept taking those pills the psychiatrist prescribed, she stayed out of trouble and she was her own sweet and decent self. But whenever she stopped, as she had twice before, she ended up in the state hospital. And she hadn't gone there of her own free will.

At the restaurant, Drew was in the middle of telling Mrs. Fairchild what had happened at the Johnsons' when she looked up to see Raymond Ordway beside the table. Her heart gave the same heavy thump it had at his house.

"Ah, Drew," Mrs. Fairchild said, "Raymond asked me if I thought you'd mind if he joined us and I said no."

"I'd like to make up for my rudeness," he said.

Drew gave him a warm smile. "I don't mind at all," she said honestly. "I'm glad you came."

"Thank heaven you said that, Drew. Otherwise Raymond would be sulking through the entire meal."

"Harriet—please," Ordway said, sitting down. "Order anything you like," he said to Drew, "on or off the menu. I own the restaurant and they'll make it for you."

"Raymond owns everything," Mrs. Fairchild said. "It's a habit he's picked up."

She went on to relate to her brother how worried she had been at not finding Drew at the hotel, and that Drew had just been describing to her how she had been compelled to go to the Johnson house.

Drew told them what had happened there.

Ordway was grim. "You sensed that Betty went there two days before she was murdered, and Luther admitted it?"

"Yes."

"And he said Betty told him she was in love with Ed . . ."

"Raymond, perhaps Luther misunderstood Betty," his sister said. "Remember, she and Ed worked in the civil rights move—"

180

"He said he threw Betty out, did he," Ordway said.

"I don't think he said it exactly like that."

"Where I made my mistake," Ordway told his sister, "was in not getting rid of the whole bunch when I had the chance."

"You certainly tried your best," his sister said.

"I didn't try hard enough," he said. "Everytime I see one of them I'm reminded all over—"

"Raymond, you made life miserable for the whole family. Why don't we order?"

Ordway called to a passing waitress, but she didn't hear him. Their own waitress was approaching an adjoining table and he signaled her.

When she smiled and indicated she'd be right there, Ordway picked up his serving plate, held it out over the floor and dropped it. It shattered on the hardwood floor and Drew jumped.

"Come here," he said to the waitress. He reached for another serving plate, but she was beside the table now, completely flustered.

"Bring me a phone," he said.

Drew was ready to go through the floor.

Harriet Fairchild patted her hand. "Try not to be upset," she said. "It is Raymond's unique way of showing he feels unappreciated."

The waitress came back accompanied by the head-waiter. He put down a cordless phone before Ordway. "I'm sorry, sir," he said. "The young lady is new and didn't know who you were."

While Drew tried to concentrate on giving the waitress her order, Ordway tried to reach Turnage.

"Why are you calling Mark?" his sister asked.

"I want to know why Luther never told the authorities about Betty's visit."

"He said he was afraid of what could happen if he did," Drew said.

181

"He should have been—throws my niece out of his house two days before his sonofabitch son—"

"Raymond!"

Ordway put a hand up, spoke into the phone. "Mark, Harriet and I are here having lunch with Drew Summers. She just came from the Johnson house . . . That's right, she went to see Luther Johnson . . . I don't know, she just went. She's right here—you want to ask her? She said that Luther told her that Betty came to see him two days before she was murdered. That's right, Drew got him to admit it . . . She also got him to admit that he yelled at Betty and threw her out . . . Wait. Did Luther threaten you in any way?" he asked Drew.

"Not at all," Drew said.

"No . . . Is that all you have to say? I want the man questioned . . . I said I want him questioned," he insisted, then he hung up. "Yelled at her, did he?" he said to Drew, tight-lipped. "How bad?"

"He said she was scared."

"She had every right to be," Ordway answered. "He and his son killed her."

His sister kept her eyes on the menu. "I believe we can do without further discussion of this for the remainder of lunch," she said. "Drew, what would you like?"

Ordway said his sister was right, and the two became as pleasant as though nothing out of the ordinary had occurred.

Drew was nervous and ate lightly.

GG had just gotten up to pour herself some more coffee when the phone rang. She handed it to her mother.

"Mrs. Johnson?"

"Yes."

"This is Chief Turnage."

She'd known it was him right away. She would never forget his voice. The few times they met over the past twenty-three years, he touched his hat and greeted her

182

respectfully and she nodded to him. But she had never spoken a word to him. "Yes," she said now.

"Like to speak with Mr. Johnson, please."

"Hold on, please." Her heart was beating very fast. "It's Mark Turnage," she told her husband.

GG said, "What's he want?"

"Now you be careful," she said to Luther. "Don't you lose your temper with him."

Her husband cleared his throat. There was no friendliness in his hello. Mrs. Johnson moved her chair beside his and put her ear close to the receiver.

". . . that I'm doing some work on the Betty Fairchild murder. It's possible we might reopen the case, and I got a report here says Betty paid you a visit a couple of days before she was murdered. That right?"

". . . It's right."

"Like to have a talk with you about it. Maybe you wouldn't mind comin' down here some time tomorrow . . ."

"What time'd you have—" He broke off as Arlie pulled away from him shaking her head and motioning for him to cover the phone. "Hold on," he said.

"You are not going down there," his wife said. "He wants to talk to you, he can come here."

"I don't want him in my house."

"Then you talk with him in the street, but you are not going down to that police station."

He looked into Arlie's eyes for he didn't know how long, then he said, "You better come here."

"I'll have a man out there about ten o'clock tomorrow morning—that okay?"

"That's fine." He put the phone down.

"He comin' out here?" GG said.

"One of his men—tomorrow morning," her father answered.

"That's your little white doll baby's work," GG said to her mother. "Went straight from here to the police—right

183

to the man who killed Sonny. Your darling darling Betty. I'm gonna kill that girl, Mama."

"GG," her mother said, "you know where that kind of talk leads."

GG knew, and she made herself calm down. Every time she spoke her mind, truly said what she was thinking, they thought she was crazy and wanted to put her away. She made herself smile. "You're right," she said. She got up and started to clear the table. "I gotta go."

"Oh Lord," her mother said. "I left the hose running."

Her father went in to lie down for a while and GG gave him a peck on the cheek, said she'd see him again soon, then she put the dishes in the sink.

Outside she was sweet as pie, told her mother she hadn't meant what she said inside, and she could see her mother was surprised and pleased. They talked for a minute about this and that, and when her mother asked her in an offhand way if she was taking her pills, GG's answer was just as offhand. "Of course, Mama," she lied.

When she drove off, she felt good. Outsmarted her. Her mama was against her, the way she always was, and her daddy, he was just too good. So she'd kept her mouth shut. But this was the last time that girl was going to make trouble for them.

This time when she went after the bitch, she'd get her good. This time she'd catch her when nobody could help her.

Once Raymond left them to return to work, Harriet Fairchild had a glorious time. Avoiding the tourist attractions, she showed Drew Betty's old elementary school— now the library, the little park where Betty used to play, and then, despite the fact that Drew had found the diary there, she showed Drew their old house and described the inside for her as it had once been.

"Juleen has done some things to it I would not," she said, "but I'm glad that she made Lee buy it. She always wanted to be like Betty, copied her in every way. She never had Betty's innate good taste, of course, or breeding, but she loved the house."

At first Drew had felt self-conscious riding in the limousine, but then she sat back and relaxed, letting Mrs. Fairchild talk about what things had been like in the Greenview that Betty had grown up in.

"It's almost all gone now," Harriet Fairchild said as the limousine headed toward Main Street. "We used to be just a little country town. Now we're becoming a city. Raymond likes what is happening. I don't. 'Raymond, it's your world,' I keep telling him, 'I'm just trying to keep up with it.'"

"You must be happy living way out where you are now," Drew said.

"In a way. Here in town every year the patches of woods between homes become smaller. However, I would not say I enjoy the most exalted position in life."

"You come pretty close."

"I am a glorified caretaker is what I am, my precious. Someone has to keep the tea towels fresh and ironed, and who is better suited than I—one foot in reality and all my weight on the other, as Raymond is fond of telling me."

Drew smiled. "What are tea towels?"

"Tea towels, honeybunch, are linens. They are like large napkins. You cover tea trays with them, or cucumber sandwiches, or ham or marmalade, or anything else you do not want the honey bees to get. Southern women have more of them and thus are able to find more uses for them than any other group in the world."

When they drove down the old part of Main Street, Drew said that it looked almost residential—shops and offices set back from wide sidewalks, and no building over two stories.

"Oh, you should have seen it twenty-five years ago," Mrs. Fairchild said. "It was graciousness personified, the best part of town. Now it's quite touristy. There," she said, pointing to a low brick building shaded by giant oak. A white sign on the lawn said GREENVIEW ELEMENTARY SCHOOL. "That was Betty's high school. A few years after integration the high school was relocated out of town."

She asked Drew about her work and the kind of life she led in Manhattan, but just as she had when she asked Drew other things about herself, she quickly went on to something about Betty that she felt was interesting. Drew didn't mind. She'd have liked to visit a few historical places, but she was just as happy to sit back and relax.

When the phone rang, Mrs. Fairchild debated whether to answer it. Finally she picked it up. "Yes," she said. "Yes, Mr. Pennington . . . Do hold on, I'll see if she is here," she said, handing Drew the phone and making her laugh.

"What's this I hear that you paid a visit to Ed Johnson's family," Pennington said.

"How did you find out so fast?"

"From somebody at the police station. What made you do that?"

"I'll give you one guess."

"Is that true—Ed Johnson's father threw Betty Fairchild out of his house a couple of days before she was murdered?"

"Yes. It doesn't mean anything though."

"Maybe not. What are you doing?"

"Having a wonderful time. Mrs. Fairchild is giving me the deluxe tour of Greenview and I'm . . ." Her voice trailed off and she put a hand to her forehead. "Chuck, hold on a minute."

Mrs. Fairchild was concerned. "Are you all right, Drew?"

". . . Yes, but I think I have to go somewhere."

"Whatever you wish, but there is nothing wrong?"

"No. Excuse me. Chuck," she said into the phone, "could you meet me at the hotel in fifteen minutes?"

186

"What is it?"

"Something's going on . . ."

"Uh-oh. Betty?"

"I think so."

"You want to go somewhere, but not with Mrs. Fairchild."

"Very much."

"How bad do you have to go, if you'll pardon the expression. I've got a date with Lee Caldecott at five and I'd hate to miss it."

"I can do it on my own if I have to."

"Are you kidding? The hotel—fifteen minutes."

When she hung up, Mrs. Fairchild said, "Are you sure I can't take you wherever it is you are going?"

Drew thanked her and said it would be better if she didn't. Mrs. Fairchild was disappointed, but did not feel it was her place to question Drew. She made Drew promise, however, that she would call her later to let her know that she was all right. Drew promised.

11

He'd been driving her around for almost a half hour now. They were ten miles from Greenview, heading east, and what they were doing out here in the boondocks, almost out of the county, Pennington had no idea. What was worse, neither did Drew.

Occasionally she'd given him directions, but none of them led anywhere. He glanced at his watch. He had an hour before his appointment with Caldecott. "We could knock off and try again tomorrow," he said.

"We're going to find it now," she said shortly.

"Find what for Christ's sake?"

"Chuck, do me a favor. Don't make me any crazier than I am already. Left here," she said. "This may be it."

"May be what?"

"I'll tell you as soon as I know."

Pennington knew where they were—on the outskirts of Clinton's Corner, land flat as a chessboard, thin woods, an occasional small house. The road turned into the main drag, two blocks of stores. Drew told him to make a turn at the second signal light. It brought them to a run-down residential section and the old brick courthouse. Next door was the Municipal Building, a two-story elongated green box set back from a token lawn, the county's monument to law enforcement and civil service.

"It's behind that building," Drew said. Her heart began to hammer as Pennington turned into a gravel driveway. It led into a parking area for the sheriff's cars. Past that were more buildings, one uglier than the next.

"There it is," she said. She pointed to a long, low, brick-fronted structure, the county garage. Pennington had been in it once before, steel superstructure, sheet-metal walls. Two of the four overhead sliding doors were open, all kinds of county property visible, from motorized lawn mowers to sanitation trucks.

A deputy was talking with a mechanic by one of the doors and for a few seconds Pennington wondered how he'd get past. He knew a second later when he spotted something inside. "I'm an active Sheriff's Department volunteer," he said as he slowed beside the deputy. "Want to check on the condition of the float."

Not particularly interested, the deputy nodded and let him glide past.

The Sheriff's Department Crime Prevention float was made of papier-maché on a wooden frame. It had bright aluminum foil, flashing lights, and was thirty feet long when it was assembled and dragged out for the Christmas parade. Pennington parked beside it, gave it a glance so that he couldn't be called a liar, then he and Drew went to look for what it was that had drawn her here.

Drew saw its ghostly outline less than five minutes later through a window yellowed with grime. It was in a corner of the building, inside a shedlike corrugated enclosure. A tarp rotting with age covered it, and Drew didn't have to go into the shed to know what was underneath. When she told Pennington, he nearly flipped.

He ran to his car for his camera, forced open the padlocked door. Then he proceeded to take pictures from every angle of what remained, after twenty-three years, of Betty Fairchild's once-gleaming red '68 Mustang.

Pennington was able to drop Drew off at her hotel and still breeze through the glass door of Caldecott's

189

outer office ahead of time. He was impressed: old wood and leather. The man was a class act. He called Arnold Stiggs while he was waiting.

"Arnold, I'm going to drop something in your lap you're not going to believe."

"What is that?"

"What if I told you Drew Summers just found the car that Betty Fairchild was murdered in?"

"Chuck, has it occurred to you that anybody might do the same simply by going through records?"

"Good observation. What records do you think she went through before she went to Willow Creek this morning and told Chief Turnage flat out that Betty Fairchild wasn't murdered there? Or before she went to the Johnson house this afternoon and made Ed Johnson's father admit that he flew into a rage with Betty Fairchild two days before she was murdered?"

"Cut to the chase, Chuck."

"Okay, a few hours from now I am going to finish a story about a girl who discovers an important piece of evidence that has disappeared for over twenty years. I'm suggesting you call Turnage, let him know the car is around, and if all the chief's horses and all the chief's men can't find it in the next two hours, give me a call. I'll be glad to let you know where it is. In return all I want is an intelligent comment from you."

He hung up, thinking, Drew, you sweet honeybunch, don't let them find it.

Bulging briefcase under his arm, he was ushered into Lee Caldecott's office. "Nice of you to see me," he said, taking Caldecott's outstretched hand.

Pennington complimented him on the office and admired the wet bar hoping for a drink. When he didn't get it, it proved to him what he'd always known: if he'd had the same advantages of being tall, good-looking, and as well-familied as types like Caldecott, he'd be President of the goddamn United States. Or Vice-President.

190

"Did Drew Summers call you last night?" he said.

"What makes you ask?" Caldecott said.

"Drew asked me to. She had one of those blackouts of hers last night and carried on with somebody over the phone. She's afraid it might have been you."

"Uh-uh," Caldecott said.

"She'll be glad to hear it. She wants to talk to you, but she was afraid to call you. She's a nice kid by the way."

"So . . ." Caldecott said, keeping his tone breezy, "I hear that you and the young lady met with the police at Willow Creek."

"Yeah. I wanted to talk with you about Betty Fairchild, but maybe we can talk a little about Willow Creek too. I read what you said to the police way back in 1967. You remember?"

"I never thought of it as being 'way back,' but yes, I remember quite well."

"You said you went out to Willow Creek to meet Betty Fairchild to lend her some money. You have any idea why she wanted to meet you there in particular?"

"No."

"Drew thinks it was because Betty intended to meet Ed Johnson there too—that they were going to run off together. She says they were in love."

Caldecott began to feel uncomfortable. "Not to my knowledge. Are you going to write that?"

"Why shouldn't I?" Pennington said.

"I don't know but that people might not like that sort of gossip—especially her family."

"Are you saying it's not true?"

"As far as I know it's not. But you haven't told me what went on at Willow Creek today. I'm interested."

"I'll do better," Pennington said. "I'll let you hear a little of what she said when *I* was there with her, the day before. It's essentially what she said today, but more dramatic." Pennington dug into his briefcase and came up with his tape recorder. "Getting back to what you told

191

the police, though—you said that when you got to Willow Creek, you saw Johnson looking through Betty's purse, toss it away, then look in the trunk of her car. As soon as he spotted you, you said, he ran off with the cosmetics case."

Caldecott said that was correct.

"Drew said something different," Pennington went on, searching for the place on the tape. "You don't want to hear the whole thing so I'll fill you in. What Drew did was point out where Betty's car was parked. It may be hard to believe, but she even described a trail that isn't there anymore, and she more or less identified you and Johnson."

"Did she actually describe us?"

"Sketchily. Johnson was young, black—you young, white."

"Not very much of a description."

Pennington let that pass, found the place he wanted. Before he played it, he said, "By the way, Drew said that you arrived before Johnson, said you were waiting behind a tree. Here, listen."

Drew's voice came on.

". . . He *is* waiting for someone, watching . . . There, he sees the person now and he's ducking back . . . It's a young man. He's coming along a trail by the edge of those woods. He's black. I think he's carrying something. Now he's leaving the trail and he's coming this way . . . He's heading for the car. He's leaning down and peeking in—"

Drew's voice broke off, and Caldecott waited, his stomach knotting. He couldn't believe what he was hearing: The girl was describing what had happened as if she was actually there watching him, pointing the finger of guilt at him.

Her voice began again. "I lost him. I—No, wait. There's something strange going on. I think there's someone else on the other side of the car. Yes there is. He's

192

standing up . . . Now it's getting confusing. I can't really see. Somebody is taking something out of the trunk. Some kind of a small case . . . The young black guy has it now. He's going away. He's running."

Pennington snapped the recorder off. "Hear that? She said there was someone behind a tree—you?—and someone else on the other side of the car. What do you think would make her say something like that?"

Caldecott forced himself to appear unconcerned, but inside he was screaming. *How did she know? How the fuck did she know?* Swiveling his chair so that he faced away from Pennington, he locked his hands together to steady them. Now he wished he'd offered the reporter a drink. He needed one himself.

"I had a thought," Pennington said. "Do you think it's possible Drew saw something that even *you* didn't know about?"

"You'll have to explain that."

"You said you arrived after Johnson. Suppose somebody was holding a gun on him, heard you coming and hid behind the car, waiting for you to leave. Instead you start for the car, Johnson sees his chance to get away and takes off."

"If there was anybody besides Ed behind that car, I think I would have seen him, don't you?" Caldecott said testily. "Did she describe the man?"

Pennington shook his head. "She came up with a beauty today, though—she said that Betty Fairchild wasn't murdered at Willow Creek, but someplace else."

How did she KNOW?

"She have any idea where?" Caldecott asked him.

"No, but as Cyrano de Bergerac would say, so far she's been on the nose with everything else. And I mean on the nose . . . I just left her at the Marriott after she took me on what I thought was a wild goose chase. Instead she led me to Betty Fairchild's 'sixty-eight Mustang."

"Are you serious?"

"You'll read about it in the paper tomorrow. I'll tell you what I think. I think that girl is here to find Betty Fairchild's murderer." He watched Caldecott closely to see how he reacted. He didn't. "By the way," he went on, "there's a strong possibility she's going out to Willow Creek again. Would you want to come along?"

I am going to make that girl Drew go back to Willow Creek, Lee. Hear?

"I never want to go out there again, Mr. Pennington. Not unless I have to. No."

He told Pennington he did not have much more time and they talked for another ten minutes about Betty, what she was like, her friends, her family.

As soon as Pennington was out the door Caldecott poured himself some vodka. He drank it down, hoping he could bring on a buzz fast enough to shut out the girl's voice. He failed. *I am sending that girl back to Willow Creek and I will find a way to make her tell what you—*

His secretary rang to inquire if he needed her any longer. He said no, asked her before she left to give him the number of the Marriott.

He was desperate now. He couldn't take any more of this. He had to meet with the girl, privately, nobody but the two of them present.

When the phone rang, Drew thought about not answering it. She'd been trying to take a nap, but so far Harriet had called, then Chuck, and then Raymond Ordway.

She picked it up. "Hello?"

"Ms. Summers, this is Lee Caldecott."

She didn't have to force herself to wake up. "Oh," she said. "Oh. Hello, Mr. Caldecott."

"You sound as though you were sleeping. I hope I didn't wake you."

"Doesn't matter. I just want to tell you, by the way, how sorry I am for what—"

194

He interrupted her. "I know what you're going to say, and there's no need. From what I gather, what happened at the airport was worse for you than for me. I'm calling you because I thought it might do us both good to have a chat."

"I'd like that," Drew said. "I'm at a point where I just don't know what's going to happen next."

"Do you have anything to do right now?"

She hesitated. "Not right now, no. Somebody's picking me up here for dinner about eight."

"It's only a little before six now. I'm at my office, and you're only a few minutes away by car. Why don't you come on over? We can talk awhile and you can be back there in plenty of time for your dinner date."

She thought for a moment. ". . . Let me see. Hey, why not? It shouldn't take me too long to get out of here . . . Is half an hour okay?"

"Perfect, I have work to do in the meantime," he said, "so don't you worry about keeping me waiting."

He gave her the directions and said he was looking forward to meeting her.

After he hung up he sat without moving until he realized his jaws were clamped together. Opening his mouth wide, he spread his fingers flat on the desk. She was coming over. Good. Very good. This time he'd be ready for her, meet her on his own turf, in private, pick her brain, find out once and for all what she knew.

He became aware of the quiet. He wasn't used to being alone in the office this late. Usually if he was here at this time he'd be with a client and potential buyers or sellers. But tonight there were no clients, no deals to negotiate, no questions to answer. He could sit and pick his nose if he was in the mood.

He got up and went to the bar, made himself a vodka on the rocks. He started to put the bottle away, changed his mind: If he had to worry about one drink more or less when he was dealing with a twenty-three-year-old girl, he was in deep shit.

He went to the window, separated the slats and looked down at the parking lot. Couple of cars there: A few people were still in the building.

Going to the couch, he lay down and sipped his drink, thinking about the best way to deal with her. He'd take the fatherly approach, be understanding, find out exactly what she knew. He'd tell her that besides the unwelcome publicity he and everyone else were receiving, she was opening up old wounds. He might even hint gently about possible legal action. He'd get tough if had to.

As the minutes crawled by he became conscious of faint sounds from all over the building: water running, the clatter of the porter's pail downstairs, the murmur and beep of an answering machine somewhere. Getting up, he went to the window again. It was still light outside.

By the time it was close to her arrival he felt very capable of handling her. Until a thought struck him: Suppose she turned into Betty? Suppose she just walked right in here and became violent—tried to kill him?

He thought of the gun in the bottom drawer of his desk. Up to now he'd almost forgotten about it. Juleen had bought it for him a couple of years ago when somebody working late in the building had been assaulted by an intruder. On impulse he opened the drawer, pulled the hanging files forward. He started to reach down behind them, stopped when he heard the slam of a car door. He went to the window again.

It was the girl. He watched until she disappeared into the entrance, then emptied the last of his drink and put the bottle back in the cabinet, the glass in the sink. As he heard the elevator rising, he wondered what he would do if she did turn into Betty. The image of the bloody wrappings in Betty's car again began to form in his mind, and he quickly erased it.

Look for me by moonlight.

196

The elevator stopped, and when he heard the door slide open he listened for footsteps, but the hallway carpeting deadened them.

Somebody rapped at the glass outer door.

"Come on in," he called.

The rapping was repeated, more urgently, and he glanced at his own door. It was partly ajar, darkness beyond it. A faint voice called, "Mr. Caldecott?"

The outer door was locked, he realized. He got up and had to steady himself as he moved around his desk.

In the gloom of the outer office he saw her outline through the thick glass. The light of the hallway was behind her and she had a hand above her eyes, trying to see in. He switched on the lights with some apprehension. The girl staring at him could have been Betty.

"Mr. Caldecott?"

It wasn't Betty. She didn't know him.

He opened the door and put out a hand. "I'm glad to meet you," he said, forcing his best smile. "And I do mean *you*. Call me Lee."

"Drew. It's nice to meet you too," she said. Her hand was warm, young, brought him back twenty years.

He indicated the open door to his office, and she went ahead of him. She had Betty's ass, Betty's legs. Unbelievable. "You got here fast," he said.

"Couldn't have done it in New York." She looked around appreciatively. "What a beautiful office," she said. "Do you ever get any work done?"

"Never," he said. "That's why I'm the boss. Care for a drink, or a soft drink?"

"A soft drink sounds good."

She was looking at a painting as he went behind the bar. Leaning down, he opened the refrigerator and reviewed what was there for her. "Perrier . . . Coke . . . apple juice." She didn't answer and he raised his head. "Drew?"

197

She was frowning, rubbing her forehead. "I'm sorry. What did you say?" she asked. She looked dragged out.

"Asked if you wanted a Perrier, Coke, or apple juice. Are you all right?"

"I think I'm getting a headache. Juice is fine."

He took the small can out, poured the contents into a glass, and offered it to her. She thanked him, but when their fingers touched she looked at him strangely.

". . . Did you say something?"

"No."

"That's funny, I thought you did."

"What did you think I said?"

"Something like, 'Meet me at South Fork.'"

He felt resentment knotting his stomach. "What?"

"It was almost like I heard you saying it to Betty Fairchild. Is there such a place?"

"Yes there is," Caldecott said guardedly.

"What kind of a place is it?" she asked him.

"State land. Woods mostly. Park."

She glanced at the glass in her hand. "It popped into my head when you handed me this. Did you and Betty Fairchild make a date to go there once?"

How could she know that, goddamnit? How could she know!

"You're talking maybe twenty-five years ago," he said, irritated. "What I'd rather talk about are some of the things you've been saying that seem to concern *me*."

"I can't blame you for being annoyed." She put the glass on top of a pad, leaned against his desk. "Ever since I've been here I keep hearing things, getting crazy feelings about things. It's really getting to me. Sometimes—" She broke off as something in the outer office caught her attention.

"What's the matter?" he asked.

She put her fingertips to her forehead, then let them slide down to her chin. "I think I'd better go," she said, staring at the floor.

"Hey," Caldecott said. "You just got here."

"I know, but my head is killing me. I'm sorry . . ." She went to the chair and picked up her handbag.

"I can get you some aspirin if that'll help . . . I'd hate to have stayed here for nothing—"

She started for the open door, then hesitated, averting her eyes. She looked drawn. "It's not the headache. It's . . . I don't know how to say this . . . Mr. Caldecott—Lee—but . . ." She glanced furtively toward the outer office again. "There's somebody out there."

Concerned, Caldecott started for the door.

"I know what you're going to tell me," Drew said, closing her eyes. "There's nobody there."

"There isn't," he said.

"There is for me."

"What does he look like?"

Eyes still closed, she said, "He had some kind of a jumpsuit on—coveralls. And a hat, a leather hat . . ." The office was cool, but Caldecott felt a chill that had nothing to do with the air-conditioning. "I can't really tell what he looks like," she went on. "He's wearing dark glasses . . ."

Opening her eyes, she made another quick glance outside. This time an expression of revulsion appeared on her face. She made a choking sound and leaned over his desk. Caldecott—anger rising in him—was afraid she was either going to throw up or faint. But she did neither, just kept leaning on the desk, gagging and taking in big gulps of air.

Then she turned around, stared past him and breathed a sigh of relief. She was about to say, Thank God, he's gone, but she didn't get the chance. All of a sudden Caldecott slammed the office door hard enough to make the room shake and advanced on her, infuriated.

Her hands flew up to ward him off, but he grabbed her wrists. "Don't say another word," he warned her through clenched teeth. "I don't want to hear a sound out of you unless I ask for it. I don't want to know what you think, I don't want to know what you feel."

She started to protest, but he dragged her to a chair and forced her down into it, twisted her wrists when she tried to resist. She grimaced in pain. "I called Chuck Pennington before I left the hotel," she said quickly.

"I don't give a fuck who you called." He knew he sounded coarse, strictly low class, but he didn't give a shit. "There's not a soul on this floor to help you," he said. "Try to run and I'll break your fucking jaw, is that clear?"

She nodded and he let her wrists go and went behind the bar, took the vodka out. Hands shaking, he sloshed some into a glass and drank it down. He had to think what to do next. Think.

"What did he look like? The man you saw."

"I couldn't tell."

"Are you saying that because you're afraid of what I might do to you?"

"No. He had a wide-brimmed hat and dark glasses. He was all covered up. He even had on rubbers. And gloves." She shuddered. ". . . He was covered with blood."

Caldecott felt sick. God only knew what the girl was capable of finding out, of saying. He'd made a mistake, a bad mistake. He shouldn't have brought her here, shouldn't have let her get near him. And she wouldn't ever get near him again if he could help it. As much as it mattered now: She had to know she saw Betty's murderer, and she'd make the connection to South Fork. *I'm gonna get you, Lee* . . .

He felt violent anger rising in him and he tried to curb it. He had to deal rationally with the girl. He spotted her handbag on a chair. He got it, tossed it into her lap, stood over her. "You've come after me three times," he told her. "At the airport, at the Spengler, and last night you called me on the phone."

"Mr. Caldecott, I'm sorry, I really am, but I don't remem—"

"You remember saying things at Willow Creek that just about call me a liar, though, don't you?"

"I never mentioned you."

"You didn't have to. You did it by innuendo."

"I'm sorry, Mr. Caldecott, I don't blame you for being upset with me, but I can't help what I see."

"Sorry isn't good enough. I'm putting you on notice—stay in this town, and I'm going to make life miserable for you."

"I *tried* to leave here."

"Try again. Besides knowing where you live, I know where you work. After you walk out of here I'm going to start making calls to people I know. They know other people. One of them will get to someone in your firm who has clout, and I promise you—if you're still in this town after noontime tomorrow, you will lose your job. That's for starters. If you're still here day *after* tomorrow, I'm going to have you raped and beaten and thrown into a garbage bin." He leaned down, his face close to hers. "You believe me?"

". . . Yes." His breath was sickening.

"Good." Without warning he grabbed her arm, and she hugged her handbag to her as he jerked her to her feet and dragged her, stumbling, into the outer office. There, unlocking the door, he opened it and propelled her down the silent corridor.

At the elevator he jabbed the button and she was grateful when the door opened almost instantly. He shoved her in with such force that she spun around and her elbow hit the railing. Pain jolted her and she let go of her handbag. It dropped to the floor, everything inside spilling out. She leaned against the wall, not caring.

Caldecott held the door open and stared at her pitilessly. "I told you what's going to happen to you if you stay here. I meant every word."

He stared at her until the door completely closed. Numb, she didn't try to move even after the elevator started its descent. She closed her eyes, rested her head against the wall and massaged her elbow.

Downstairs, when she came out of the entrance, dusk was settling. She headed for her car, the fear beginning to catch up with her. She knew that Caldecott was watching from above, and it didn't matter to her. All she wanted was to get out of here as quickly as possible.

It made her careless.

When she opened the car door and smelled the rank odor of stale tobacco, she disregarded the warning alarm that went off in her head until after she slid in behind the wheel.

Then she scrambled to get out, but it was too late. Someone was already rising up from behind her, an arm was going around her throat, and her head was cruelly jerked back against the headrest.

12

When her car didn't leave, Caldecott was afraid the girl was going to come back. He checked to make sure the outer door was locked, then switched off the lights and went back to the window. Her car was still there.

Suddenly the horn began to blare.

After a minute or so the colored janitor came out, and as he got near the car the horn became silent. The rear window was rolled down and he talked with someone. Caldecott couldn't hear what was said, but when the janitor turned and trotted back toward the entrance, there was a flash from the rear window followed by the snap of a gunshot and the sound of breaking glass below.

He ducked back. He thought about calling the police, then decided to stay out of it. Whatever happened, it was no fault of his.

The dispatcher at Greenview Police Headquarters clocked the call in at 6:48. It came in on 911 and was from a janitor at 322 Hampton: An armed black female was holding a white female hostage in a car in the parking lot of the building. The woman had already fired a shot and was threatening to kill the hostage. She had demanded to see the chief.

The dispatcher asked the man to stay on the line, alerted all available units, then spoke to the man again.

*   *   *

Drew knew she was close to death. GG wouldn't let up, cursing and threatening her, jamming the gun muzzle against the back of her head.

"Gonna beg for your life, bitch?" GG hissed in her ear. Holding a fistful of Drew's hair, she jerked Drew's head back beside the headrest. Drew gasped in pain. Her scalp was already cut, the back of her neck tortured.

"GG, you're breaking my neck," she managed to say.

"That right? You hurting?"

". . . Yes."

"Then you lucky, bitch. You ain't screaming in pain yet. But you will be, don't you worry, you will be."

She eased up. Drew was able to raise her head, and the pain lessened.

"Why you come back here?"

"I told you, GG—I haven't come back. I've never been in this town. I'm not Betty Fairchild. I don't have any connection to her."

"Then how you know my mama? How the hell you know about that girl comin' to see my daddy all them years ago?"

"I told you that too. I don't kn—"

Drew cried out in pain as GG jerked her head back again. "I said don't lie to me, bitch!"

"I'm telling you the truth," Drew said, close to tears. "What do you want from me?"

The question hit GG like a man's punch. Dumbfounded, she leaned forward so the girl could see her face in the rearview mirror, see her rage. "What do I want from you?" she said. "Girl, you took my mama away from me. I want my mama back. You got my brother Sonny killed. I want my brother back. Now you here to take my daddy from me. But I ain't gonna let you. You ain't gonna take no more from me or my family, you hear me? No more!"

She kept control of herself by remembering that she

must not kill the girl. Not yet. But the girl kept talking, distracting her, begging for GG not to hurt her, and her begging was mixed up with the sound of sirens that grew louder and then went silent when two cops' cars appeared. They skidded to a stop right outside the parking lot. Officers spilled out and then the janitor came out the door and was pointing her out to them.

The girl was still begging and GG yelled, "Shut your damn mouth." She couldn't think straight. She knew she'd had a purpose for doing this, but she'd forgotten again. And now those cops were flashing lights at her. Too much was happening and she was getting more and more upset. She felt herself losing control again and she pulled harder on the girl's hair, prodded her with the gun. It brought more crying and begging, and GG swore to herself that if the bitch kept it up she was going to get this over with and pull the trigger.

Cousin Wendell had done a good job: Raymond Ordway's desk—usually as well-ordered as the grounds of his estate—was littered with faxed reports and taped interviews flown in by couriers. Some of the interviews had been made in person, others over the phone. They included some of the girl's former neighbors in Sherman Oaks, California, a teacher in high school, coworkers in New York, a cop from the Thirty-fourth Precinct, the girl's fiancé, and a couple of tenants in her apartment house.

One of the tenants, a Mrs. Metzger, had said some things that fascinated Ordway, and he was replaying the tape for the third time. The interviewer had posed as an insurance adjuster investigating the girl's claim for her stay in the mental hospital. He'd been shrewd: When the woman related what had happened in the hallway, the interviewer suggested that maybe Drew had been shamming. The suggestion antagonized the woman, and the interviewer capitalized on it.

". . . Well, you never know. Maybe she wanted to avoid an uncomfortable situation or get out of work . . . For instance, I once had a hospital claim where—"

"Forget it. It was terrible for her—all those shmucks standing around out there gawking, one shmuck saying, 'Duhhh, she's on dope.'"

"You have to admit dope is a big problem . . . If this claimant was on dope, by the way—"

"Are you kidding? This is a kid that works for a living. Decent. Gives you a smile, a hello. A human being. And good-looking? Beautiful. Gorgeous. Like a model. Forget dope. I told you, I took her back into her apartment and stayed with her till the cops arrived, so I know. She was scared to death. Petrified."

"And it wasn't a nightmare."

"I suggested that to her myself, but she said no, she couldn't remember a thing—*nothing*. Hey, the cops talked to her. Ask them."

"I will . . . You said you saw her when she came back here from the mental hospital, is that right?"

"Must've been—but I didn't even know she was *in* a hospital. Lemme see . . . that was, uh, three days ago. Yeah. We both came out in the hall about the same time. She looked very nice, but different."

"Different in what way?"

"Different. Not the way she usually does. *You* know—smart. This time—"

"By smart do you mean expensive?"

"Nah. That kid could wear stuff from the thrift shop and look chic. I mean . . . I don't know how to describe it. She didn't look cheap exactly. Just a little much with the makeup. And the sex. But sweet. Right away she gives me a nice smile the way she always does. Only this time she says, 'How do, ma'am,' which meant she was in her Southern Period."

"What do you mean by that?"

206

"I'm kidding, but *you* know—like Picasso had his Blue Period, he painted blue, this kid has her Southern Period, she talks with a southern accent. Anyway, she's got a suitcase with her, so I says, 'Where you going?' She says home for a visit, and I said, 'Ah, that's nice. How long since you been back?' First I thought she said twenty-three years, then I figured she must've said three. Then she says she wants to thank me for what I did for her the night she went bananas."

"Did she say it like that, that she went bananas?"

"Oh, no."

"How did she phrase it?"

"Very courteous. Lemme see . . . 'I want to thank you,' she said, 'fo' evuhthing you did fo' me.' She didn't say *fo*. I can't talk the way she did, but it wasn't like one of them thick accents. It was sweet . . . Anyway, we go down in the elevator and I ask her if somebody was going to water her plants, and she said her boyfriend probably would. Now *that* I thought was strange, but I let it go."

"Why was it strange?"

"'Cause she said *her* boyfriend, not *my* boyfriend. *You* know, like she was referring to somebody else's boyfriend. Anyway I told her have a good time and she—"

Ordway switched off the machine when his secretary rang.

"Mr. Pennington just called. He said he didn't have time to talk, but to tell you that Drew Summers has just been taken hostage in Greenview. By a black woman, at 322 Hampton Street."

Ordway was so stunned that at first he could not make sense of her words.

"Mr. Ord—"

"Call Arthur," he snapped. "Tell him I'm coming down right now."

He stood up, feeling unsteady. He was going to lose her, he thought, and it made him so weak he had to lean on his desk. The sight of the reports and the tapes suddenly filled him with self-disgust. "You stupid *stupid* sonofabitch," he muttered, sweeping them onto the carpet.

When he came out of his office, his secretary stared at him in alarm. She had his chauffeur on the line. ". . . He's coming down right now, Arthur, and he's in a terrible, terrible hurry."

She was getting up as he went out the door and she called something sympathetic after him that he disregarded. He was in no mood for professional expressions of concern.

In the street outside the parking lot, Warren Hawkins caught a whiff of smoke from Rich Pauley's cigarette and fought the urge to ask him for one.

He leaned on his car door wishing he could see inside the girl's car, but it was too dark to make either her or GG out. There wasn't anything he could do now anyway. Twenty minutes ago, when he'd gotten here and thrown a light on the car, GG had screamed and carried on and threatened to kill the girl if they didn't turn it out right away. He was glad he wasn't the chief.

"What's going on?" Turnage's voice crackled over the radio.

"Still quiet," Hawkins said. "Where are you?"

"You'll hear my siren any minute. What about the Johnsons?"

"Someone's gone to pick them up. Sure be glad when you get here . . . Hold on, Mark, she wants something."

The car horn was sounding and the rear window rolled down.

"Richie?" GG called.

On the other side of the cruiser, Rich Pauley reached in and picked up the bullhorn from the seat. He and GG were distantly related, and she wouldn't talk to anybody else.

"Yeah, GG."

"Where's that damn chief of yours?"

"Should be here any minute. He's on the radio right now."

"You better not be lyin'!"

"It's the truth, GG. He said we ought to be catching his siren just about now."

Inside the car, GG rolled up the window two thirds of the way. She was glad that she'd remembered her plan, but she wished that Turnage would get here. The gun was heavy and she was sick of holding it. She propped the barrel on the seat back beside the girl's head.

"You know where I got this?" she asked the girl. "It belongs to my daddy. He bought it when everybody was cursing us, calling us on the telephone saying my brother Sonny killed your mama so they gonna kill us."

Drew could still smell burnt powder from the muzzle. She didn't answer. She knew better than to chance saying something that could set the woman off.

"How could they say Sonny do a thing like that?" GG went on. "How could they treat us that way? Couldn't walk down the street without some cracker cussin' me out . . ." The memory of being shoved into a car rushed at her. Four big white men in it. Scared her. But she couldn't remember anything else.

Drew said sincerely, "GG, I know what you must have gone through and—"

"How the hell would you know what I went through?" GG said savagely. "You knew you wouldn't be here now wantin' to hurt my daddy—" She hesitated as they heard a siren in the distance, then she said, "What my mama tell you 'bout me?"

"Not a lot," Drew said, thinking GG was referring to her visit to the house. "We didn't—"

"'Not a lot,'" GG said sarcastically. "Well she always told me plenty about you. You were her darling, sweet Little-Betts."

She'd misunderstood, Drew realized: GG was back in the past. She heard what had to be Turnage's siren.

"You know how sick I got hearin' about you?" GG went on. "'Oh that dear little girl,' my mama'd say. 'She so swee-e-t. She so goo-o-d.' Well, who wouldn't be sweet and good when they got what you had? I was sweet. I was good. But I never had all them dolls, never had all them clothes, never had no car, nothin', an' I gotta hear 'She so swee-e-t. She so goo-o-d.'"

The chief's car, lights flashing, was coming down the street now. GG's features twisted with remembered rage. "Girl, I hate you so. I hate you!"

The car shrieked to a stop near Hawkins, and Drew saw Turnage pile out. Even if she hadn't known him as well as she did she'd have recognized him right away. He was that tall.

The effect of his presence on GG was immediate. She lowered the window, put her head out and cupped a hand to her mouth.

"Mark Turnage," she yelled. "Mark Turnage!"

Pauley handed him the horn and he said, "GG."

"You know who I got here?"

"I heard. Hope you didn't hurt 'er."

"Tell him," GG said to Drew.

"Chief, this is Drew Summers—I'm all right," she called. Then she realized it hadn't been loud enough. "I'm all right!" she shouted.

"But she's not gonna be all right for long," GG shouted. "'Cause I'm gonna kill her."

"You have a reason why you want to do that?"

"You have a reason why you kill my brother Sonny?"

". . . I didn't kill your brother, GG."

"Liar! You liar!" she screamed. "You killed him. Everybody knows you killed him. You want to see this girl dead you tell me again you didn't. Say it. Say it right now, go on!"

210

GG grabbed Drew's hair again and pulled her head back. Drew prayed silently. One word, she knew, and GG was going to kill her.

Turnage bit his lip.

An officer—Hart—came over to him. "Chief, I can pick that woman off."

"How you gonna do that?" Turnage said.

"I got my hunting rifle in the trunk." He pointed to his cruiser close by. "I couldn't miss from over there."

"Suppose you did?"

"No way. She even puts her head *near* that window, she's history. . . ."

As much as the idea turned his stomach, Turnage forced himself to consider it. It might have to be done. Hart wasn't certified as a marksman, but he was good. . . .

"You go on and set yourself up," he said. "That's all. You don't do anything—you don't put in a damn shell— before I come over there and see how it looks. Clear? *Nothing.*"

Hart said it was clear and moved off.

"Mark Turnage!" GG. Head out the window again.

"Still here, GG," he said through the horn.

"You gonna say how you killed my brother?"

"If that's what you want."

"You write down how you did it and where you did it and what you did with Sonny's body. Then everybody knows you did it. And I want that Mr. Caldecott here too. He's another liar. You *all* lied!"

"Gonna take time to find Mr. Caldecott, GG," he called.

"Then you find him quick."

"I just got here. You give me some time to work on all this now, will you?"

"I'll give you five minutes."

She disappeared inside the car.

"Caldecott in the building?" Turnage asked Hawkins.

Hawkins started to answer when Turnage's phone rang. It was Raymond Ordway wanting to know if the girl was all right, and when Turnage assured him she was, he told Turnage to make sure he did everything possible to ensure her safety. Turnage said he would, and Ordway told him he was on his way there right now and hung up before Turnage could get in another word.

"Gonna have the governor callin' next," Turnage complained.

"Caldecott's not in the building," Hawkins said. "The janitor says that's his car there in the lot, but his office is locked up. Everybody else is out."

"What'd you send for the Johnsons, horse and buggy?"

"They'll be here any minute, but I wouldn't depend on her listening to them. She's out for blood, Mark."

Two minutes later GG rolled down the window again and asked about Caldecott. Turnage said they hadn't been able to reach him so far.

"Well, you find him," GG yelled. "And you keep writing out how you killed my brother."

"GG, I need more time."

"You write," she shouted, "and you get it over to me in five minutes or I shoot this girl—and next to killing you it be the best thing I ever did in my life. Five minutes, I said, and I don't want no more talk!"

"GG, listen to me . . ."

But the window was rolled up again and GG disappeared. Turnage cursed under his breath.

"Get me a damn piece of paper," he told Hawkins. "Never mind," he said as he spotted the flashing lights of a cruiser a couple of blocks away.

The flashing lights went off, and as the car sped toward them, Turnage had the first upbeat feeling of the night. "Hallelujah," he muttered. He started walking, not wanting the cruiser to stop where GG could see the occupants before he talked to them.

212

As it came to a halt beside him he was able to make out the two figures in the backseat. Turnage opened the door and Mr. Johnson got out first, helped his wife out, and when the two of them faced him, as always when Turnage confronted one or the other of them, he felt their pride and their anger and he would not look them in the eye.

Inside Drew's car GG held the pistol in both hands and cocked it. Drew felt the prod of it through the back of the seat.

"You got five minutes, bitch." Her tone was mean again. "You think that cracker gonna admit he killed my brother? Bet your life he won't, and I mean you bet your life. But you know something? Don't matter. No matter what he say it ain't gonna bring Sonny back. Ain't gonna change nothing."

The interior was splashed with yellow light then darkened again as GG lit another cigarette. Smoke came Drew's way. Resting her arms on the steering wheel, she put her head down.

GG dragged on her cigarette and stared at the back of the girl's head, feeling a little sorry for her. Suppose she *wasn't* Betty? She didn't talk like her, didn't act like her. But if she wasn't Betty, why did her mama like her just as much as she'd liked Betty? She had to be Betty. Or her daughter. You looked at her you could tell easy it was one or the other.

"You know how many times I killed you in my head, Miss Little-Betts? Everytime my mama come home too tired to even hug me, too tired to listen about what I did at school. Everytime she come home too late to play with me. Everytime she mention your name."

Her tone had become mean again. "She cleaned for you and she dressed you, wiped your ass and ironed your clothes, but she never had time to—"

"GG," Turnage's voice broke in, magnified by the bullhorn, "can you hear me?"

GG rolled the window down. "I hear," she shouted. "You finished writing?"

"Not yet. Somebody here to talk to you."

"I'm not talking to nobody but you and that Lee Caldecott, so you keep on writin', 'cause—"

She and Drew jumped as a hammer blow struck the car's engine. Neither of them knew what had happened until a second bullet ricocheted off the asphalt.

Turnage knew what it was immediately.

"Down—down everybody!" his voice thundered through the bullhorn, and he was already herding the Johnsons behind the cruiser as two more shots came. Hart jumped into his mind and he swore he'd kill the man.

When another shot hit the asphalt close to the car and a sixth hit the trunk, GG was enraged. She pulled Drew's head back again. "That dirty bastard," she screamed. "You see what he's like? He don't care about nobody, not even you!"

"GG," Drew pleaded, "please don't hurt me, please. Maybe he had nothing to—"

"Shut your damn mouth," GG spat. "I swear to God I hear one more shot I'm gonna kill you. You're gonna die, you white bitch!"

She jabbed the gun at Drew's head so hard this time that, between the pain and the terror, Drew gave up. "Please, GG," she begged. "Please don't kill me, please. Listen to me . . ."

She was going to make a final plea, one that at least would give her some precious seconds, but before she could say anything, another voice was speaking over the bullhorn. This one came into the car calmly, clearly, with quiet authority.

"GG," Mrs. Johnson said. "I am here, and your father is here too. We are coming to talk to you."

Helpless, able to see little else than the ceiling,

214

Drew held her breath. The gun barrel trembled against her head.

"GG." Mrs. Johnson's voice came again, not magnified this time. "Do you hear me?"

". . . Mama? Mama, don't you come here. You stay away," GG shouted. "I don't want you comin' here."

"Your father and I must talk to you, GG. Please, darling." Her voice was closer.

"No!" GG's grip on Drew's hair tightened. "Mama," she shouted, "don't you come here. Daddy, you stop her. I don't want to talk to y'all. Stay away!"

Please God, Drew prayed, let them keep coming. Please. Please.

"Mama, you stop right now." GG's voice was unsteady. "You won't save her, I'm tellin' you. You stop right now or I kill this girl. Mama, you stop!"

From the corner of her eye Drew saw the Johnsons appear beside the car and her hopes surged.

"Let that girl go, GG," Mrs. Johnson said.

"Mama, I'm tellin'—"

"Please. Let that poor girl lift her head."

Mrs. Johnson peered at Drew through her gold-rimmed glasses. Drew thought it was the most beautiful face she had ever seen in her life.

"Are you all right, child?"

Before Drew could answer, GG said, "I ain't gonna let this girl go, so now you both get outta here."

Mrs. Johnson put a hand on the rear door. "We have to talk, GG," she said.

"Mama, you don't go 'way I swear I kill her!"

"You can't do that, GG. We don't hurt other people in this family. We're not that kind."

Her father leaned down. "You all right, miss?" Drew nodded slightly and he said, "Give me my gun, GG."

GG said nothing.

"Honey," Mrs. Johnson said, "this girl never hurt you. She never hurt anybody in our family."

"She did. She got Sonny killed. She hurt us all. She—"

"That's not this girl, honey."

"Now she got Daddy in trouble, went and told Mark Turnage about when Betty come to the house that time—"

"Your daddy won't be in any trouble, GG."

"Why you taking her part?" GG's eyes were filling with tears. "You always that way, always take her part. Why you do that, Mama? Why you love her more than you love me?"

Mrs. Johnson said, "That's not true, sweetheart."

"Oh yes it is," GG said. "You always saying, 'Oh my, how pretty that girl is. What pretty clothes she has.'"

"Honey, whatever I said about Betty, it didn't mean that I didn't love you."

"Then why didn't you say how pretty *I* was, how much you loved *me*? Why you never tell me that?"

"I did, baby. I did. You forgot."

"No you didn't, Mama. You never say anything like that to me. You always say, 'Oh my what a smart little girl that little Betty is. She a beautiful little doll.' You never say that to me."

"GG, that couldn't be. You know how much I loved *all* of you."

"Sure, Mama, I know, but you never tell *me* how smart I am. You just tell me I got to do better in school. You never say to me, 'GG, you so beautiful I just want to hug you.' You say, 'Now GG, you make sure you stay clean. I got enough ironin' to do all day 'thout you gettin' your dress all messed up.'"

She lowered the gun and let go of Drew's hair. She'd forgotten her.

"You remember that day, Mama, when you took me to the Fairchild house 'cause you had to go somewhere when you finished work? Remember? I went into Betty's bedroom and I never saw anything like it. All that lace and all them pretty pinks and blues. It was so beautiful I wanted to cry. I lied down in that bed and I felt like a princess. Mama, it was like floating away in a cloud. I fell asleep and you come in and you pulled me out and you smacked me on the butt and you told me *never* do anything like that again—never! I didn't think I done anything bad, but you were so angry . . . The way you pulled me out, I felt like dirt. Oh, Mama, that hurt so bad. So bad . . ." The corners of her mouth turned down and tears rolled down her cheeks.

Mrs. Johnson's eyes were filling. Drew, fearful moments before, felt terrible for her.

"Why'd you do that, Mama?" GG went on like a little girl. "How come you be so awful mad at me? All I wanted was to lie down in that bed 'cause I never touched anything so beautiful. I wasn't a bad girl, but you made me feel like I always was and always would be."

Mrs. Johnson was trying to control her tears. "GG, my baby, why you never tell me you felt like that? Why didn't you ever say that to me?"

Her face twisted with grief, Mrs. Johnson opened the rear door, reached in and took her daughter's hand. "Come out here, GG. Come out here to me."

She drew her daughter out and there beside the car she hugged her close. "GG," she said through her tears, "I wouldn't hurt you for anything. My little baby, you the most beautiful girl in the world, and no one, no one, will ever come before you to me."

"You really mean that, Mama?"

"Yes I do," her mother said, patting her.

GG's eyes were shining. "Oh, Mama, I love you so much."

Unable to talk further, the two of them hugged each other and cried while Mr. Johnson, holding back his own tears, simply touched his daughter's shoulder.

They didn't know the police had moved in until they were suddenly caught in a flood of blinding lights.

"Stay as you are," Turnage called sharply. "Don't move—anybody!"

Barely visible behind the glare, he and his officers had their weapons trained on the three. "Where's the gun?" Turnage said, coming closer.

Drew shielded her eyes, unable to see. She was scared. Anything could happen now, she realized. Everyone was on edge.

"*I said where's that gun, damnit!*" Turnage demanded.

Drew realized for the first time that GG no longer had it. "It could be down on the floor behind my seat, Mr. Turnage," she said quickly.

Turnage moved past the two women, reached down behind Drew's seat. When he came up with the gun the officers visibly relaxed. At the same time one of them reached for GG and tried to take her arm. GG flinched, and almost as one Mr. and Mrs. Johnson shielded her.

"You got the gun," Mr. Johnson said. "She's not about to hurt anybody now."

The officer looked at Turnage.

"It's regulations," he said. "That's the way it has to be."

GG shrank into her mother's arms.

"Don't scare her," Mrs. Johnson said. "This is my little girl. This is my beautiful little daughter, and you must be gentle with her. Don't you worry, GG, nobody will hurt you or mistreat you. Your daddy and I are here. We love you and we will stay beside you." She looked at Turnage. "Can we ride with her?"

"Be better for everybody," Mr. Johnson said, and Turnage nodded wordlessly.

GG was staring at her mother like a little girl. "You really love me, Mama?" she asked. "You really do?"

"Yes, little baby, I do."

218

The officer said, "This way," and her father on one side and her mother on the other, GG followed him.

"I ain't afraid, Mama," Drew heard her say. "I ain't afraid—not with you and Daddy here." And the last thing Drew heard was, "You really do love me . . . ?"

Then she was gone.

Turnage leaned down and looked into the car. "We got a doctor here. You need one?"

Drew was massaging her neck.

"A couple of cuts on my head, but I think I'm okay," she said. "I'm getting the shakes though."

"Bad?"

Before she could answer, he turned at the sound of a commotion, someone coming toward them protesting to an officer trying to stop him. The bright lights made it difficult to make him out, but the voice was well-known.

"Don't you tell me I can't see that girl!" Raymond Ordway was almost shouting. "You try to stop me and I'll make sure your chief has your hide. Now get your hands off me. I want to know if that girl is all right, and by God I'm going to!"

Turnage automatically shut the car door as Ordway materialized from the glare. "Is she all right?" he demanded. "Is she all right? What did the nigger do to her? I want to see her." With surprising strength, he tried to shove Turnage out of the way.

Turnage held his ground. "Slow down, Mr. Ordway. The girl's been through a bad time, but she's not hurt. Give her a chance to calm down."

"I want to hear from her that she's okay. Drew?"

"I'm all right, Mr. Ordway," Drew said. "I really am."

Turnage gave enough ground for Ordway to put one hand on the door. "You're sure—she didn't hurt you?"

Drew assured him she was fine, and he said, "You're staying at my house tonight with me and my sister."

"Gee, that's really nice of—"

"I won't take no for an answer," he said. "You're not going to stay in a hotel room all alone, with no one around who cares about you. Furthermore, Harriet said that if I come home without you she'll never talk to me again," he lied.

"Mr. Ordway, I honestly appreciate it. I do," Drew said. "I was just going to say that before I do anything, first I really have to go to the bathroom."

That made Ordway chuckle and even Turnage smiled. He cut the smile short when he saw that people were crowding his officers. A camera flashed from behind them, blinding him, and he heard Pennington's voice. "Why can't we go through? It's all over, for God's sake."

Turnage acted.

"Keep those people back," he yelled to his men. "All of 'em. Mr. Ordway, that goes for you, too. You're gonna have to move." He pulled open the door, forcing Ordway to back up, and told Drew to scoot over.

"Where are you going?" Ordway demanded as Turnage got in and slammed the door.

"Taking this girl over to the station, where she'll be attended to and where she can make a statement." The key was in the ignition and he turned it. "And where she can go to the bathroom."

Sitting outside Turnage's office, Raymond Ordway again looked around with distaste. The wood-paneled walls were battered and dirty and the plastic tiled floor needed mopping. If this was a police station God help the citizens. He glanced up as the air-conditioning kicked in and he felt a breath of cool air. There was a brown stain around the vent. Close to it, electric conduit and other wiring was visible through an opening in the ceiling.

Down the hall near the exit a colored woman behind a sliding glass window was talking to patrol car officers and answering the phone. From somewhere in the opposite direction he heard a drunk carrying on. The whole place smelled of second-rate authority and losers and it only increased Ordway's sense of guilt toward Drew. And Betty.

He could not forgive himself. The girl might have been killed and it would have been his fault. Instead of taking her under his wing, he'd treated her with suspicion and cruelty. How much convincing did he need? Everything turned up by Lee's investigation and his own proved what he should have known by instinct: Drew was genuine. Everything she said, everything she did, indicated she had no idea what was happening to her, that she was a victim of circumstance. No. How did that reporter phrase it? *The victim of a cosmic error.*

Betty's spirit was inside of this girl—her touch, the smell of her hair, her youth, her sweet bounciness, and every feeling he'd ever had for her twenty-three years ago had come back as violent as hunger.

He was thinking of knocking at the door when it finally opened. He got up as Turnage came out. "Where is Drew?"

"She'll be right out."

"Well hurry it up." He looked around in disgust. "This place is a pigsty."

"Glad you noticed. You might mention it to the city administrator. I keep complaining that our janitorial and maintenance services aren't the best, but I don't get anywhere. You still plan on taking the girl home?"

"Any objection?"

"Well, I know you're taken with her, but maybe you ought to—"

"Ought to what? Wait for someone to kill her? Let me tell you something, Mark, I realize something now. I realize that Providence has brought this girl here—to me, to Harriet, to all of us. And so far all we've done is make life miserable for her, haven't we? I'm putting a stop to it. On my way out here from town I swore to myself that if Drew came out of this ordeal alive I'd take care of her. I'm going to keep that promise."

Turnage shrugged. "Well, I'd still be careful. She's swearing out a complaint against Lee."

"Against Lee? For what?"

"Says he threatened her and assaulted her."

". . . Is that why she was there, to see Lee?"

"Yeah. Says he asked her to drop over. I tried to call him, can't reach him so far. You ask me she might be a good young lady to stay away from."

Ordway was unconvinced. "I'll take my chances."

"I'm sending an officer out to guard your house."

"What for? We have alarms. The house is safe."

"You never know. Whoever took those shots at her in the parking lot might try again. From now on I'm assigning an officer to her 'round the clock."

At that point Drew came out with Hawkins. She looked wan, and Ordway's heart went out to her. He herded her out of the place as quickly as possible.

Once in the car, he had them driven to Drew's hotel so that she could get a change of clothes.

All the way out to the house, a police car following them, he kept an arm around her, comforting her. There were dark stains on her scalp where it had been dabbed with iodine—cuts from the gun barrel, Drew told him. Ordway felt that if he had GG Johnson there right now, he'd kick her to death.

Harriet met them on the porch. "Oh, I am so glad you're safe," she said, hugging Drew. "I was too cowardly to go into town. If anything had happened to you . . ."

She dabbed at her eyes with a handkerchief, then asked Drew if she was hungry. Drew said she'd had a hamburger in Turnage's office, so the three of them sat on the upper veranda and looked out over the pond.

"I'm calling the solicitor tomorrow," Ordway said after Drew described what had happened. "They'll throw the book at that madwoman or I want to know why."

"She didn't know what she was doing, Mr. Ordway," Drew said. "It's not her fault."

"She knew. She was trying to finish what her nigger brother started twenty-three years ago."

"Raymond, that is both unkind and untrue."

Ordway disregarded her. "I don't want to hear any more of this 'Mr. Ordway' stuff," he said to Drew. "From now on you'll call me Ray."

"And you'll call me Harriet," Mrs. Fairchild said.

A few minutes later Drew was too tired to talk anymore and went to her room. Ordway asked his sister what her feeling was about Drew.

"I have so many, Raymond, it is hard to sort them out. A few minutes ago I caught myself wanting to braid her hair into pigtails as I used to do with Betty."

"I want to have a party for her," Ordway said.

"It's a wonderful idea, but I doubt that Drew will even be here by the time it could take place."

"She'll be here. We'll make it day after tomorrow."

"Raymond, you're not serious!"

"I am. I want a big party. Invite everybody. If you can't manage it, I'll have my secretary do it."

"You cannot give people such short notice."

"They'll come—they'll be too fascinated not to. We'll turn the clock back—tell people to come dressed the way they did back in the sixties—jeans, anything."

"Raymond, *no* one will have time to do that."

"Make it optional. I want everybody to see this girl. I want her to see everybody." He was smiling in anticipation. Harriet hadn't seen him this enthusiastic and happy in years.

"At least give me until two days from tomorrow."

"Saturday. You've got it," he said.

Getting up, he went to the den and called Lee. He started to leave a message on the machine, but Lee came on the line. Ordway made it brief—told him he wanted to see him as soon as possible, and Lee said he'd call him in the morning after he looked at his schedule.

"Keep Saturday night open," Ordway said. "Harriet will call Juleen." He hung up before Lee could answer.

After he made a few more calls and was headed for his bedroom, he switched off the hallway light, switched it back on as soon as he saw light under Drew's door.

He knocked softly. When she opened it she took his breath away. She was in her robe, a bath towel turbaned around her head. She looked fresh, clean, and youthful, smiled as soon as she saw him. She was holding a magazine.

"I didn't mean to disturb you," he said. "I wanted to make sure you're all right."

"I'm fine," she said. "I was just going to read for a few minutes. I knew it was you."

"How did you know?"

"I just did. I was thinking about something that I mentioned—" The magazine slipped from her fingers and she quickly bent down and picked it up. Her robe parted, and before she pulled it closed he saw the swell of her young breasts. "I can't hold on to anything," she said, looking distracted. "What was I saying?"

"Something that you mentioned . . ."

"Yes—I was thinking of a line I mentioned to Chuck Pennington. He found out it was from a poem called *The Highwayman*. Are you famil—"

"Of course I know it," Ordway said quickly. "It was Betty's favorite. She won first prize for reciting it in the Sixth Grade Recitation Contest."

". . . You helped her, didn't you?" Drew said. "You tutored her."

224

Ordway's throat was dry. "Yes," he said.

Drew looked into his eyes. "'Look for me by moonlight,' it went. 'Watch for me by moonlight, I'll come to thee by moonlight, though hell should bar the way . . .'"

She'd said it without a trace of her normal accent. Ordway would have sworn he was listening to Betty.

"I *must* have heard that somewhere," Drew said, frowning. Ordway said nothing. "Well, good night, Ray," she said.

"Sleep well," he said. He walked away as she started to close the door.

"Good night," Betty's voice came to him softly. "Sleep tight, don't let the bedbugs bite."

He turned and caught a glimpse of her before the door shut completely. He'd have sworn Betty was smiling at him, the way she did when she was a little girl and he'd kiss her good night and tuck her in.

In that moment he had a flash of insight. He knew without the slightest doubt why Betty had come back. The reporter had been wrong: She was not here because of a cosmic mistake. She was here by cosmic design. She had come back because of him. Not for anyone else or for any other reason but to be with him.

Pennington was clicking away at his word processor when his phone rang. He glanced at the clock, saw he had plenty of time to deadline, and reached for the phone.

"Pennington," he said.

"All right, where is the car?" Stiggs asked.

"Car? What car?" Pennington said, rubbing it in.

"The last record Turnage's office has on that Mustang is 1978, when it was stored at a county yard."

"What does that tell you?"

"That some poor overworked and underpaid civil

225

servant neglected to note when and to where the car was moved—not at all unusual. I'm surprised it is still around at all. Where did you find it?"

"Ah ah ah. First, I want to be there when you look at it. I want pictures and an exclusive."

"Who says I am going to look at it?"

"Arnold, as Charles Manson once asked his disciples, do you really hate the idea of being involved in what could be *the* murder case of the decade? And do you know, may I ask, where the young lady involved has now taken up lodgings?"

"Fort Sumter."

"Close. She is within the House of Ordway, and I will bet you one hundred to one that if she gave her consent, he and his sister would file adoption papers on her forthwith."

"You're being carried away, Chuck."

"Man, what do I have to do to convince you to get with it? You're aware that Drew was just held hostage by Ed Johnson's sister, aren't you?"

"Yes."

"Are you also aware that Drew Summers went to see Luther Johnson—Johnson's father—and made him admit that he threw Betty Fairchild out of his house two days before she was murdered?"

"Yes."

"Okay, let's *still* say Drew is a phony. Fine—pretend this is Crime Prevention Week and interest yourself in the case on the grounds that you're out to protect the Ordways from a possible con job. But interest yourself in it. Personally."

"I am interested, Chuck. Very much. In fact I would like to meet with the young lady."

That was what Pennington wanted to hear. He went on to make a suggestion Stiggs loved, they made a deal, and then Stiggs asked him where the car was.

226

"Arnold, you're going to love this," Pennington said, starting to laugh. "It's in the county garage."

Stiggs didn't blame him for laughing. The county garage was behind the Municipal Building—one minute away from Stiggs's office.

13

Raymond Ordway began to wake up. He was dreaming that Drew had thrown off her robe and was doing things with him that he had taught Betty. His member was swollen and throbbing, and, unwilling to let the delicious excitement go, he stayed submerged in half sleep. When release came he surrendered himself to the waves of ecstasy that surged from all over his body and spurted from his loins.

He lay with his eyes closed, his drowsiness rich with imaginings. Occasionally his wet fingers, as delicately as though he were inside Betty, extracted another small flicker of pleasure. When he had shrunk to complete softness he was quiet within himself, content. He lay thinking of Drew living in the house permanently. Betty wanted it. He wanted it. Drew would want it.

He got up and crossed the soft carpeting to the bathroom, where he rinsed his hands with warm water. Then he brushed his teeth and showered.

Later, in the hall, he paused outside Drew's door. If he were to go in and wake her up, would he find Betty smiling at him, opening her arms to him?

He hated to leave the house, but knowing she was in it made him feel more whole and complete than he had in years.

Drew woke up with a stiff neck. She closed her eyes, thinking she'd drowse, and when she woke again it was a little before seven. She explored her scalp tentatively for the tender places, then lay back, staring at the bed canopy. Beyond it, the ceiling was striped with sun from the window shutters. The sound of birds came into the room, and she thought how beautiful it must be outside.

The soft pillow beneath her head and the crisp sheet covering her felt good. She threw her arms out and smiled: The bed was so big she couldn't reach either edge. The canopy must have been eight feet above her. The room was huge too, high ornate ceiling, carved moldings. When she sat on the edge of the bed she felt like a little girl: Her feet dangled above the floor.

She started to think about GG, and Lee Caldecott, and anger rose in her.

Cut, she said to herself. Don't think of them. Relax and do nothing. Pamper yourself.

Going to the doors, she opened them and walked out onto the wide veranda and into heaven. The last time she had seen grounds as beautiful as these was in Kew Gardens outside London. But that had been a place for tourists. This was a private home, private grounds.

Twin rows of giant oaks led to the entrance in the distance, and from the entrance to the gardens and the huge pond below, acres of thick grass carpeted the ground. On one side, again in the distance, were stables and white fences, on the other thick woods with a stream that flowed to the river.

Directly below her, two mallards were swimming in the pond, and Harriet Fairchild was tossing pieces of bread to them.

"Good morning," Drew said.

Mrs. Fairchild looked up. Shielding her eyes, she pretended she was seeing Betty. "Good morning, sleepy-head . . . How are you feeling?"

Drew stretched. "Like Alice in Wonderland."

"You have had a few calls," Mrs. Fairchild said.

"Would you know if one of them was from a Susan?"

"I'm sorry, I don't. My secretary took them. Dial the asterisk, then two-three. Her name is Mary Jo."

Drew asked if Mrs. Fairchild minded if she used the phone to call out, and she told Drew to call anywhere and talk for as long as she liked.

They arranged to have lunch—brunch for Drew—by the azalea garden, wherever it was, then Drew called Mary Jo.

A pleasant-voiced lady, she told Drew that yes, Susan had called, and a Norman O'Neill also. After she ascertained that Drew had no plans, she said that subject to Drew's approval a masseuse would be coming at one-twenty, a manicurist at three, and someone to do Drew's hair at five.

"For me?"

"Mrs. Fairchild felt you would enjoy it."

Drew's first impulse was to say no, then she thought, What am I—crazy? She told Mary Jo she wouldn't dream of refusing.

"In between," Mary Jo said, "you can swim in the pool, use the gym, or the hot tub, or the sauna, and do whatever else you like. If there is something you need, why you just let me know."

She asked if Drew would like coffee sent to her room and Drew told her thanks, no, then called Susan.

"You're not going to believe this," Susan said. "Belle's decided to stick with their present agency."

Drew groaned. "All those hours for nothing."

"Don't let it get to you. I've seen accounts call for a review, have three or four agencies doing spec work for a couple of *months* and then say forget it. We were lucky to put in just a couple of weeks."

"Norman knows I'm down here, huh?"

"I had to tell him. He wants to talk to you."

"About the Belle's thing?"

"I don't know. I guess so. By the way, he got a call from an insurance adjuster and had me talk to the guy,"

230

Susan said. "I figured it was okay to tell him about the southern accent jazz and what happened at the meeting."

"Sure."

"And a couple of detectives were here asking questions."

"About *me*?"

"About a disturbance in your hallway, they said."

"That was a month and a half ago. What took them so long?"

She told Susan she was going to try to be back Monday, then she described where she was and, starting with the masseuse, she reeled off her schedule for the day. Susan said it sounded disgusting and she was flying right down to join her.

"How are you feeling?" Drew asked her.

"Wonderful. I think it's a girl."

They talked another minute before Susan switched her over to Norman's office. Drew waited nervously.

"Got some good news and some bad news," Norman said. "Belle's is dead."

"I heard," Drew said. "What's the good news?"

"*That* was the good news. I've been told that if you're not back to work by Friday, I have to let you go."

That riled her. "Oh shit."

"You don't sound surprised."

"I'm not. I think some creep down here did it."

"I can push it to Monday if it'll help."

"I'll do my best, Norman."

"Don't worry. If I fire you I know two agencies that'll grab you for more money than you're getting here. Try to make it back, I don't want to lose you. By the way—what the hell are you doing down there?"

"Finding out I'm not crazy."

"Why be different from the rest of us," Norman said.

"Norman, I mean this. I not only love you, when I come back I want to marry you."

"You don't make enough. Try me in ten years."

231

After she hung up she started to call Corey, hesitated, then decided she wanted to. As usual, she got the recording and left a message that she was still in Greenview. She was okay, she assured him, had even called her boss, and he wasn't to worry about her. "I mean that. I'm fine . . . Believe it or not," she ended, "I'm a guest on a plantation."

On the west patio, which adjoined the azalea garden, Mrs. Fairchild brushed aside Drew's thanks.

"My motive is purely selfish," she said. "We are giving a party for you on Saturday and I want everyone to see how beautiful you are."

"I don't think I'll be here, Harriet. My boss said if I'm not back in a couple of days I'm out of a job."

"Did you explain what has happened to you?"

"It didn't matter. I think Mr. Caldecott did it."

"Lee?"

"Yes." She related how Caldecott had threatened her.

Mrs. Fairchild was shocked. "Lee has always been such a very fine . . ."

There was a cordless phone on the table. Mrs. Fairchild called her brother.

"Lee told you that?" Ordway asked when she put Drew on.

"Ray, I don't want to cause any troub—"

"You're not causing any trouble, but I will. If I can straighten this out and fix things so your job won't be jeopardized, will you stay for the party?"

"It sure would be easier. I wouldn't have to leave my car here and—"

"Think about what you want to wear. You'll hear from my secretary inside of an hour."

A half hour later, while they were still eating, Norman himself called.

"Honeychile, who you messin' with down there? I done got another call from upstairs. You're in good shape."

232

"Norman, that's terrific. I'll try to be back on Monday."

Mrs. Fairchild, still disturbed by what Drew had told her about Caldecott, felt a little better. She left Drew alone to answer the rest of her calls, saying she had many many things to arrange for the party.

Drew called Ordway to thank him, but his secretary said he was in a meeting. Then she contacted the repair place in town and was told she couldn't have her car for another three days.

Chuck Pennington had left a message, and when she called him, he said that the county solicitor wanted to see her.

"Why?" she asked him.

"He's thinking of reopening the Johnson case."

"I think I've given the Johnsons enough grief already—especially Mr. Johnson," Drew said. She said she'd have to think about it.

A few minutes later, however, the solicitor himself called. He assured Drew he had no preconceived notions about anyone's guilt or innocence and that he wanted very much to talk to her. "You might very well be able to help a lot of people, including the Johnsons and Mrs. Fairchild."

Drew agreed to meet with him the next morning.

The masseuse showed up promptly at one-thirty and Drew spent a wonderful hour having every muscle in her body squeezed and pleased, then she had a manicure by the pool. By the time the beautician came to do her hair, she felt she really *was* Alice in Wonderland.

"Raymond, you have hardly eaten a thing," his sister said when dinner was almost over.

"I had a late lunch," he lied. The truth was that he was so taken with Drew, he had no appetite.

She had gotten some sun and had lazed around all

day and she was glowing. She looked softer, more feminine, as fresh and as youthful as Betty.

He'd loved her reaction when he and Harriet led her into the dining room. He had told Harriet he wanted it gleaming, and it was. Drew took one look at the glowing chandeliers, the draperies, the muraled walls, the antique table set with fine old crystal and silver, and her jaw dropped.

"Wait . . . just . . . a . . . minute, guys," she said, pointing her thumbs at the blouse and slacks she was wearing. "*Moi?* I? Dressed like this? I'm eating *here?*"

Harriet and he had both laughed. "You are *dining* here," Ordway had told her, "and no one who's dined here has ever been more welcome, have they, Harriet? Or more beautiful."

Drew was sitting back now, finished eating, and he asked her if she'd enjoyed it.

"It was wonderful," Drew said.

He suggested they have dessert and coffee outside near the pond, and as they were going out through the French doors, Drew said, "All I can say is I'm sure going to hate leaving here."

"That is the last thing Harriet and I want you to think about," he said, ushering her out.

"Ray, I really appreciate your hospitality," Drew said, "but I'm going back to the hotel tomorrow morning."

He felt as devastated as when he had driven around the estate the morning after Hugo. The sun had been shining, the day perfect, but his world was in shambles. The stables were destroyed, centuries-old trees uprooted and flung at buildings, miles of fencing gone.

"You won't leave," he said. "Betty won't let you."

He wasn't smiling, and Drew wasn't sure if he was serious. "I have to," she said. "Chuck and I have a meeting with the solicitor in the morning."

He found himself resenting the girl.

"Do reconsider, Drew," Mrs. Fairchild said. "We so

234

want to get to know you. As Raymond said, no one has ever been more welcome here."

"I think I know how you feel," Drew said, "and I appreciate it, but I really would like to go back to the hotel."

"You are coming to the party, though," Ordway said.

"Of course. I'm looking forward to it," Drew said honestly.

She went to the balustrade and leaned on it, looking out at the night. It had showered a while ago and the air was crisply perfumed. Faint light fell on the black surface of the pond, and Drew made out the two mallards floating near the bank. They were so still that hardly a ripple marked their presence. It was exquisite here, Drew thought, easy to forget the world outside.

A servant had brought coffee and was asking Drew if she wanted cream and sugar when a bloodcurdling cry made her jump. It was from one of the mallards, and she caught a glimpse of it, wings outspread, just as it disappeared beneath the water. It reappeared a moment later gurgling and shrieking, wings beating the surface, while its mate swam away quacking hysterically.

"What is it?" Drew asked Mrs. Fairchild. "What's happening to it!"

Instead of answering, Mrs. Fairchild shut her eyes tightly and clapped her hands over her ears.

Horrified, Drew watched as the bird was again pulled down and again rose, its shrieks filled with the pain and terror of a death struggle.

The next time it was pulled down it didn't resurface. The dark waters stirred and shifted as a silent struggle went on beneath them.

Ordway came beside Drew and put an arm around her shoulder. "A snapping turtle got it. The pond is full of them. Once in a while they'll grab on and hold a bird down until it drowns. Then they eat it."

Mrs. Fairchild had remained frozen, unable to hear, unable to see. "Is it over?" she pleaded.

Later, Drew lay awake listening to the occasional low rattle of grief from the remaining mallard. Each time she closed her eyes she saw its mate, contentedly floating, unaware of danger. Then the beak snapped onto its leg, dragging the bird down into darkness.

She shivered. She was glad she was leaving. She would come back for the party, but she did not want to spend another night here if she didn't have to. The same with the town. She wanted out—to go home as soon as possible. There were too many unexpected dangers in this place, and she was more afraid than ever of what might happen to her.

Rich Pauley drove Drew back to the hotel at ten the next morning, but before he let her enter her room he checked the bathroom and the closet. For good measure he glanced under the bed. On his way out, he reminded Drew to make sure the bolt on the connecting door was always in place. Even though there'd always be an officer right outside, he said, the entrance to the adjoining room was around the turn in the corridor and somebody might try to get in that way.

Chuck picked her up a little later, and at eleven o'clock they were in Arnold Stiggs's office in the Municipal Building.

In his early thirties, Stiggs was homely as sin, had a high-pitched voice, and Drew liked him. He was from South Carolina—Columbia, he told Drew—but he had no accent.

"What's going on?" Drew asked. "Hardly anybody I meet down here has a southern accent."

"Oh, we got 'em," Stiggs said, "we just don't use 'em roun' you Yankees."

Drew laughed and they talked amiably for a few more minutes before Stiggs got down to business. His line of work made him a little dubious of the existence of ESP, spirits and such, he told Drew, "but I do like to keep an open mind. At least that is what I tell myself. I like that word dubious," he added. "Has a ring to it."

He went on to say that he was going to ask Drew some questions that she should not take to be doubtful of her sincerity. He did not intend them that way. He was aware that she was presently under psychiatric treatment, he said, sitting back, and asked her about the events leading to it.

After she explained, and he had questioned her about what had occurred since she had been in Greenview, he asked how she liked staying with Raymond Ordway and his sister. He was mildly surprised and seemed pleased when Drew told him she had gone back to the Marriott this morning. He asked her why.

"One reason was that I felt that Mr. Ordway and his sister could become too attached to me. They acted as though they knew me, but I don't know them and it made me feel a little uncomfortable."

"I heard the tape of what you said at Willow Creek," Stiggs said. "Between that and what Chuck here has told me about you, I was impressed. I am even more impressed now that I have met you. But for you, we might not have found the murder car. Because of you there is a strong possibility we may reopen the Johnson case. By the way," he added, "Mr. Johnson was questioned this morning. He verified what you said about Betty Fairchild paying him a visit."

"I really feel bad about that," Drew said. "I didn't intend to make it look like—"

"Nothing for you to feel bad about," Stiggs said. "Mr. Johnson is not a suspect. The detective who questioned him said he was a concerned parent, not a killer."

Drew was relieved. "That's great."

"But how did you do it?" Stiggs asked. "How did you

know Betty Fairchild had been there? Did you feel her presence?"

"No. Not that time. Sometimes I do, though."

"What is it like?"

"It's the one thing I can't describe. I can't see her, I can't hear her, I can't touch her, but she's there. I feel her, and sometimes I know what she wants."

"Ms. Summers, I'd like to ask you—and should you refuse I will certainly understand—if you will come with me to take a look at Betty Fairchild's car."

"You mean right now?"

"I do. I know it is not a pleasant task, to say the least," he said, letting Drew ponder the idea, "but with this ability you have to tune in on matters relating to Betty Fairchild you might be able to tell us more of what happened on that day she was murdered."

Drew said okay, she would do it, and Pennington silently congratulated himself: He'd come up with the idea of going to the car, and although Stiggs had liked it, he'd said he wanted to question Drew before he committed himself.

"I hope you won't mind," Stiggs said now. "I informed Chief Turnage of our meeting this morning. He said if we went to the car and he was available, he wanted to be present. Is that all right with you?"

". . . Sure, why not?" Drew said after a pause. "I owe him one."

Pennington said, "He's got an officer guarding her 'round the clock." He indicated the door. "One outside there right now."

"I'm not surprised. Mark Turnage does not let his personal feelings interfere with his work."

He excused himself to take a call from his wife, then haltingly gave her a recipe that included a couple of lemons and Tabasco sauce. When the call was obviously taking longer than he'd expected, he started to blush, making Drew smile.

238

Putting his wife on hold, he asked his secretary to call Turnage, then asked Drew and Pennington if they minded waiting in the outer office a few minutes. Drew said not at all, asked if the recipe was for Bloody Marys.

"Cocktail sauce. We're having a dinner party this evening and my wife is a bit anxious."

In Stiggs's outer office his secretary, a pleasant, gray-haired lady, called Turnage and found out that he'd be at the county garage in fifteen minutes. That done, she told Drew that she'd been fascinated with what she had read about her in the paper and thought it would make a wonderful book.

"That's what *I* keep telling her," Pennington said.

Fifteen minutes later, he, Drew, and Stiggs were heading for the garage.

A deputy by the entrance accompanied them to the shed, opened two sturdy locks that now secured the door.

The interior was airless and damp, heavy with the odors of urine and mold. What was left of the tarp had been removed. The Mustang was up on blocks.

Drew felt her skin crawl. It was an exact duplicate of her own car, but dust and the erosion of time made it look as though it came from another dimension. It made her think of a Kienholz construction—quiet terror.

The windows, too dirty to see through, were raised, and the canvas top hung in tatters from the rusted frame. Drew looked over the windows at the interior. The leather upholstery, formerly white, was dirty gray, veined and cracked with age. Rats had built nests in the seats, and their droppings were everywhere.

It didn't take any special powers to imagine the grisly horror that had taken place in the car. Drew forced herself to look at an ugly rent in the dash. Even after twenty-three years strands of hair still sprang from it. She was glad she was not here alone. She felt nauseated.

"I have to go out for a minute," Drew said. "Could we open that window?"

Pennington and the deputy started for the window at the same time. The deputy was closer. He unlocked it and was banging on it as Drew and Stiggs went out. From outside she heard it slide up.

Stiggs told her she was very pale and advised some deep breaths, and by the time Turnage drove up a few minutes later, she was feeling better.

He was courteous but aloof, asked if it was true that she had left the Ordway house. She said yes, and his reaction was noncommittal.

When they all went into the shed, the door was left open. Between that and the open window, the air was breathable.

Stiggs asked Drew if there was anything they could do to help her.

"No." She began to move around the car, unsure as always of what she was going to do.

Standing beside Turnage, Pennington made a face. "Is that the girl's hair there on the dash?"

Stiggs cleared his throat, gave Pennington a mock frown and shook his head.

Drew walked completely around the car before she stopped at the trunk. "Can I open it?" she asked.

The deputy did it for her. The rubber lining inside the door adhered to the metal, and the deputy had to use force. When the trunk opened, the acid odor of rats filled the room. It was empty except for the spare tire and a Tootsie Roll candy wrapper. Drew stared into it, trying to keep her mind empty.

"There were suitcases in here," she said.

After a respectful silence Turnage cleared his throat. "That being the trunk," he said quietly, "I'd say that's true."

Drew blushed. The deputy wanted to giggle, cut it when Stiggs chastened him with a look.

"I meant that there were suitcases in here the day she died," Drew said.

"Can you tell how many there were?" Stiggs asked.

". . . Three."

"How about the color?" Turnage said.

"All the same . . . Blue, I think."

Stiggs and Turnage exchanged glances, and Stiggs decided to go ahead with a thought he'd had before he left the house that morning.

"Drew, might I prevail upon you to sit in the car?"

She hesitated and he said, "Ah . . . wait." Going to a briefcase he'd left beside the door, he opened it and pulled out a bedsheet. "We'll spread this. But I certainly will understand if you are not of a mind to."

Drew said she'd do it.

After the seat had been draped, Drew got in gingerly, trying not to touch anything. What she saw was hideous: Blackened and dried gore clung to the door on the passenger side, and after one glance, she avoided looking at it. Blood had been spattered on the windshield too. There were smears where it had been carelessly wiped off.

"The top and the windows were down," Drew said.

Stiggs was standing beside Drew, and she got out while he and the deputy struggled to lower the windows and finally got the remains of the top down. Pennington started snapping pictures.

When Drew was in the car again Stiggs closed the door. "You've been studying the evidence, Mark. Maybe you can tell Drew about the victim's last known movements."

"Last anybody saw of her she was driving out through town along Macon," Turnage said. "The end of Macon she and a girlfriend waved to each other. Girl named Theresa. She's the last one saw Betty alive. That was maybe two hours before the body was discovered."

Drew sat with her hands in her lap. "I think she had

241

the radio on," she said. She turned a knob. It clicked. After a long pause she said, "She was on her way to meet somebody."

"Do you know where she was going?" Stiggs said.

Pennington glanced at him and Turnage. She had their full attention. Stiggs was disappointed when she shook her head.

"Do you want me to say anything that comes into my mind?" Drew asked him.

"Go ahead," Stiggs said.

She glanced at Turnage. "Maybe I'm wrong," she said hesitantly, "but I'm getting the feeling that you drove this car that day."

The other three men looked at him. He was scowling. "Little lady," he said, "you are something."

"Is she wrong, Mark?" Stiggs asked.

". . . No. She's not wrong."

Stiggs was visibly shocked. "You did drive the car that day?"

"Damn right I did—like I did all the other Fairchild and Ordway cars—oiled 'em, lubed 'em, repaired 'em. My father owned a garage. I finished repairing this one and test drove it eight o'clock the morning of the day Betty was murdered. My father had died 'bout a week before. It was one of the last cars in the shop. Keep going, Ms. Summers, you're doing fine."

Stiggs accepted the explanation without comment. He was impressed with the girl now.

"You said Betty Fairchild was on her way to meet someone. Do you have any idea who it was?"

"No."

"Was she going to Willow Creek?"

". . . No. No, she wasn't going there. She was— Wait . . . She *was* going to Willow Creek, but first she had to go someplace else."

"Do you know where?"

"I . . . I'm not sure."

Again Chuck Pennington shot a look at Stiggs and Turnage. They were oblivious of everything but Drew.

". . . South Fork," Drew said finally. "She was going to South Fork." She frowned. "Wait a minute—that was the place I mentioned to Mr. Caldecott when I was in his office. I asked him if he ever went to South Fork with Betty Fairchild and he got mad."

Stiggs tried to control his excitement, but they all felt it. "Drew, South Fork takes in a lot of miles. Do you know where she was going in South Fork?"

". . . No. But she did go there. She got there and she waited." Drew was quiet again, then she smiled. "She was really happy. So happy. Happier than she'd ever been in her life. She was just sitting there, waiting for a friend—"

Drew broke off, then after a pause she went on. "She was thinking about somebody. Not the person she was waiting for. Somebody else . . . She thought about the suitcases in the trunk. About . . . She was wonder—"

Drew broke off again, this time as though she'd been surprised. She turned and stared open-mouthed at a point close to Stiggs, who was on her side of the car. The air was suddenly charged with electricity as everyone became aware of what was happening.

She said, "Oh God, Oh God—" and her eyes widened in shock. She said, "No—oh no, please don't. Oh no, please— Oh please, oh—" Her words ended in a shriek as she flung an arm up to ward off a blow. She fell back on the seat then struggled up and tried to get to the passenger door. She barely cleared the steering wheel before she let out a groan of pain and a look of shock appeared on her face. For a moment she didn't move, then she whipped around in the seat, flung an arm up again. Then she began to scream, fending off an unseen attacker, her arms flailing.

Everyone was gaping, too stunned to move as Drew, shrieking in agony, squirmed for the passenger door.

Not until she was cringing against it, her legs drawn up, her shrieks of pain becoming fainter, uglier, did anyone think to act.

"Get her outta there! Lord's sake get her out!" Stiggs yelled to the deputy.

The deputy moved fast. Pulling the door open, in almost one motion he had Drew out and on her feet, then he wrapped her in his arms. She clung to him, still screaming as he assured her she was okay, she was okay.

"Take her out!" Stiggs commanded.

The deputy made his way to the door with her, Stiggs helping him. Turnage followed them out.

Pennington was left alone, his ears still ringing from Drew's shrieks. He didn't move. The sheet had been dragged out of the car along with her, uncovering the grim evidence of the butchery that had taken place. He stared at it, realizing for the first time the full horror of what Betty Fairchild had gone through.

Holy shit, he thought, what a fucking story.

When he walked out Drew was sitting on the bumper of Turnage's car, her head in her hands. Stiggs was comforting her. The men stood to the side quietly.

Pennington stooped down in front of her. "How is it?" he asked.

She took her hands from her face. "I have to go back in there," she said.

"Sure," Pennington said, surprised.

"I mean now." She got up.

"Are you certain you want to do that, Drew?" Stiggs asked her.

"No, I don't want to," she said wearily. "I don't want to at all."

"Then why do it?" Turnage said.

"Because it's what she wants, and I can't take much more of this. Let's get it over with."

Inside, Drew stood as far from the car as she could at

244

first. Then she moved closer—testing the waters, Pennington thought.

"I'm not getting anything," she said finally. Pennington thought she sounded relieved.

"May I ask you some questions, Drew?" Stiggs said. "Sure."

"Are you certain Betty Fairchild was murdered at South Fork?"

"Yes."

"Have you any idea who the murderer was?"

". . . No. But I think it was someone I saw in Lee Caldecott's office that day I went there. Not a real person," she said quickly, "—it was like a vision. He wore coveralls, like a mechanic wears, a wide-brimmed leather hat, sunglasses. He had on gloves and rubbers. He was all covered with blood."

Like a mechanic wears. Pennington glanced at Turnage. No reaction.

"Could this person have been a woman?" Stiggs asked.

"I didn't think of that. It could have been."

"A little while ago you said that Betty was waiting at South Fork for a friend. Do you know who the friend was?"

". . . No. Not for sure."

"Your answer will not be taken for fact, but do you have a feeling about who it was?"

"Yes, Lee Caldecott."

"Do you know why Betty Fairchild would want to meet Mr. Caldecott there?"

"She needed money. She was going to have a baby."

Jackpot! Pennington thought. Go, you beauty.

"Are you certain of that, Drew?" Stiggs asked.

"Yes."

"Why?"

"I just am."

Not unkindly, Stiggs said, "Drew, do you believe Betty Fairchild is communicating these things to you?"

She looked him in the eye. "Yes."

He accepted that. "Can you think of anything else that you believe occurred at South Fork relative to Betty Fairchild?"

Drew shook her head. "Ms. Summers's answer was no," Stiggs said for the tape.

"Wait. There is something else," Drew said. She had gone close to the car, rested a hand on the passenger door. "About Willow Creek. When I was there with Chuck I saw Ed Johnson coming toward the car . . ." She glanced at Stiggs. "You know what I mean by that?"

"Yes. I heard the tape."

"Now I get the feeling Johnson was carrying a cardboard box . . . He got here to the car—the top was up—and he looked through the window." She walked around to the front of the car, hesitated there a moment, then moved past the passenger door to the rear fender. She touched it. "Someone was right here," she said. "He was hiding, watching Johnson. He was the man—the person—in the coveralls. He had a gun. . . . I'm not sure what happened next, but he and Johnson talked. Then another man came over to them. Lee Caldecott."

"Are you quite certain the man was Lee Caldecott?" Stiggs asked.

"I'm positive."

"How about the individual behind the car?"

". . . I don't know."

"Is it the murderer?"

"I think so . . . I'm not clear on the rest of this, but Johnson tossed something to the man behind the car. Then the man hugged him."

"Hugged him?" Stiggs said.

"Yes. After that Johnson opened the trunk. He took a small case out of it and ran off. He ran toward the river. Then he was shot."

246

"You're quite sure about that, Drew . . ."

"I can almost see him. The man who shot him dragged his body to the river. A hunter."

"Have you any idea what the man looked like?" Stiggs asked.

Pennington would have sworn Drew started to look at Turnage, then checked herself.

". . . No," she said.

"Could he have been one of the three people at the car?"

"I don't think so."

"Do you know what happened next?"

"He dragged the body to the water and pulled it a ways."

"How far?" Stiggs said.

"I don't know, but he buried it. That's about all I can tell you."

"If you're facing the river," Stiggs said, "which way did he pull the body?"

"That way." She pointed left.

Stiggs said. "What do you think, Mark?"

Turnage cleared his throat. "If she's right, it tells us why Johnson's body never turned up."

Stiggs nodded.

"Why?" Pennington asked.

Stiggs said, "Well, everybody took it for granted that after Johnson's body was dragged to the water the current carried it downriver. That's where a search was made. But Drew here says that the individual who shot Johnson floated the body *up*river—"

"Then buried it," Pennington said quickly. He looked at Turnage. "Wow, wouldn't that be something if Drew was able to find it?" he said innocently.

"Yeah," Turnage said.

Later, as Pennington drove Drew back to town, Officer Pauley following them in a police cruiser, he asked her if it was really true that she didn't have any idea who'd shot Ed Johnson.

". . . Yes," Drew said.

He didn't believe her. "Turnage didn't look too happy when you came up with what you did."

"I know."

"If he did shoot Johnson and buried the body, he's going to be even less happy about the possibility that it'll be dug up."

"Why?"

"Because the slug that killed Johnson might be there too, and if the weapon is still around . . . Come on, Drew, the truth—he shot Johnson, didn't he?"

"I don't know," she said very quietly. "Off-the-record, I have the feeling he may have. And I mean off-the-record. There's something that's *really* bothering me, though, and I don't like it at all."

"What's that?"

"I feel I'm being used."

"By who?"

"By Betty Fairchild. She's holding back on me, hiding things from me. Why, I don't know. Maybe she's trying to protect somebody."

"Maybe the guy in the leather hat."

"I sure hope not."

When they drove into the parking lot of the hotel, a man who was getting ready to pull out saw Drew. After waiting over an hour for her, he was on his way to see someone he'd just called.

Turning off the ignition, he watched as Drew and the guy she was with got out of the car and headed for the side entrance. Getting out of his own car, he waited until he didn't think Drew would see him, then bore down on her.

At the last minute Drew saw him coming out of the corner of her eye and cringed. He didn't reach her. Before

248

she knew what was happening, Rich Pauley, who had been following her and Pennington, shoved her aside and reached for his revolver.

Almost falling, Drew got her balance in time to see a look of fright on a face that she knew well, and then she was really scared.

"Rich, don't!" she screamed to Pauley, "I know him!"

Jim Hendricks was almost frozen with shock.

"Rich, it's okay," Drew said, still not sure she wasn't seeing things. "Really, it's okay."

Pauley holstered his gun, and then Jim was hugging her, almost gratefully.

"God," he said, "I forgot how beautiful you are."

She was flustered. "Jim, what are you doing here?"

"Here to see you. What are *you* doing down here is the question."

After introductions Pennington took off and she and Jim went into the restaurant.

She couldn't get over seeing him, hardly knew what they were saying to each other until after Jim had ordered drinks. "Why the police guard?" he asked, indicating Pauley, watching her from a spot near the door.

So much had happened, she didn't know where to begin, but she told him as best she could about her resemblance to Betty Fairchild, the revelations she'd made, the antagonism, the violence, and finally her acceptance by Raymond Ordway and his sister.

"Is that *the* Raymond Ordway?" Jim said. "The developer?"

"I think that's what he does."

"Drew, do you know who that guy is?"

". . . He seems like a very nice man."

"A very nice man? Jesus Christ, he's the South's answer to Donald Trump," Jim said. "And you look like his dead niece?"

"Yes."

He started asking questions about Ordway and his

sister, and when he kept it up the thought struck Drew that he was more interested in them than he was in her.

As if he realized it himself, he said: "You've really been through it, haven't you?"

"Kind of."

"Why are you even staying down here after all that? Why don't you just leave?"

". . . I can't."

"What do you mean you can't?"

"I tried. I can't."

"The police?"

"No, it's nothing like that, but it'll just sound stupid right now."

"You're coming back to New York with me."

"When do we leave?" she said lightly.

He put his hand on hers. "I mean it."

She'd left her drink untouched. He asked her if she wanted it, and when she said no he signaled for the check. "Come on, I'll take you to your room."

"I wish you wouldn't, Jim."

"What's the matter?"

"I want to be by myself for a while," she said. "I can't think right now. I can't do anything."

"Oh." He was disappointed.

"I'm glad to see you, I really am, but try to understand. I've just gone through so much. How did you even know I was here? From Corey?"

"No. I got a call from somebody. A guy. I don't know who. He just called and told me you were here, even told me what hotel. So here I am."

"He didn't give his name?"

"No."

"Why didn't you call me and let me know you were coming?"

"Wanted to surprise you." He put some money on the table, saw the cop get up when they did. "I'll take you to the door," Jim said.

250

"No you won't," Drew said. "I know you."

He smiled. "Cold shower time. Couple of hours enough?"

"Sure."

"I love you," he said. He gave her a kiss on the cheek and watched her to the elevator.

Then he went to call Lee Caldecott and say he'd been held up but was on his way.

14

Caldecott thought it was taking annoyingly long for Hendricks to accept the obvious: that Betty Fairchild was the cause of Drew's strange behavior. At first he had completely refused to believe it, but after a while the preponderance of the evidence began to get to him: the blackouts, Drew's compulsion to come down here, her finding the diary, her remarkable resemblance to Betty, and the highly personal things she knew about people which only Betty would have known.

"Look," Caldecott said finally, impatient to get down to business, "the only alternative is that she's pretending. She's your girl. You know her a hell of a lot better than I or anyone else. Do *you* think she's pretending?"

Hendricks's head shake was automatic. "No. But are you *sure* about everything you've told me?" Caldecott stared at him stonily, and he shrugged. "Well, I'll tell you this. As hard to believe as it is, I'm sure glad it's not what I thought."

"Then let's get down to business," Caldecott said. "Can you convince Drew to go on home with you if I make it worth your while?"

"That's why I agreed to come down here."

Caldecott started out by appealing to Hendricks's feelings, telling him about the close call the girl had had with GG and the dangers she might still face. Hendricks stayed cool, waiting, and Caldecott realized he'd better get to the bottom line.

He was about to make an offer when his secretary told him that Raymond was on the line, the last person he wanted to talk to right now.

"I asked you to hold all calls," he said.

"Mr. Ordway said it's an emergency, sir."

He picked up the phone, pretended concern. "Raymond. Is anything wrong?"

"You'd better drive down here to my office, Lee. We have to talk."

"I'm tied up at the moment. Can it wait?"

"Afraid not."

Caldecott cursed silently. "How about in a couple of hours?"

"Be here in thirty-five minutes—and bring Hendricks with you."

While he was waiting for them, Raymond Ordway sat thinking how interesting it was that up to now he'd only remembered Betty's tenderness and affection. She hadn't been that way all the time, though. Sometimes she'd been downright unfeeling—a bitch of the first order—when she had a mind. Gave him trouble. Like the first time she'd up and announced to him that she wasn't going to let him do it to her anymore. He found out pretty quick what the trouble was: She'd gotten too interested in some boy, an eighteen-year-old. Had a crush on him.

He tried to tell her the boy was too old for her, that all he wanted was to use her and brag about it to his friends. She insisted she wasn't doing anything with him, but Ordway felt she was lying.

He was convinced of it when he got her in her room one afternoon and she started screaming and fighting him, fought him so hard it brought that nigger bitch Arletta knocking at the door. He accused her of putting out for the boy, and she cried and got hysterical and said she wasn't. He didn't believe her, he said, made her swear on the bible and on her mother and father's life.

After that she was impossible, never came home unless Harriet was there, and kept her door locked. He wasn't worried at first because she'd acted like that before, cried and told him she didn't want to do it, but he'd always gotten into her finally, or at least got *something*. That time she wouldn't even give him a hand job and it made him boil: He'd given her everything he could think of, never refused her anything, and there she was denying him and getting him upset because of some kid who just wanted to stick it into her. He tried to be patient, figuring she'd come around, but he knew she was seeing that boy, and no matter what she said, he couldn't believe she wasn't doing anything.

He had to smile when he thought about it now. He'd brought her around finally: Gave her a Persian kitten and told her he still loved her and that he understood how she felt. She was so surprised and happy she hugged him and told him she loved him. That was nice. He'd almost felt sorry he had to teach her a lesson.

Just as he figured, she let down her guard, and one night when Harriet was out Ordway had her bring the kitten out into the garage so he could show her something he'd bought for it. What he'd bought was a pair of heavy work gloves and a meat cleaver, and right in front of her he chopped the kitten into three pieces. When he finished he said that if she didn't start acting nicer to him that's what he was going to do to her and her mother and father while they were all asleep.

She didn't give him trouble for a long time after that.

He tried to think how old she was then. Fourteen maybe. Yes, she was, because it happened a month or two before she cut her wrists, and he recalled telling them in the emergency room that she'd just turned fifteen.

He started thinking about Drew, remembering how he'd felt the night he'd knocked at her door. Was all he could do not to pull that robe off her and get her up on that bed. He was imagining doing it when his reverie was interrupted by his secretary: The two men had arrived.

He glanced at the clock on his desk: forty minutes. Not bad. He told his secretary to send Lee in and have Hendricks wait.

He was leafing through a financial proposal as Lee walked in. "Lee," he said pleasantly, "how goes it?"

"Fine," Lee answered. He was on his guard, which Ordway did not want. He had to make some things clear to the man and he wanted him receptive.

"What made you bring Hendricks down here?" he asked. He kept his tone pleasant, flipped a couple of pages and finally dropped the proposal on his desk.

"I thought that if anybody could get her to leave, he could. How did you know he was here?"

"You'd be surprised at what I know. Drew moved out of my house today. Did she know Hendricks was coming?"

"No."

"You should have mentioned to me you were going to do something like that," Ordway said. He swiveled around in his chair, looked out the window. "I want Drew Summers to stay in Greenview, Lee."

"Raymond, the girl is making life miserable for me. She'll do the same thing to you."

"She hasn't so far, has she?"

"When she was in my office that night, she said she saw someone in bloody coveralls."

"Did she say who it was?"

"No, but—"

Ordway turned, waved a hand to dismiss it. "What was she doing in your office?"

Caldecott explained how and why he had invited her, and Ordway questioned him closely for details. When he finished, Ordway said, "You were too rough with her."

"I lost my temper."

"Did you check her for a wire?"

"A what?"

"A listening device."

"No I didn't."

"After what you said and did to her, you should have. I did when I brought her home from the police station—everywhere but her crotch. She was clean."

"That kind of thing wouldn't occur to me."

"I have this room swept every few days to make sure it's not bugged, have the phone lines checked too. Cousin Wendell taught me that. I do the same at home."

"What for?"

"Easiest thing in the world to eavesdrop electronically, Lee. I like to learn personal things about people—it's helpful—but I don't want them learning about me. I told you you'd be surprised at what I know. Take Juleen's stealing, for instance. Got her arrested for shoplifting in New York once, didn't it?" He smiled. "I got a kick out of it when you asked her one night what I'd think if I knew about it. Laughed, didn't she? 'Raymond?' she said. 'He's the one person in Greenview who couldn't care less.' She was right."

Caldecott gaped. "You have my house bugged?"

"Not for years now. I know all about you I want to know. Read this." He offered Caldecott a page.

"Just tell me what it is."

"Good detective work. The girl had some gas station receipts in her purse. I got copies of them, never mind how. One was particularly interesting, and my investigative people checked it out. They interviewed an attendant, a kid who remembered her. Listen to this." Ordway read aloud from the page. "Question: 'What makes you remember the girl so well?' Answer: 'I remember how she signed the wrong name there.' Question: 'Any other reason?' Answer: 'Well, she was nice. And beautiful.' Question: 'I'm sure you see a lot of nice beautiful girls. Why do you remember this one so well?' 'She acted kind of funny.' 'In what way?' 'Well, she pulled up to the

256

self-serve and then she just sat there until I went over and told her I could only serve her at the full-serve. She didn't even know what that was.'"

"Raymond, what's the point?" Caldecott asked him.

"The point is that Betty wouldn't have any idea what full-serve and self-serve are. Look at these." Ordway shoved copies of two receipts at Caldecott. "This one has Betty's name crossed out and Drew's name signed over it. This one is signed with Drew's name."

"Yes . . . ?"

"*All the signatures are in Betty's handwriting.* You were right—Betty is inside that girl."

"Thanks. It doesn't make me feel any better."

"Lee, what the hell is the matter with you? Why do you think the girl went to the Johnson house?"

"You tell me."

"Because Betty is going after the people who were *really* responsible for her death."

"She's also going after me, Raymond."

Ordway was silent, then he said, "Lee, did you fire those shots night before last? We know each other too long to fool around. Just tell me." Caldecott murmured an assent, and Ordway said, "You took a big chance."

"I was very careful," Caldecott said, going to a cabinet. "I got out the rear of the building fast." He found the vodka, but no glasses.

"I moved them," Ordway said. Getting up, he went to another cabinet and found an old-fashioned glass, took the bottle from Lee. "What kind of a deal did you make with Jim Hendricks?" he asked.

"I haven't made one yet. Why don't we bring him in?"

"In a minute. Does he know you want him to take Drew home?" He finished pouring and put the bottle down.

"He knows I didn't fly him down here to talk about his love life."

Caldecott reached for the drink, and the next thing

he knew his face was wet, his eyes blinded and stinging. It was only the beginning of his bewilderment and pain. His tie was grabbed and he was jerked across the room like a puppet, then spun around and shoved backward. He braced himself to hit the floor, but a couch broke his fall and he lay half on it, his heels on the carpet.

Ordway got between his legs and pushed a knee into his stomach. He tried to scream, but Ordway had grabbed his throat and all that came out was a strangled sob. His head was crammed between the cushions, and the pain in his stomach was so awful he was afraid he was ruptured.

He found Ordway's chin, lodged the heel of his hand under it and tried to push, but Ordway easily pried the hand free. At the same time he tightened his grip on Caldecott's throat. His strength was frightening.

Caldecott's eyes were still on fire and he saw only a black hole above him where Ordway's mouth was.

"You have to understand something, you sodden piece of shit," the hole said. "First, if that girl had been hurt bad or killed you would not be alive right now. You understand me?"

Caldecott managed a sound, and Ordway shoved his knee in deeper. The pain was excruciating. Tears welled from Caldecott's closed eyes, streamed into his ears.

"Second, you don't ever do anything regarding Drew Summers unless you talk with me first. I want her to stay in Greenview, and if you ever lay a finger on her again or try to get her out, I'll gouge your fucking eyes out. Is *that* clear?"

Caldecott gasped a yes and the pressure of the knee finally eased, but Ordway remained over him, clutching his throat. "Do you know why Betty's come after you?" he said. "Do you? She told you, didn't she, but you didn't understand. You betrayed her, Lee."

Caldecott tried to pry Ordway's fingers free. "Raym—"

258

"Oh, not 'cause you got her to go out there to South Fork," Raymond said, his grip still strong, "but 'cause you knew what was going on between her and the nigger and you never told me until it was too late. *Y'all* knew—all you kids, didn't you? Y'all betrayed her."

Caldecott was able to see Ordway's eyes now. There was no feeling in them, only the calculated coldness of a predator, something that couldn't see past its own hunger. "*I* betrayed her?" Caldecott croaked. "Raymond—for God's sake, *don't you remember what you did!*"

The eyes came closer. "I'm going to ask you a question. You be careful how you answer." He spoke slowly. "Do you think I ever, *ever* had anything but Betty's best interests in mind?"

The question made him feel as if the man's fingers were slipping into his brain, manipulating him. He told him what he wanted to hear. ". . . No."

"You think I ever did anything but it was for Betty's own good?"

"No."

"You know it," Ordway said. "And Betty knows it too." His grip loosened and he helped Caldecott up, nudged him toward the bathroom. "Tidy yourself up."

Ordway heard him start to cry before the door closed behind him, shook his head in contempt.

Don't you remember what you did?

He remembered well, and he'd do the same thing today. Lee was still a little boy, tippy-toeing around, as afraid to face facts as the day he'd finally told Ordway about Betty and Ed Johnson. Even then he wouldn't come right out and just say it. No. He had to start by saying Betty had asked him to lend her a thousand dollars and he wasn't sure he should. Ordway had almost laughed. *A thousand dollars? Boy, whut the hell for?*

Ordway'd had to pull it out of him that Betty was going to run off with Johnson, and it cut the ground from under him. Worst blow he'd ever received in his life. He'd been good to that girl, trusted her, loved her, and she'd lied to him. *Lied* to him. Not only did she go sneaking around corners, but she went and did it with a . . . And there was something even worse.

She's gonna have a baby, Lee said.

That had done it. Made him cold. Cold. He went right home and sure enough, one of the suitcases in Betty's closet was already half packed. He found her bank book. She'd withdrawn all but five dollars.

Right then he knew he was going to do something drastic. Had to. He questioned Lee, found out that Betty and the nigger planned to leave in two days from Willow Creek. Three o'clock in the afternoon. *You tell her you'll give her the money*, he told Lee. *Draw it out of the bank. I'll give it back to you, but don't you tell her you told me and don't you mention this to anyone. ANYONE.*

Two days later he was ready, told Lee to call Betty and say he'd meet her at South Fork. At the old mill picnic grounds. One-thirty. By the five oaks. He'd give her the money there. *And you tell her not to say a word to anybody, hear? Not a word.*

But he didn't give Lee any money. And Lee wasn't going to South Fork either, Ordway told him. He was going to Willow Creek, and Ordway would meet him there at 2:15.

Thinking about it now, he remembered that day perfectly. Hazy and warm, hardly a car on the road. Didn't see a one that he recognized. He got to South Fork over a half hour before Betty was due to meet Lee there, parked his car way beyond the five oaks, where she wouldn't see it. Wasn't a soul around, probably not a soul for miles.

He opened the trunk, stripped naked, and began to put on the longjohns and the other things he had in the canvas bag.

Inside of a few minutes he was pulling on the rubbers over his shoes. Then he carefully folded his clothes and put them in the bag. After that, hatchet in one hand and canvas bag in the other, he went deeper into the woods, circling around toward the five oaks so she wouldn't see him if she showed up early.

He could have saved himself the trouble. She'd never been early in her life. He unbuttoned the coveralls and the longjohns down to his waist, did some push-ups and some running in place to stay limber.

When she finally drove up—fifteen minutes late, damn her—she parked just about where he figured she would, the back of the car to him. He was sweating, but he was glad it was warm out: The top of the Mustang was down. Easy to get at her. She turned the engine off and left the radio on.

He buttoned up, put on his sunglasses and gloves, took the wide-brimmed leather hat from the branch it hung on. Then he eased out the razor-sharp hatchet from where he'd embedded it in the tree.

He wasn't nervous. He had no feelings. What she'd done with Johnson was so disgusting it had taken all his feelings away. He'd had more feeling about chopping up her kitten. Now he was just getting rid of garbage.

He made his way carefully to the edge of the woods, where he put down the canvas bag, then started for the car. She was so involved in listening to her stupid rock 'n' roll she didn't even know he was there until he was right alongside her.

When that blond head turned around and those blue eyes saw him she got so scared he almost giggled.

It cost him. He wanted to split her head with the first chop, but she threw an arm up and the hatchet cut into it. She started to scream and dived for the passenger door, but he stopped her with a good one on her hipbone, whipped open the door and was on her. He thought of punching and kicking her, but he kept using the hatchet. She twisted around, got a knee up, and he split it open, but then she went berserk. He didn't realize she'd fight so hard and he started hitting the dash and the seat as much as her.

He tried to get a grip on her for a solid crack at her skull, but she was spurting so much blood she was too slippery. Then she kicked him in the chest and that made him furious. If it'd been in the face he'd have trouble explaining it. He went crazy—split her forehead open and kept chopping long after she was dead. When he got his mind back, what was left of her was splayed like a gutted chicken and was sliding down to the floor.

He tried to keep her on the seat so he could shove her down under the dash neatly, but she was too slippery and he didn't have the strength. He let her slide down. She was well below the window anyway, so it was fine.

It was almost two when he started the Mustang. Late. He was about to pull out when he got a jolt of fright: the canvas bag. He ran back for it, then drove the half mile over to Willow Creek with the top and the windows up. The smell was godawful, but he didn't want anybody seeing in.

He didn't pass but one car and that had an out-of-state plate.

Like he expected, Lee was waiting by his own car when he drove up. He got out and left the door open, and Lee took one look at him and what was inside the car and went gray. He stumbled back and heaved his lunch.

When he was done he just stood there taking in gulps of air and quaking, trying not to look at Ordway or the Mustang. Ordway told him to pull himself together, put it to him straight. "You know who did that?" he said. "Ed Johnson. Listen to me, Lee. You

262

see what's going on in this town. You see all them niggers pushing in where they're not wanted, crowding into Jepson's, into Sears, into the five 'n' dime, taking what don't belong to them. They want to dirty us, Lee, take what belongs to us and mongrelize us all. Well, there's a way we can stop it, a way to set the whole goddamn bunch of 'em back by showing this whole town, this whole state, what they'll do when they get the chance. Goddamnit, Lee, you hear what I'm saying?"

Lee nodded weakly and Ordway said, "Then listen . . . I'm telling you Ed Johnson did that as soon as he laid his black hands on her. He wanted her and she didn't know any better, so she let him mislead her and dirty her. Then he killed her."

He took out the revolver he'd brought and asked if Lee was with him or not. If he was they'd wait together for Johnson to show up. But he didn't want Lee lying to him and then going back on his word, 'cause if Lee did, by God, he'd find a way to chop him up too.

"Raymond this is terrible, this is awful," Lee said. He said it three or four times.

But in the end he came around.

"I got your word?" Raymond asked him.

Lee said yes, and Raymond told him what they were going to do.

And Lee came through for him, Ordway thought. Not that he'd had that much to do. Mainly what Ordway had needed was for Lee to drive him back to his car. He'd been good with the police, though—told them exactly what he was supposed to, and that had helped a lot. He'd been loyal.

When Lee came out of the bathroom, Ordway poured a drink and offered it to him. He grinned when Lee hesitated before he took it.

"Let's talk about this fellow," Ordway said, motioning to the door. "How much you think it will take to get him out of here?"

After they discussed it and Hendricks was ushered in, Caldecott watched what followed with fascination.

Raymond did not smile during the briefest of handshakes and greeted Hendricks's admiration for the harbor view with cold silence. Then he let Hendricks struggle to make conversation for a couple of minutes before he got to it.

"Is it your intention to bring Drew back to New York?"

"Yes. Mr. Caldecott and I talked about that over the phone. That's why I came down here."

"That's too bad," Ordway said. "Mr. Caldecott has changed his mind. Like my sister and me, he wants her to stay."

Hendricks's face fell as fast as the Dow Jones on Black Thursday. He turned to Caldecott.

"Is that right?"

"I'm afraid so," Caldecott said.

"I assume you have seen Drew already," Ordway said. "Did she tell you about her resemblance to my dead niece?"

"Yes, she did. It's remark—"

"My sister and I are convinced that her problem is far beyond being mental, and that if she returns to New York it will worsen."

He let that sink in, then he said, "You're an associate with Carson and Ellerbee."

"That's right—mergers and acquisitions."

"Are you aware that I own the Chapman Woolen Mills?"

"No, sir, I am not."

"I do, and I'm thinking of getting rid of them." He let that sink in also, and Caldecott shifted uncomfortably in

264

his seat. Business was one thing, but they were dealing with the man's fiancée here.

Hendricks was silent. So was Raymond. Caldecott took a quiet sip of his drink and crossed his legs. Hendricks cleared his throat.

"Okay, where do we go from here?"

It was as simple as that.

During the business discussion that followed, Caldecott felt that he was back twenty-five years. At that time Raymond was well-known for the talks he'd given to boys to keep them away from Betty. This talk was on a different level, but the purpose was the same and the conclusion exactly what Raymond wanted: Hendricks agreed to leave town immediately.

Ordway got up, and this time the handshake he gave Hendricks was as solid and impersonal as the deal they'd made. "Mr. Caldecott will drive you back to Greenview," he said, and as soon as both men were gone he called Drew's hotel.

She picked up on the first ring—probably thinking it was her boyfriend, Ordway thought. "Just calling to find out how you are," he said. "I'm concerned about you."

"You don't have to be anymore, Ray. Somebody just got here who's going to keep an eye on me."

"What's his name?"

"Jim. How'd you know it was a he?"

"By the sound of your voice. I'd like to meet him, so you make sure you invite him to the party."

She didn't answer and Ordway said, "You there?"

". . . Yes."

"Something the matter?"

". . . I don't know," Drew said. "I just had the strangest impulse . . ."

"What is that?"

"To say, 'I'll be coming home soon.' Isn't that weird . . . ?"

Ordway felt a tug. They talked about what it could

mean, and although he thought he knew, he offered no suggestions. Finally Drew said she wanted to get off the line in case Jim was trying to call her.

He hung up, elated. He'd been right, goddamnit, he'd been right. Betty was coming back to him. She'd loved him then and she loved him now, and she was coming home. To him. He knew it.

The note was waiting for her at the desk.

Drew—I decided to go back to New York. I hope everything turns out all right for you. We'll be in touch. Good luck. Jim.

She read it over, thinking she'd missed something, then she read it again. *We'll be in touch. Good luck.* Nothing else. No *Love*, or *I'll call you later.*

Had she been that distant, made him feel that he wasn't wanted? She had to admit to herself that even after she'd gotten over the shock of seeing him in the parking lot, she'd still felt uncomfortable, hadn't known what to say. But that was because she hadn't seen him in over two weeks. He hadn't come to see her at the hospital, and then suddenly he showed up here. It had happened too fast and she hadn't known what to do.

Now he was gone. But then why had he come all the way down here to see her in the first place? It had to mean he cared for her . . . A thought struck her—the thought that someone—Caldecott—had asked him to come down here. . . . No. She didn't want to think that. She didn't like herself for thinking it. But then she heard herself asking Jim if he'd known from Corey that she was here. *No. I got a call from somebody . . . I don't know who . . .*

She tried to blot out the whole idea. She'd rather think that it was her fault he'd left, something she did, and that deep down he still cared for her as much as he ever had. Because not until this moment did she realize what a lift his being here had given her.

Now she felt abandoned, and suddenly more alone than ever.

In his bedroom that evening Raymond Ordway made certain that his door was locked before he went to the bureau and opened a drawer. Taking the clothes from it, he lifted the false bottom and removed two folders of photos that lay side by side. He hadn't looked at them in a long time because they'd lost their ability to excite him. Occasionally he'd thought of destroying them, but he was glad now that he hadn't. They were alive for him again, as alive as Drew.

Most of them were of Betty when she was past fourteen, but one was taken when she was eleven. He was sitting on her bed naked while she, also naked, was on the floor between his legs, looking up at him adoringly and cuddling his stiff "dolly" against her cheek.

The photo didn't excite him. He wasn't having real sex with her at that point. He'd only kept it because of how sweet she was then. With that face and those budding tits, she looked like an angel.

She'd been something, his Betty. All charged up with sex even when she was ten. He could tell. All she needed was a fuss made over her.

He went slow with her. Made it fun. She had dolls to play with, but none so fascinating as the one he told her he had hidden in his lap. He taught her that it was a lollipop too. He was careful with her, didn't break her cherry until she was close to thirteen.

There were a couple of years there when he did everything with her: He'd bend her over the sink in the bathroom and watch himself in the mirror, or get her in the car, or in warm weather lay her down in the high grass at Carlton Meadows. Even had her in the kitchen a couple of times while Harriet and her husband were at church.

Then she changed, didn't enjoy it anymore. She'd lie back while he did it to her, tears in her eyes, those gorgeous hooters jiggling, and she'd pretend she wasn't feeling anything, but *he* knew. She didn't make a sound, but he could feel her coming. She wouldn't put her arms or her legs around him, wouldn't look at him. She'd just lie there and let him do it to her.

He was sitting on his bed looking at the photos and he thought about Drew in her bathrobe, nothing on underneath. He thought about having her under him, helpless with passion. It was going to happen. Soon. Here in this house.

Betty was coming back to him the night of the party.

Jim didn't get home until after ten, and there were four messages on his machine. His mother and a buddy had called. Drew was the third.

"Hi, Jim—'bye, Jim. Hey, what happened to you—me? I really was glad to see you. I'm sorry if maybe I didn't act like it, but I'm kinda fragmented right now. There's just too much going on. I'm hoping I'll be back in a few days and we can get together." She didn't say anything for a few moments, then before she hung up she said, "I miss you."

He thought about what he'd done. He'd been a shit. On the other hand, Ordway obviously was taken with Drew and she could end up with big bucks. He listened to the last message then went into the bathroom, pointed a finger at himself in the mirror. "Are you aware, buddy, that in three or four months from now you are going to have an income of four hundred K a year?"

"Yeah," he answered, smiling.

15

The evening of the party, Drew had trouble getting past the gate. First the guard asked for her invitation and then her ID. Finally, followed by one of Turnage's cruisers, she was allowed to drive through.

When she reached the house, it literally took her breath away: Every balcony, every staircase and balustrade was festooned or garlanded with flowers. The whole house looked as though it was in bloom.

A parking attendant took her car, and when she got to the door she wondered if she had been the first to arrive: The house was silent.

But when the door opened and she stepped into the entry hall, she was stunned. It was so filled with people that her first reaction was to back out—until some of them made way, and there was Raymond Ordway and his sister standing before a massive antique pendulum clock.

He beckoned to her, and as he did, she realized why the guard at the gate had delayed her.

"Come in, Drew," Ordway said. "We've all been waiting for you." He was beaming, aware of the whispers and murmurs, and the heads that craned to see the portrait in the hallway ceiling.

The glass door of the clock was open, the pendulum motionless. Glancing at his watch, Ordway reached up and moved the minute hand to the correct time.

"Over twenty-three years ago I stopped this clock," he said when Drew was beside him, "and it's been silent ever since. It won't be silent any longer."

He started the pendulum swinging, glanced at his sister as the slow, measured tick of the clock began.

Her eyes filling, Mrs. Fairchild moved to Drew with open arms. "Welcome *back*, my child," she said.

Drew heard sighs and murmurs from the admiring throng as Mrs. Fairchild hugged her, and she forced herself to smile. But suddenly she was afraid, frightened by an image of being confronted and caught by Betty Fairchild's murderer, just as she was now caught in Harriet Fairchild's fervent embrace.

Then Harriet released her, the image was gone, and Drew was in control of herself again. A band began to play somewhere and Raymond Ordway, claiming the first dance with her, slipped his arm around her waist and led her off.

A while after the party had started, Chuck Pennington surveyed the ballroom and figured there had to be a hundred people in it, probably four hundred more crawling all over the house.

Spotting Ordway, he was about to go over to him when he saw Mrs. Fairchild talking to a servant in bell-bottoms and leather vest. He got to her just as she was turning away, and she smiled at him blankly.

"Ah, yes," she said after he told her his name. "Mr. Pennington . . . How do you like our little affair?"

"*C'est magnifique,* as my Russian father used to say." He knew what he said had gone by her, but he was impressed. The flowers everywhere were what got to him: camellias, pink roses, and magnolias. Even the railings were garlanded. He asked her if it was part of the sixties motif. "You know, the Flower Children," he said when she gave him another blank look.

"Why no," she said, "but how astute of you to think of it."

How come she always says the right thing, Pennington thought, and I always get the feeling she's saying lines? He asked her for some statistics about the party, took some notes, then asked how it felt having Drew here.

"Oh, I couldn't possibly describe it. If I try, I shall begin to cry and you will think I am unhappy."

"I bet you can't spend enough time with her."

"Unfortunately I have not had time to do anything but tend to this mammoth whatchamacallit."

"Well, you did a great job," Pennington said as she excused herself and went off. He looked for Ordway again, but didn't see him.

He glanced at the slides of late sixties *Sentinel* pages being projected on a screen: CHINESE REDS REPULSE CHARGE BY MARINE BATTALIONS IN SAIGON. DOGS A PROBLEM IN GREENVIEW; SHOT IN THE STREETS. CARY GRANT MAKES GETAWAY IN BEVERLY HILLS; ARRIVES IN LONDON TO MEET HIS MOTHER. Television schedule: *T.H.E. Cat. The Avengers. Rawhide. Combat* . . .

Way on the opposite side of the room, *Woodstock* was playing on another screen, acres of kids listening rapt to a folk-rock group. The sound was off, while the dance band Ordway had hired—pretty good too—was playing the Beatles' "Something."

He wondered if any of the dancers had ever been to Woodstock or if they'd ever worn what they did tonight: Indian bedspreads and ponchos, bib overalls and tie-dyed slacks. Not many in the A crowd, he thought—the physicians and the corporation lawyers, the big property owners and the ones with family money.

A few of the women had ironed their hair, and the black lights in the chandeliers helped the mood, but this was not a crowd for sandals and beads. Correction: Juleen Caldecott looked like the real thing, and he made a note of the burgundy miniskirt, the hand-embroidered

271

blouse and the floppy burgundy felt hat. Good-looking woman, that one.

She was talking to Drew, who was wearing the party dress she'd shown up in at the charity gamble. Drew was probably the only one here who couldn't remember the sixties, he thought, and she looked like she belonged in them more than anybody else.

He started writing in his head: "The Flower Children were in their forties and fifties now. They'd become the Establishment, and if any of them had once been radicals, they were now the very people they'd viewed with suspicion. They'd been part of a revolution that was only a quaint memory: Affirmative action was now indifference, hippies and yippies had become yuppies, and the Sexual Revolution had ended in AIDS. Drew was the only one among them who had remained the same. She was like a symbol—a lovely reminder—of all the hope and expectation of the sixties."

He liked it, took notes so he wouldn't forget it. It would go in the book.

"How does it feel to be the center of so much attention?" Juleen was asking Drew.

"I'm not sure," Drew said. "People keep coming up to me and asking if I know who they are."

"Mary Ann told me you knew her—Mary Ann Stokes."

"Not really. Her name just came to me."

"She told me you knew she was in the Junior Debs with me and Betty in high school. I have to tell you it's very spooky," Juleen said. "I keep thinking you're Betty, and I have to stop myself from asking you where you've been and what you've been doing."

After some more friendly conversation, Juleen felt comfortable enough to bring up what she really wanted to talk about. "Drew," she said, "I was hoping—"

She interrupted herself when the reporter joined them, a big smile on his face. "Chuck," she said quickly,

272

"I wonder if you would mind letting me talk privately with Drew for a little bitty minute." His face fell, he said sure, and walked off.

"I didn't want to do that, but I was hoping you and I could talk about the charges you've brought against Lee . . . He knows he overreacted and he wondered if there was a way he could make it up to you."

"He could spend some time in jail."

"You don't mean that."

"Did he tell you what happened?"

"He said y'all had some words."

"*He* had the words. He started off by threatening to break my fucking jaw—I'm quoting him—and he finished by saying that if I didn't get out of town, he was going to have me raped and beaten and thrown in a garbage bin. In between he got physically rough."

"That doesn't sound like Lee at all," Juleen said. "Do you think that maybe, looking like Betty as you do, you could have said something that antagonized him?"

"Whatever I said there was no excuse for what he did. It was cowardly."

"I am surprised to hear that, Drew. Truly. Lee never did anything like that before."

"Well he did it with me and—"

She broke off in mid-sentence, and Juleen, prepared to argue, waited for her to go on. Instead Drew gave her a brief smile, one Juleen thought she recognized. It was momentarily disconcerting, then it was gone.

"Do you mind if I ask you something?" Drew said.

". . . Why, no."

"Did you know Ed Johnson well?"

Juleen shrugged. "Only to see him in school, or around town."

"Strange," Drew said. "I just got this picture of the two of you alone. In back of a store, I think. By some shelves. You were touching his shoulder—"

"How dare you," Juleen cut in.

Beet-red with fury, she made sure no one was close enough to hear her before she said, "I am warning you—if you ever say another word to me, or to anyone else *about* me, *I'll* break your little fucking jaw."

She started to turn away.

"Hold it, Bigfoot," Drew said. "Here's that other word for you—I'm sick of being pushed around by you and everybody else in this town. I took your husband's crap because I had to, but I don't have to take yours. You want to break my jaw, lady? Try it and I mean right now!"

Trembling, Juleen seemed to debate it, then she turned and strode off.

Drew stared after her feeling great, better than she had all evening—the best, in fact, since she'd hit this town. Juleen was headed in Raymond Ordway's direction, she saw. Giving Ordway a wave, Drew headed for the bar again.

Ordway watched her go, the room suddenly empty for him. He'd inhaled her freshness during that first dance and hadn't been able to take his eyes from her since. Those moist lips, that youthful ripeness, and that delicious ass made all the other women look dry as dust. Alongside of her even Juleen, whom he'd occasionally had a yen for, looked matronly.

"Whatever you two were talking about," he said when she reached him, "you didn't enjoy it, did you?"

"I was trying to talk to her about the charges she's bringing against Lee."

"And?"

"I know how fond of her you are, so I will not say anything further."

"Go ahead." He took a sip of his wine.

"She can be a very nasty young lady."

As nasty as Betty could be was what he felt she wanted to say. Interesting, because for the past hour he felt that Drew had been acting more and more like Betty, same mannerisms, same way of holding herself.

274

"How does it make you feel, having her in the house again?" a voice beside them inquired. The reporter.

Juleen walked away. Ordway gave him a statement, then asked him how Drew had felt about her boyfriend leaving. Pennington said she'd been upset.

Ordway noticed that Drew was gone and excused himself.

She was at the bar, just getting a drink. Her fourth or fifth, if he was correct. She was talking with someone and he watched the way she held her head, the way she gestured. Betty, all right. She even kept looking down at her tits every so often in that self-conscious way Betty used to. He'd had a lot of wine, but he wasn't imagining it. Betty was inside that girl and she'd come back here for him. Drew wasn't aware of it, but he was.

When she left the bar she went to the bathroom. Going in after she came out, he inhaled the scents of her body and her perfume, even the faint smell of her pee.

He thought of Betty's Sweet Sixteen party. She'd been gorgeous, and he'd wanted her so bad he'd shoved his way into the bathroom with her before she could lock the door. Made him smile now to think of how mad she'd been. She tried to push him out, but he said he needed her to do him real bad or it would ruin the whole party for him. She'd gritted her teeth and said it was gonna ruin it for her if she did, but he made her feel how hard he was and he raised his voice and that scared her. Ray, she said, be quiet, somebody's gonna hear.

He said he didn't care, told her she knew how nervous and high-strung he got when he felt like this. Now, come on, baby, come on . . .

She took his handkerchief, and even mad she knew how to touch him and hold him. After he came, she sat down on the toilet and started crying, said she felt like a slut. Just thinking about it now got him all excited . . . But then someone knocked at the door and he calmed down and went out to look for Drew.

He wanted that girl. Wanted her wanted her wanted her.

Lee Caldecott waited for Drew to walk away from the bar before he went to it. So far he'd made sure he kept his distance from her: He wasn't going to let her do another number on him in front of people.

He found Turnage leaning on the player piano in the men's smoking room. He had on bell-bottoms and a T-shirt, about on a par with the way he dressed anyway, Caldecott thought.

"Long way from Backlick Road, isn't it?" he said.

"What's that mean?" Turnage said, knowing damn well what it meant: rusted sinks and pull-chain toilets.

"Nothing at all," Caldecott said. "Forget it." He should have known better. Besides having no class, Turnage had no sense of humor. He wished he knew how to deal with the guy. Turnage was nothing, always had been, yet for some reason, as far back as high school, Caldecott could not get respect from him.

Maybe because of Betty. Everybody knew Turnage had been in love with her, but if he was mad because Caldecott got her, he could have saved his resentment. Betty would never have had anything to do with Turnage anyway. He was coarse and had about as much taste as a . . . as a cop.

"How are the wife and kids?" he asked, not really interested.

"Fine," Turnage said.

"Your wife still up in Chapel Hill?"

"Yeah."

Caldecott couldn't remember her name for the moment, but he'd heard that she and Turnage had been separated a while. He'd dated her a couple of times when he and Juleen had been separated. She'd been a cocktail waitress at the Spengler then. Years and years ago. Sharon, that was her name. Good-looking—skinny with big tits—but he decided it wasn't worth the work to get her into bed. When he heard she married Turnage he knew he'd been right.

"What do you think is going to happen with these stupid charges this kid has brought against me?" Caldecott said.

"Be dismissed. Lack of evidence."

"That's what my lawyer said. But I want a public apology from her."

Turnage gave him a look of pained tolerance.

"Why not? The girl has been harassing me."

"She's not done with you yet either. She maintains she saw Betty's murderer when she was in your office. Add that to the stuff she's come out with about you being at Willow Creek before Ed, and him and Betty being in love, and it puts a new slant on the case."

"In what way?"

"Nobody's still gonna believe Ed murdered that girl, so nobody's gonna believe you. That makes you a suspect."

"How about Luther Johnson? The girl said he flew into a rage at Betty."

"Forget Johnson. This isn't twenty years ago. Had a man interview him. He said all Johnson was was a worried parent. Whatever he was, it leaves you with the story you told."

"Look, Mark, I was there, she wasn't."

"There's evidence supports what she says. The county solicitor has it now. I'll have to ask you to come in for questioning, by the way, so I hope there's nothing in that evidence that contradicts your story."

"Such as?"

"Lot of stuff nobody ever went over carefully before. Casts of footprints, tire tracks. One thing in particular— lot of Betty's blood was smeared on the right rear fender of her car, and there were footprints alongside it. Somebody wearing rubbers leaned against that fender, which is what the girl indicated."

Caldecott felt weak. "I told the truth."

"No you didn't, Lee." Turnage's expression was hard. "I never said anything because it wasn't any of my business, but things are different now. If Ed didn't do it then somebody else did—and I happen to know you were there before Ed, and before Betty too."

Caldecott could barely talk. "What makes you think that?"

"'Cause I saw your car there."

"You couldn't have."

"I saw it, all right—on my way over to Grady's Hill. Look, let's not go into it now. I gotta question you anyway, so instead of me doing it officially and going through all kinds of rigamarole, why don't we just have a talk? I got some time tomorrow if you do."

"How about my office? Say five-thirty . . ."

"Sunday?"

"I'll be there from noon on. Have some work."

Turnage was already moving away. "That's fine."

"I appreciate this, Mark."

Turnage waved it off, and Caldecott stayed where he was for he didn't know how long before, ready to scream, he headed for the bar and ordered a double vodka on the rocks. He couldn't take much more of this, he thought. He was not going to take the blame for what Raymond had done. He imagined himself talking to Turnage. *I had nothing to do with what happened to Betty,* he said, *nothing at all. But I know who did, and if we can make a deal, I'll tell you the whole story. I had no idea something like that was going to hap—*

He broke off as the bartender handed him a drink. He finished half of it before he went to look for Juleen.

Ordway was dancing with Drew, and she fitted into his arms as snugly as Betty. She was a little tipsy, and it only made her more charming. Guests had begun to leave, and he hated the idea of her leaving too. He asked

278

her if she'd had too much to drink and she smiled up at him.

"I think I had just enough," she said.

"I think you had just a wee bit over the limit," Ordway said playfully.

She said no she didn't, then lurched against him, making them both laugh. "Oh how awful," she said. "Believe me, I don't usually drink this much."

"You've been through a lot. Anyone deserved to have a few drinks, it's you."

"Thanks, Ray," she said. "You've been wonderful to me. I appreciate it."

"Is that why you moved out of my house?" he said impulsively. He immediately regretted it, and added, "It wasn't my place to say that."

She waved it away. "I was really scared of you at first," she said. "Now, I don't know why, I just feel like—I feel so comfortable with you."

There. He saw her giving a quick glance down to his pants when she thought he didn't notice. But he noticed. Betty *was* inside this girl, trying to get to him. He was certain of it.

Drew nestled closer to him, and he had to use his will to suppress his mounting excitement. He was almost certain she was coming on to him, but he wanted to be sure. He didn't want to make a wrong move.

She made a slight misstep, stopped and touched a hand to her temple. ". . . Hold the phone," she said.

It was so like Betty, he held her away from him.

"Am I stepping all over you?" she said apologetically.

"Not at all," he said.

She moved back into his arms. "Funny—as soon as you said that, I felt as if I'd talked with you and danced with you many times before."

"Maybe you did," he said.

"You know what, Ray?" she said. "I think I did have too much to drink. I'm not feeling too good."

She was a little pale, he thought. They were close to the side entrance that led to the rose garden.

"You need some fresh air," he said.

He guided her through the door and out onto the flagstone. Below them was the rose garden, and benches that lay in leafy darkness. "Careful here," he said. He put an arm around her as he guided her down a few steps.

She took a deep breath. "Oh," she sighed, "you were right. This is what I needed. Is that a bench way over there?"

"Yes." He took her hand and started for it, but she pulled back. "I can't really see, Ray," she said.

He slowed down. "Don't worry, I won't let you fall," he said.

He led her to the bench and she slumped down onto it, then stretched her arms into the air and closed her eyes. His own eyes swept over her body, and he wanted to take her in his arms and make love to her. Go slow, he said to himself, you'll get her.

"Uh-oh," she murmured. Her eyes popped open.

"What's the matter?"

"When I close my eyes, everything starts spinning. Whoo. What's that?" she asked, pointing.

"Harriet's greenhouse," he said. The glass roof was visible above a hedge.

"I've never been in a greenhouse," she said.

"In that case . . ." He took her hand and helped her up. "Now you stay right behind me so you don't trip."

He was going to have her. He knew it. She followed him along the path, down a few stone steps, and finally around the hedge.

He opened the door for her and she went ahead of him, weaving slightly. "It's like the tropics," she said when the door closed behind them.

He moved beside her. "Steady," he said.

"Wouldn't it be nice to own a big big big big greenhouse," she said, "about ten times as big as this? It could be a private Garden of Eden, and every time you wanted to come to it and be natural you could . . ." She smiled at him. Her eyes were languorous, sleepy. He wanted to kiss her. More.

Drew looked at him fondly. "Thank you for being so nice to me, Ray," she said.

"Easiest thing I ever did," he said. "What you said back there about feeling that you talked with me before and danced with me before . . . I feel the same when I'm with you. For me it's like being with Betty again. We were very close."

"I know you were."

He took her hand. "I loved her more than I loved anyone else in the world. She loved me the same way."

"Yes," she said, "I felt that."

"I wonder if you know what I'm saying?" he asked.

He drew her to him, and he saw that she was slightly surprised. If this was Betty, he'd already have had her panties down. His pulse was racing and he wondered if he was making a wrong move. Then he thought he saw something happen to her. A change. Something. He wasn't sure. Then suddenly he *was* sure. Her surprise was gone. In its place was Betty's mocking smile: She knew what he wanted, knew exactly what he wanted.

"Hello, Ray."

It was her, and just hearing her breathe his name made him excited. He drew her closer, all her softnesses familiar, inviting. She leaned her head against his chest and her hand slipped to his waist. But he still had to be careful. He touched her chin, lifted it.

Betty was staring into his eyes with a look he knew well, a little fear, even defiance, but a defiance he could break easy, that he'd broken over and over. And made her glad he did.

"You still get excited as fast as you used to, Ray," she said.

"Only with you, girl," he said. "Who was my little filly?" he asked her.

"I was."

"What was I?" he asked her. When she didn't answer he said it again. "What was I?"

"A big, big stallion," she answered.

That made him feel strong, sure of himself, the way he'd always been with her.

His hands dropped to the roundness of her behind, hiking up her skirt. "I need you bad, honey," he whispered. He pulled her against him, wanting to kiss her, but she put her arms against his chest.

"We just got here, Ray, and you're all over me already."

"That's how I get when I'm around you."

She pushed him back against a table loaded with clay pots, and he smelled her hair as she leaned her head against his chest again. "I know how you get and I know what you want."

"What do I want?" he said weakly.

"What you taught me to do to your dolly."

"Yes."

"Did I do it good?" she said. Her hand dropped to his belt.

"You sure did."

"Even when I was a little girl?"

"Even then."

"Want me to do it now?" she asked him.

"Yes," he said hoarsely. "I want that bad. Take out my dolly, little baby." He got ready, rested his hands on the table, trembling with eagerness as her fingers went to his belt buckle. Oh Betty baby.

She stopped. "Get me a little hot, Ray," she said. "Tell me what you used to do to me when you took me to Carlton Meadows. Remember how you used to lay me down there in the tall grass and take off my panties?"

"Oh yeah," he said. "And I used to open my little girl's

legs and get down there and kiss her and lick her little honeypot for her."

"You know how that used to make me feel when you got my legs open and did that?"

"You loved it," he told her. "You loved everything I did." She was taking too long, and he reached down to open his pants himself.

She stopped him. "I didn't love it at all, Ray. I loved you, but I hated that."

His eyes met hers. Hers were accusing, and he hoped it didn't mean she was going to give him a lot of talk. Goddamn. "Honey, why you want to bring that up now?"

"Because I couldn't tell you then. I was only a little girl and I was scared. I used to lie there and look up at the sky, pretending I wasn't there, pretending your mouth wasn't between my legs."

"Ah, honey, you—"

"I'm telling you how I felt, Ray. Don't you care?"

"'Course I do, but—"

"I felt like there was a hog down there, Ray, a big ugly hog slurping and slopping between my legs, making all kinds of hog sounds and making me afraid he was gonna hurt me and bite me."

"Oh, girl, we can talk about all that stuff later."

"You mean after you get what you want, like you always did. Sneaking into my room all the time and forcing that thing in me every chance you got, hurting me. I couldn't even go to the toilet without being afraid you were gonna come in."

"That's enough," he said.

"And you threatening and begging. 'Oh Betty, come on honey, you know what it means to me. You know how I get. Goddamnit, girl, I done a lot for you, and you're gonna give me what I need or I'm gonna beat the—'"

"Shut your mouth," he said. He started to rebuckle his belt.

"Givin' up so easy, Ray?" she taunted. "How come?

You used to be able to make me do anything, didn't matter how I felt. C'mon, Uncle Ray, what do you want? I'll do it, and if I don't, you can punch me around."

He stared at her evenly, touched the knot of his tie to make sure it was in place, then turned away from her and adjusted his clothes.

"I hated you, you bastard. You stole everything from me. You stole my childhood, you stole every decent feeling I ever had. You made me feel like I was worth as much as a condom, then you stole my life."

"Be off these grounds in five minutes," he said. He started for the door.

"There's another diary, Ray," she said.

That stopped him. He stayed with his back to her.

"That's right," she said. "Another diary. And I'll tell you what's in it. Not that sickly sweet shit I wrote when I was a little girl, but what I wrote later. Everything you did to me, how I hated to come home when you were there, how I'd of changed places with the poorest girl in town if I could of just been like them. It's in another diary, Ray, and that girl Drew is gonna find it when I want her to."

He turned around. "I don't believe you."

"Good. Then you don't have to worry about what I wrote the day before I was gonna leave."

"What was that?"

"About how Lee was gonna meet me at South Fork and lend me the money I needed so I could go away with Ed. I wrote how happy I was and how much I loved Ed and how much I hated you, you sonofabitch."

"And did you write that the nigger made you pregnant?" he said, coming back.

"No, you bastard. I wrote the truth—that *you* made me pregnant and I was gonna get an abortion. If it was Ed's baby, I'd of kept it."

He slapped her without warning.

She fell against the table behind her and the load of clay pots stacked on it tumbled to the floor, broke into

284

pieces. Dazed, she found herself hanging on to the table with one arm, not sure for a moment how she got there. Ordway leaned down and dragged her to her feet.

"Tell me more about this diary," Ordway said. She was afraid now, he saw. That made him feel good. "Tell me," he said. "I want to know where it is so I can read it myself, you little slut!"

"You'll find out. But first I'm gonna make that girl go back to Willow Creek with that reporter. This time she'll tell what you made Lee do an' you know what? Lee's gonna be so scared of the electric chair he's gonna tell on you, an' *you'll* go to the electric chair!"

He slapped her again with force enough to send her sprawling. She lay where she had fallen, eyes closed. Going to her, he kneeled beside her, infuriated. And excited too. Always excited him when Betty fought him.

He was going to kill her—he'd have to do that as soon as possible—but she looked good. He started touching her, then realized he was being stupid. He was thinking of what to do next when he felt a slight draft.

Someone came in. Turnage.

He took in the scene. "What's going on?"

Ordway thought fast. "Glad you're here," he said. "The girl had too much to drink and I may need help with her. She fainted. I think she hit the table."

Turnage squatted down beside him, raised Drew's head. There was a welt on her cheek, but she looked okay. He was about to lift her when her eyes opened.

"Are you all right, Drew?" Ordway asked her.

When she nodded, the two men helped her up. She asked them what happened, and Ordway told her what he had told Turnage, watching her carefully for the slightest sign that she remembered. There was none. She was embarrassed.

"Oh God," she said, brushing herself off. "You mean I keeled over just like that?"

"Don't let it bother you," Turnage said. "I'm getting kinda used to seeing you that way."

"That's enough of that, Mark," Ordway said. He asked Drew if she was sure she was all right.

"I think so," she said.

"I'll take you back to the party," he said. He looked at Turnage inquiringly. "What brought you here?"

"Came to find you. Some of your guests want to say good night."

Ordway put an arm around Drew, told her to lean on him and he'd see her back to the house.

He did not waste any time. He left Drew at a bathroom, said good-bye to a few guests, then went looking for Wendell Barnes. He found him in the conservatory, playing the piano for one of his women. He was bringing him to the den when he spotted Lee. He told Wendell to go on, he'd be right there, and pulled Lee aside.

"I want to talk to you in a few minutes."

"We'll have to talk tomorrow," Lee said. "I'm leaving as soon as I find Juleen."

"You are not." Ordway squeezed his arm. "Didn't you hear me? We have to talk about Drew. I want to know everything the little bitch said to you when she turned into Betty, everything she knew."

Suddenly the truth dawned on Caldecott. His fear of Ordway became secondary. "She turned on you," he gloated. "She turned on you. Just when you thought you were going to get a little of it—whammo! She did the same thing to you she did to me. Well, now you—"

"I wouldn't be so happy if I were you. That girl is threatening to tell everything to that reporter tomorrow. Everything—you understand? Means that you're in for it too, doesn't it, so you stay here. Wendell is waiting for me."

"Hold it, Raymond." Caldecott stopped him. "I didn't like having to do it, but I've made out a statement. I've left it where it will be found in the event of my death. It

286

tells what you did at South Fork and what happened at Willow Creek, God help me."

Ordway tightened. "Why would you do that?"

". . . I thought it best."

"Best? Doing that to me? Think this is some kind of a melodrama, do you, where I am going to kill you to shut you up? I'll remind you that I have looked out for you ever since you been out of your teens . . ."

"And I appreciate it. But after what you did to me in your office I don't know what you're going to do next. I'll tell you something else—Turnage knows I was at Willow Creek before you came there with Betty."

"What are you talking about?"

"He saw my car there."

"I don't believe it."

"Whether you believe it or not that's what he just told me. I'm having a meeting with him tomorrow, off-the-record."

"For what?"

". . . I want to find out what he actually knows."

Ordway felt like choking him. "Are you crazy? The man'll chew you up. He's a police official. There's no such thing as off-the-record with him. Can't you see he's going after you because he's getting pressure on himself? Now I'm telling you, you stay here, and as soon as I finish with Wendell I'll talk with you."

"I . . . said . . . I . . . am . . . going . . . home," Caldecott said through clenched teeth, "and I mean it."

"Lee, you just better calm down. Because if you turn on me I swear—statement or no statement—I will have Wendell Barnes find some doped-up lunatic who will douse you with gasoline and burn you alive."

"Raymond," Caldecott said measuredly, "fuck you."

In the den, Wendell Barnes displayed his best smile when Ordway walked in. "Cousin Raymond, to what do I owe the pleasure of this gracious interlude?"

287

If anybody could get him out of this it was Barnes, but Ordway was in no mood for his good ol' boy banter. "I want someone murdered," he said quietly.

"Raymond, I declare you beat all," Barnes said with mock admiration.

"I am serious, so you keep your voice down and don't give me any of your country bullshit. I need this thing done and I need it done before tomorrow morning."

Barnes sobered. "As you know, Raymond, I am delighted to help you with minor illegalities such as those connected with feminine companionship and eavesdropping, but what you are suggesting is—"

"Is something you know all about. You have had people murdered, and I know it. You have men who do it. You can do this."

Barnes became serious. "Even if I could, Raymond, tomorrow—"

"This has to be done . . ." His voice trailed off when there was a soft knock at the door. "Who is it?"

"It's me, Ray." Drew's voice was barely audible.

Ordway motioned Barnes out of sight and opened the door partway.

"I'm leaving, Ray," Drew said. "I wanted to thank you for inviting me. It was a lovely party."

"You made it lovely," Ordway said. Frowning, he touched her cheek. "Does that hurt very much?"

She shook her head. "It was my own fault. I shouldn't have drunk so much. I feel really stupid."

"You were very charming. We've only known you a short time, my sister and I," he said, taking her hands, "but we feel very close to you. You are tired. We'll talk tomorrow."

He kissed her on the forehead, then closed the door. Signaling Barnes to wait, he opened it again a trifle. When he closed it, Barnes expected him to be mellowed out. But his eyes were cold.

"You have to do this," he went on in an even lower voice. "I have no one else to turn to."

"Who is this lucky person?"

"Her." He indicated the door. "Don't be surprised. The girl looks decent, but she's evil."

"That hardly seems like a reason to kill somebo—"

"Don't tell me what she is or she isn't," Ordway said angrily. "She's a *demon*. She has to wiped out of existence—sent back to wherever she came from. I'd do it myself if I could."

Barnes wasn't sure how to handle this. He'd always known his cousin was a little crazed—it ran in the family—but now he was talking like a maniac. Barnes went over to a decanter, picked up one of the brandy snifters beside it. He decided he'd take a reasonable approach.

"Unless I am wrong, Raymond, I do believe that pretty child is under *police* protection. . . ."

"If you won't do it," Ordway said as Barnes poured himself a drink, "starting with your money-laundering operations, I'll see to it that you get so much police pressure put on you you'll be out of business."

Ordway knew he'd gone too far, but he didn't care. If the creature went back to Willow Creek or came up with that diary he was finished anyway. She had to die. No mercy for her.

Barnes sloshed the brandy around in his glass. As always, cold anger made him smile. "You are a cunning man, Raymond. But you don't want to say something like that to me. It is beneath you. And fraught with danger," he added, inhaling the fumes before he drank.

"I don't give a damn," Ordway said. "You can't do anything worse to me than that girl can. I told you we're dealing with a demon here and I mean it. She's unholy."

"Perhaps we can put a stake through her heart . . ."

"Don't you laugh at me, you sonofabitch!" Ordway's face was twisted in rage. "Don't you understand? This girl is infected with Betty's evil spirit. I never told anybody, but before Betty died she sank low. Low. You couldn't sink any lower. What's come back from the grave is worse. If you don't do this for me you're finished!"

Barnes knew his cousin well enough to know he meant what he said. He also knew enough not to accept his first offer as final. "I have not said no, and I have not said yes. What is the emergency?"

"She is going to talk to a reporter tomorrow. She can't be allowed to."

"It won't be easy to take her out."

Ordway looked at him blankly.

"Take out . . ." Barnes said. He pantomimed holding a rifle, clicked his tongue. "Who is the reporter?"

"Chuck Pennington."

"Ah-ha." He indicated the door. "The one out there I gave you that stuff on. Chubby fella." Barnes took a sip of brandy. "I am not committing myself, mind, but suppose—we only spozin' now—suppose the reporter was out of the way."

Ordway considered it. Not a bad thought. "What do you have in mind?"

"The obvious. Buying time until we can either take out the girl or get her away from the police and—"

"What do you mean, get her away from the police? *Kidnap* her? You couldn't do that."

"Given world enough and time, Raymond, I could kidnap the pope. At this moment, however, we are simply considering an option."

"I want her kidnapped," Ordway snapped.

"Raymond, you have already pushed me." Barnes smiled again, an edge to his voice. "Do not shove."

"You wouldn't have mentioned it if there wasn't a chance you could do it."

"I do admire you, cousin Raymond. As soon as you find something is within your grasp, you set your sights beyond it. The elite call that vision. My daddy called it greed."

"She has something I want."

"I'll make some calls. No promises."

"There's a secure phone in the desk drawer."

"I don't carry around those kinds of numbers. I have to go back to Charleston."

"Then you go now. Get her for me, Wendell. You won't be sorry. If you can't kidnap her, kill her. But get her."

"I shall let you know in an hour or so, suh, if I shall attempt anything at all. But I must tell you, Raymond, that besides being cunning, you have always had luck. That is a blessing. I am not sure but that in this situation you may even have phenomenal luck."

After Barnes left, Ordway was calmer. What Wendell had said about luck meant that he had something up his sleeve. Ordway was sure of it.

But there was still Lee. Getting violent with him had been a stupid mistake. He had handled Lee all wrong. Alienated him. After the girl was out of the way, he might get Lee to promise he'd destroy the statement, but there was nothing to guarantee he'd keep his word. If *he* was Lee, he certainly would not.

The man was shaky, no doubt of it—too shaky. God knows what he was liable to tell Turnage tomorrow. Everything maybe. He had to get him back somehow.

Caldecott wished he could get rid of the *Sentinel* reporter without offending him. He'd been on his way to meet Juleen out front when the guy had cornered him and started asking him questions: Did he think Drew Summers was sincere? How did he feel about the complaint she had filed against him?

Caldecott insisted he would rather not comment, and he was on the point of excusing himself when all of a sudden Drew herself appeared in front of him.

It was all he needed. He tried to get away, but Drew

said, "Please don't. I'm leaving, and I just wanted to tell you something. For whatever it's worth, a few minutes ago I got the feeling that tomorrow I'll be able to tell exactly what happened at Willow Creek."

"Drew, are you serious?" Pennington said.

"Not only that, but I think I'll know who that third man was."

"Spectacular," Pennington said quickly.

Caldecott felt as though he were coming apart. "I wouldn't say it's spectacular," he snapped. "I'd say the young lady is simply repeating what she said before."

"I can't help what I feel," Drew said. "I'm trying to be honest. If I feel differently tomorrow, you'll get an apology from me."

Thankful for an excuse to get away, Caldecott walked off.

"Drew, what happened?" Pennington said, touching a finger to his cheek. "Where'd you get that?"

Drew dismissed it. "An accident. Chuck, I'm going to split." She started off and he went with her.

He was flipping out. "This isn't spectacular, it's beyond spectacular, it's— Look, are you sure about this?" Pennington said. "That guy can sue your ass."

"I'm positive."

"What time do you want to get together?"

"I don't know," she said. "I can't even think right now. It'll have to be in the morning because I'm going into Charleston with Mrs. Fairchild."

"Suppose I call you about nine. How's that?"

"That's fine."

"I gotta go back," Chuck said. "Hey, take care of yourself, will ya, you look out of it."

Drew stopped. "You know what," she said, "there's something else too—there's another diary."

"*Another* diary? Jesus! Where?"

"I don't know yet."

Fantastic, Pennington thought. "Get a good night's

sleep," he said. He gave her a quick hug, then went to look for Ordway. Wait'll he hears this, he thought, he'll love it. What a story.

The Atlanta *Constitution* jumped into his mind. Fuck 'em, he thought. If he got a book out of this he'd head for Washington. Or New York.

16

Drew was scrubbing off her makeup in the bathroom, working around the sore place on her cheek, when she started to feel dizzy. The washcloth dropped from her fingers and she held on to the sink for support.

She was in crappy shape. She knew that. What she'd gone through with Caldecott and GG had worn her down, but this last confrontation with Raymond Ordway had pushed her close to the edge.

She should have been more careful. She knew Ordway was vicious, she just hadn't realized how fast he was—like a shark. He'd have ripped her apart right there in the greenhouse if he'd thought he could get away with it, and he wouldn't have felt a thing. She remembered the way his hands felt on her and she shuddered.

She thought about how wonderful it would be to leave all this behind right now and go back to New York. She used to think her job was hectic. Now it seemed like a vacation. But she couldn't go back yet. Not after what happened tonight. She was worse off than ever.

The sensation hit her that a lot of this had happened to her before. She straightened up and tucked in the collar of her robe, stared at herself in the mirror. As always, she saw a little of her sister staring back at her, Gena's lips, a look in her eyes. Now she saw Betty Fairchild too. Maybe there *was* some of Betty in her. Why not? Everyone here acted like there was, and she was beginning to *feel* like Betty. Jim had let her down just like Caldecott had let down Betty. Drew couldn't be certain—she hoped to God she was wrong—but she had the feeling that he hadn't come down here off some mysterious phone call.

She made the water warmer, rubbed more soap into the cloth and started scrubbing again.

She was unaware that, behind her, outside of the bathroom, the door to the adjoining room was opening. It opened so slowly and soundlessly that even without the water running, Drew would not have heard the man who slipped into the room. He heard the splash of water, padded across the room quickly and silently and hugged the wall beside the door. He looked in to see Drew leaning over the sink.

She had just gotten the soap out of her eyes and was lifting her head when she felt someone come up behind her. A powerful arm wrapped itself around her waist, a hand was clapped over her mouth. Eyes wide, she saw Turnage's face in the mirror. She didn't struggle, and as soon as he knew she was okay he took his hand from her mouth, put a finger to his lips.

She was unsteady on her feet, and he didn't let her go until she indicated she was all right.

She dried her face, then followed him quietly out into the room. He stopped, held up a warning finger and pointed toward the phone. Drew nodded knowingly, but he shook his head, indicating the underside of the table itself. She gave him a look of disbelief, kneeled down and peered up beneath it. He was right: there was a listening device there.

Getting up, she followed him into the adjoining room, closing her door behind her. Waiting for her there was a tall bearded black man. He stared at her with concern, and not until Turnage had shut the second door did he go to her.

"You did it, Drew," Ed Johnson said, hugging her. "You did it."

Surprised to see him here, Drew said nothing, afraid she would start to cry.

Johnson felt her tension. He held her away from him, shocked by the change in her. Turnage had been right: the hostility and the violence—and the pretense—had all taken their toll. She was haggard.

"I'll never forgive myself for what happened with GG," he said.

"Don't blame her, blame Ordway," Drew said. "Ed, what are you doing here? I thought you were in New York. Is something wrong?"

"Wrong?" Impulsively, he hugged her again. "The only thing wrong is what you've had to go through. Drew, you've been remarkable."

"I'll second that," Turnage said. "C'mere. I got one of those for you too."

Holding her, he felt great. She was safe, and he couldn't wait to see Ordway's face, and Caldecott's, when they found out Ed was alive.

"You *better* hug me," Drew said. "You were so mean I almost believed you."

"And you were terrific," Turnage said when he let her go. "Sorry I scared you back there"—he indicated her room—"but I was afraid of that bug."

"My fault," Drew said. "I opened the bolt, but your door was locked."

"We just got here," Turnage said.

"And now that we are here . . ." Johnson took a bottle of champagne and some plastic glasses from a paper bag. "We are going to have a toast. Drew, I can't tell you how proud of you I am. Do you realize how far you've gone beyond what we expected?"

"That's not the half of it," Turnage said. "I talked with Caldecott tonight. I got a date with him tomorrow, and I'm gonna try to break him. As soon as—"

Drew interrupted him. "What do you think the chances are he'll break?"

"I don't know, but you got that wimp so scared he's near crazy. One way or the other, after I finish with him Ed and me are gonna meet with Stiggs. We'll let 'im listen to the tape you made in Caldecott's office and the one you just made in the greenhouse. We'll tell him the whole story, and if we don't convince him that Ordway murdered Betty, I'm not chief of police. In the meantime, you're gonna keep a low profile."

"I can't. I'm going back to Willow Creek with Chuck Pennington tomorrow," Drew said.

Turnage was surprised. "For what?"

"To put more pressure on Caldecott. I'm going to tell Chuck exactly what he and Ordway did there."

Turnage smiled. "Hey, I just told you, I'm gonna see Lee tomorrow. I'll be wired, and after the number you been doing on him, if I can't bring him to the admission stage I'll sure as hell get him damn close."

"Close isn't enough," Drew said.

"Not enough? Drew, all we set out to do was show that Ed would never have killed Betty and that Ordway did, and Lee helped him. We got ten times that!"

"Enough to convict Ordway of murder?"

Turnage hesitated. ". . . Not unless Caldecott confesses and—"

"Then he has to confess. And he will when he hears what I tell Chuck."

Turnage shook his head. "No. I'm not letting you take any more chances."

"That's up to me, isn't it?" Drew said sharply.

Johnson exchanged a quick glance with Turnage. Something was wrong. "Drew," he said gently, "the reason I came here is that Mark asked me to. He feels that you can't take any more. I tend to—"

"I'm all right," she said stubbornly.

297

"No you're not. You're worn-out. Let go, Drew. You've done a wonderful job, but it's over."

"It's not over," she said. She looked from one to the other of them, and what Johnson saw in her eyes made something inside of him shrivel. Suddenly he knew why she was haggard, and he almost knew what was coming next.

She swallowed hard, trying to control her emotions. "Ordway is going to kill me."

"No way," Turnage said. "Soon as he finds out this is a scam, the man won't dare go near you."

Drew knew better. "Yes he will. I saw it in his eyes in the greenhouse, and I saw it when I said good-night to him. He's going to kill me. If he doesn't do it here he'll do it in New York or somewhere else."

Both men were shocked into silence.

"I'm so scared I don't know what to do," Drew said, slumping into a chair. "He's a maniac, and I'm Betty to him. I know what's going to happen. If he's not locked up I'm going to be walking down a dark street some night, or I'll come into my apartment and that's it." She looked at Turnage, swallowing hard. "So you have to break Caldecott and I have to go back to Willow Creek."

Turnage was grim. He shook his head in helplessness. "Drew, it's too dangerous. I told you about this cousin of his, Wendell Barnes. He's southern mafia. I can't compete with him. Half my men don't have the training they need. They're rookies, shoe salesmen, pizza delivery drivers. My damn cruisers have ninety to a hundred thousand miles on 'em before I buy 'em." He jerked a thumb toward her room. "These dudes are heavy duty. You saw. They had your phone tapped hours after you moved in. They put that bug in yesterday. You need more protection than I can give you."

"There's the cop you've got with me day and night."

"It's not enough."

298

"It's more than I'll have in New York. Look, forget about *me* for a second, all right? Don't you want to get that man? Don't you remember what he *did* to Betty? What he did to GG? How much—" She broke off, realizing her mistake too late.

Johnson looked at the two of them. "GG?" It took him a few moments to absorb what Drew had meant. "*Ordway* did that to her? How do you know that?" he asked her.

"I told her," Turnage said.

"The night he took me to the stationhouse . . . I'm sorry, Mark," Drew said.

Johnson felt rage building in him. Turnage had told him what his family had gone through, and what had been done to GG, but not until long after they happened. He had never told him this. He struggled to keep his voice down.

"Ordway was . . . He was one of the filth that . . .?"

"No," Turnage said quickly. "No, Ed. Get ahold of yourself. He wasn't one of 'em. But he paid 'em."

"And you knew that?" Johnson said. "You always knew that?" When he didn't get an answer, he went to Drew and touched her shoulder with trembling fingers. "You don't have to worry. Ordway won't hurt you. You'll be safe. I promise you."

"Now that's just great," Turnage said. "If that doesn't just crack it I don't know what does. What are you gonna do—shoot 'im, stab 'im, or kill 'im with your bare hands?"

Johnson regarded him coldly. "You knew he ordered that done to my sister. You knew it and you didn't tell me. . . ."

"Damn right I didn't! For the same reason I didn't tell you what happened to GG *at all* till years later. I knew what you'd do. I knew you'd come back and not be able to do a damn thing except get the rest of your family hurt and get yourself killed."

"You had no right to make that choice for me!"

"I had every right! We agreed you couldn't take the slightest chance of that insane sonofabitch finding out you were alive."

Johnson was silent.

"Jesus Christ, man—are you forgetting what the hell it was like here twenty years ago? *You* were the one who said we couldn't even let your mother know you were alive. There was no way, you said, that she could look in your father's eyes day after day and not tell him. And you were right. I'll testify to it because I've had twenty years of passing that woman on the street and biting my tongue every time I saw the grief in *her* eyes!"

He paused, his anger suddenly gone. "Ed, look what the man did to your family when he thought you were dead and gone. He knew you were alive, there'd have been a dozen KKK goons starting on them all over again. And now what are *you* gonna do—try to kill that maniac and blow everything this girl here risked her life for? Then what?"

Johnson nodded: He agreed. His shoulders sagged. "I am so sorry, Drew," he said, his fingers brushing her shoulder again. "I am so sorry I got you into this."

Drew put her hand on his, glanced up at him. "You didn't. Remember? I'm the one who got *you* into it."

The three were silent again, struggling with their emotions.

Drew was the first to speak. "Did Jim come down here because of a deal?"

Wondering if he should lie and say no, Turnage finally muttered a yeah.

It hurt more than she thought it would.

Johnson went to the window and stared out. Turnage picked up the champagne and set it down again.

Finally Drew said, "Guys, it's getting late . . . What are we gonna do?"

300

* * *

After he changed into pajamas and bathrobe, Raymond Ordway took the folders from their hiding place in his bureau and brought them to the fireplace.

Putting a match to the first of the photos, he watched with disgust as the flame crawled across the face and body of the girl he had once loved. She was repugnant to him now.

He hadn't felt that way after what he had done to her at South Fork: He'd done it because he believed that Betty had been misled. She'd been a victim of the times, of civil rights do-gooders and communists, and other mongrelizers. At the same time, she could not be allowed to bring shame to her family. He had mourned for her as deeply as Harriet had. For a long time he had missed her so badly he'd wept over her.

Not ever again. She was worse now than she'd been twenty-three years ago. She didn't see that she'd done wrong. She thought *he* was the one who'd done wrong.

He burned the rest of the photos, checked the ashes, then looked at the clock. Almost one-thirty. One way or another he should have heard from Wendell by now. Wendell wouldn't let him down. If he did, though, Ordway thought, there was one slim possibility. Turnage. The girl was in his hair too.

The only thing was you couldn't be sure of Turnage, could you? Too private. In all the years Ordway had tried to find something on him, he couldn't. He'd killed the Johnson nigger—he'd more or less admitted that to him—but he wouldn't take money for it. He was either crafty or stupid. Maybe both. Either way you couldn't trust him.

In the bathroom, he was brushing his teeth when the phone rang. Wendell. Snatching it from the wall, he willed that he would hear what he wanted to, then he said hello.

"Forgot to mention it, Raymond," Wendell said. "I got

301

a new car that I want you to look at. Drop by tomorrow morning before you go to your office."

"I'll do that," Ordway answered.

He hung up exultant: It was a go.

He'd been right. Ol' Wendell *did* have something up his sleeve. Let it be kidnap, he prayed. He wanted to get his hands on that girl. If he did, she'd tell him where to find that diary of hers damn quick. She'd be grateful to tell him anything he wanted to know.

He got into bed feeling serene—and powerful—and fell asleep right away.

Pennington was just walking into the brick dependency he rented—former slave quarters converted to a guest cottage—when the phone rang. The screen door banged closed at the same time he picked up the phone.

"Hello."

He got dead air. He watched the insects bat against the outside light while he said hello a few more times, then hung up. "Jerkoff," he muttered.

The place was an oven. Going to the screen door, he hooked it shut, turned off the outside light, and opened all the windows.

In bed a few minutes later, he set the radio clock. He'd call Drew about nine, he figured, meet her around ten. Jesus, if she came through with the name of that third man, what a story. He'd done a sidebar on it: FAIRCHILD LOOKALIKE PROMISES MORE MURDER SCENE DETAILS.

He read for about fifteen minutes, then turned out the light.

In his room, Ed Johnson lay awake, his mind in turmoil. He thought of his mother and father a short distance away. All the joy he had envisioned in surprising them faded each time he saw Drew sitting hollow-eyed and frightened.

302

Ordway is going to kill me. If he doesn't do it here he'll do it in New York. He's going to kill me.

He glanced at the window as a faint breeze nudged the curtain. There was no point in trying to sleep, he realized. Getting out of bed, he lit a cigarette, sat down by the window.

Why had he let her do this? Why hadn't he listened to himself? So many times during the months he had coached her—going over names with her, faces, places, incidents—he had suggested that they call the whole thing off. It was too farfetched, he insisted, too difficult, too dangerous. But Drew had said no, she could do it. She *wanted* to do it.

Selfishly, he had allowed her, watched fascinated as she transformed herself so completely into Betty that at times, even knowing she was pretending, he almost convinced himself that by some miracle Betty's soul had found its way inside of her. He had felt something tug at him at those times, a yearning for what he had thought forever lost.

He had never allowed it to go beyond that, and as he came to know Drew better, saw her resourcefulness, her quickness and her intelligence, something strange happened: The more he was around her, talking, having laughs, exchanging ideas, the more he saw what Betty could have become had Ordway not abused and molested her. His hatred for the man, seething before, became venomous.

It had impaired his judgment, he realized now, made him shortsighted. He could be excused for not anticipating danger from Caldecott and GG, but if anyone knew what Ordway was like, he did. He should have realized that as foul and evil as the man had been twenty-three years ago, he would only become worse.

A breeze touched the curtain again and it swayed inward. His thoughts turned to Betty and himself, and he smiled faintly as though remembering two kids of whom he had once been fond. Until she had started coming to his house occasionally—to avoid being home alone with Ordway, he realized much later—he had never thought of her as anything but the spoiled girl whose family his mother worked for.

He got to like her, saw why his mother was so fond of her, and coming from a woman whose treatment by white people did not encourage affection for them, that fondness said a lot.

Betty could do no wrong as far as his mother was concerned, despite what anybody said about her. *That girl has her cross to bear,* his mother would say, and not until years later did he connect it with what he had once overheard her tell her father.

She was crying and screaming in her room something awful, Luther. I ran fast as I could, but the door was locked. When I knocked, she broke off crying right away, like somebody put a hand over her mouth. I kept knocking and calling, and finally she said in this little voice she was all right. Later I saw Mr. Raymond come down the hall and go out. I didn't even know he was in the house. I went to her room right away, and Luther, I know that man did something terrible to her. I know it. She looked old. I don't know what to do . . .

You mind your business, his father had said. *We say something against that well-to-do buckra, that might be the last thing any of us ever say.*

His mother kept silent about it, otherwise he and others might have understood why Betty was so unstable. It did not square with her warmth and her gentleness. After she joined the civil rights movement and he came to know her better, fell in love with her, he wondered how it was possible that she could have lived through what she had and still possessed so much goodness and generosity.

304

Because she finally told him about it. Not all at once. She hinted about it at first, and as they became closer, she told him more, but it was months before she could get past the shame and the self-hatred. Then she opened up completely and told him everything. Or what they both thought was everything. It was never everything because there was always more. Even after they became lovers, the repressed memories of what Ordway had done to her from the time she had been a child kept pouring from her—every conceivable act of degradation: threats, beatings, rape, sodomy.

And Johnson could do nothing. Wanting to kill Ordway, he could only console Betty, hold her, tell her it was not her fault, kiss her eyes, her hair. Often what she said made him cry, made them both cry, bringing them almost as close as the act of love. Years later, in Paris, when he told some of it to Drew, she wept with him as he had wept when Betty had related it to him.

His thoughts went to Willow Creek and to what had happened there those many years ago. In Africa, and finally in Paris, he had succeeded in relegating the tragedy to another life. But now he was home. Greenview's scented air was coming in through the window on the night mist. Greenview's streets meandered somewhere in the darkness below, and the road that led to Willow Creek was out there.

Once again he saw himself leaving his parents' house. He'd wanted to leave a note, he recalled now, but he and Betty had needed as much time as possible before their disappearance was connected. Her Mustang was a standout, and if they were stopped, God help him. He couldn't even chance being seen with a suitcase, so he had thrown a few clothes into a cardboard box.

He took two buses to reach Willow Creek. The second left him about half a mile from where he was to meet Betty, then he took a short cut through the woods . . .

He was grinning like a fool when he was close to the clearing, wanting to sing and yell. He saw her Mustang as soon as he rounded the turn in the horse trail, and he wondered why she'd put the windows and top up. It was so warm out.

He almost didn't see the vomit on the ground, made a hop around it. She had morning sickness again. Poor kid. He bent over and looked through the window.

The inside was a butcher shop.

He turned away, trying not to heave, suffocating. Darkness began to close in on him, and he thought he was going blind until he realized he was fainting.

He forced himself to take in gulps of air and his sight came back. He knew that a maniac had done it, and he looked at the silent woods, fear churning his stomach, feeling that any second he could be hacked up too.

He didn't want to look at what was in the car again, but he had to. Why he opened the door he did not know. The warm thick smell that came out was as hideous as what was halfway on the seat, dripping. He slammed the door and rested his arms on the canvas, groaning, taking in more gulps of air.

He almost screamed when a voice said, "You see what you did to her, boy?"

A blood-covered maniac. Behind the rear fender on the other side of the car. Perspiration and blood running down his face. Blood on his dark glasses. Hat covered with blood. Coveralls soaked with it. He was smiling. Pointing a revolver.

It was Raymond Ordway, Johnson realized, and he was sure that he was going to die.

"You hear me, nigger?" Ordway said. "I said you see what you did to that girl? Now I better hear an answer or I'm gonna blow your fuckin' head off."

"I didn't do that," he managed to say. "I couldn't do anything like that."

"Oh yes you did, boy. The minute you touched her. The minute you put that black body on her you turned her into garbage, didn't you? I just went over to South Fork and chopped it up for you." He came around the car. "Reach in there and bring out Betty's purse . . . go on."

Johnson opened the door and leaned in, holding his breath, trying not see. The purse was partly under her. He didn't want to touch it. He was going to black out.

Ordway prodded him with the revolver. "Bring it out."

It was wet, and it slid free easier than he thought it would. The clotted blood on it was warm and sticky.

"Take out the money and put it in your pocket."

After he obeyed, Ordway told him to drop the purse on the ground. "What's in that box?" he asked.

The box with his clothes. Johnson could not remember dropping it. "My . . . my stuff."

Ordway backed off. "Get over here. Come on, move. Open that trunk."

Betty's keys and her pink rabbit's foot dangled from the lock. Johnson raised the lid. Two suitcases and a smaller case were inside.

"Lee!" Ordway called. "Lee, come on out here!"

Johnson turned. Lee Caldecott appeared from behind a tree, sickly gray. When he reached them Ordway said, "Pick up that box there, then tell this boy what you saw him do . . . Come on, talk up. We don't have all day."

". . . I saw him—"

"No!" Ordway said, "you talk to *him*. You look him in the eye and you say, 'I saw *you*.' Say it."

"I saw you . . . take money out of Betty's purse."

"Go on."

". . . Then I saw—you—look . . . in the trunk," Lee said.

"Then what?" Ordway asked. "Then what'd you see?"

"I saw him—"

"I saw *you. You!* Look at him and say it."

"I saw you take out a blue case from Betty's car."

"That's right," Ordway said. "Then you asked him what he was doing there and he ran off, didn't he? So you came over here to the car and looked in and saw what he did to Betty."

Ordway raised the revolver and pointed it at Johnson's face. Shutting his eyes, bracing himself, he hardly heard what Ordway said next. "I said give me your keys," Ordway repeated. "Your keys. Hear? Toss them to me."

Johnson was shaking so bad he could barely get them out of his pocket. Ordway didn't bother to catch them and they landed under the rear bumper.

Then Ordway came to him and pushed the muzzle of the gun under his chin. "Lift your head, boy," he said, and suddenly Ordway was hugging him with his free arm. He felt the man's privates half swollen against him, the smell of him sickening, like the inside of the car, and when Ordway let him go he knew he had clots of Betty's blood on him.

"Now you get out of here, boy," Ordway said. "You run and you keep running, because Lee here is going back to town and tell what he saw you do. After that there's gonna be men come looking for you with rope and fire, you see. And when they find you, you will beg 'em to kill you. Run to your family and the men'll come for them too. G'bye, boy."

Johnson started to back off, but Ordway said, "Hold it. Take out that cosmetics case . . . *Now* run," he said. "You run like hell, you nigger sonofabitch."

He ran, expecting to be shot in the back.

He kept running. He didn't know for how long. He knew he'd gone pretty far because he was breathing hard. He realized he was heading for the river. He didn't know what he was going to do when he got there. He had to keep moving. If he didn't he would fall down and cry and he couldn't afford that. When he got to the river he would stop, think what he was going to do.

White men would come hunting for him. He knew that. He remembered how when he was a kid four white men came for a man who lived next door. They took him out behind his own car in his own backyard and what they left was moaning through broken teeth.

What was left of him, Johnson knew, would be charred.

Close to the river, he began to think. A boat. There were always rowboats tied up along the bank. He'd get one. He took a look behind him to see if anyone was after him, then he sped up.

He was aware of dodging limbs now. The growth was thicker here by the river and he had to be careful. But as careful as he was he did not see the elegant animal ahead until it turned its head and glanced at him, startled—a deer. He thought he was going to run into it, but just like that the deer launched itself out of his way.

Sunlight took its place. And something else. He saw it too late to yell or do anything about it: someone way ahead there, sitting with his back against a tree, facing him, knees raised. He had a rifle and he was going to . . . Oh God—!

He woke with his head pounding, somebody wiping his face and neck with a wet cloth.

Ed, you all right? "Ed, are you all *right*?"

It was Mark Turnage—one eye half-closed,

mouth still swollen, scared. He didn't have a shirt on, and he kept saying the same thing over and over: how sorry he was, that he didn't mean it, that Johnson had come out of nowhere and he'd shot him by accident.

Johnson finally understood. He tried to get up but he was too weak. His head was wrapped up, and the torn shirt Mark was cleaning him off with was full of blood. He looked down, saw he was drenched with blood and it made him feel even weaker.

He was here by the riverbank, but he couldn't remember how he got here, couldn't remember being shot.

Mark told him he'd dragged him here to clean him up, asked what the hell he was *doing* all the way out here. He didn't answer. He'd come to meet Betty—he knew that—but he couldn't remember what he'd done after he left the house.

Until Mark said, "What's this?"

It was Betty's blue cosmetics case, and as soon as he saw it, Johnson knew that something terrible had happened, something worse even than his getting shot.

And then gradually it came back to him . . .

Now, as he stared out the window at the darkened pasture below, he unconsciously touched the scar near his temple. He'd blurted out the whole story to Mark, couldn't stop, and when he'd finished Mark was sick. *Ordway? And Lee?* he'd asked. *You sure? You sure?*

He'd kept asking questions until he finally accepted it. *Shit, man,* he said, *you are dead meat.*

And without Mark he would have been. He had been helpless, and to this day he wondered at the innate decency of the man, his guts and his fairness. Mark had sat calmly thinking, and when he'd finally proposed what they should do, Johnson was too weak to do anything but assent.

310

They'd heard the first sirens as Mark had eased him into the water. He'd even thought to take the cosmetics case, then towed him upriver to where his pickup truck was parked.

Looking back now, Johnson could barely recall the rest of that day. Half the time he wasn't lucid. Not until he woke late the next morning in Mark's house did he learn that Greenview was ready to explode. Self-styled vigilantes had driven through his section of town the previous night, shooting at darkened houses and tossing Molotov cocktails. A mother and her fourteen-year-old son caught at a bus stop were badly beaten, the boy's skull fractured. Ed knew them: They lived down the street.

Recalling the guilt he'd felt, the despair and the impotent rage, he shook his head.

He put out his cigarette and got up.

In the bed a few moments later, he stared at the ceiling, his thoughts shifting to Drew. He tried not to think about the danger she was in. But it kept him awake.

It cooled down in the early hours of the morning and Pennington became aware that the sheet was sliding down his body. He groped for it, but it kept moving. What finally woke him was pain: Someone had grabbed his hair in a tight grip.

He opened his eyes, rigid with fear. A misshapen face floated above him, and pointing down at him was a gun fitted with a silencer. He realized that the face was a rubber mask, but it didn't lessen his fear.

He saw it all clearly by the reflected light from a bright spot on the ceiling.

The spot moved. It came from a flashlight held by another intruder. This one also wore a rubber mask. He let go of the sheet and it settled onto Pennington's feet.

Pennington was terrified. He was convinced that he was not only going to be murdered but that first he was going to suffer unbearable pain.

17

Turnage drove into the station house parking lot at his usual time, a little before seven, and felt the usual comedown. Like all the other shortages in his department, there were never enough parking spaces. A few of them were already occupied by sanitation workers' vehicles, a sore point with his men: Not only wasn't there enough parking, but garbage trucks were considered more important than police cars.

He stuck his head in the dispatcher's window after she buzzed him through. "Tell Baker he's gonna be on duty with Pauley at the Marriott starting this morning, and I want them both to check in with me before they leave."

When they were in his office, he told them that from now on there was going to be two officers guarding Drew, "and y'all listen to me good. That girl came close to buying it once," he reminded them. "In addition, whoever took a shot at her is still around, besides which there's other people in this town that's not too fond of her. That means you guard her like she's the First Lady."

"What do we do if she does something crazy?" Pauley said. "Hawkins said she can be pretty spacey."

"You let her do what she wants—unless you think it's dangerous for her or for somebody else. But you don't let her out of your sight."

Baker grinned. "Suppose she's in the bathtub?"

Turnage stared at him till he squirmed, then told them what Hawkins and Pauley already knew—that he wanted Drew in the hotel as much as possible. "She's going out to lunch with Mrs. Fairchild, and then you bring her right back. Unless it's an emergency, you don't move her. Clear?"

He waited till they both said yessir before he went on to caution them to be careful. They were wondering what the hell had bitten him, and that was fine with him: he was as worried about them as he was about Drew. If they were injured because he couldn't tell them what was going on he would never forgive himself.

After they left he made a note on his desk calendar to put Hart on with Hawkins at four, then he penciled in his meeting with Caldecott for five-thirty.

He was looking forward to it. He intended to break the bastard. This time Drew was going to tell Pennington exactly what happened at Willow Creek and Turnage was going to bring a copy of the tape along. He'd break Lee, all right. He felt it in his bones. He'd lied to Lee at the party when he said he'd seen his car at Willow Creek, and Lee had believed him. When he met with him at five-thirty he'd be wearing a wire and he'd put on all the pressure he had to: There was no formal arrest involved so he was free to do what he liked.

He made some notes, then read over the previous day's log his secretary had typed up. When he was done he automatically reached for the phone to call the city administrator. He paused with his hand on it. He'd like to skip a get-together this morning, he thought. The only thing was they hadn't met for three days and there was a long list to discuss: a suit brought by a private citizen against two of his officers, a couple of civic problems, and increasing turnover and morale problems.

Morale was the worst, the lowest it had ever been, and he didn't see an end to it. It was one reason why he was going to offer his resignation after he arrested

Ordway and Caldecott. He didn't want to leave, he loved this town, but no matter how many times he'd begged for larger salaries and better health benefits, he'd been turned down. The result was he kept losing all his good officers.

And he'd almost lost Sharon and the kids.

"Mark, I can't live like this," she'd told him time and again. "You're putting in seventy hours a week and when you're home you're still thinking about the job. Don't you see, honey? They're never going to give you the budget you need. They don't care because they know that somehow you'll keep things running. Mark, I love you, but I need you to be with me. The kids need you."

She was right. He knew it, but his pride wouldn't let him quit. Not until she threatened to leave. Then he promised her he'd start looking. But by the time he started putting out feelers this chance to get Ordway and Lee had come up. And finally she told him she was leaving with him or without him.

He'd gone up to see her and the kids every chance he could get, and after today, thank God, he'd be able to give her a definite date for when he was going to quit.

Picking up the phone, he dialed the city administrator, and as the number rang he thought about Drew. He'd made her promise that after she had lunch with Mrs. Fairchild she'd come right back to the hotel. "And you don't budge unless I say so," he'd told her.

She'd agreed, but he didn't like it. He was a small-town cop, half his force untrained and uncertified, and he had the awful feeling he was into something way over his head.

He didn't like it at all.

As soon as Pennington felt movement from somewhere in the house, he got out of the bathtub. It was gloomy, but at least he could see. It was pitch-black when they locked him in, and there was no bulb in the light

314

fixture. Not that it mattered a hell of a lot. At dawn the little bit of light that seeped in under the door showed him what he'd made out by touch: bathtub, toilet, sink. No window. After a while he'd gotten in the tub and dozed.

He tilted his watch toward the bottom of the door: 8:43. He heard faint voices from somewhere, too faint for him to make out what was being said.

He wondered what they wanted with him. He'd tried to find out when they were driving him here, but the one with the Freddy mask started cursing and threatening him and told him if he didn't shut up, they'd push him out of the car while it was doing eighty-five.

They'd probably come for him soon, and the anxiety made his feet sweat. He wished again that they'd have at least let him put socks on before they'd taken him. Shirt, pants, shoes, pillowcase over his head, out the door, into a car: wham-bam, thank you ma'm.

He was out in the sticks. He knew that by the night sounds when they got here. He'd heard roosters at dawn, and a horse had whinnied a little while ago.

Somebody walked into the next room—the kitchen— turned on a cheap radio. Shitkicker music. He heard water running. Coffee being made.

He wondered if he should say something. He didn't want to antagonize the one with the Freddy mask. The other one, Frankenstein, didn't talk much, but Freddy was nasty. What the hell, he thought. Very quietly he said, "Hello?" Too quietly. "Hello," he repeated.

He reeled back as someone charged the door and kicked it so hard he felt it like a blow. The whole bathroom shook as Freddy kept kicking and pounding in a rage. "Whud I tell you, asshole? Did I tell you not to talk unless you're talked to? Did I tell you that? You hear me? I said, you hear me? You gonna answer or I come in there and I beat on your face?"

315

"Yes," Pennington said. His stomach was hollow. "You told me. I hear you . . . I'm sorry."

"You better be sorry, dickhead. On account of you I gotta get outta bed in the middle of the night and spend my good time in this here shithole. Now shut up!"

With a last kick, Freddy walked away.

Pennington sat down on the toilet seat, shaking. When his ears stopped ringing he got up and peed, then he sat down again.

He smelled the coffee, heard the murmur of the two men talking somewhere. He was drying his hands on the pillowcase after he'd drunk some water from the tap when another kick at the door made him jump.

The key turned in the lock and Freddy pulled open the door. He had his mask on. "Get out here, you flabby fuck."

Pennington didn't move fast enough, and Freddy grabbed his shirtfront, swung him around and flung him across the kitchen. He stopped himself at a speckled Formica counter and waited, rigid with fear.

Frankenstein walked in with a phone, a long cord trailing. "Time to reach out and touch someone," he said. "We'll tell you what to say and you better say it right. Don't do anything stupid." He jerked a thumb at Freddy. "This guy wants to kill you."

Drew murmured a sleepy hello.

"Wake you up?" Pennington said.

"That's okay. What time is it?"

"About eight forty-five. Listen, something came up and I had to go out of town early this morning. Won't be back until after lunch."

"Ah, that's too bad, Chuck."

"Okay if we get together about three?"

Drew thought fast. Mark wasn't meeting Caldecott until five-thirty. "Sure, we can do that," she said.

316

"Great," Pennington said. "You want to meet me at the shop or where you are?"

"Here's fine."

"What are you going to do today?"

"Spend some time with Mrs. Fairchild."

"What time you gonna meet her?"

She was about to answer when she remembered the tap on the phone. *Don't tell anybody where you're going or what your plans are,* Mark had said. "Hold on a second, Chuck, got something in my eye," she said.

She took the time to think, then making her voice husky with sleep, she said, "What'd you ask me? Oh yeah, Mrs. Fairchild. I don't know. She's gonna call. Chuck, I'm going back to sleep," she said. "See you at three."

Her eyes stung and she was awake now. She thought about what she was going to tell Chuck later on. More playacting. She'd gotten to hate it, she'd told the guys last night, especially with somebody like Harriet Fairchild.

"You have nothing to feel guilty about," Ed had reminded her. "Just remember—maybe Harriet Fairchild wasn't aware of how bad it was, but deep down she knew what was going on between Ordway and Betty and she did what she always did—she stuck her fingers in her ears and shut her eyes."

Like her own mother, Drew thought. She'd known what was going on too—she'd always known—but it was easier to deny it. Keep the family together no matter what . . .

"They all knew," Ed had said bitterly. "Betty once told Juleen when they were kids. She was so naive she thought it was something every little girl did with her uncle. Lee knew, my mother knew, *everybody knew.*"

Drew got up. There was no point in trying to sleep. Instead she took a leisurely bath. She didn't want to think about Jim, but she did. Maybe he *hadn't* made a deal, she tried to tell herself. Maybe he left because he felt that she had to work this out by herself. Sure. *We'll be in touch. Good luck.*

A little after ten, when she sat down in the coffee shop with Pauley and Baker, she felt that people were staring at her. She realized why when she opened the *Sentinel*. Along with her picture, a sidebar on page one said she had promised to reveal the identity of the third man today.

A woman approached the table. She started to ask Drew for her autograph, but blushed crimson and changed her mind when Baker touched his gun and Pauley rose.

The incident made Drew feel highly visible, and more of Turnage's words popped into her head: *Stay in your room as much as possible. Get in and out of places fast.*

Caldecott hated when someone walked into his office without knocking. He glanced up, and his annoyance immediately changed to apprehension.

"Don't blame your secretary," Ordway said pleasantly. "I told her I wanted to surprise you. Take a short walk with me, Lee. It's a beautiful day. Come on—couple of minutes, that's all."

Caldecott told his secretary he'd be back in five minutes. Out in the hallway, not wanting to be alone with Ordway in the elevator, he suggested they take the stairs. "I need the exercise."

The street was bright and humid, and Caldecott blinked in the glare. Ordway's limousine was at the curb.

The flowered greenery of the old plaza was a block away, and as they walked toward it Ordway said, "You had more sense then me, Lee. You were right about that girl. She's here for an evil purpose. I owe you an apology."

"Big of you to admit it."

"Better late than never. I never did much like bullshit for bullshit's sake, so I'll get right to the point. You read

318

that little piece in the paper today about what the girl's going to tell that reporter . . ."

"Yes."

"Made you nervous, did it? Well let me tell you this," he went on not expecting an answer. "Before anybody can do anything to me—or you—they got to have evidence, Lee—hard evidence. Nobody's got that, not Turnage, not anybody."

"What makes you so sure?"

"If they did they'd have used it in the original investigation. And you just remember, that was twenty-three years ago. More to the point, and the reason I dropped by, is I know how sensitive you are. You're not like me."

"Raymond, please . . ."

"It's the truth. You are sensitive, and you do get upset easy. I just hope you're not so upset you'll do something you wouldn't do under ordinary circumstances, something you might regret. I'm not threatening you, mind," he added. "I'm talking about what you got to lose—your business, your home, your family—everything you built up here. Let's start back."

"Don't you think I'm aware of that?"

"I know you are, so I won't say any more. As for what you told me last night—about that statement—it's my fault you did that. I was blind there for a while—forgot how much you mean to me."

"I appreciate that, Raymond."

"I just came by to tell you there's nothing to worry about. I'll take care of everything. That little girl won't be talking to the reporter anymore, and after today it's going to be as though she never showed up—never existed, for that matter."

"What do you mean?"

They'd reached Ordway's car. He squeezed Caldecott's arm affectionately. "I'm on my way home to pick up a change of clothes, Lee. Leaving town. Won't be back

319

until tomorrow. Don't you run scared. There's nothing to be scared of."

He got into the rear of the limousine and Caldecott peered in at him. "Raymond—"

Ordway held up a warning hand. "Just remember," he said, leaning forward, "she never showed up, never existed. *Never.*" He grinned and put a finger to his lips, held it there, then pulled the door shut.

The car moved off and Caldecott stared after it. What he had seen in Ordway's eyes made him glad he'd told him about the statement.

Drew felt smothered. Almost from the moment she'd sat back in the quiet confines of the limousine, Harriet had not stopped talking about what a dismal failure the party had been. Drew had assured her over and over that it had been a big success—and Harriet admitted that others had told her the same thing—but her brother's reaction this morning had convinced her otherwise. He had been in a terribly nasty mood and would not even talk about the party. Harriet was deeply wounded, and said it was her own fault: Having already wasted the best years of her life as Raymond's caretaker-woman, she should have known better than to take on such a thankless task. It could have been done just as well by one of Raymond's secretaries.

She was inconsolable, so that when the car finally swung off the highway and headed for the center of Charleston, Drew was relieved.

She liked the city right away. New York was all noise, grime, and pressure, so much going on you couldn't keep track of it. Charleston was laid-back and sophisticated, meant for sightseeing.

They drove along Bay Street's row of elegant, old single-houses. Set back behind wrought-iron fences, they lounged half hidden in lush greenery. "They call them single-houses because, as you can see, the side rather

320

than the front faces the street," Harriet explained. "There was a tax on frontage when they were built. The narrower the house, the lower the tax. Pure southern genius."

After they had walked along the Battery, then seen Courthouse Square and a few other places, Harriet said she had made reservations at a fine restaurant.

Drew groaned inwardly. She did not want to be trapped in a fancy restaurant. "Harriet, where would you go if you wanted to pig out?"

Taken aback, Mrs. Fairchild managed a smile. "I haven't 'pigged out' in a very long time. . . ."

"Ah, c'mon, Harriet, suppose you were eighteen and you were with a guy you liked."

Harriet and the chauffeur held a conference, finally agreeing on the Gourmetesserie.

Drew was hopeful when they stopped near it: The streets were filled with shoppers, tourists, and young people. And as soon as she and Harriet walked into the huge old brick warehouse Drew liked the place: a couple of dozen stalls offered everything from hamburgers to Greek salad and Near East delicacies.

"Harriet," Drew said, "you really came through. The treat's on me."

Pauley wasn't sure if they were being tailed or not. He and Baker were following the limo back up the interstate and he'd spotted the car in the rearview mirror a couple of miles back. It kept hanging on, always three or four cars behind, speeding up or slowing down when they did. He and Baker decided they'd wait one more mile.

Inside the limousine Drew listened without comment as Harriet Fairchild kept talking about Betty and how proud of her she had been.

"Every one of my friends, Drew—*everyone* who saw that child—was jealous of me," she was saying. "'Harriet, I am going to steal that little girl from you one day,'

321

Juleen's mother used to say. Did I tell you, Drew, that Betty received straight A's in school?"

She had, but Drew said no. She felt edgy and didn't know why.

"Oh, she was an exceptional child, Drew, simply nonpareil. She could have been anything, an actress, a dancer, anything. Her teachers were simply astounded by her talents. Her piano teacher told me once that if Betty wished to she could be a world-famous concert pianist . . ."

Finally Drew realized what was bothering her: Harriet never talked about Betty except as a baby or a little girl. As far as Harriet was concerned, her daughter had never gone past the age of ten.

She remembered Harriet's definition of herself: one foot planted in reality and all her weight on the other. *Like my mother,* Drew thought. When Gena had finally gotten the courage to tell their mother what their father had done, she did not want to believe it. And even after they hammered the truth into her, Gena sometimes screaming in frustration, their mother found a dozen reasons to forgive their father, none to find him despicable. And Gena killed herself.

As Drew thought about it now, she felt as angry as Harriet as she had at her mother. How was it possible for this woman not only to have closed her eyes to the torture her daughter had gone through, but now to only recall her as a storybook child—and herself as a storybook mother?

". . . We adored each other," Harriet was saying. "I cannot recall a bad word between us or that Betty ever gave me a moment's anxiety. As hard to believe as it might seem, our relationship was perfect."

"I had the feeling that your brother and Betty sometimes had some pretty bad conflicts," Drew said.

"Oh, occasionally," Harriet said. "But Betty *loved* Raymond—even more than she loved that feckless father of hers."

"That doesn't mean you can't have conflicts."

Harriet smiled tolerantly. "What do you mean?"

"You know—arguments, getting mad at each other."

"Rarely. Occasionally, when Raymond tried to discipline her, Betty might have exhibited the normal display of temper, but other than that—"

"Did you have any idea she was in love with Ed Johnson?"

"I have thought about that too, Drew. I don't believe she was. She would have told me."

"Maybe not. I did things I never told my mother."

"That was never the way with Betty and me," Harriet insisted. "She told me everything."

"Even if she felt you might get upset?"

"Why of course, lamb. She knew I would never interfere."

Drew tried again, relating how Lee Caldecott had treated her in his office. Harriet said she was very surprised: Lee came from a good family. She went on to say how much in love with Betty he had been at one time, and again began talking about Betty as a child when the limousine slowed and moved onto the shoulder.

"Why are we stopping, Roy?" Mrs. Fairchild asked the chauffeur.

"The police officers are signaling, ma'am."

The two women turned to see the police cruiser stopping behind them, headlights flashing. Mrs. Fairchild pressed the button to lower the window as Officer Baker came up.

"Sorry about that," he said. "Thought we had a problem, but everything's okay."

Drew was lying back against the pillows, trying to read a magazine and getting nowhere. It was almost three-thirty and Chuck still hadn't shown. The phone rang.

"Chuck?"

"Yeah. Jesus, Drew, I'm sorry to hang you up like this. My damn car broke down in the middle of nowhere."

"I figured something must have happened."

"I'm in a station about two hours away, and it's going to be another hour before I'm out of here. That should get me there about seven. How about if I come by the hotel, we grab a bite and talk?"

She had no choice. "Sure, we can do that."

"The main thing is we'll have plenty of time to make the morning edition. Anything else come to you about that third man?"

"I know who he is."

"You're kidding."

"No. I'll tell you when I see you."

"Around seven," Pennington said.

She thought for a few moments, then ripped a page from a yellow pad. Turning on some music, she got off the bed quietly and opened the connecting door. She slipped the page under Johnson's door and briskly moved it from side to side. A few moments later she heard the faint sound of the bolt being slid.

Ed Johnson got in to see Turnage using the name they'd agreed on, Jonathan Edwards.

"The reporter called Drew about twenty minutes ago," he told Turnage. "His car broke down and they won't be getting together until seven. Drew would like you to hold off seeing Lee until tomorrow."

"Shit." Turnage wanted to say no, nail Lee while he was ripe.

"She has a point," Johnson said. "When the story breaks in the morning paper, if anything can scare Lee, that certainly will."

Turnage chewed his lip. "I'm worried about that goddamn Ordway." But when he thought of what Drew had said about walking into her apartment some night, he knew there was no choice.

He leafed through his Rolodex, then picked up the phone. "If Lee can make it tomorrow morning, okay," he said, stabbing buttons. "If not—"

"Lee," he said when he was put through, "I got something that just came up. Can we get together tomorrow morning instead of at five-thirty?"

Caldecott said the morning was fine with him and they settled on eleven.

"Okay, that's that," Turnage said after he hung up. Not wanting to think about the situation, he asked Johnson how the town looked to him after all these years, then studied him, hardly listening to his words.

There was still something special about him. Even after all he'd gone through, he thought, he'd ended up the way Turnage always figured he would. Everything about him—clothes, manner, the way he talked—said he was class. He had it. He himself didn't, Turnage knew, and it used to make him feel bad. Not anymore. You made do with what you had.

"How'd it feel being around Drew so much?"

Johnson hesitated. He and Chantal and the children spoke French most of the time, so his immediate thought was *étrange*.

"Peculiar at first, then delightful. . . . That boyfriend of hers must be an idiot."

"You never told me how you met her."

"In the Louvre of all places," Johnson said. "I hadn't been there in years." His mind jumped back to that first astonishing moment he had seen her in a quiet room hung with Rubenses. "I couldn't believe it. I went up to her and introduced myself and my wife, and the three of us started talking. She came to dinner the next night, and . . . and this is very strange, Mark." He hesitated. "I'd never told anyone except Henry Attucks what happened—"

"The Liberian guy . . ." Turnage said.

"Yes. I hadn't even told Chantal. But that night, I don't know why, I told Drew and Chantal the whole story.

It just poured out of me. It was quite an emotional evening, as you may gather. All three of us cried. On top of it Drew told us about her sister . . . I don't think she would mind my telling you," he said when he saw that Turnage didn't know. "Her sister was molested by their father. She committed suicide."

"What the hell is it in this country?" Turnage burst out. "Got one of my officers in court right now trying to nail a stepfather for the same thing. She tells me that one out of every four women—can you believe this?—one out of every four women are sexually molested before they're adults." He shook his head in resignation. "Sorry, Ed. Go on."

"That was it. She was in Paris for a week, and Chantal and I saw as much of her as we could."

"What did she mean last night when she said she got you into this?"

"Just that. This whole charade was her idea. I laughed it off. My initial reaction was the same as yours—it wouldn't work. But she kept talking about it, saying she could do it, that Betty sounded exactly like her sister. 'Ed, we can get those guys. I can be her,' she insisted. And I'll never forget this. One day we were having lunch and she asked me to turn away. When I turned back . . . Mark, it was uncanny. She was Betty—or almost Betty. The same look in her eyes. Wounded. Angry . . ." He made a gesture that said it was beyond description.

"Don't tell me," Turnage said. "Back there at the Spengler I had a coupla times when . . ." He couldn't find words either.

"Then you can imagine what it was like working with her," Johnson went on. "I flew into New York every chance I had. I think that on and off over the past year we probably spent an average of ten to fifteen hours a month together. She was like a sponge. Everything I told her about Betty, everything I showed her she absorbed, made

326

it a part of her. Sometimes I'd interrupt her in the middle of an impersonation, disparage her, call her a phony, do everything we thought someone might do to trip her up. After the first few times nothing threw her. She could slip in and out of being Betty in the blink of an eye. What rankles me is I can't get her to accept anything but expenses. She's like you."

Turnage shifted uncomfortably and Johnson got up. "It's interesting," he mused, "how she and Betty could look so much alike and be so different . . . This may sound strange, but I've sometimes thought that, in a way, Betty and I were like Othello and Desdemona in reverse."

Turnage arched his eyebrows, making Johnson smile. "I'm serious, you character. I only realized it when I saw the play in the West End. Years ago. 'She loved me for the dangers I had pass'd,' Othello said, 'and I loved her that she did pity them.' With Betty and me it was the opposite."

Turnage didn't get it. "You pitied her?"

"I loved her. But she was totally different from what we thought she was, Mark. We all believed she had everything—envied her—and she had nothing. As hard as my folks had to scrape, I was rich by comparison. She never had any of the warmth I did, none of the love. And yet there was so much honesty and sweetness still in her . . ."

He stopped and Turnage cleared his throat, swallowing the jealousy stuck there after all these years.

They were quiet, and Johnson broke the silence.

"Mark, I meant what I said to Drew—if we don't get Ordway, I won't give him the chance to hurt her."

Turnage didn't want to talk about it. "I'll be here a while. Stick around the hotel in case I have to reach you."

And keep an eye open, he wanted to add, but then he'd have had to tell Johnson what to keep an eye open *for*, and he didn't know.

He thought of Sharon. It was going to feel good to be

able to tell her what had been going on all this time. She'd suspected it was something important, something he couldn't talk about. And she knew it wasn't another woman. They didn't play those kind of games. But she'd still kept asking him when he was going to make the move and all he could tell her was soon. Lately he'd told her *very* soon.

The phone rang, and after he hung up he got so busy he almost forgot that he wanted to brief Hawkins and Hart before they took over at the Marriott. He caught them in the squad room, brought them into his office and told them more or less what he'd told Pauley and Baker.

Knowing the ground rules already, Hawkins asked Turnage if he had anything specific in mind as far as trouble was concerned.

"Specific in what way?" Turnage said sharply.

"Nothing, I just thought that if you're edgy maybe you had a special reason."

"I do." Turnage leaned forward. "You were there when the girl almost bought it from GG, but maybe you forgot. Maybe you both forgot that somebody took shots at the car they were in. You do remember that . . . ?"

They both murmured that they did and he said, "Pauley and Baker reported that a car might have followed them on the way back from Charleston. The girl's agreed to stay in the hotel for the rest of the day, but be on your toes."

After they went out he was tempted to take a shot of bourbon. He looked at the clock on his desk: 3:54.

Outside the door he heard an officer call to Hawkins and say something that made Hart laugh. Right then his instincts told him that something was going to go wrong. He felt it so strong he wanted to go out and tell the two men to get over to the Marriott on the double and bring Drew back here right away.

But he didn't.

* * *

"Who is it?" Drew's voice came through the door.

"Hawkins"

"Be right there, Warren."

While they waited Hart slapped his paperback against his thigh.

"How is it?" Hawkins asked him.

Hart glanced down at the cover. "Gettin' good."

"Greenview's finest reporting," Hawkins said when Drew opened the door. "Ralph'll be up here the next couple of hours and I'll be downstairs."

"I feel more secure already." Drew smiled.

Hart looked toward the elevator as the door opened and a man carrying an attaché case got out. The guy glanced their way, and Hart kept an eye on him while he consulted the sign that showed how the numbers ran.

"Only person you're expecting is Chucky baby," Hawkins was saying. "Is that right?"

"About seven. How do you like it here compared to Detroit?" she asked him.

The man disappeared into a room a few doors down.

"No comparison," Hawkins said. "How about you?"

"It's gorgeous. I saw a little of Charleston today too. Nice. If Detroit is anything like New York, I can see why you came here."

"Tough town."

"New York or Detroit?"

"Both."

Drew smiled, said that she'd probably be eating here in the hotel with Chuck, then closed the door. As soon as Hawkins left Hart sat down and started reading.

In his room a few doors down from the cop, DeWitt Williams had left a wakeup call for 5:45. When the call came he thanked the operator cheerfully: He'd had a good nap. He did the crossword puzzle in the newspaper for a while, then went to the bathroom.

He'd left the attaché case there, and after he washed up, he brought it out with him.

At 6:47 he finished taping it to the room door, dropped the roll of duct tape into the basket beside the bureau, then peeled off the rubber gloves he had on and stuck them in his pocket.

He did a few yoga exercises, then shook his hands out and let them hang loose.

At 6:55 he strapped on his shoulder holster and put on his jacket. Examining himself in the closet door mirror, he liked what he saw: average-looking, quietly dressed type.

Taking a last look around the room, he carefully opened the door to the corridor and listened. Silence. He walked out.

Outside Drew's door, an ankle resting on his knee, his hat under the chair, Hart glanced up unwillingly from his book. The man who'd come out gave him a shy nod, and Hart realized it was the same guy he'd seen when he came on. He lost interest, and by the time the guy reached the elevator, Hart forgot he existed.

His lurching heart reminded him when he heard the click of a hammer and stared into a gun muzzle.

"I'll kill you if I have to," the man said with quiet authority. He indicated the stairway exit, and Hart, his foot asleep, limped to it.

The man walked him up the stairs, stopped him on the roof landing. He was cursing himself for being careless and stupid when—

DeWitt hit him cleanly, watched the red line on the cop's bald spot overflow as he eased him down to the floor. He tied the cop's hands and feet expertly and fast, taped his mouth. Wouldn't be long before he woke up, but his head was bleeding like hell. DeWitt didn't like the idea of hurting a cop bad.

He glanced at his watch: 6:58. What the hell, he thought, what goes around comes around. Rolling the cop onto his side, he took out a handkerchief, pressed it against the cut and held it there while he rolled the cop onto his back. Perfect.

Down in the lobby Hawkins saw on his watch that it was exactly seven. Taking his radio from his belt, he tried to raise Hart. No answer. He tried again, then headed for the stairs and took them two at a time.

Revolver in hand, he saw what he expected when he broke out onto the third-floor corridor: Hart was gone.

Reaching Drew's door, he jiggled the knob, pounding and calling her name.

"Drew—Hawkins. Open up, fast! Is Hart with you?" he asked as soon as she appeared.

Drew was wide-eyed. "N-no."

"C'mon, I'm gettin' you outta here."

"What is it?" Drew said. "What happened?"

For answer a muffled explosion shook the floor under their feet. Smoke billowed into the corridor from a room a few doors down and an alarm went off.

"Let me get my handbag," Drew said as alarms began going off all over the hotel.

Doors were opening, guests coming out.

"All of you people stay calm," Hawkins called. "Use the stairways at either end of the corridor and walk out of the building as fast as you can. I said walk! Drew—let's go!"

The smoke was getting thick as someone rounded the turn in the corridor, a bearded black man. "What's going on?" he asked.

Hawkins motioned with his revolver. "Mister, don't ask questions and move it out. Drew!" he called again.

Drew came out clutching her handbag, but stopped short when she saw Johnson.

"I won't tell you again, mister," Hawkins said. "Either start out of this building or get your hands up!"

"Warren, it's all right," Drew said, "he's a fr—"

"I don't care who he is." Hawkins didn't take his eyes from Johnson. "Make up your mind!"

Johnson backed off, hands half raised. "Go ahead, Drew," he said.

Hawkins grabbed her hand, and then they were dashing past Johnson to the exit door.

No one else was on the stairs and they went down fast. They were almost to the ground floor when there was another tremor and another explosion.

At the exit to the lobby Hawkins told her to stay back, then took a look and waved her to him. "C'mon!"

He grabbed her hand, and as they dashed for the parking lot exit, Drew got a quick flash of smoke coming from the opposite side of the lobby. Then they were through the door and outside and Hawkins was propelling her to the parked police cruiser. Sirens sounded in the distance as he opened the rear door, eased Drew in and slammed the door shut.

Then he was behind the wheel, the engine roared to life, and Drew was pressed back against the seat as the car screeched off.

He was on the radio before they were out of the parking lot. "One-oh-six to Greenview. Lemme hear," he said.

"Go ahead."

"I had two explosions here at the Marriott and a couple of ten-seventies and I can't raise Hart. You better send ambulances. Tell the chief I'm seventy-six seventy-five with Drew Summers."

Turnage came on. "I'm here. What's the status of Hart?"

"Unknown," Hawkins said.

"How about Ms. Summers?"

Drew laced her fingers through the grill. "I'm okay, Chief," she called. "Thanks to Warren."

"I heard that," Turnage said. "What's your twenty?"

"I'm passing the car wash," Hawkins said.

". . . I'm ten-eight. Meet me at the K mart lot, north end," Turnage said.

As Hawkins hung the microphone on the dash, Drew heard sirens in the distance. "Warren, thanks," she said. "You were terrific."

"Don't thank me yet."

"Think Ralph is okay?"

"Don't know."

The radio was on, officers giving terse messages and getting terse answers from the dispatcher. The flashing lights of a cruiser appeared, coming fast. A voice said, "One twenty-seven to one-oh-six," and Hawkins took the mike from the dash.

"Go ahead."

"Everything ten-four?" the voice asked.

"Affirmative," Hawkins said, putting the mike back. He and the officer waved as they passed.

"Why is the chief meeting us halfway?" Drew asked.

"He wants to find out what happened at the hotel and doesn't want to talk about it over the radio. I'm the only one who—" The rest was drowned out when a fire truck came at them, siren screaming.

"You must've scared someone awful bad," Hawkins said, making a diagonal left.

"You're telling me," Drew said.

"Got any idea who?"

"I wish I did," Drew said, feeling guilty. He'd just risked his life to save hers, and she didn't like lying to him.

It was getting dark, Drew realized: A few cars had their lights on. Something was bothering her, but she was still so upset she couldn't put her finger on it.

Hawkins made a sharp left this time and she realized what it was: This wasn't the way to the station.

"Warren, I think you're going the wrong way."

"How's that?"

"The station's over that way."

"Don't you worry, I know," Hawkins said.

"Why are we going this way?"

"It's what the chief wants."

He cut the flashing lights and the siren.

"But you just told him on the radio you'd meet him at the K mart."

"Yeah," Hawkins said, "but that was just in case anybody was listening in on our frequency."

"I don't understand."

"Simple," Hawkins said. "If somebody *was* listening they'd think we're headed for the station. We're not. I'm taking you to a safe house."

"Where?"

"Just outside of town."

They were nearing the edge of town now, and a police car approached, siren on—a sheriff's car, Drew saw as it sped by.

The streetlamps were dim here and farther apart. Drew was confused. She tried to tell herself that there was nothing wrong, nothing to worry about. Except that Mark hadn't said anything to her about this.

She leaned forward, grasped the grill.

"Warren, are you sure this is what the chief wants?"

"Hey, get off my case, will you?" he said sharply.

"Nobody ever mentioned it to me."

"We didn't want to take the chance you might let it slip."

She tried to catch his eye in the rearview mirror, but he kept watching the road ahead. She willed him to look at her, and finally he did. He looked away fast, and what she saw in his eyes confirmed what she felt: He was lying to her.

Wherever she was being taken, it was not to a safe house, and as the police cruiser passed a final old-fashioned streetlamp and plunged into rural darkness, Drew realized with a sick feeling that something had

334

happened that she didn't know about. A deal had been made.

Keeping one hand on the grill, she felt for the door handle. There was none. Same on the other side.

Her heart was pounding now and she had to use all her willpower to keep the shakiness from her voice.

"Warren, where *is* this safe house?" she asked him.

He didn't answer.

18

Turnage kept looking for Hawkins's cruiser all the way to the Marriott. He hadn't shown up at the K mart and Turnage couldn't raise him on the radio. Neither could dispatch. Either he wasn't answering or he couldn't, and by the time Turnage approached the Marriott driveway he had a bad feeling in his gut.

One of his officers waved him on and he felt a slight lift. His men were on the ball: They'd kept the area clear for vehicles and herded everybody—guests, potential witnesses and potential suspects—onto the lawn a safe distance from the building. A couple of sheriff's cruisers had also arrived. The deputies were lending a hand, and seeing their crisp, new uniforms made him momentarily angry. His own men's were wilted, their shirts so old they wouldn't hold a press.

Smoke was coming from a blown-out window on the third floor, and Turnage rolled over broken glass as he maneuvered past a fire engine. A couple of men were cranking a ladder up to the window, while two more men at another engine were unreeling hose.

Driving around to the east parking lot entrance, he pulled up behind an ambulance, and at almost the same time he started for the door one of his lieutenants pushed it open.

"Hart is okay, Chief," Keagy said. "The EMTs are bringing him down now."

"What happened to him?"

"Somebody slugged him." He let Turnage go past.

"Anyone else hurt?"

"No, but there's a witness wants to talk to you in the lobby."

They were heading there when the techs came toward them with Hart on a stretcher. Seeing Turnage, they stopped.

Hart's head was bandaged, shirt and undershirt bloodied. He was sweating and pale but conscious.

"You hurting bad?" Turnage asked him.

Hart gave him a scared grin. "Can you hurt good?" He told Turnage what happened and said he gave a description of the suspect to another officer.

Turnage squeezed his shoulder. "Glad you're okay," he said. He started for the lobby again, Keagy still with him. "Where were the explosions?"

"One in a room on the third floor, second in a room on the other side of the lobby," Keagy said. "Both were empty and there's only minor fire upstairs."

Another thing to feel good about, Turnage thought. But something wasn't right: An officer down, two explosions, Hawkins and Drew get out with no trouble, but now no Hawkins. The image of gunmen commandeering Hawkins's cruiser flashed through his mind and he rejected it, but not before his stomach went sour.

The smell of smoke was strong in the lobby, a haze of it hugging the ceiling.

Keagy pointed. "There's the witness—that black guy over there. He saw Hawkins leave with the girl."

Johnson was standing by the front desk with a couple of people. As soon as he saw Turnage he started for him. "Mark! Is Drew all right?"

"I don't know," Turnage said.

"What do you—"

Turnage cut him off. "Ed, tell me what you saw."

"Not much. There was an explosion and I went to check on Drew. Your officer was just getting her out. He held a gun on me and wasn't any friendlier even after Drew said she knew me."

"Tall, slim, black curly hair?"

"Yes."

Hawkins all right. He turned to Keagy. "Anybody else see them?"

"Nobody we've questioned so far."

Turnage pulled out his walkie-talkie. "This is one hundred to Greenview."

"Go ahead," the dispatcher answered.

"One-oh-six show up?"

"Negative."

"See if you can raise him," he said, and when she tried and there was only dead air, the image of the gunmen jumped into his mind again. One of them was the guy who slugged Hart.

"Greenview to one-oh-six," the dispatcher repeated while Turnage stared at Johnson in silence.

When there was no answer Turnage swore to himself and told her to keep trying. "How many of our men we got here?" he asked Keagy.

"Six."

Just about the whole shift. "Divide the city into quadrants north and south of Main, east and west of the highway. I'll take the northwest, you pick the men for the other three. Tell them to cover every street, every alley, every driveway. Got it?"

"Yessir."

He tapped Johnson. "Come on," he said as Keagy got on the walkie and started calling men in to huddle.

"Mark, what's going on?" Johnson asked as they piled into his car. "Is Drew safe or not?"

"I don't know. I wish I could tell you, Ed, but I don't know. I don't know a damn thing."

338

* * *

Heart pounding, Drew tried to keep her tone light. "Warren, I think this house is so safe we're not going to be able to find it."

Hawkins slowed and turned onto a dirt road.

"Put on your seat belt."

No sooner did she do what he said than the car began bouncing and swaying from ruts and potholes. Even with the seat belt on she had to brace herself.

She told herself she had to stay calm and not panic. She still had a chance. She was pretty fast on her feet, and Hawkins didn't know she suspected anything. It was dark now: When they reached where they were going maybe she'd get the chance to make a run for it. Maybe.

Turnage took a different route back to the station house. For the second time in as many minutes he listened grimly as the dispatcher failed to raise Hawkins.

"Where the hell could they be? *Where?*"

Johnson tried to be reassuring. "Mark, if they weren't okay, wouldn't you have heard some—"

"Hold it," Turnage said. Keagy was calling him. He snatched up the mike.

"This is one-hundred. Go ahead, one-oh-three."

"Chief, you better hear this," Keagy said. "A deputy here just found out we got an officer missing and he thinks he saw him."

"Put him on."

"Deputy Gibbons, sir. On my way here to back up your officers, I was coming east on Garden Grove and I passed one of your cruisers headed west. Near Macon. It was getting dark, but I thought I saw a white female in the back."

Turnage felt like he'd been punched. "Was the car's emergency equipment on?"

"No sir."

339

"How fast was he going?"

"Maybe a few miles over the speed limit."

It all fit suddenly, and Turnage felt things slipping away. He kept his voice steady. "Ten-four, Deputy. Appreciate your help." He tried to remember Keagy's badge number, but he couldn't. He had all he could do to think straight. ". . . Keagy, you know what we got."

"Yes, sir."

"Go ahead and reroute your available units to the Garden Grove vicinity. Use ten-zero," he added, knowing he didn't have to. Like the dispatcher and every man listening, Keagy knew Hawkins was dangerous.

Keagy signed off and Turnage told dispatch he was coming in and to start putting out a BOLO for Hawkins. Then he hung up, and, slapping the blue light into the metal bracket on the windshield, he cut on the siren and all his lights.

Turnage was gray, and Johnson tried to contain his own mounting anxiety. "What's going on, Mark?"

"You heard it," Turnage said. "That deputy saw Hawkins's cruiser headed out of town. No blue lights, no siren." He lost his voice and had to clear his throat.

"I still don't—"

"If the sonofabitch was getting Drew back to the station, he'd of been lit up like a Christmas tree and breaking speed records. And he put Drew in the back. You put a goddamn prisoner in the back, not someone you're guarding. I got a bad cop, Ed. Somebody assaulted my officer and left Hawkins free to get Drew out of the hotel. *Ed, I gave her to them.*"

"You didn't give her to anybody."

"I gave her to them. As sure as—"

Johnson cut him off, angry. "You're acting like a child. *What are you going to do?*"

That shut him up. Ed was right: he was wasting time on self-pity. "The only thing I can," he said. "Get to the station and give the dispatcher a hand putting out a

340

statewide BOLO—be on the lookout—then I'll head out Garden Grove myself."

Johnson was silent, then he said, "Mark, what about Lee? Do you think he might know something?"

Turnage looked at him in amazement. It was so simple he almost choked. "Why the hell didn't *I* think of that?"

Checking for traffic behind him, he screeched to a rolling stop, made a U, and seconds later they were speeding in the opposite direction.

Reaching above the visor, he pulled down a notebook and turned the pages with fingers that did not want to obey. Finally he found what he was looking for, thrust the open book at Johnson.

"He won't know your voice. Call his house. Find out if he's home. If they say he's not, give me the phone and I'll try to find out where he is. It's a long shot, but we don't have anything else."

Johnson had already picked up the phone between them before Turnage finished. As he did, Turnage grabbed the mike and advised the dispatcher he wasn't coming in and she was to put out the BOLO without him.

Johnson heard the phone on the other end ring.

"Caldecott residence." A maid.

"Hello," Johnson said. "Is Mr. Caldecott home, please?"

"Yessir. May I ask who is calling?"

"My name is Mr. Rexford. Uh, Mr. Ordway suggested that I—"

Johnson depressed the cutoff button. "He's home."

The ruts and potholes had come to an end, and they were moving through a lane of brush that scraped and slapped at the car. The lane ended and the headlights picked up an area of knee-high grass. Hawkins pulled up near a doorless and windowless hut and stopped.

Drew said, "Can't say I admire the chief's taste in safe houses, Warren."

Hawkins made an amused grunt and turned off the engine and the lights, bringing total darkness.

"Where are we?" Drew asked.

"Out of town," he said.

"I kinda gathered that." She unlocked the seat belt, laced her fingers in the grill. "Can I get out and stretch my legs? I feel car-sick."

He rolled down his window, then the window on the passenger side. He wasn't going to let her run anywhere.

Her eyes were becoming accustomed to the dark and she could faintly make him out. It was time to stop pretending.

"What are you going to do with me?" she said.

"Not going to do anything with you."

"Please, Warren, I know what's going on. I can't do anything about it, so at least tell me the truth."

He pulled a pack of cigarettes from his shirt pocket. ". . . Turning you over to somebody."

"Who?"

"What does it matter? You'll see when he gets here." He fumbled with a book of matches.

"Are you doing it for money?"

"I gotta do it and that's that. Let's cut the bull." He opened the door and got out.

She got as close to the open door as the grill would allow. "What's going to happen to me?"

"I don't know. . . ." He struck a match and his face appeared, then was gone. "And I don't want to know. I'm stuck. I owe somebody."

"You're talking about Raymond Ordway, aren't you? Warren, you don't have to lie, I know it's him."

"Raymond Ordway?" He sounded surprised.

"Whatever you did, whatever he's got on you, Warren, it can't be that—"

342

"He hasn't got anything on me. I don't even know the man. Wendell Barnes is the one wants you."

"Then he's doing it for Raymond Ordway. Warren, they're going to kill me."

"I don't know what they're gonna do and I don't want to know. I hand you over and I get paid and I'm outta here. That's all I know."

"Warren, please, if you're in trouble, Mark Turnage can—"

"Mark Turnage can't do diddly, so just lay off."

The glow of headlights appeared, bouncing crazily, and a minute later a car broke out of the brush. It turned and waded slowly through the grass toward them, brights on. When it came to a stop it lit up the interior of the cruiser. Drew heard a door open.

"Warren, listen to me," she pleaded. "Please, I'm begging you—"

He slammed his door and Drew swung around, shading her eyes from the blinding glare. She watched his silhouette through the rear window as he undid the flap on his holster and walked toward the car.

He said, "Hey, dim those lights, pal. I can't see a—"

A firecracker sound cut him off and he staggered back as if a giant fist had slammed him in the chest. He hit the ground with a sickening impact, and Drew turned away as he tried to get up and failed.

When she looked again, the grass was quivering around him and he was making pitiful wet sounds. Drew wanted to put her hands over her ears.

Whoever had shot him came out from behind the open car door holding a big revolver.

When he paused beside the front bumper and Drew saw who he was, she had to fight to hold on to her sanity.

It was Raymond Ordway, and he was wearing coveralls and a wide-brimmed hat.

He blotted out one of the headlights as he made his way to Hawkins's body, and Drew turned away as he pointed the gun down and pulled the trigger. When she looked again, he was stooped down beside the body searching for something.

Drew began to shake uncontrollably.

A block away from the Caldecott house Turnage cut all his emergency equipment, and when they pulled up, he and Johnson were out of the car and dashing for the door at the same time.

Turnage knocked and pounded until the maid peeked through a side window.

"Catherine, open up," Turnage said. "This is an emergency."

When she did, she found her arms held. "Don't get upset and don't get scared," Turnage said. "Where is Mr. Caldecott?"

"He's in the family room," she blurted and Turnage let her go. She thought she heard a faint "Sorry" from the black man who chased after him down the hall.

Lee Caldecott had one leg draped over the arm of his favorite chair. He was watching a good flick with Juleen and Tricia, and he was thinking of putting the tape on pause and getting some ice cream when footsteps came pounding down the hall.

He barely had time to move before two men charged in. Tricia let out a scream, and Caldecott thought it was a robbery until he saw Turnage.

It was worse. Turnage was on him like a crazy man, pulling him out of his chair, dragging him over to the bar and slamming him against it.

Caldecott braced himself to be hit, but instead Turnage was yelling at him and he was so confounded and frightened he didn't understand what the man wanted.

Juleen charged over to them shrieking. "Mark, what are you doing? Are you crazy? Leave him alone!"

She started clawing and kicking at him until the black man grabbed her.

344

"Woman, stay out of this!" Johnson yelled, shoving her toward the couch. Instead she stumbled for the phone and Johnson went after her. He jerked the receiver from her hand and almost flung her onto the couch this time.

She was getting up when Turnage yelled, *"Juleen!"* He pointed a warning finger at her. "You stay the hell out of this and take care of your daughter or by God I'll have you thrown in jail.

"Now, you sonofabitch," he said, his face inches from Caldecott's, "Drew Summers and one of my officers are missing and I want to know where they are."

"Mark, how would I know that?" Caldecott said.

"You know. Don't tell me you don't! Raymond Ordway's got 'em and you're gonna tell me where they are or I'm gonna—"

"Mark, believe me, I swear I don't know!"

Turnage pulled him forward and shook him, then slammed him back against the bar. There was murder in him. "Lee, where did he do it? Where did he kill Betty? We have to know!"

"I don't know what you're talking about. Why are you asking me all these ques—"

"Lee, there's no more time. Ordway's got that girl Drew and he's gonna kill her. We got but one lousy chance to find her and it ain't too good. Now tell me!"

"Believe me, Mark, I don't—"

"Believe you? Believe *you*, you sonofabitch? I'll tear you apart. Tell me, goddamnit!" he shouted, drawing back a fist.

"No!" Johnson said.

Turnage knew what was happening, and all his instinct and training went against permitting it, but in the next moment it was done. Johnson had his gun.

"Give him to me," Johnson said. He made a threatening motion. "Give him to me!"

"No, Mark!" Juleen shouted. She was holding her daughter protectively.

"He'll tell me," Johnson said, his eyes burning into Turnage's. *"Let me have him!"*

Juleen's voice was almost a whisper. "Mark, for God's sake . . ."

Johnson shoved Turnage aside, then trembling with repressed fury he pushed the muzzle of the revolver against Caldecott's throat.

"Lee," he said, his voice almost conspiratorial. "You know who I am?"

Caldecott shook his head.

"Yes you do. Sure you do, Lee. You simply think you don't. Twenty-three years ago I went to meet my Betty at Willow Creek. I went to meet my lovely, lovely Betty. And you know what? My Betty was there, but she was no longer lovely. . . . You know who I am now, Lee?"

Caldecott's jaw dropped.

"I see you do. You remember. Because you were there too. You and Raymond Ordway. Waiting for me. And you watched while Ordway came out from behind Betty's car and held a gun on me and then called out for you to come over and rehearse the lies he told you to tell. You remember all that, Lee?"

Caldecott swallowed, the only movement he made.

"Then you remember what Ordway did to me? This." He pushed the muzzle up under Caldecott's chin, his voice filled with contempt. "'Lift your head, boy,' he said to me. *'Lift* your head!'"

Paralyzed with fear, Caldecott raised his chin.

"Yes, you remember, all right. You watched him put that revolver of his right . . . up . . . there." Caldecott's head went back even farther. "And now you disgusting piece of dogshit," Johnson said, "you're going to tell me where Raymond Ordway murdered my Betty. You knew it and you lied for him. Now he's going to murder

346

Drew or he may have done so already. Where was Drew taken?"

He pushed up harder. Caldecott could barely talk. "I swear . . . I don't know."

"But you know he plans to murder her, don't you?"

". . . Yes."

"He told you."

"Yes."

"Where did he kill Betty?" Sweat beaded his forehead. He was all hatred now. "Whatever you do, Lee, don't tell me you don't know. Drew Summers has been taken somewhere and she is going to be murdered. There is a chance that Ordway is insane enough to do it in the same place he murdered Betty. You know it's in South Fork because you drove him back there to his car. Now you tell me, you cowardly degenerate, and you tell me *now!*"

He shoved the gun up farther.

"Mark," Caldecott whispered, "Mark!"

"Tell me!" Johnson roared. He pulled back the hammer. *"Tell me!"*

Caldecott's voice was a rasp. ". . . Five . . . Oaks."

"You're lying!"

"I . . . drove him . . . back to . . . Five Oaks."

Johnson's lips twisted in a sneer. He drew the gun back and Caldecott shut his eyes and waited for the blow.

"Don't be dumb," he heard Turnage growl. He opened his eyes to see Turnage gripping Johnson's wrist, taking his revolver from him.

And then suddenly Johnson let Caldecott go and the two men were slamming out of the room. Caldecott brought his head forward. His hand went to the back of his neck.

When the front door slammed, he looked at his wife and his daughter. They averted their eyes.

He turned and reached out a trembling hand for

the vodka bottle, but before he touched it he began to cry.

He was aware of Juleen and Tricia silently leaving the room, and he was aware of the video still playing.

It sounded mocking and stupid, but it was better than silence, so he left it on.

Outside, Turnage's cruiser screamed down the street and took a right on two wheels. Turnage floored the accelerator.

"Ed, we're ten minutes from the picnic grounds. If Hawkins is listening and I call for backup they'll finish Drew off fast. If they're not there yet, they'll take her somewhere else and do it."

"Suppose you don't call for backup . . ."

"We got surprise going. But then there's no help for Drew but from us. If I call in there might be a sheriff's car in the area that could get to those picnic grounds before we do."

"How good a chance?"

"Small."

"What do your instincts tell you?"

"Don't give 'em a warning."

"You have good instincts, Mark. Follow them."

By the time Ordway got up from Hawkins's body and came over to the car, Drew had regained some control.

He peered in at her, one side of his face lit by the headlights. The brim of his hat touched the window.

She forced relief into her voice. "Ray? Ray, oh thank God it's you."

"You all right, are you?"

"Yes, but I'm locked in. Could you let me out?"

He studied her. "You ever think of where that other diary is?" he asked.

". . . Other diary? I don't know what you m—"

"See this?" He showed her the revolver. "I'm going to

348

hand you in these." He held up a pair of open handcuffs, and she realized what he'd been bending over Hawkins's body for. "Put one around your left wrist."

"Ray, what for? Can't you just let me out?"

"Be a good girl and do as I say." Opening the door a little, he thrust the cuffs in. "No, on your left wrist . . . That's it . . . Little tighter," he said when it clicked. "Good. Now reach that hand out to me."

Grabbing the chain, he opened the door all the way and pulled her out.

"Ray, why are you doing this to me?"

"Doing what I have to, girl. Come along now," he said, starting for his car.

"No!" she protested. She pulled back.

"Well now," he said, "you're going to act like Betty, I'll have to treat you like Betty, won't I?"

A sharp pain stabbed her wrist as she was suddenly jerked forward. Ordway sidestepped, forcing her to stumble around in a circle before he again started for his car.

"Ray, please—I can't go that fas—"

But he wouldn't slow down and, fighting dizziness and pain, she tripped and went sprawling.

The chain was pulled from Ordway's grasp as something soft stopped her. She raised her head to see the gleam of blood soaking Hawkins's chest. His dead eyes stared into her own.

Before she could think to do anything, Ordway had grabbed the chain and was pulling her up.

"Now let's go, girl, and don't give me any more trouble."

When they were beside the car he opened the passenger door, put a hand on her head and pushed her down onto the seat. Dazed, she let him pull her left arm up and snap the remaining cuff to a handhold above the door.

He tapped her thigh. "Get your legs in," he said. She obeyed, her arm crossed before her face as he slammed the door. Then he was beside her, starting the car and maneuvering back toward the entry road.

When they were on the asphalt again, Ordway told her he felt bad about having to do this to her. "I mean it, girl. I had plans for you. Wanted you. Still want you. You're a beautiful, beautiful girl, Drew," he said. "Beautiful as Betty was. But you don't have control of yourself, and that's a pity. There's a bad, evil girl living inside you, and I have to do something about it."

"Mr. Ordway—"

"'Mr. Ordway' is it now . . ."

"There's no one inside of me but me," Drew said.

"You don't know that, do you, because you can't remember what Betty makes you do. She is inside you, all right."

"No she's not. I can remember everything I said and everything I did. I've been acting. It's all been—"

Ordway wasn't listening. "I'm sorry it turned out this way. Betty wasn't always bad. She just turned bad one day and there was nothing I could do about it."

"Ray, listen to me, please. *I'm not Betty.* I was imitating her. I'm telling you I was acting."

He shook his head. "Honeybunch, I knew that girl better than anybody else in the world," he said. "You weren't acting. You had that same nasty mouth of hers, knew things only she knew. You were *her*. You *are* her. Where could you learn all that?"

"From Ed Johnson."

"Who?"

"Ed Johnson. He told me everyth—"

"What the hell are you talking about, girl? Mark Turnage shot Ed Johnson twenty-three years ago."

"Yes he did, but only by—"

Only by accident, she was about to say, and then she was going to explain how Mark was in on this too when a sign appeared in the headlights that froze the words in

350

her throat. She saw the sign only a moment before it was swallowed up by darkness, but its message sliced through her like the sharp edge of cold metal.

It read:

SOUTH FORK
4 mi.

19

Turnage glanced at the speedometer. He was doing close to sixty-five. The limit was forty-five.

"You let me take your gun back there, didn't you?" Johnson said.

Turnage murmured a yeah.

"How did you know I wouldn't kill him?"

"I knew."

The dispatcher came on and he listened as she reeled off the BOLO on Hawkins. It was perfect—brief, all the information that was needed: *Marked Greenview police car . . . description of Hawkins as arson and kidnapping suspect . . . white female Drew Summers . . .*

"Mark, how much farther?" Johnson asked as soon as the radio was silent.

"You asked me that."

"I don't know this road. It's new." He was talking too much, he knew, but he couldn't bear to think of what might be happening to Drew. "Maybe they won't hurt her," he said. "Ordway has to realize he has nothing to gain by it."

"Yeah." Turnage said.

"Are we close at all? And don't tell me yeah."

"Few minutes." Turnage remembered something. He unlocked the glove compartment, took out the Smith & Wesson he kept there. "Just before we turn into the picnic grounds I'm gonna call for backup. I don't know if

352

we're gonna need it or if we're gonna get it in time if we do. You know how to use this?"

"Yeah."

Turnage gave him a quick glance and handed it over. Then he pushed the needle past seventy.

Drew was getting desperate. No matter what she said, Ordway insisted that she was Betty and she could not convince him otherwise. Even after she explained to him how she had met Johnson in Paris and how they had planned all this with Turnage's help, he questioned her relentlessly: Why did Turnage help Johnson? Why did he let everybody think he'd killed Johnson?

Every answer she gave made him more agitated. He couldn't, or wouldn't, accept that he'd been taken in. He sneered, saying she could never have imitated Betty the way she did. "You hear? You *think* you were imitating her. But you weren't. How else could you have recognized everybody—Lee and Juleen, me, all those other people?"

"From photographs. Mark got me photographs of everybody. He even told me who was going to be at the charity gamble that night and let me in."

"How did you know your way around town like you did?" he shot at her.

"I flew down once and spent a whole day driving around. And I had maps. And Mark made a videotape of—"

"What about those spells you had in New York?"

"Mark said that you and Caldecott would find out everything you could about me. That's why I went to the psychol—"

He wouldn't let her finish. "How did you know about that time I pulled Betty out of the water?"

"Ed's mother was there when it happened, and she told the family . . ."

Her voice trailed off as they slowed and turned at a sign that said FIVE OAKS/PICNIC GROUND. In her mind she saw Hawkins falling, saw herself slide into his body . . .

"Ray, where are we going?"

"You keep your mouth shut and answer *my* questions. How did you know the diary was in the attic? Talk up!" he demanded when she didn't answer fast enough.

"Mark put it there," she said wearily. She was exhausted and hurting from tugging against the handhold above her.

"You're lying!"

"I'm not, don't you see—"

"Where did he get it?"

"It was in Betty's cosmetics case."

"Where is the other diary?"

"There isn't another one. I made that up."

"Don't you lie to me!"

"It's the truth!"

"Oh no it's not, Miss Smartmouth. But don't you worry. You'll be telling me the truth very soon. Oh, you'll be screaming the truth before I am done with you."

He drove past the parking area and onto the ample picnic grounds. The lights swept over huge clusters of tables, and he drove down a lane of them three deep on each side.

"Who else is in on this?" he demanded.

"Nobody," Drew said as they came to the end of the lane. "Just the thr—"

She broke off as he made a right and the headlights swept over a car parked beyond another section of tables. The car had appeared and was gone so quickly that she tried to tell herself that she couldn't have seen it, that it couldn't possibly be there. But sudden weakness and the terrible pounding of her heart told her that she had.

Ordway skirted the section, then made a left, and the

354

car sprang into the beams again. He stopped a short distance from it, wanting her to see it.

Her Mustang. Waiting for her. The top down.

Her heart was thundering now and she wanted to scream, but she could barely breathe. All the energy was draining from her.

Ordway turned off the ignition and the lights. His voice came from the darkness, heavy with sarcasm.

"Welcome back, my child."

"Mr. Ordway—R-R-Ray . . ." Her teeth were chattering. "If you hurt me you'll m-m-make it worse for yourself. Lee Caldecott told me what happened at Willow Creek. It's on tape. Everything you said in the greenhouse is on tape."

"You weren't wearing a wire the night of the party, so don't you tell me—"

"Mark put a tape recorder in the greenhouse."

"Very clever," he said, turning to her in the darkness. "Mark still got the hots for you, Betty? Does he? Always did. The poor fool was in love with—"

"I'm not Betty!"

"Now don't you say that," he chided. "Say yes. I used to like it when you said yes to me. Liked it most after you kept saying no. Got me all excited. Say yes for me. Hear me, girl?" he warned. *"I said say yes."*

". . . Yes."

"Better. Much better. I like that."

His arm went around her and he drew her to him, began to touch her.

"No, don't—" Panic rose in her as his hand kneaded her breast then moved down between her legs.

She searched frantically for the door handle, found it, and with all her strength she shoved herself from him and almost fell out of the car.

She'd have hit the ground, but the handcuff held her fast. She struggled to break free as Ordway unhurriedly got out and came around the rear.

"You stay away," she said. "Don't you touch me!" Sweating and wild-eyed, she aimed a kick at him.

He avoided it easily, slid the revolver from his pocket. It looked huge as he leveled it at her. "Want your face blown off?" He came closer and held out a key. "Unlock the cuff on the handle. Remember—on the *handle.* Don't try to be smart."

She took the key from him, searched for the slot with shaking fingers. The key fell.

"Pick it up," Ordway said.

Hampered by her upraised arm, she ran a hand over the seat then the carpet before she found it.

This time she was more careful, and as soon as the cuff clicked open Ordway grabbed it.

Drew hung on to the door as he started for the Mustang. "Please, Ray, don't hurt me."

He turned on her, his eyes glittering. "Hurt my little Betty? My innocent, loving Betty? Never. I could *never* do that. Why I'm not even here, you see. I am in Savannah now. I flew there this afternoon, so how can I possibly hurt you?"

He tugged on the chain cruelly, and Drew was wrenched from the door. She grabbed at the chain and dug her heels in, but he pulled her relentlessly forward until she lost her balance and fell. Struggling and protesting, she was dragged along the grass, still pleading with him when she was on her back beside the car.

Breathing heavily, he pointed the revolver down at her. "You don't shut up, goddamn you," he snarled, "I'll shoot you like an egg-sucking bitch hound."

Drew lay still and he opened the door. It swung out over her head, and as soon as it did, the .32 under the dash flashed into her mind.

He tugged on the chain. "Now you get up and get in there. Go on, get up."

She was breathing as heavily as he. "All right," she said. "All right, just . . ."

356

She started to get up, then pretended she had to lean on the ledge below the seat to rest. As she did so, she saw Ordway's revolver drop to his side.

It was the chance she was praying for. Bracing herself as though she were getting up, she dove for the button. Magically, she found it immediately, pushed, and the panel sprang down. Then she was reaching for the gun, gripping the handle, pulling.

She screamed, recoiling in pain as she broke her fingernails against metal that would not move. In shock, she heard Ordway giggling.

"Wired it to the panel, my smart little miss. Now you get up and get in there." Grabbing the back of her shirt, he lifted her and forced her onto the seat. "Thought I'd forget it was there, did you? Oh, you're my Betty all right. Not very bright. Not bright at all. I don't forget anything, you see," he went on. "I don't forget disloyalty and ingratitude."

He'd transferred the revolver to his left hand. It was inches from her face.

"Ray . . ." She was going to plead with him, beg him, tell him she would do anything for him if he let her live, anything he wanted, but before she could say it he had reached down behind the driver's seat.

When he straightened up his teeth were bared in a death's-head grin. In his hand was a gleaming hatchet.

He searched for his pocket with the muzzle of the revolver and thrust it in.

"Where is the diary?" he said.

She couldn't take her eyes from the hatchet. "Ray . . ." She started stuttering again. "I tol—told you—"

Without warning the hatchet came down inches from her, slicing open the back of the seat all the way to the bottom.

"Oh yes, my little darling, you haven't changed a bit. You're as stupid as you always were. Stupid and disloyal."

357

Drew felt her lips moving and she knew that sounds were coming from her, that she was moving away from him crablike. She heard her own voice say, "Oh please. Please don't. Please don't!"

The car dipped as he stepped onto it and steadied himself on the steering wheel. He towered over her.

"Where is the diary?" he said, enjoying himself.

He hefted the hatchet, raising it, and Drew saw in his eyes that this time when it came down he was going to kill her. She flung up her hands and a scream tore from her throat, then another. Over them, Ordway kept yelling at her about the diary, and she wanted to say there was none, there was none, but by then her tears were blinding her and she was shrieking insanely, waiting for the horror to bite into her. She heard him howling above her and she thought he was torturing her, waiting for her to open her eyes before he let the hatchet fall. He was howling like a maniac now, howling so loud it drowned out her own shrieks.

And then suddenly she realized he was not making a sound or a movement—and the howl was not coming from him. She opened her eyes to see him turned from her, staring off at something, and her heart leaped when she too saw it: a glowing halo of light racing above the trees, and racing somewhere below it, the piercing, blissful howl of a police siren.

She almost missed her chance. Ordway was already turning back to her as she pushed herself up from the seat, hands out like claws to shove him with all her strength. The soft seat made her clumsy and one hand missed, but the other hit him hard enough to make him grab for the windshield and step back onto the ground.

Scrambling onto the backseat, she was trying to clamber onto the trunk when Ordway lunged for her and grabbed her ankle. In desperation, she twisted and swung the handcuff with all her strength and felt the

358

instant satisfaction of metal landing solid on cheekbone. Ordway cursed in pain and his fingers slipped away as she slid off the trunk headfirst and tumbled onto the grass.

Yet no sooner was she on her feet and running than he was behind her.

A flashing blue light had burst into view and she ran for it screaming as Ordway's outstretched fingers touched her.

She dodged him, dashing for a mass of tables to her right just as the police car turned in their direction. They were caught at the edge of the lights, and out of the corner of her eye Drew saw Ordway's shadow reaching for her, made herself run faster. It didn't help: He shoved her and she went sprawling toward a bench.

She squirmed under it just as he grabbed for her and missed. Knocking the bench over, he reached under the table for her, but she was already coming out from under the bench on the other side. She was on her feet and running as he came around after her.

The police car had come to a stop, its searchlight snapping on, but Ordway would not give up: He kept after her as she dashed down the lane of benches screaming for help. Dodging between a row of tables and into another lane of benches, she again scrambled under one. This time Ordway anticipated her: Leaping onto a bench, then a table, he jumped down almost at her feet as she crawled out the other side.

She turned to see him above her, grabbing her foot just as the bright glare of the searchlight whitened him. Rolling onto her back, she shook him off, and somehow, screaming and kicking hysterically, she managed to throw him off balance. And this time, before he could raise the hatchet again, a shot rang out.

Ordway uttered a grunt and started to topple. The hatchet dropped to the ground and he almost fell on her.

Instead a bench broke his fall. Sitting up, Drew scooted backward. Then she was on her feet and running. She didn't look back, dodging down rows of tables until she broke into the open, running for the police car and a man who was emerging from behind the open door.

Astounded that she was alive, she ran into Ed's outstretched arms sobbing with relief.

"Get 'er back here!" Turnage barked at the same time that the light went off, and as Johnson pulled her behind the door, she felt she had never seen two more beautiful and wonderful men in her whole life.

"You hurt?" Turnage asked her, revolver in hand.

She managed to gasp a no.

"How bad's Ordway hit?"

"I don't know," she answered, fright still with her. "He almost fell on me."

"Stay here," Turnage said to them. He moved to the rear of the car, keeping low, and disappeared around it. They heard him moving away.

"Sure you're okay?" Johnson's arm tightened around her.

She nodded, shivering. He had a gun, she saw, but she wasn't going to feel safe until Turnage came back and said Ordway was helpless or dead.

She followed Johnson to the rear of the car where they watched Turnage move like a shadow from tree to barbecue. Ordway's car was off to his right, the tables ahead of him. Drew lost sight of him when he reached them.

"Can you see him?" she whispered.

"I think he's over there."

She thought she saw movement where Ed pointed, but she couldn't be sure. Seconds later she heard a shot.

More seconds went by.

"Mark?" Johnson called. "Mark!"

360

When there was no answer, he told Drew to stay where she was and started on the route Turnage had taken. Drew followed him

"Get back there," he hissed.

"I'm not staying by myself."

"Drew, listen to me."

"I won't get in the way."

She kept her word, stayed well behind him until he reached the rows of crisscrossed legs and benches, then moved into them. She ran after him and reached a spot a few tables from him when an engine roared to life and backup lights flashed on.

"Ed," Drew yelled, "it's Ordway!"

Johnson was on his feet and moving before the car had barely started backing. Drew ran after him as he dodged around tables, heading for a section where they were stacked top to top and Ordway would have to pass.

She was behind him when he reached the place, and at almost the same time, bright lights blazing, Ordway's car finished backing and turning and started toward them.

It picked up speed fast and, holding the gun in both hands, Johnson took quick aim. His first shot sent sparks flying from the front bumper. A second bullet went through the windshield on the driver's side. He got off one more shot as the car suddenly swerved and came at him.

Unaware that Drew was there, he turned to run and almost knocked her over. Grabbing her around the waist, he propelled her forward with him as the car plowed into tables and benches, sending some of them crashing out of the way and plowing the rest forward.

Ed's arm around her, Drew didn't think they were going to make it. She steeled herself as the ground shook and she heard a grinding and groaning juggernaut of benches and tables rising up behind them.

Johnson felt it too, and before it overtook them, he heaved Drew ahead of him with all his strength.

Fighting to keep her feet, she finally fell and went skidding along the ground on outstretched hands.

When she came to a stop she lay dazed. She was safe. There was quiet behind her.

A broken length of board lay across her legs. She kicked it off and winced from a stab of pain in her calf.

She sat up. The lights of Raymond Ordway's car gleamed through a pileup of crisscrossed wood. The engine was silent and she could hear the steady tick of contracting metal.

Escaping steam hissed and curled up in the light beams.

She saw Johnson. He was doubled over under a huge tangle of wood.

She listened for a sound from Ordway. Not hearing anything, she started to rise. Pain lanced her calf. Her fingers went to it, touched a jagged piece of wood sticking out of her jeans. She took a deep breath, pulled—and nearly passed out. Blood began seeping down to her ankle and she fought off nausea.

". . . Ed?"

She crawled to him. A table lay across his back, wood piled heavily on top of it. Under him, the leg of an overturned bench pressed into his midsection. She thought the worst until he groaned and she realized he was conscious. His breath was coming in short gasps and he was braced under the weight pressing down on him. Perspiration dripped from his face.

There was room for her to crawl under the table and get beside him. Bracing herself, she pushed up with all her strength. Nothing happened. She tried again.

"Ed, I can't move it," she said. Panicked, she eased herself out and got to her feet. The wood above him was all interlocked. None of it budged.

She looked around desperately. A bench. If she could wedge one end under the table and lift the other . . .

She was dragging a bench over, telling Ed to hold on when she heard a sound that froze her: The door of Ordway's car had opened. Through the crisscross of wood she thought she saw movement, but it was behind the lights and she couldn't be sure.

Johnson tried to say something and she put her fingers to his lips. "Ed, we have to be quiet," she whispered. She held the free handcuff tightly.

It couldn't be Ordway, she told herself. Not after all she'd gone through. He couldn't come after her again. It was impossible.

She waited, listening, but the sound was unmistakable: *Someone was moving around the pileup.*

She prayed she was wrong, steeling herself for the worst, but when Ordway's outline appeared in the faint glow from the headlights, she had to stifle a scream.

She ducked as he looked in her direction. "Betty? That you there, little miss?" he asked playfully.

When she looked again, he was closer, standing on a bench, revolver in hand. Half his face was covered with blood.

"Yes, indeed, it's you, all right. I may have misjudged you, girl. I just settled accounts with Mark Turnage, and that could be Ed Johnson there with you . . ."

She had to run, Drew told herself. Save herself. Ed was caught. No matter what she did, she couldn't help him. There was no reason for her to die too. If she ran now she might get away in the dark . . .

"I wouldn't dream of separating the two of you again," Ordway said. "If Ed's still alive, I'll make sure he joins you after I send you back where you came from."

He put the revolver away, and even before his hand slid into the other pocket she knew what he was going to take from it.

"Now don't you go running away," he said, stepping down from the bench.

She could still get away, she thought, and she was bracing herself to do it when Johnson gasped her name.

It was so faint and tortured she almost didn't hear it. He had raised his head, his lips working as he desperately tried to tell her something.

Then he did a remarkable thing. His eyes boring into hers, despite the crushing weight above him, he lifted a hand from the ground and pointed a trembling finger at something a few feet in front of her.

His lips formed a word he could not finish.

And suddenly Drew understood, understood what he'd tried to say when she had told him they had to be quiet. Frantically, she scanned the ground before her, praying she could see it in time.

And there it was in plain sight: his gun.

She dove for it feeling the wonderful solid weight of it in her hand as she lifted it and in almost the same motion wheeled and held it before her.

Ordway stopped, and it flashed through Drew's mind that she should be afraid. He could still hurt her. He could still charge across the few feet between them and chop her to pieces. Yet she had no fear. She was not a helpless victim now. If she *was* going to die it would not be like Betty. She had as much power as he now, and as she pointed the gun at him, her free hand expertly steadying her wrist, she stared into his eyes, waiting.

All her senses had speeded up, so that a moment before Ordway made his decision and started for her, her lips twisted in contempt and she pressed the trigger without panic. The explosion jolted her arm and stopped Ordway short. She didn't see a mark on him, and thinking she'd missed, she pressed the trigger again. This time he cried out in pain, dropped the hatchet and clutched his thigh.

Blood spilled through his fingers, and now she knew for sure she could not be hurt. She was not Betty and she was not her sister. If anyone was going to die, it would be him.

"Mr. Ordway," she said, "this is from Betty."

Coldly and calculatingly she squeezed the trigger. The gun roared, and he clutched his chest.

"And this is from my sister," she said, shooting him again.

This time he fell to his knees, his face twisted in pain. It made her feel so good she shot him again and watched without pity as he fell against a tipped table, slid down and finally lay still against it.

"That one was from me, you dirty sonofabitch."

She let the gun slip to the ground, feeling the start of tears even while she knew she had no time for them.

From then on she believed she was being very clear-headed. She knew what she had to do and she went about doing it.

Telling Ed to hold on, she finished dragging the bench over beside him. *You're going to be okay, Ed,* she assured him. She said it over and over as she worked the bench in beneath the table, but she wasn't sure if she was saying it out loud or if it was in her mind. *I'm going to get you out, Ed,* she told him. *I'm going to get you out, and then we'll go help Mark.*

She got one end lodged where she wanted it and told him to get ready. *I'm going to lift this end, Ed. Try to get out of there when I do, okay?*

Grabbing the free end of the bench in both hands, she began slowly and carefully to raise it. When the bench was waist high she kneeled down and somehow got her shoulder under it, straining to lift it farther. The wood above Ed groaned and the table rose a little. She'd done it: the weight was off him. *Ed, see if you can get out now,* she said. But he didn't move. She spoke to him again, but he still didn't move. She hadn't helped him at all, she thought. She should have gotten something to prop under the bench because now if she let it down, he might be crushed.

She heard the howl of sirens, and lights were appearing, and she wondered if she could hold the bench up until someone got to her.

She didn't know how long she'd been screaming for help, but she knew she was shaking badly and having trouble remembering where she was by the time she finally heard voices. Flashlights were shining and cops were picking their way toward her and she was afraid they might not realize what was happening and that Ed could be hurt.

She tried to explain that to one of the cops, and he told her he understood and that she could let go of the bench. She asked him if he was sure, and he said yes ma'm he was, and she liked that—somebody saying yes ma'm to her. "Ma'm you can let go now," he said again. "We got that man out."

"But what about Mark?" she said, and he said something she didn't understand. Words just weren't making sense to her now. Her brain was going. She decided it was time to let go—of the bench and everything else—and she felt herself falling. She didn't worry about it, though. She was safe. She could fall and she wouldn't be hurt. And sure enough she was right because suddenly she was weightless, floating up through air filled with excited voices and lit with flashing red and blue lights.

She floated above everything, going higher and higher, until she was so high she couldn't hear any voices, she couldn't hear anything at all, and all the lights faded away. Then she drifted gently downward . . .

Riding beside Luther in the police car, Mrs. Johnson tried to believe with all her heart that she was on her way to see her son, but the goodness of it was so rich and the

366

impossibility of it still so strong within her that tears came to her eyes and she began to cry again.

Luther put his arm around her and held her to him and said "Now Arlie . . ." as if there just was no reason he could think of for her to cry, but she knew his heart was as full as her own and that he wanted to cry himself and that like her he was afraid it was all a dream.

It was not though. It could not be. GG's friend Olivia had called them from the hospital and told them, told them Sonny was alive and that there was a police car on the way to bring her and Luther to the hospital. And sure enough, like she said, the police car arrived a couple of minutes later and the colored officer who was driving told them it was the truth. Her son was alive.

But now, only a couple blocks from the hospital, Mrs. Johnson tried to prepare herself for disappointment. It could not be possible that after all these years Sonny was alive, she told herself. She had given him up to God, had buried him in a little graveyard in her heart, knowing that someday, somewhere, when the time came she would be reunited with him wherever he was. But she had not ever expected to be reunited with him in this life, and the goodness of it and the sweetness of it was almost too much to bear.

And yet here they were pulling into the parking lot of the hospital in front of Emergency and there were all kinds of police cars here and people gathered. She and Luther were helped out of the car by two officers and then they were being led in through a door and into a wide corridor. Then they were going up—no, floating up—some stairs, mounting them to the first floor, and she was calling Sonny's name in her mind. And even before she reached the top of the stairs she was already calling his name out loud, shouting his name out loud, because she knew, she knew he was going to be there.

"To the left, Mrs. Johnson," a voice said, and people

made way for her, made way as she walked toward a tall lone man who waited for her near the end of the corridor, a tall bearded man, and even though she didn't recognize him, she hoped and she prayed he was her son. He had to be her son.

And he was. O, Lord, he was. He put his arms out to her and he said "Ma . . . Ma!" and she knew it was Sonny. Her Sonny standing tall as he'd been all those many years ago and handsome and fine-looking, oh my what a fine-looking man, and he was coming toward her and she was saying to herself I won't be able to stand it I won't I won't I won't.

And then he was in her arms and she was touching him, kissing him, hugging him, hugging her flesh, her blood, her being, her life, and she was crying so she couldn't see a thing and saying his name over and over. *"My Sonny, Oh my Sonny, my Sonny. Oh my Sonny boy."*

Alone with his parents in a private room, Johnson was trying to explain what had happened to him following Betty's murder, but Turnage was on his mind. Drew was under sedation and was going to be fine, thank heaven, and although he himself was all taped up and it hurt him to breathe, he was all right. But Turnage was still in the operating room, a bullet in his stomach, and even GG's friend Olivia hadn't been able to tell him anything, so he was preoccupied.

It wasn't easy for his parents to absorb it all either. When he started to relate how, after shooting him by accident, Turnage had kept him hidden, his father became confused.

"Don't see how Mark Turnage coulda done that, Sonny," he said. "That redneck father a his never would of allowed him to hide you in the house."

"His father was dead, Dad," he said. "He'd died about a week before, and Mark was alone."

368

His mother was overcome. "Mark Turnage did all that and never said anything to us all these years? Oh, Sonny, you know how I treated that man?"

"He understands, Ma."

He told them how at first he wanted to call the SCLC and the ACLU and every other organization he could think of and then turn himself in.

His father automatically shook his head and Ed said, "I know. Mark felt the same way."

"It was bad, Sonny. Everybody was afraid to go into work, afraid to leave the house."

He knew that too. He'd seen the photo of himself, fist raised, that the *Sentinel* had run. Originally taken at a sit-in, it had been cropped and placed beside a picture of Betty in her Sweet Sixteen gown. The story left no doubt of his guilt, or of Lee Caldecott's bravery in chasing him off. All that, and the $10,000 reward offered by Ordway, had brought all the scum from Summerville and Goose Creek and every other nearby town pouring in.

Even then he'd considered surrendering himself and accusing Ordway—until Turnage was taken down to the police station for questioning. Only then did he realize that this was no march or sit-in. He was on his own, and for the first time he understood the cold fear that had made his father take a strap to him a few nights before.

"You mean that, Sonny?" his father asked. "You understood? I always felt so awful about that."

Johnson took his father's hand in both of his. Its frailty touched him. "I understood."

With the police believing Turnage had killed him, he continued, he thought of going up to Canada and losing himself among the draftees who were there to avoid the Vietnam War. Instead he called his best friend at Howard University, Henry Attucks, and as soon as he said he was in trouble, Henry told him to come ahead.

A Liberian, Henry lived in Washington, D.C., and more than once he had invited Johnson to come to Liberia.

The timing couldn't have been better: Henry was planning to leave for home in about a month, and after they talked, he promised that Johnson would be with him.

Johnson knew Henry's father was a cabinet minister in Liberia, and a powerful man. Yet he still could not believe it when four weeks later, a Liberian passport in his hand and all the necessary clearances, he boarded a plane and was on his way.

"Sonny, you went to Africa?" His mother looked at him as if he'd said he'd gone to Mars.

"For a few years," he said, glancing anxiously at the clock: Olivia had said that Turnage would be in the operating room for at least an hour.

A few years had been all he could take. At first he couldn't believe his good luck at being in a black-run country, but when he began to see the poverty, the graft, and the corruption, he understood how easy it had been to get him a passport: in Liberia anything could be gotten for a "dash"—a bribe.

He'd settled in Monrovia, the capital, working at whatever he could while he looked around for an opportunity. It came when he realized that Monrovia had no decent ice cream. Within two years he and a partner had opened ice cream parlors in every major city and were on their way to a small fortune.

With his business flourishing, he went to Paris with Henry for a vacation, and as soon as he set foot there he knew it was going to be his home. When he returned to Monrovia and was hit by its sweltering humidity, its smells and its slums, he could not wait to sell his half of the business and leave.

After six months in Paris he was speaking fluent French. Within a year he had found a *gerant,* a capable

Frenchman with whom he partnered, and went into his first business, one he knew something about—*glaces et sorbets.*

He was about to tell his parents about Chantal and the children when the phone rang.

"Mr. Johnson," an operator said when he picked it up, "I'm sorry to disturb you, sir. There's a reporter here named Chuck Pennington. I told him you weren't talking to anybody right now, but he said to tell you he was kidnapped last night and it has to do with Drew Summers. He says he'd appreciate a few words with you."

Johnson hesitated, took the call against his better judgment.

"Hi," Pennington said, "is this Ed Johnson?"

"Yes, Mr. Pennington."

"You're not putting me on—you really are Ed Johnson."

"I'm not putting you on."

"I don't know if Drew told you about me, Ed."

"Yes, she did. I trust you're all right." He knew he sounded stiff-necked, but he didn't like the man.

"A little shook up, but I'm fine. Couple of goons grabbed me and let me go about an hour ago. I know it was related to you and Drew and I'd like to come up there and talk with you."

"I'm afraid not, Mr. Pennington. There is simply too much turmoil here at the moment. When I talk to Drew I will tell her you called, however."

"Hey, can you just tell me—"

"Mr. Pennington, I don't wish to be rude, but I cannot talk with you now. Good-bye."

He held the cutoff lever down, then asked the operator to hold all calls except from his family or Turnage's wife. He'd started to talk about Chantal and the kids again when Olivia pushed open the door. She was smiling. "He's out of the operating room now. Gonna be okay."

It was ten-thirty by then and Johnson urged his

parents to go home. He wanted to be there when Mark woke up, he said, then he'd come over. But his mother and father wouldn't hear of it. They'd wait for him, they said.

Before he finally was able to see Turnage he had to get by a curious hospital staff, a few patients and two police officers.

Turnage was pale and still doped up, but he immediately asked how Drew was.

"Like youth in general—indestructible," Johnson said. "She's sleeping now and the doctor says she'll be fine."

Turnage's speech was thick. "What about Ordway?"

"Critical. Drew put four bullets in him."

Turnage managed a smile. "Coupla real heroes you and me . . . Hope he lives. Want that bastard to fry . . ."

"Your wife is on the way down. She should be here in a couple of hours . . . I'm sorry this happened to you, Mark."

Turnage made a face. "Seen your folks yet?"

"They're here."

". . . Flipped out, huh?"

"My mother said something very touching. About you. She said that all those years when she thought she had lost a son she had another son she didn't even know about."

Turnage felt good. He liked Mrs. Johnson. His eyelids drooped. He was fading. His hand lay at his side and Johnson took it. He was about to say how grateful he was when Turnage's grip tightened and he opened his eyes.

"Remember that fight?"

He was almost hostile, and Johnson wasn't sure he was lucid. "Sure do . . ."

"I should of taken you."

"You were drunk."

Turnage shook his head slowly, fading again. His

372

voice came from far away. "I was wrong. I'd of taken you otherwise."

He closed his eyes and his hand relaxed. Johnson squeezed his shoulder. Then he went out.

Turnage shifted in his wheelchair and exchanged another glance of annoyance with Johnson. Neither of them had liked Pennington's attitude from the beginning, and they liked it less as the interview went on.

"That must have given you a big charge, putting everybody on the way you did," he was saying to Drew.

"No, but there was nothing else I could do."

"Have you talked with Mrs. Fairchild since you guys nailed her brother?"

". . . No."

"How do you feel about the number you did on her?"

"Not good."

"Let's back up," Pennington said to Johnson. "You were living in Paris when you two met."

"Yes," Johnson answered stiffly. "I still live there."

"How come you never got in touch with your family?"

"Fear for them. Mr. Ordway was and has always been a very powerful man with some very nasty friends."

"Chuck, let's get off Ordway," Turnage said. "I don't feature his lawyers claiming he's being tried in the press. Off-the-record, Ed had every right to be afraid for his family. You found that out yourself."

"What do you do in Paris?" Pennington asked.

"I have a number of enterprises."

"Now that it's safe for you to come home, will you?"

"No, I will continue to live in Paris, but I will visit here often."

"How come?"

"My friends are there, my wife, my children. My life is there. And frankly, the economic and social climate for African-Americans in this country is in many ways as bad as it was before the civil rights movement came into being."

Pennington changed the subject. "Okay," he said, turning to Drew, "so you meet Ed here in Paris, he tells you a story that tugs at your heart and you decide to do something about it. Whose idea was it?"

"Mine, I guess," Drew said. "We just started talking about how people might act if I showed up and pretended I was Betty. Especially Lee Caldecott and Raymond Ordway. Ed got a charge out of the idea, but felt it was too far out. Anyway, we wrote and talked after I got back from vacation, and I finally convinced him."

"Why did you do it?" Pennington asked.

"Because what Ed told me made me mad."

"It must have," Pennington said. "You risked your job, your boyfriend, your life. . . . You getting paid?"

"Why is that important?" Johnson interjected, an edge to his voice.

Pennington bridled. "I'll tell you why. I've been conned, kidnapped, and nearly killed because of this kid. I'm led to believe she did it for a principle. Well, as my sainted grandmother said when I once introduced a hooker to her as my girlfriend, I'd hate to find out that's a lot of crap and that you're paying her."

Johnson said, "When Drew decided to do this I offered her a handsome sum of money."

"Now we're getting down to the nitty-grit—"

"—And she refused it," Johnson went on heatedly. "I am paying her expenses, which is all she will accept. What I will do, however, is contribute the sum I offered her, plus any more I can afford, to some national organization dedicated to helping victims of child abuse."

"You mind if I check that out?"

"Not at all, but now that I know how your mind works I want to make something clear in case you are tempted to touch on it when you write your story. There is nothing

374

between this young lady and me but deep affection and respect. My wife, with whom I am very much in love, shares my feeling towards Drew, and if you so much as hint that there is more between us than I have just told you, you will have to account to me and to my lawyers. In the meantime, if you don't pay a little more attention to your manners I just may throw you out the door."

"The hell you will," Turnage said. "I'll throw him out the window first."

Pennington was mad. "Did it ever occur to you people that you used me, and that if it hadn't been for me you'd probably never have gotten as far as you did?"

"Damn right," Turnage said. "'Cause every time you got some information you figured Ordway might want you ran to him with it. It happened to fit in good with what we were doing or believe me I'd of hung you out to dry a long time—"

"God," Drew interrupted, "will you guys stop? Chuck, you were a big help," she went on, the three of them looking a little sheepish. "You really were. We all did the best we could, including you. So mellow out, everybody, okay? Next question."

The next question, when he asked it, was close to what Turnage and Johnson were thinking.

"You sure you're only twenty-three?" he said.

It was lovely here, the grass thick and the grounds well-tended. The sun was bright, the air sultry, but the shade trees and wildflowers made the heat bearable.

Drew found Betty's gravestone easily.

Her Soul and Her Beautiful Spirit Forever Remain . . .

For a few moments she stood holding the flowers she'd brought, then kneeled down and laid them by the stone. She thought she felt Betty's nearness.

"Hi," she said quietly. A faint breeze stirred, but it was gone before it could do anything about the heat.

". . . Ed wanted to come with me, but I wanted to come by myself."

From somewhere she heard a girl's laughter and for a second she thought she had imagined it, but it had been real. A teenager.

"I just wanted to tell you that we got him. I guess you know, though. I hope he doesn't die because I don't want it on my conscience, but if he lives I sure hope he suffers. . . . I knew we'd get him. The more Ed told me about you the more I knew we would."

She thought of all the work they had done, the videotapes they'd made, and the dozens of pages of notes Ed had prepared. Each time he'd flown in he'd brought more—more details, more facts, more conversations that he kept dredging up from that fantastic memory of his.

"I can see why you fell in love with him," she said. "He gets a little stuffy sometimes, but he's so smart. And good-looking."

For no reason she suddenly thought of Gena, how much she had wanted to die. And she, Drew, had never been able to help her. She'd even made things worse.

Guilt and melancholy took hold of her suddenly, and she had all she could do not to cry.

Tell someone.

The words had been as clear as the laughter, as clear as if they'd been spoken right beside her. She wondered if she really *was* hearing things this time.

Bending down, she took a flower from the bouquet she had brought. A yellow iris. On impulse she put it to her lips and kissed it. Then she placed it gently where Betty slept.

Tell someone.

The words sprang into her mind again, and she looked around at the bright slanting sunlight and dark shadows. A carved angel, worn by rain and time, stared at her from beside an ivy-covered vault.

Who could she tell? And what for? What good would it do?

The three of them drove to the airport together, and after Drew checked in at the flight desk, they had a drink in the bar. Turnage was still in a wheelchair and Johnson sat up abnormally straight because of the tight bandage around his middle. Drew's leg was bandaged.

Going back over what had happened, they had some laughs now about what had scared them the most, and the mistakes they'd made. The two men agreed that they wouldn't have done it if they'd thought the risks would be a tenth of what they had turned out to be. They'd been lucky, they all admitted.

Not until a voice announced that her flight was boarding did Drew realize how fond she'd become of them. They were like two older brothers.

In the departure area she said, "I'm going to miss you guys. I really am." She stooped over and gave Turnage a big hug. He was as awkward as a teenager, and for a moment Drew knew exactly what he had been like around Betty—decent and dependable, and painfully shy. She kissed him on the cheek and he glowed.

Johnson took her hands, openly admiring her.

"I can't possibly tell you how grateful I am, Drew," he said.

His eyes had always fascinated her, yellow-green. Now she was the awkward one. "You don't have to," she said.

"I'm sorry about your fiancé," he said.

She was going to say something offhand like Well, you can't win 'em all. Instead she shrugged. He kissed her on both cheeks, then embraced her. She fitted comfortably in his arms.

When he held her away from him, those wonderful eyes studying her, she saw why he had appealed to Betty. She'd have gone for him herself.

It was time to leave.

"I'll be seeing you at the trial, I guess, huh?"

They said yes, and she said so long and started for the gate.

The two of them stared after her, waiting for her to turn for a final wave.

She stopped sooner than they expected, as though she'd just remembered something. Then she turned slowly and gave them both a long appraising look. It was a look they were familiar with, as was the radiant, almost shy smile that went with it. It got to them both— especially when she put one hand on her hip and her smile became deliciously innocent and seductive at the same time.

"If y'all happen to be in New York? Give me a call. Will yuh?"

With that they thought she would drop the pose and they'd share one more laugh. Instead she wrinkled her nose, sashayed off, and did not turn back.

20

Berringer was one of the first people Drew called. She made an appointment to see him, and in his office a week after she returned, she explained everything.

"You were really nice, Corey, and I'm sorry about all the pretending, but I had to do it. I felt that the least I owed you was an explanation," she concluded.

She'd brought along a copy of a southern newspaper. It lay on his desk, and Berringer glanced down at it. The story of Raymond Ordway's crimes, and Drew's role in capturing him, filled the front page.

Drew said, "I just hope you're not mad."

Berringer looked up. "Are you kidding? I'm so impressed I'm speechless."

That made her feel good. "So you don't think I was being underhanded or anything?"

"You were terrific. You sure had me fooled." He shook his head. "I didn't think you were sick to begin with, but I couldn't figure out what was wrong with you."

"You mean we're not going to go into all the deep, dark secrets I've kept hidden up to now?"

"Not when you tell me you weren't here for therapy in the first place. You must feel very proud."

"That's the funny part of it," Drew said. "I wanted to get that bastard Ordway so bad it scared me sometimes. But for some reason . . . I don't know—now I just don't feel as great as I thought I would. Isn't that weird?"

"Well, maybe whatever made you want to get him that badly is still unresolved," Berringer said.

"What do you mean, unresolved? I did it because it was right."

"It certainly was. All I'm suggesting is that maybe some of your motives came from feelings you're not aware of."

Drew didn't know why, but she felt suddenly defensive. "What are you saying—I did the right thing for the wrong reason?"

"Not at all. And if you have the slightest notion I'm criticizing you or attacking you, forget it. But look at this from another angle—you risked just about everything you had to accomplish what you did, including your life. That's pretty extreme."

"Maybe it is, but Corey that man Ordway is a disgusting human being. If you're trying to tell me that wanting to catch him was neurotic or sick . . . Wow."

Berringer smiled. "Hey, how come you keep writing my copy for me?"

She managed a smile herself, and he went on. "Let's see if I can say what I really mean. What you did was right. It wasn't only right, it was fine, it was extraordinary. But it was also very dangerous, which means you had powerful emotions driving you, so powerful that as you just said yourself, they scared *you* sometimes."

He waited for her to say something, and she sensed that he wasn't going to pursue the subject if she didn't want to. She heard herself say, "Go ahead."

"Okay. All I'm suggesting is that those emotions could have come from feelings you've never dealt with, or talked about with anyone."

"Such as . . ."

He'd brought it up because he was concerned. She'd done a lot to reverse her role as victim, but as time passed, he felt, she'd be just about where she was before.

380

"Such as your feelings about your sister. I think you were telling me the truth about her suicide."

"Yeah. It just kinda came out."

"It's understandable. And I'll bet there were dozens of times when you believed you could have done something to save her."

She wondered how he knew.

"That's not surprising," he said. "We all do that, especially when something terrible happens. We think that if only we'd done this, or that, we could have prevented it."

"I *could* have prevented it, though, Corey. It was my fault Gena committed suicide."

Berringer leaned forward. "Drew, I think you are one of the bravest, loveliest, and nicest people I have ever met, but that is complete and utter nonsense."

"What makes you so sure?" Drew said stubbornly.

"All the pain you still have—and the guilt—over your sister's death."

"It's justified. You know, I really don't know how we got on to this," she said, a little annoyed, "but as long as we have . . ." She hesitated, then decided the hell with it. "Gena wanted my father to stop. She always wanted him to stop but he never would. Finally one time she just said 'No more,' and he knew she meant it. She hated it, hated him, hated herself. So he started on me . . . You knew it, didn't you?"

She'd gotten it out. Corey was glad. "Kind of. There was no reason for me to think your father would have treated you any better than he did your sister."

Drew shifted in her chair, overwhelmed suddenly by nausea and self-disgust. Once again she could almost taste her father's mouth on hers. And once again she remembered how she'd tried to deny to herself what he was doing to her, tried to find a place in her mind he couldn't reach while he invaded her body . . .

"How old were you?" Berringer asked. For the first

time he saw what she had successfully hidden up to now: the bewilderment, the self-blame, and the hurt.

"Almost twelve. Look, feel sorry for Gena, not for me," she said quickly. "She had it a lot worse than I did. She made him leave me alone . . . She took my place. And I let her. I shouldn't have, but I did. I sure paid her back, didn't I?"

"What do you mean?"

"I mean I killed my sister, Corey, let's not—"

"Drew, listen to me. I know you loved your sister deeply, but you're assuming guilt for something that—"

"What am I supposed to do—feel good about it!"

"Not at all." She hadn't come here to be treated, but he couldn't let this pass. He chose his words carefully. "Just be aware that for you to say you killed your sister is . . . well, it's avoiding the *real* issue—that you were only eleven years old. You were a child." He paused. "You were a victim, Drew, not a murderer."

She was silent, weighing the idea, and it flashed through his mind how much he wanted to know her personally.

She managed a humorless smile. "I thought you said I wasn't a sick wick."

"You're not. I think you're damn healthy."

"You're a good guy, Corey," she said. "I mean it. If I ever decided to go into therapy I'd come to you."

He hesitated. "Well, that's something we'd have to talk about. We started off in a cockeyed way here. Don't misunderstand me. If you wanted some therapy and you need me I'm here. I'm not abandoning you. But I honestly think that for what you'd want to talk about you ought to see a woman."

She shrugged. "It was only a thought. Like I told you—in my family we didn't talk about all that stuff."

"That was your father's idea, I'm sure. 'Shhhh, don't tell anybody what's going on. Keep it a secret.'"

They talked for a few more minutes, and just before

382

she left Berringer gave her the names of some therapists. "One of them has had a lot of experience working with AMACs—adults molested as children. If you should be interested," he said, "shop around a little. Find someone you can talk to easily."

After she was gone he sat thinking. He understood now how she had managed to reveal so little about herself. She was strong, able to push the pain back and be assertive and giving. He hoped she'd get therapy. She could go on without it, but the ease with which she had been able to take on the persona of a tortured girl was an indication of the depth of her own torment.

He wondered if she had any idea how attracted to her he was. He'd work with her if she wanted him to, but he hoped she'd decide against it. He had too many feelings that weren't appropriate in a therapeutic context. He could deal with them if he had to, consult with a colleague, but he'd prefer not to.

If he didn't hear from her, he decided, he'd wait a suitable length of time, then he'd call her and ask her out to dinner. Whether or not she went into therapy with someone.

At various times over the next couple of weeks, Drew wanted to call Corey. Once, when she was feeling particularly down, she dialed his number and then hung up before the phone began to ring.

And once she almost called Jim. Just to say hello, she told herself, then decided there was no point to it. It was over, and if she was willing to be honest with herself, they really hadn't been as close as she'd wanted to believe. Jim had always been so busy with work—and she as well—that if they'd seen each other twice a week it was a lot.

The more she thought about their relationship, the more aware she became that Jim hardly knew anything about her. She hadn't told him that much about her inner feelings. Him or anyone else.

She didn't even have that many friends, she realized. Most of the people she knew she'd met through Jim. It made her feel suddenly alone.

The only person in the world who really knew anything about her was Corey.

One night, as she was taking a TV dinner out of the toaster oven, she remembered the time at the rest home when she came on to Corey, and it made her smile.

He was a good guy, someone you could trust. He wasn't abandoning her, he'd said. That was nice. She had the feeling he really liked her.

Again she had a strong urge to call him. It didn't have to be for therapy, she thought. She could tell him frankly and honestly that she was grateful to him, which she was, and invite him out to lunch.

She peeled the foil off the top of the aluminum tray and brought it into the living room. She didn't turn on the TV as she usually did. She sat and ate, slowly and deliberately. She was not consciously thinking about anything, but she knew that she was making a decision. When she finished eating she got up, dropped the tray into the bag under the sink, then went back into the living room.

Her handbag was on the couch. Opening it, she took out her address book and removed the slip of paper folded up inside of it.

Glancing at the number she wanted to call, she dialed. While it rang she decided she was going to fly back to L.A. over the Labor Day weekend and visit Gena's grave.

She saw herself there, telling Gena how much she loved her and how sorry she was that everything had happened the way it had. She thanked Gena for every-

384

thing she had done and then told her she had come to say good-bye and that she would never forget her.

She had brought flowers with her and she saw herself laying them on Gena's grave when a machine cut in on the other end.

"Hello," a woman's pleasant voice said, "this is Dr. Carlson. I am not able to talk with you now, but if you will leave a message I'll return your call as soon as possible."

She sounded nice, Drew thought. Clearing her throat, she said, "Dr. Carlson, my name is Drew Summers. Corey Berringer gave me your number, and I'd like to make an appointment with you . . ."